DECENT DECEIT

For my friend, Diann — Enjoy! Marie Pinschmidt

Destiny of Deception

MARIE BUSH PINSCHMIDT

outskirts
press

Decent Deceit
Destiny of Deception
All Rights Reserved.
Copyright © 2017 Marie Bush Pinschmidt
v2.0

The opinions expressed in this manuscript are solely the opinions of the author and do not represent the opinions or thoughts of the publisher. The author has represented and warranted full ownership and/or legal right to publish all the materials in this book.

This book may not be reproduced, transmitted, or stored in whole or in part by any means, including graphic, electronic, or mechanical without the express written consent of the publisher except in the case of brief quotations embodied in critical articles and reviews.

Outskirts Press, Inc.
http://www.outskirtspress.com

Paperback ISBN: 978-1-4787-7951-3

Cover Photo © 2017 thinkstockphotos.com. All rights reserved - used with permission.

Outskirts Press and the "OP" logo are trademarks belonging to Outskirts Press, Inc.

PRINTED IN THE UNITED STATES OF AMERICA

One

*"Accept the things to which fate binds you, love
the people with whom fate brings you together, but
do it with all your heart." Marcus Aurelius*

Drake Dawson entered the Bucket of Blood with some reluctance—but he'd come too far to change his mind. The bar was a little spot on earth where it had all begun—a lifetime of feeling misplaced, misunderstood, messed up and unable to determine what he really wanted of life, or where his life might lead him. Now it was spelled out right before his eyes—the story of his early existence condensed to a rundown local bar on the corner of an insignificant trashy street in the tiny Midwestern town of Porterville. More a burg or village than a town, it held no claim to fame as far as he knew, certainly his previously unknown family had contributed little or nothing of value to the town's survival or status.

The dated and dingy interior of the dive held no memory for him, yet a profuse sweat beaded in his armpits and cascaded over his ribs. His restless pulse would send a cardiologist to the medical textbooks. Bottles of spirits sat on shelves long in need of dusting. The colors and labels of the bottles satisfied his visual senses more acutely than the yellowed print of poker-playing canines hanging slightly askew on the wall above them. But then color always fascinated him. He smelled the senility of the place, felt the scratched and peeling red Formica countertop beneath his elbows, heard the drunken laughs and slurred mumblings of a million boozers before him. But how could that be? He had been but a child when he made his first appearance in this godforsaken sorry excuse for a town. His life had been a tree with no roots but now the gnarled tentacles of his past were unearthed. The question was where did he go from here, from this mound of decadence where his innocence and sense of unrest had begun? He took a second cursory look around, and before the boobs-and-butt waitress appeared for his order, he left the premises, slamming the door behind him.

The following morning, a block and a half from the Bucket of Blood, he stared at a silent, dilapidated cottage sitting alone as if it had been tossed aside like the butt of a cigar. Next door, a vacant lot was partially hidden by overgrown weeds and carelessly tossed debris. Unexpected ghosts of his past glimmered before his eyes. He didn't need to enter the sagging front door to see in his mind the tattered and food-stained sofa where the old man had napped, when he wasn't shuffling his way back and forth from the kitchen, a bottle clutched in his blue-veined talon-like hands. For the first time, Drake remembered the door to the cellar. His mind descended the wooden steps to the damp storage room below. He smelled the sweet dusty odor of rotting and dried sweet potatoes and apples, heard the scampering of rodents in the obscured ominous corners, and saw the thin slash of light sneaking in from beneath the bolted door. Once again, he felt the fear, but ignored the tears that dampened his eyes—the first tears he had shed in he couldn't remember when. A mirage of images floated before his eyes—the black iron bed, the fringe of the chenille bedspread. He felt the tightness of the old man's belt tethering his small emaciated wrist to the cold post. He shook his head. Why was he remembering now, after so many years? Was it memory, or had his imagination gone bipolar after learning of all the deceit he had been fed?

Drake Dawson spent the previous night in a Motel 6—about a mile down the road. It wasn't exactly the Ritz Carlton. No flowers, no champagne, no chocolates on the pillow. Rust stains in the sink, broken tiles around the tub, reminded him of other unsavory places in which he'd found respite during earlier brief drinking bouts. He'd showered in public restrooms, even slept in his car. His thoughts shifted back to sober times when he had his own room with a clean bed to sleep in, a nice home, and a father and mother who took him to places as foreign as the moon while he was growing up. But now, he didn't need glitz and glamour—his small apartment in Coopersville sufficed.

He turned away from the scene in front of him. An awakening sky opened its gaping mouth and spewed out a stream of glorious brilliant color. Years of unshed tears ran freely down his whisker-bristled cheeks. The unexpected tears dried before he turned once more to face the humble structure of old timber, roof with missing shingles, and haunting memories. He moved cautiously across the weathered, rotting, splintering boards of the narrow porch, reached out and touched a broken hinged shutter by the door. It fell, striking his foot and causing him to wince in pain. He vowed it would be the last time he would allow his past to hurt or confuse him.

Without thought or hesitation, he removed a lighter from the pocket of his denim shirt. He flicked it on, placed the flame deliberately to a tattered piece of fabric on the abandoned Lazy Boy by the window—its guts exposed to the elements—letting it all hang out. He watched with disinterest as the fingers of fire quickly spread until the red glow competed with the colors of the sunrise reflected in the cracked and dirty windowpane. Drake sighed, sniffed, turned and sauntered across the neglected dandelion-invaded yard as rapidly changing colors in the eastern sky merged with the reds, orange, and smoky grays of his past. Subconsciously, he murmured: *That's it—finished—a deceitful past he had never known he owned.*

While the tiny town still slept, Drake sat upright on his Harley as it caressed the soft hills and valleys of the highway. No longer in any particular hurry, numb from coming to grips with recent events, he basked in the beauty of a surrounding landscape he had previously only viewed blindly. Behind him, his newly discovered past lay smoldering in ashes where it belonged. As he rode along the peaceful rural highway, the corners of his mouth stretched upward as his thoughts finally embraced a future—a future as obscure as his past had been.

As Drake approached an intersection, he touched his helmet in salute to a gentleman checking a sign on a farm post—the man raised an arm in response. Now a lone traveler in more ways than one, he gunned his Harley and his smile widened as he leaned into an approaching curve. Frown lines softened and disappeared as he headed into the welcoming sunrise. He felt as free as the bald eagle that soared in the sky above him.

For the first time in his life, Drake knew the truth of his past, a past that had been wiped clean of buried memories and questions—until now. Now, he would have to figure out where he was headed with his new-found identity. It had taken modern technology to trace his early beginnings and bring an awareness of his secret past. He guessed he would now have to claim the spoils of his early childhood as well as his often troubled adolescence. Would it ever make sense? Would he ever fully understand? For now, his future belonged to him alone, and he might as well embrace it—hopefully it would be brighter than his past. Some changes would have to be made, but future success or failure would be his own doing— no one else left to blame.

Even as a child, Drake had felt restlessness within him. During his adolescence, he had intermittently become like those hobos of long ago—lonely and lost, escaping from commitments and responsibility. Unlike a hobo, even during his drinking bouts, he hadn't needed to steal food from those living by railroad tracks or bus depots. He'd managed with others willingly coming to his aid. But relationships with others never lasted—they passed through his life like a hot air balloon lifting from the solid earth in search of airborne dreams.

In bus stations and public restrooms, he read books, newspapers and discarded magazines left behind by other travelers. Back home, there were well-tended books in shelves free of dust—books with substance: philosophy, archeology, history, even poetry and novels—books found in libraries of professors and other learned men and women. Many of the books he read—others he cast aside after a chapter or two—the texts offering no words of insight for him.

Always, he had felt an affinity for nature: the mountains, the trees—they could be counted on —always there—solid, standing against nature's harshness and man's callous touch. He found brief solace in the liquid, ceaseless, ever-flowing ocean. It, too, could be counted on—the natural ebb and flow of waves in perfect symmetry—each breaker pausing to let another pass, awaiting its turn to make its strength known. Would that humans could show such courtesy.

His parents—he would have to get used to thinking of them as his adoptive parents—in spite of his adolescent rebellion, had begged and cajoled him throughout high school. After graduation he had another love affair with the bottle, but it was short-lived after seeing his only buddy draw his last breath following an overdose. Eventually, in a sober moment, he asked his parent's forgiveness for all the grief he had caused them. It was a grownup moment, a moment when he felt a shift in his attitude. Would it last?

Two months later, he decided his Dad actually was too good to be true. The only man he ever believed in was capable of weakness—a fraud. His law practice, Dawson & Walker, had grown by leaps and bounds and Drake, during good times, had been proud to call him Dad. Brian, his father's law partner and long-time friend, came onto him while visiting their home. Drake hadn't respected Brian for a long time. He took only cases that fed his ego, or fattened his coffers. At least that had been his mother's impression when she had told him about Alice, a woman who had no money for lawyers, and a low paying job. She had begged Brian to take the woman's case and he refused. "What do I get in return?" was his response.

That afternoon Drake was alone in the house. His father was playing golf, his mother off to her garden club meeting. Brian stopped by to discuss a case with his father – at least that was his excuse. The man had brazenly approached him with his filthy suggestions and retreated only when Drake threatened to mess up his pretty face.

After the episode was over, Drake had gone to his room and locked the door behind him. A few minutes later, from the back door, he heard his father's cheerful hello, indicating a successful round of golf. Drake was tempted to burst his bubble by confronting both of them but was too shaken to deal with it. Where had the man gotten the impression he would cooperate in such a tryst? Later that evening his dad came to his door dressed in a pinstriped suit and paisley tie. "Brian said you were upset with him—you know how he loves to kid around."

"Dad, he was not kidding around. What kind of a man would come onto his best friend's son? Jeez, is there any decency left in this world?"

"Drake, you can't make a big deal out of this. He's my law partner. Forget it ever happened. This is an imperfect world and you would be wise to accept that fact and get on with building your future."

"I can't believe you're so blasé about this, Dad. He's a sleazebag. I feel sorry for his wife."

"Another reason you have to let this go—too many people would be hurt." He placed his hand on Drake's shoulder and added, "You have to do what's best for the family, son—for all of us. Be a man and put it out of your mind."

His mother called from the foot of the stairs, "Come on, Jim, we're going to be late."

"Coming, Emilee," his Dad replied.

That was the last time Drake saw his dad alive—he died the following day in his office of a massive heart attack. Drake later wondered if his dad had confronted Brian after all, and an ensuing argument had brought on the attack. One more uncertainty he would have to live with.

After his father's death, Drake once again was tempted by the bottle but the shock had sent his mind into a period of more mature thinking. His mother had needed him to be strong during the period of mourning. In a fog, he tried to deal with his own guilt—if he had just kept quiet about the confrontation with Brian. He was no longer a grade school kid and should have been able to handle things on his own. On the other hand, was the reputation of the law firm more important to his father than his own son's welfare? But he wasn't his flesh-and-blood son, was he? Would he have handled it differently if he had been a legitimate off-spring?

Somehow, he got through the necessary protocol of the funeral—the endless line of family friends, colleagues and clients paying their respect. Drake scarcely heard their condolences—his mind was reliving his life with parents who had given him a nice home and the appropriate care, much of which he had not fully appreciated. His mother had always been there to support and encourage him to make a name for himself in the world. She believed in his intelligence and abilities and she made her love known in many ways. Nonetheless, he always felt a gap in their relationship, a feeling of not belonging. His father had not been as loving—oh, he supplied all the necessities and many of the perks, including a vintage car Drake had admired. He awoke to find it parked in their driveway on graduation day. He doubted if he'd ever not feel remorse for destroying the trust his father had in his partner, whether or not the trust was deserved.

Still in a state of disbelief, Drake, much to his mother's dismay, enrolled in Kaiser College, a local liberal arts school.

"But Drake, your father wanted you to go to his alma mater and follow in his footsteps—join the law firm."

"Sorry, Mom, that wouldn't work for me. We've talked about this before. You know being a lawyer is not the least appealing to me. I'd rather study Literature and Fine Arts—become a writer or a painter." His mother didn't know about Brian's indiscretion and he wasn't about to tell her at this fragile time of her life.

"Drake, I admit you have some talent for the arts, and that's fine, but I want a more stable profession for you."

"Then, I'll teach, but I won't become a lawyer."

Drake began his college studies with a different attitude than in high school but remained ambivalent about his future. After weeks of searching and analyzing his inner feelings, he thought he finally had it figured out. Even a snake could shed its skin and leave it behind like a discarded gum wrapper, un-tanned by a blistering sun, pores breathing—free to start anew. Surely, he could do the same and make a decent job of it.

There were choices to be made. He didn't have to accept what the non-attending world offered—the injustice and prejudices, the bent-for-destruction thinking his short life had offered. The world seemed to be intolerant of anything spiritual. It turned away from the face that was not beautiful, the body that was flawed, the mind that dared think or opine on its own. He felt he had grown old overnight. He would have to face his future without a father's advice or influence—but then he had never felt an abundance of either. From now on, unlike the snake, he wouldn't allow himself to crawl under a rock or camouflage himself around a tree branch hoping to be passed by as something insignificant. He wouldn't stick out his serpent tongue to scare away those in his path, or rattle his words in order to drive away those who might try to help him. For the present, he wished to be left alone to sort out his new identity and to paint the canvas of his future.

Drake sensed what he wouldn't do, but not what he would do with his new maturity, his new-found identity—his choices? He could sit idly by and wait for the world to change, or he could change himself. Could he accomplish both? It was doubtful. The first would lead to disappointment— a profession in which he had already earned a Ph.D. No, he couldn't change the world but he could do his bit to eliminate some of the ugliness. He could try to change ugly ducklings into swans just to give them a taste of what it was like—a glimpse of beauty or the sublime. His jumbled and lofty thinking made him doubt his sanity sometimes, but the feeling remained. He would shed the skin of his past, the genes and flaws of his ancestors. Anything was possible. For the most part, he had turned his back on accepted or traditional learning because of his adolescent *just don't think about it* attitude. Could he possibly make up for lost time?

The booze would be the greatest challenge, perhaps an impossible one, but he took on the "learn as you go" stance. No more living for the moment but for an unforeseeable but positive future. Was it possible to erase the past, cast it aside, reduce it to ashes, as he had the hell hole of his childhood nursery—his cradle of discontent? Had he really crawled into his last hole, under his last rock, or beneath rotten floorboards and woodpiles of uninvited memories?

Yes, one had choices. If he couldn't change the so-called human condition he could change the habitat. He would strive to be happy with the fruit of his own labor. He would change from a deceitful loser to an achiever. By the sweat of his brow, he would become a decent man.

Thinking it was time to loosen the apron strings, Drake found a small apartment near campus. His first year at Kaiser was challenging. He learned all he could from mediocre instructors in literature, completing the assignments without difficulty. His art classes were a bit disappointing. He wanted to learn from the Masters, absorb all he could of light and shadow, foreshortening, color harmony and drawing, but the instructors were more focused on individual expression. How could an artist express himself if he didn't have the basic tools to bring the expressions to fruition? Feeling he was getting nowhere, he became discouraged and once more found himself tempted beyond resistance.

The bottle remained a clever seducer, calling the shots. Was there such a thing as destiny? If there was a God, where was He when hope was most needed? Instead of asking God for help, when he was reasonably cognoscente, he turned to women to satisfy his basic needs. It worked momentarily. He used them. They couldn't possibly know he meant nothing he said—just words to appease, and for him to bask in the euphoria of briefly feeling cared for. He went from one relationship to another, kept his drinking to a minimum and came out, not exactly unscathed, but not destroyed either.

Months passed. Drake went through the motions but still had not figured out his purpose in life. He hadn't experienced that solid knowledge of what he wanted to do in the future, so he continued drifting and dreaming. He never stayed with one interest long enough to know whether or not he had talent in a specific field. In relationships, he could always start an argument when he became tired of whomever he was with. Nothing could hurt him permanently if he didn't allow himself to care—that was the secret to a tolerable life. Life was just a prep school for higher learning and he sensed he had been a student too long. He was as matter-of-fact as a piece of cutlery. Life was as ridiculous as watching a parade of hedge-clipped poodles. If his father's death had not changed him—he wondered if anything would make a difference. He hated himself for his weakness.

One interlude was with a woman to be reckoned with—a woman who stood out from the rest and took on his problems as her own—at least for a while. Her name was Patricia—not Pat, Patty or Tricia—but Patricia, like a porcelain doll—so perfect if you removed one eyelash it would no longer be a Dresden. At first, he feared if he touched her face it would be cold and unyielding, her fingers too delicate to squeeze, with legs too rigid to slip between. She wore the air of a lady who might own a flock of peacocks—yet she intrigued him. Would she, too, cast him aside at the least sign of imperfection? She had sneaked into his life like an unexpected weather front, changing the atmosphere and ruffling his feathers of complacency.

Drake soon learned. If nothing else, he learned that a lovely smile or hair the color of a seal—and just as shiny—did not make a woman of easy temperament or compassionate capabilities. A face of innocence didn't make it so. He found himself often ruminating about their importance, other than continuing the emergence of the human species. Would she be capable of caring for a needy child, or would she cast aside the idea as an assault against her own perfectness? Why did women strive to be alike in talk, dress and appearance, even suffer the pain of the knife in pursuit of that end? When provoked, Patricia's voice could scrape your auditory senses like a rasp. Lies tumbled out of her mouth like a child doing cartwheels. Patricia's biggest lie was denying being in love with a man who was supposed to be "just a friend".

Drake, in all fairness, had not been much better. After a brief separation he had again approached Patricia clothed in nothing but pure and hopeful thoughts. But when he saw her in front of the stainless steel sink, looking like a butterfly that had just left its cocoon, flipping the dish towel like a perfect Monarch specimen, desire arose in him like a phoenix out of the ashes determined to control its destiny. He approached from behind, snaked his arms beneath hers and intertwined his hands over her small waist before moving them higher to encompass the globes of the world. But her racing pulse was not from desire. She pried his hands loose and without turning in his arms as she would have previously, he heard the still-familiar words. "Where have you been?"

"Come on, honey, I haven't had any..." his voice was slurred from one too many.

Once again, the monarch had turned into a bipolar wasp, ready to dispense her venom in one fell swoop. He felt history repeating itself in her words of disappointment. And who could blame her? Once again, deflated and indifferent, he had only made things worse. The next morning he awoke on the sofa with only snippets of memory of the previous night. With only slight remorse, he opened the front door and walked through, vowing never to return. There were other arms waiting, other lying lips and other fleeting passions. Once again, *hello* had turned into *goodbye*.

Time heals all things? Rubbish. With women, facts blended like a watercolor painting— explanations and excuses blurred, undependable and of little importance, the palette so over-mixed that all the colors turned gray. He began to think of women as manikins with no other purpose except to show attire for the exterior of the body, nothing to display the inner spirit. Non-conformity was more appealing. In the future he would sneak only a peek beneath their Botox enhanced and airbrushed artificial façade.

He had accused Patricia of lying, but during a brief period of clarity of thought, he had to admit that he was the liar where women were concerned. He could understand lying to escape punishment—he's done it as a child more than once. But he wouldn't lie or cheat for profit, not because of his personal piety but because money never meant that much to him. Sure, he had known some whose bodies grew fat along with their wallets, thinking it was an asset to be fat—to authenticate success in the world. Their girth only necessitated bigger cars, bigger houses, and usually bigger egos. Others made fitness centers their stimulant of choice, getting high on brawn instead of brains. Brian came to mind uninvited, but Drake quickly deleted the image. Thinking of Brian brought back thoughts of his now permanently absent parents and it was easier not to allow his mind to go there.

Drake had never put much emphasis on religion although he had attended Sunday school as a youngster. For a brief time, he had believed. As he grew older his parents had not appeared upset at his lack of interest since he showed little interest in anything— including his school work. In spite of it, fortunately, and with little effort, he managed higher than average grades. At least he was not considered scholastically inept. He felt that man could be capable of almost any sin if not kept in check—his need for the bottle was probably a sin. He didn't allow himself to analyze every instance of right or wrong-doing. It was better not to think about it, or at least not dwell on his misdeeds.

In matters of love, he made sure he left no available room to be tricked, trapped or enslaved. Love—he wasn't about to allow himself to fall in love, if such an emotion existed. He'd seen guys lose all sense of judgment over a mini skirt, or fall for a pretty face, even though she would probably lie about what she had for lunch. He wished he could believe in a woman's goodness, but for some reason he had never been able to do so—except for his mother who had given him encouragement as well as space when he needed it. Why give your heart to someone you might lose or be a part of something that isn't in your best interest? He'd rather live independently—live or die on his own. Depending on others for survival was shameful. He knew that from experience. Only with Patricia, in sober moments, had he a glimpse of real love—a glimpse of how the love of one woman could make a huge difference.

Once he had suffered rejection, he found rejection where it didn't exist, drew it forth from people simply by expecting it. He had been unaware—the process had been gradual. He built a wall of self-sufficiency around himself as defense against the world. He learned to choose from whom he would accept devotion and for how long—always short lived. No true or lasting friends—he had stayed close to his own path as if cast in a mold he couldn't crack or break his way out of. A psychiatrist wasn't needed to figure that out. Since Patricia and his new sobriety, there was a deep desire to do more than just take up space.

Drake finally came to his senses, had returned to Kaiser with new determination and dived into his studies like a man in search of the Holy Grail. If he was to become an artist, writer or teacher he wanted to be at the top of his game. He had a better understanding of his professors and of what they were teaching. Consequently, he graduated at the head of his class and was immediately offered a position of Associate Prof. at the small college. He wondered if his prominent name had played a part in the offer. His mother had seen his dedication to learning and no longer worried about his future. Two years after his father's death, she died of bacterial meningitis, leaving him a lone pilgrim with no family. At least she died knowing her son was sober and on his way to accomplishing a decent life.

Drake inherited the family home but chose to remain in his modest apartment near the college in Coopersville. His main interest was in learning all he could—to make up for the time he had wasted. Text books became his friends. His inheritance was not a staggering amount, but after the debts had been paid and the legal affairs settled, it was enough to warrant careful consideration of its future use. His father had made plenty of money but he also enjoyed spending it. Drake did not lack for much, but then he had never craved much as long as life's necessities were supplied.

Five months after his mother's death and during the summer break from teaching, he was lounging lazily in his apartment feeling restless and ambivalent concerning his future direction. Miraculously, this time the bottle didn't suddenly appear as a solution. When his doorbell rang, he took his time answering, expecting it to be a solicitor. Instead, he came face to face with a man in a navy blue suit, carrying a briefcase. After confirming that he was Drake Dawson, he carefully read the attorney's business card.

Drake soon learned his entire life had been a lie. The man with the briefcase held the truth— unraveling his world, leaving him deceived and totally alone. He learned he had a biological mother whom he hadn't known existed. He also learned he would never know her—she had recently died—and had named him the sole beneficiary in her will.

"Your biological mother, and your grandfather, lived in the small town of Porterville—just thirty miles away." The attorney then removed several legal forms from his briefcase while Drake tried to wrap his mind around this startling information.

"But how did you find me?"

"Your mother left detailed instructions and asked that I deliver the forms to you in person." He smiled and added, "I don't usually make house calls. This is all quite legal in case you have any doubts. She lived a very humble existence, owning only the small piece of property in Porterville—a property that now belongs to you to utilize as you wish."

After receiving all pertinent information regarding his previously unknown family roots, Drake was left in a state of utter disbelief—like awakening from a scrambled dream or being anesthetized. He signed the legal papers, using the only full name he had ever known. At least he hadn't been stripped of his first name. At the time of adoption only his last name had been changed.

Two

*"And though of magnificence and splendor,
your house shall not hold your secret nor shelter your longing.
For that which is boundless in you abides in the mansion of the sky,
whose door is the morning mist, and whose windows are the
songs and silences of night."* Kahlil Gibran

After igniting the fire and leaving remnants of his past in ashes, Drake's thirty mile trip back to his apartment had been without incident although his mind remained cluttered with the bizarre events leading up to his present situation. His apartment building was at the edge of town— to the north, nothing but raw nature. He secured his Harley—his only transportation after trading in his vintage car—when a glowing light on a distant horizon caught his attention. Inside, from a window, he watched as the fire danced it's rhythm like a pianist practicing arpeggios. The glow crept menacingly along the spine of the hill, leaving smoldering ashes, the fragrance of burning pine and poplar, and probably the cry of trapped animals in its wake. Drake watched the now blazing tongue of destruction as it lapped toward the deep depth of the valley, ebbing and flowing like the surf of a sea. Tomorrow, there would be no birdsong, no chirping of crickets or cooing of doves, no frolicking squirrels or rabbits. What a shame.

Drake remembered another night, a similar scene. He was lying on a bed in the window of a non-descript motel room, also on the rim of a hill, and wondering if the fire in his gut would ever be extinguished. That fire, too, had caught him unaware. While his back was turned, the flames had been pushed along in both directions by a spiraling wind, a potent fuel, leaving nothing untouched.

This enemy was not just something interesting to watch. It had approached like a thief from behind as he had complacently steered his Harley around the curves of the highway, putting as much space as possible between himself and the fire he had lit in a thoughtless attempt to erase his past.

Distant sounds of sirens filled the night air and only then did he turn his back, stretch out in his recliner and doze. In a semi-awake state, and no sense of time, memories of his encounter with the ashes of his secret childhood came flooding back. He remembered taking out his lighter and holding it to the tatters of the old chair, smelled the odor of burning fiber, but the memory was aborted by the colors of the most beautiful sunrise he had ever seen.

Sometime later he jerked upright as fingers of fear pressed on his windpipe. What was he thinking? Had he committed a crime—of arson? He owned the property, so why couldn't he burn it down if he liked? The old house was unlivable and of no use to him. But what if, like the fire on the distant hill, it had spread to other property?

Drake had a decision to make. Enough time had been wasted by brooding over the situation he found himself in. After learning of his biological parents, he realized he had been very fortunate indeed to have been adopted. He hadn't been a foundling, hadn't experienced the feeling of abandonment because he had not known his true history. Yet, that lost feeling had been there. Can a person be hurt or influenced by circumstances of which they are unaware? The things that had gone wrong—his drinking—his biological grandfather an abusive hopeless drunk. Could he have inherited the RNA? Had his inability to accept his lot in life, his feeling of something always missing, been his lack of knowing or understanding the circumstances of his birth? But the past was the past. It was time he took charge of his life and put away childish things.

Tomorrow, he would go back to Porterville. He would face the music. He would find the local sheriff and confess that he burned down the house—his house. Perhaps the sheriff would turn out to be a reasonably decent man and understand why he had started that fire. Even if the house was totally gone, the lot would be of some value. It was difficult to destroy a plot of land.

Having made his decision, Drake slept better that night than he had since his fictitious world had caught up with him and smacked his spoiled ears. What did it matter whose RNA he carried— he was now an adult and responsible for his own future.

The next morning, Drake left his apartment with an unfamiliar feeling of clarity. The sun cast a warm glow over the trees and roof tops. He secured his helmet and gunned the Harley. Perhaps he had even outgrown his Harley.

Drake relaxed and enjoyed the picturesque rolling terrain, past golden wheat fields near ready for harvest, corn fields the same, only severed stalks remaining—crows making a picnic of the kernels left behind. Farmhouse yards showed remnants of summer flower beds, awaiting the onset of autumn. He was only a few miles from Porterville when he passed the farm where the farmer had tipped his hat the previous morning. He slowed to read a crude sign nailed to a split-rail fence post: *Garage Apartment for rent in exchange for work.* A country apartment—an interesting concept: Living quietly in the country would certainly be a new experience—one he had never thought of trying, for sure. He made a mental note to check it out on his way back to Coopersville. He had already tendered his resignation from the college. He was definitely not returning to academia where students appeared interested in everything but learning. He doubted if any of his former students could describe him if asked to do so—their eyes incessantly glued to the latest electronic gadget. In a few years teaching and traditional schooling would be outmoded— relics of the past.

His palms grew damp on the handle bars as he got closer to the scene of the crime. He wasn't thinking straight when he had set that fire, but the excuse might not interest the sheriff. So be it—he was through shirking responsibility. If he was busted for arson he would face it and accept the punishment. He hoped it wouldn't come to that.

He slowed as he approached the edge of town, passed a service station on his left, the Motel 6. Garden spots showed remnants of summer vegetables, some already tilled for winter's rest. A church, painted white with nondescript steeple came into view—a cemetery alongside that he didn't remember seeing before. He wondered if his biological parents were buried there. Now he had another graveyard to visit—graves of parents he hadn't known existed except for very early childhood— and the ghost of memories the morning he set the fire. Two worlds—only thirty miles apart but could have been a continent away. If he had a choice, he wondered which life he would have chosen.

Questions remained that still needed answers. At the end of the block, *his* vacant lot stood out in its non-glorious splendor. He wiped the sweat from his forehead with his sleeve. Thankfully, the fire he had watched the night before on the rim of the hills had not been his doing. He stopped his bike and planted his boots firmly on the ground and removed his helmet. Leaving the motor running, he walked, for the second time, onto the humble patch of earth where he had been born. The old house had burned to the foundation but there were no signs of the fire extending into the surrounding neighborhood. Except for a few blackened pots and pans and the metal frame of a bed, sofa, and kitchen appliances, only ashes remained.

He felt no remorse for what he had done. No flash-backs this time, only charred remains of a childhood he had been fortunate enough to tune out but his mind apparently had not forgotten.

He was about to walk away when in the ashes a shiny object sparkled in the morning light. He rescued it from the debris, rubbed the ashes away to find a necklace with a single linked charm— a profile or silhouette of a child's head. He turned it over to find an engraving: *"Drake – My Son"*. He walked away with the charm held tightly in his hand, across the yard to his bike, his gait somewhere between a dirge and a sprint, his mind in turmoil. Was it possible she had loved him—enough to give him up to a better life?

Drake continued his ride through the tiny town, past the Bucket of Blood bar he had previously visited, continued on to a non-descript cement block and stucco building that housed the fire department, and next door the sheriff's office. An American Flag, symbol of justice for all, furled from the sharp roofline. Drake gritted his teeth, carefully parked the bike, clinched and unclenched his fists, and breathed deeply. Sheriff Webster's name was spelled out in a plaque to the left of the door. Drake slowly turned the doorknob at the same time a voice called out from inside. "Come in."

A tall, Clint Eastwood replica, and about as skinny, arose from behind a large metal desk. Drake took in the black hair with a few streaks of gray, slightly receding from the forehead. He approached with timidity. "I'm Drake Dawson…."

"I know who you are—been expecting you. I'm Sheriff Charlie Webster." They shook hands.

"I don't understand. Have we met?"

"I'll explain later." He turned abruptly and introduced his Deputy, Tom, who arose from a smaller desk to the right, and his secretary, a middle aged woman named Ethel, who found it difficult to smile. But then, what did she have to smile about? Life couldn't be very exciting in such a small town.

Grabbing his hat from a rack of deer antlers on the wall behind his desk, Sheriff Webster wasted no time coming forward. "Okay, young man, let's go grab a cup of Joe."

He instructed his staff to buzz him if he was needed, held the door for Drake to exit, and, with an air of authority, slammed it behind him.

"I've had an eye on you since the fire. Been wondering how long it would take you to show up."

Alice's Diner was half a block away. They walked in silence—Drake once again baffled by the conversation as well as the sheriff's stance. He certainly hadn't expected the man's almost cordial reception. Could be a ruse, or the "good cop, bad cop" routine, but he'd go along and see what developed. The sheriff wasn't what Drake expected in a small town law-enforcer. But maybe he was expecting the movie type—a cigar smoking, over fed, pompous show-off. Instead of finding himself in cuffs, he was on his way to have coffee with a slim, rather nice looking guy who probably had the makings of a decent human being underneath the tough-guy façade. There was muscle underneath the uniform in spite of his svelte appearance.

Alice's Diner, exterior painted yellow—white window boxes bubbling over with profusely blooming petunias—brought a smile to his face. Not exactly a Starbucks. Inside, it oozed a cozy feeling of warmth, was spotlessly clean and smelled of coffee and cinnamon. Four empty sage green vinyl covered booths sat on each side of the room. Three tables with chairs filled the center space. On the counter, what appeared to be homemade sugar cookies and muffins tempted them. Alice, 40ish, with sparkling blue eyes and red hair held back from her face with decorative combs, greeted them with a big grin that didn't appear to be reserved for customers only. Drake somehow felt sure of that. She smiled with her eyes as well as her grin. What you saw was what you got. With a scrubbed face and little makeup she was still a pretty woman.

The sheriff indicated a booth in the far corner, flipped his hat onto the seat and directed Drake onto the seat opposite him. A window looked out at the two-lane street and on the other side a small wooded playground held a swing set, a yellow painted slide, and a picnic table. A lone young woman patiently pushed a swing holding an obviously happy child. Drake began to relax.

Alice appeared with two large mugs of steaming coffee, a miniature milk glass of real cream, and two large poppy seed muffins. She patted the sheriff on the shoulder. "On the house," she said, while nervously rearranging the buttons and blossoms on her blouse to better advantage before moving back toward the kitchen. The sheriff took a cautious sip of his coffee, leaned back on the vinyl with his highly polished left boot extending into the aisle.

"Okay, Drake, you have my full attention unless we're interrupted by this thing." He placed the phone on the chrome table top. "It's too early in the day for family fights, and too late for some farmer to report a missing cow." He grinned at Drake, tore the paper off the over-sized muffin and bit in like a man who had little time to eat.

"Before you say anything, I already guessed you set that fire. Thankfully, the firemen had it out before it spread to surrounding areas".

Drake's shoulders relaxed. "That's a relief. What about that fire I saw in the distance last night?"

"I understand that one started with a cookout — sheer carelessness."

Drake took a sip of coffee but ignored the muffin—too nervous to eat. The sheriff politely listened as Drake told his story, not once interrupting nor appearing surprised at the contents of the disclosure.

After several minutes of oratory, Drake summed up with "I wasn't thinking of arson that morning, Sheriff. I was still in shock at learning of my background. As I said, memories came back as I stood on that rotting porch—memories or hallucinations. I just wanted them to stop and the lighter seemed the best way to make that happen. I'm sorry I allowed my emotions to misguide me. If I've committed a crime, I'm ready to take my punishment, or make some restitution for my behavior." He gulped the last swallow of his coffee just as Alice appeared with a refill.

The silence continued as Drake nervously stirred the strong brew. The sheriff's attention seemed more on what was going on across the street—which was nothing. The only movement in the park was a gentle back and forth of an empty swing.

Sheriff Webster finally turned back to Drake, apparently having gotten his thinking over with. "Son, I've a confession of my own. I've kept track of you for a long time."

"I don't understand. The fire just happened."

"No, much longer than that—your whole life, in fact. You see, I knew your grandfather, a drunken no-good man—sorry—who ran the Bucket of Blood, the only bar in town. He often took you, as a child, to work with him. What kind of man would do that to a child? I also knew your mother." He took another sip of coffee, followed by another pause. "Yes, I knew Rhonda. In fact, I was in love with her, but the old man made our relationship impossible. He was already drinking too much and scared to live alone. He put a guilt trip on your Mom after her mother passed away and Rhonda couldn't walk away and leave him alone in his condition."

So the flashes of memory he had the day he set the fire were not figments of his imagination but something else for Drake to wrap his mind around—one more thing for him to digest.

The sheriff hesitated for some time, gazing in the coffee cup as if it held tea leaves predicting his future. When he finally lifted his eyes to Drake, a nervous half-laugh escaped. "Ironic how things happen—or don't happen—isn't it? You might have been my son."

"So what did happen?"

"Like a young fool, I gave up on Rhonda ever marrying me, spent a tour of duty in the Army, came home and went to Coopersville where I learned to be a gun-totem' sheriff's deputy. At least, in that job, the enemy wasn't so likely to shoot back at me. While I was doing my duty overseas, Rhonda married another guy. I couldn't blame her. Your grandfather had became a total drunk, lost the bar business."

All Drake could manage was a lame "That's too bad."

"I tried to forget her—never did. Eventually this little dot on the map needed a sheriff, I was the right size for the uniform, and saved the town some money. I've been here ever since. She was still here—alone except for a little boy—you—and her irresponsible father. You see, Rhonda was born with a sense of duty that finally did her in. She knew she couldn't make your grandfather well, and yet she couldn't abandon him to his fate. When Rhonda fell for your father, I knew it wouldn't last. Ed moved in with them and your grandfather became even more cantankerous—stayed drunk most of the time. After you were born, Ed did make an effort to keep the family together. Finally, I guess he couldn't take it anymore and left. Three months later he was killed in a long distance run for FedEx. Shortly thereafter, widowed and with little income, your Mom could no longer care for both you and her dad. Her greatest concern was that he would harm you during one of his binges. She felt you'd have a chance for a better life in a different environment."

"If you cared for her, couldn't you have helped?"

"Nothing I could do. I kept my distance while she was married. After the accident, I did make an effort—tried to talk her into committing her father—but couldn't get through to her. I think she just gave up after losing you. She later developed a fast-growing cancer and lasted only a short time."

"Do you think they would have gotten back together if Ed hadn't gotten killed?"

"Who knows? Apparently, he wasn't too bad a guy, but he did

walk away from you and Rhonda— maybe took the easy way out. Or, he may have intended to return. We'll never know now. I did check on him—he had no criminal record. That should make you feel better about him."

The two men fondled their coffee mugs in silence, each lost in thought, neither aware of passing time—Drake trying to process the news that he had a father he had no memory of— another mysterious branch on his family tree.

Sheriff Webster was the first to snap out of his reverie. "In spite of everything, you need to know that she loved you and found you a good home, someone who could give you what she couldn't. She didn't turn you over to some agency. She made sure your adoptive parents were good people and could love and care for you the way you deserved."

"Thank you, Sheriff, for filling me in—and for trying to help."

"Drake, you've lost and gained two sets of parents in a short time, and that's a lot to deal with. I hope knowing the facts will help you work out your future. I'm aware that you've had your own demons with the bottle off and on, but don't allow your DNA to dictate the kind of man you are. Don't let history repeat itself. You're young, not too bad looking, with a long life ahead of you. Find someone to love and something you love to do, and let that be your anchor."

"So you never married?"

"Nope— never found anyone to replace Rhonda. Now, I'm just an aging Vet trying to maintain peace in a small town, help folks out when I can. I'm too ugly to attract anyone I'd have—or who would have me."

"I've seen uglier," Drake responded with a smile. "One never knows what the future holds— I'm a perfect example, so don't give up. I'm not."

Tilting his head toward the kitchen, he added, "Alice certainly treats you like someone special." They both laughed—a panacea they both needed.

Drake finally reached for the poppy-seed muffin and held his cup up to Alice for another refill.

"By the way, I've kept track of you in one way or another since you were a tot. In spite of everything, I needed to know you were cared for. In fact, it was kind of a promise I made to Rhonda—to watch over you from a distance. You got some of your grandfather's genes but you've worked your way around them and can be a man your Mom would be proud of."

Drake remembered the necklace, removed it from his shirt pocket and placed it in front of the sheriff. "I found this in the yard, covered in ashes. I almost walked over it."

Charlie held it in his hands, rubbed it with his thumb, and swallowed deeply before handing it back. "I remember her wearing that. In fact, I never saw her without it. She did love you—no doubt about that."

The phone interrupted with a loud rendition of "Country Roads". Drake half listened while watching a concerned expression play out on the sheriff's face. He glanced at his watch and flipped the phone shut.

"Sorry, Drake—duty calls."

"What about my crime?"

"What crime? Only you and I know who started that fire. I see no reason to stir up more trouble for you, but don't make me regret it. I want to discuss this further, so you can count on me being your shadow—until you prove there's no further need to do so—deal?"

On the short walk back to the office, Drake thanked him profusely for his understanding. "Now that I know who I am, I'm making some changes in my life and I may need a wiser man than I am to help make the right decisions."

"Don't know about the wise part," Charlie said, with a smile playing around his lips. "I've had my moments, too."

"I passed a church and cemetery on the way here—is that where they're buried? The attorney didn't tell me much about them—only what was necessary, I guess."

Charlie nodded his head. "Yes, all three of them."

Back at the office, they shook hands again and exchanged business cards. "My private number is there also. Call me if I can be of help, or if you just want to talk. Either way, I'll be in touch. Don't leave town or anything stupid like that."

The deputy was waiting at the door, hat and cruiser keys in hand. Some other poor soul was in trouble.

A few minutes later, on his way out of town, Drake pulled into a typical small-town cemetery. It didn't take long to find what he was looking for. He found the humble markers—no family marble headstone here—no embellishment other than a simple empty concrete flower vase. Drake felt he had been walking the earth all his life in search of something familiar. Now, at least, he had a family tree he could call his own. He hadn't planted the tree or watched it grow but it was his tree nonetheless. Someday perhaps he could be more sympathetic toward the woman who gave him birth, but in spite of the necklace he couldn't help wondering if she couldn't have found a better solution. Drake's heart went out to orphans everywhere and wondered if they all felt disconnected in the self same way.

His life hadn't been ideal but he knew he was fortunate not to have been arrested for arson. There remained a number of problems he would have to deal with, the most urgent being his future. He couldn't alter his past but he could build a future, he hoped a totally different but more constructive one. The vacant lot—what would he do with it? No house—he'd burned it down.

As he walked away, his thoughts were on adoption. Wouldn't it be more humane to rehabilitate parents rather than break the bonds of birth? Often when placed in children homes or foster care they were further abused. In his case, his mother had willingly given him up—he hadn't been taken away by welfare authorities. How long would it be before the questions haunting his mind and heart would be answered? He looked again at the necklace, caressed the charm with his thumb as the sheriff had done, and felt his heart soften.

Three

"And in the sweetness of friendship let there be laughter, and sharing of pleasures. For in the dew of little things the heart finds its morning and is refreshed." Kahlil Gibran

Drake awakened to ribbons of sunlight streaming diagonally across the bed. His sleep had been restless and he felt a bit disoriented, recalling vague dreams of burning houses and faceless strangers coming and going. His focus finally rested on his Harley keys lying on a scrap of white paper on his bedside table—the necklace alongside it. Thoughts of the previous day swept away the cobwebs and brought him to full awareness.

Sheriff Webster's response to his visit had completely befuddled him. He hadn't expected the man's understanding or willingness to overlook his crime of arson, nor had he expected to learn of the man's connection to his biological family. Just one more person he had been denied the privilege of knowing. Every day it seemed a different curtain opened to reveal more of the obscure landscape of his past. He wondered what other surprises awaited behind the curtain, but for now he needed to maintain a clear head and not make any more stupid mistakes. With that thought, he reached for the scrap of paper containing the phone number of the farmer who offered an apartment in exchange for labor. He wondered what the real story would be.

Feeling more refreshed and upbeat than he had in a long time, Drake felt no reluctance to contact the man for the particulars about the apartment. He was certain he didn't want to remain in the university town any longer. Teaching had given him a temporary purpose but he now felt ready to open himself to other possibilities. Without hesitation, he tapped in the numbers.

After dressing and a quick breakfast, Drake was once again on his bike, following the now familiar highway back toward Porterville—this time to visit a Niles Tanner, owner of the garage rental apartment. He approached the day with a blasé attitude. If nothing else, he would meet the friendly guy who had tipped his hat at him on his first visit to Porterville.

It was a clear morning and little traffic. He made good time. As he neared Porterville he came to an intersection and turned into a narrow two-lane intersecting road. He slowed the Harley further to avoid numerous potholes—he didn't wish to end up in a roadside ditch. The Tanner farm was just up ahead, nearly hidden by a wind screen of towering trees. The large white, two-storied framed house sat slightly below road level with a fenced yard and cement steps leading down to the front porch. North of the road was a deeply wooded and wire-fenced hillside and just beyond the house a garage with a second story—obviously the apartment as advertised.

Drake parked his Harley as close as possible to the front gate. Niles Tanner arose from a rocking chair on the porch and greeted him with a friendly handshake and indicated a pair of white porch rockers.

"Let's get acquainted before I show you the loft—as my son called it—if you're not in a hurry." The man sat down and started rocking as if he had nothing better to do. "The space might need some work to make it suitable for your purposes—but you look like an able-bodied man."

Drake sized him up—the man was either trying very hard to

look like a farmer or trying not to—he wasn't sure which. His cap was hanging on the corner of his rocker, but he wore a pair of khaki trousers, neatly pressed as if they had just come from the cleaners, and a pale blue button-down shirt. He reached over to a thermos on a side table alongside two coffee mugs.

"Care for some Java?"

"Just the thing I need after a long ride. If you don't mind my saying so, you're not what I expected."

"And what did you expect?"

"A nice friendly toothy guy in overalls and a day old beard—maybe chewing tobacco."

They both laughed—cracking the ice of a first meeting.

"Sharp... you've read me rightly. This property has been in my family for over fifty years. I inherited it, but spent few of my adult years here—off doing more important things—at least I thought they were more important at the time. This was originally a large dairy farm but my father gradually sold off some of the acreage. The remainder has been leased out to other farmers."

"I see," Drake said. "I'm probably not what you expected either."

"Well, you're the first and only call I've had since the sign went up three months ago. I didn't have very high hopes of anyone taking me up on the offer. He looked Drake over—from his straight, neatly trimmed, straw-colored hair to his biker mode of dress—the black Levi's and short leather boots. He looked up to the dusty Harley parked at the gate, and back to Drake's amused smile. "You're either looking for a place to hide or you're on a search for solitude."

"Ah, you've tagged me perfectly. It's the latter, but I'm thinking the "biker" part of me would soon lose its appeal if I had to travel these country roads."

Both men sipped their black coffee in silence—except for birds arguing like a bunch of politicians in a sycamore tree a few feet from the porch. From his viewpoint, Drake noted the absence of auto traffic, or nearby neighbors. He could only guess at what existed beyond the garage and further down the rural road. He supposed in time one could learn to like the sense of isolation he was feeling.

Mr. Tanner broke the silence with an offer of a refill.

"Time seems to have stood still out here—very peaceful," Drake offered.

"Yes it is—a relatively new experience for me since my semi-retirement. But, I like it."

Drake wondered if the man lived alone, but waited for the story to continue at its own pace.

As if reading his mind, Tanner set his empty cup aside. "I retired from a career with the Feds in D.C. and came back here to refuel. The place had been rented out and well cared for. Then I got word that my twenty-six year old son was being sent home from the Middle East—the army— with post-traumatic stress disorder. Can't seem to wrap my mind around that diagnosis—could mean anything. He's being checked out at an Army hospital before being discharged. He's unmarried, and I decided this was the best place for us both to recuperate. My wife, Annabelle, died of cancer three years ago. She was "Anna" to everyone else—only I was allowed to call her "Annabelle". Drake saw an anemic smile followed by another pause.

"I'm sorry, Sir." That explained the coffee being served from a thermos, and the absence of accompanying cookies. His Mom would have served cookies or scones with the coffee.

"This doesn't appear to be a working farm, Sir." *Somehow, the man seemed to warrant the title.*

"Not yet. What we do with it depends on my son and his progress. I've kept twenty acres and the house—what you can see—so there's not a lot of upkeep at the moment. To be honest, I want someone on the premises, someone I can trust, to look after things when I'm away. I still do some consulting and I might need backup for my son. He's being discharged from the hospital in three weeks and, frankly, I'm worried."

Drake was speechless—not what he expected at all. Another surprise, but he liked this man and felt an unexpected compassion—a new experience for him. Was the empathy coming from his own personal past history?

"We can talk about all of this later. Now tell me about you and why on earth a young man like you would consider living out here in the country."

"Mr. Tanner, your story makes my issues seem terribly insignificant—makes me ashamed for my lack of participation in what's going on over there."

"A lot of the boys are coming back physically or mentally traumatized—or both. Oscar has been a good son and a good soldier. I just pray I'll be able to see him through this period of recuperation. I may have to give up my occasional consultation work, which I'll do gladly and for as long as he needs me."

Drake continued. "I've lost both of my parents—or who I thought were my parents—a year apart. Then, three weeks ago an attorney showed up at my door informing me that I had been adopted as a young child, that my biological mother had also died, leaving me sole beneficiary of her "estate"—a run-down house and lot in Porterville. That's where I'd been when you tipped your hat to me. I saw your sign on another visit I made to the Porterville sheriff, and why I'm here today. I'm all alone in the world and I need a quiet space to sort out my past and somehow make a decent future for myself.

"Good Lord, I can't imagine how you're handling all of that."

"I'm at a total loss to know where to go professionally. I have, perhaps foolishly, given up teaching at Kaiser College in Coopersville to pursue writing or painting—or both. I want to try my hand in the arts. Mr. Tanner, I feel like I've been blindfolded all my life, and now that the blindfold is off, I find the light almost blinding. I might even need a few shadows to cut the glare. Understand?"

Tanner studied him with an expression of deep thought, causing Drake to feel a bit uncomfortable under his perusal.

"Young man, I can see why you want to be a writer or painter, to devote your life to something creative. I also sense you're very close to finding your true calling. We are not responsible for the circumstances of our birth but we are responsible for the way we live —as a believer or a nonbeliever."

Mr. Tanner leaned back in his rocker and began to sing. *'I believe for every drop of rain that falls a flower grows. I believe that somewhere in the darkest night a candle glows. I believe that somewhere the smallest prayer can still be heard. I believe that someone in the great somewhere hears every word. Every time I hear a new born baby cry, or touch a leaf, or see the sky, then I know why I believe.'* Sorry—may not be the exact words but you get what I mean."

"Wow, that's an old one. I remember my mother—my adoptive mother—singing that song."

Mr. Tanner smiled and watched as two blue jays swooped down to land on a low limb of a dogwood tree. "I learned it from my mother—she always sang when piddling around in her garden, deadheading her roses, or sitting here on the porch stringing beans. She had the voice of an angel. At least that's the way I remember her."

The two men rocked in unison, lost in memories as the sun rose higher in the sky.

Drake broke the silence. "You can have that kind of faith after all the loss you've been through?"

"A man has to believe in something bigger than himself, or else be destroyed by what the world offers."

Drake repositioned himself in the rocker and changed the subject. "I hope Oscar will make a quick recovery."

"The VA doctor is optimistic. I just hope he's right in his prognosis."

"One more thing you might want to be aware of before showing me the apartment. I lived a rather troubled life growing up, struggled with the bottle off and on—things I'm not proud of— but I'm clean now and have no intention or desire to return to that way of life. Now that my new roots have sprouted, I have a better understanding of who I am. Hopefully, I'll be able to accept what I can't change and find some way of giving back."

"Sometimes it takes a bit of trauma to get us to the good stuff in life. Let's hope that's true for both of us—and especially for my son." Drake watched the man struggle for composure and was surprised at the degree of compassion he felt for him—a total stranger.

"The reason I'm offering free rent in exchange for help is the need for some refurbishing of the space. On the other hand, you may find it suitable for your purposes. You'll be free to make any improvements you need—within reason. Oscar used it primarily as a place to practice his music when we visited—to protect my parents from permanent hearing loss."

Drake laughed. "I understand. I don't play a musical instrument but as a teenager I knew to turn my music down when I heard a car in the driveway. Mom tolerated it, but my dad leaned more toward the classics—probably typical for lawyers," Drake added, but quickly changed the subject.

"Your house is not at all what I expected. I'd probably sit here on the porch and rock all day."

"I had it spruced up—a few updates for Annabelle's sake. I couldn't bring her back here to live without a few modern conveniences. She grew to love it before—well, you know." Another subject neither wished to address further.

"Come, Drake, let me show you the apartment."

Drake noticed the roof of the one car garage had been extended to form a carport and a deck extending out from the apartment above. Wooden steps led them to a cedar deck that looked out over the acreage to the east where an extension of the rural highway curved and disappeared into a covered bridge a half mile or so away. An uncovered section of deck extended around the south side of the apartment, affording a view of the main house and outbuildings, including a silo.

The apartment was no smaller than the one in the city and he immediately liked the open loft-like feel of the space. Mr. Tanner pointed out the electric heaters in the baseboard, apologized for lack of air conditioning but offered to pay for a window unit if Drake agreed to install it. A small area enclosed with shutters held a stacked washer and dryer with scant evidence of use. A galley kitchen supplied the basic appliances. In spite of the dusty windows, Drake was surprised at the light—a north window that looked out onto a steep wooded area beyond the highway. Meant as a bedroom, there would be room for his bed and dresser from his old apartment and probable space for an easel. He would have to determine which room provided the best light for painting. The living area was ample for a television, sofa, and his recliner. The thought made him smile. He hadn't felt the need for an oversized one with remote controls, or one that vibrated or played music—or opened a can of beer—certainly not an issue now in his new sobriety. He'd had a proper upbringing after all, and had some pride in his few possessions. The walnut desk he had kept from his father's home office would fit in nicely. He vowed to forget the negative feelings he had once harbored of that office.

"As you can see, Drake—no furniture except that sleeper sofa. If you don't want it, there's a Hospice outlet in Porterville. They would be happy to take it off your hands."

"Furniture is no problem—I have my own—but do you have internet connection or cable TV this far out?" Drake had no desire to be totally isolated from modern technology.

"All set—I use the internet a lot in my business so it will be no problem extending the service up here."

Drake hadn't expected that in the rural area, but then, Mr. Tanner had turned out to be anything but the stereotypical farmer.

"As I said, Oscar used the space mostly for his music." He turned aside, looked out the south facing window before continuing. "It wasn't used much. He decided to travel, see what the rest of the world looked like before settling down. He was away two years, came back unhappy with the situation in Iraq and Afghanistan. He signed up to do his part for his country—served three years and then—well, you know. Life doesn't always play fair. I was upset with him because he didn't choose a higher education, but we have to let people lead the life they think is best. He's an intelligent young man, and well traveled."

As he turned back, Drake didn't miss the tears that had formed in the grieving father's eyes. He seemed to have forgotten why they were there, cleared his throat and again turned aside. Drake had no trouble making up his mind, and the decision had as much to do with Mr. Tanner as the apartment itself. He liked the man, felt drawn to him somehow, and for the first time in his life wanted to help another human being. The solitude and raw beauty of the countryside intrigued Drake, as did the minimalist décor of the space.

"Mr. Tanner, I'd like to give this a try, but I'd feel better paying some rent. I can't imagine my helping out here would compensate for the space—much nicer than I expected, I might add."

"Let's see how things go. Just having you on the premises will be a blessing for me, and I have a feeling you and Oscar will be good for each other."

"Afraid I've never formed lasting relationships—too wrapped up in my own issues, I suppose. I look forward to meeting your son." The two shared a tight handshake and felt their hearts lighten.

"You may move in whenever you like. I'm looking forward to knowing you better and I hope this will work out for all three of us. I'll contact Comcast and get you hooked up to the rest of the world.

And now, if you're in no hurry, would you like to see what I've done with the main house?"

"I would, but first, another question—how will Oscar feel about me living in what used to be his space? I wouldn't want my presence to make him uncomfortable in any way."

"I talked to him about renting it out and he's okay with the idea. His music has been pushed aside or put on hold since all of this happened. Besides, if he does take it up again he won't have to worry about the noise, not that it ever bothered me. When I'm away, he'll have the big house to himself, unless you decide to pay him a visit from time to time."

As they entered the front door of the main house, Drake was surprised to see the interior was quite large and nicely decorated. Mr. Tanner pointed out the changes— a wall knocked out between the living and dining room to give a more open concept—with an updated kitchen beyond. The main rooms opened through French doors to a large living space with a huge fireplace, a pool table to the far side, a comfortable seating arrangement facing a large flat screen television. Another door led to the strategically placed kitchen.

"Wow, this is unlike any country house I would have imagined," Drake offered.

"Not much entertainment here in the country, so I insisted on the pool table—and there's a portable ping-pong top to go on it. Oscar and I played often. Even Annabelle occasionally beat me at pool." The smile once again faded at the mention of her name.

Through a wall of windows, Drake saw a large screened porch overlooking the valley, and a meandering creek at the foothills. He thought about Oscar and what the young man had sacrificed for his country's freedom. Drake doubted if he had any ability to be of use to the traumatized soldier, but if friendship or a little companionship would make a difference, it would be the least he could do.

Four

"You can muffle the drum, and you can loosen the strings of the lyre, but who shall command the skylark not to sing."
Kahlil Gibran

Drake left the Tanner farm around noon and realized he was quite hungry. Other than finding some food, he felt the need to talk with Sheriff Charlie again. He wanted to be sure he hadn't dreamed their first meeting at which time he was absolved of any wrongdoing in regard to the fire.

Alice's Diner served decent food, and his Harley seemed to lead the way, not to his city apartment but back to the small town of his birth. He passed the Motel 6, the church and cemetery at the edge of town, and the threatening sign to slow to twenty-five mile per hour just beyond. He slowed.

From a newcomer's point of view, Drake noted that the houses were mostly well kept—mostly white, with pots of mixed flowers on the porches—mostly petunias. He knew his flowers —his mother had been a member of the Garden Club. Main Street offered a Colony movie theatre with the neon marquee spelling out Brad Pitt in a star role. The place showed no activity—matinees only on the weekends, he supposed. Next door, an ice cream shop with small antique tables and chairs beaconed from the sidewalk—too small a town for Baskin Robbins. He passed an antique shop, the Hospice outlet Tanner had mentioned, and Porterville Hardware.

His now empty lot soon came into view—a definite eyesore—and a reminder of his past that had been forever hidden from him. He made a mental note to have the lot cleared, to clean up the mess he had created.

He slowed the bike further when the Sheriff's office came into view—the squad car missing from the parking space. He continued on to Alice's Diner hoping to find Sheriff Webster there. He recalled his feelings of trepidation on first meeting the sheriff. This time, as he hurried inside, he felt no such thing—only anticipation.

Alice was busy, flitting from table to table like a sparrow in mating season. Her smile brightened the room when she spotted him with his shiny black helmet in hand. "Well, look at what the cat dragged in," she said. "Charlie's right back there in the corner booth. I'll be there with a menu and coffee in a minute." Drake found her so refreshing he could have hugged her like a favorite aunt, except he'd never had a favorite aunt, or any aunt for that matter. He wondered if Charlie had given her his life history—probably not—until he proved himself worthy.

The sheriff hastily arose from his seat, greeted Drake with a powerful handshake and a slap on the shoulder. "Good to see you, boy, although you're not much of a boy anymore."

"Good to see you, Sir. Having a quiet day?"

"For the moment, yes—but sit down, sit down, what have you been up to?"

He was just as Drake remembered —upbeat and friendly, his dark hair neatly combed, his uniform spotless. Meeting Mr. Tanner, finding a new apartment, and now seeing Charlie again—he was having a very good day.

Charlie glanced at his watch. "I do have a backlog of paper work on my desk, but I can give you some time. What's on your mind?

Getting ready to return to teaching?"

"Not this year—talking my life in a different direction."

"Well, you're still young, and teaching, like my job, has to be a challenge these days."

"Do you know a Niles Tanner? He has a farm about eight miles from here."

"I know who he is. His family has lived in this county for years. Lost his wife some time ago, and has a son in the military, I believe. Why do you ask?"

"I just spent the morning at his farm and am about to make a decision, perhaps a foolish one." He placed his helmet on the seat beside him. "You did say you were available if I needed advice, didn't you?"

"Right—but it depends on the advice. If it's about finding female companionship, I'm afraid I can't help you."

"Sorry, that's a minor concern right now. I don't understand it myself, but I feel like some invisible force is pulling me back here—to my roots. I want to get away from the city, at least for a while. Mr. Tanner has a nice garage apartment and I'm considering renting it and moving to the country. I feel a strong need for a different lifestyle, a fresh start."

"That would be different, for sure. You've always been a city boy."

Drake told him about his morning visit with Mr. Tanner, about his soldier son with PTSD, as well as his plans for the apartment.

"I was quite taken by the man, and not only because I could relate to his losses. His wife died of cancer, he had big hopes for his son—a son now coming home with what could be serious psychological problems. This is a new experience for me, but I would like to help the man in any way I can. He seems rather alone and lost and I know well that feeling. He's not even charging me rent, providing I help out around the property, and be there for support when his son, about my age— or a little younger— is released from the hospital."

"Listen to your heart, Drake. Frankly, I'm proud of you for reaching out to help others. That's seldom a bad thing. Plus, you'll be nearby—I can keep a closer eye on you," he added with raised eyebrows.

Drake laughed. "Not too closely, I hope."

"If there's nothing else on your mind, I need to get back to my office."

"Well, yes—when you have time, I'd like to discuss my empty lot. It's an eyesore to your town and something should be done about it. I want to repay my debt to not only you but to the town. I'd like to move into my new digs at the Tanner farm as soon as possible, get the place in order before Oscar returns home. My number will remain the same, and you know where I'll be living. I'll give you a call as soon as I'm settled. You're welcome to stop by. Let me know if you have any ideas for the property."

"Good deal—great to see you again, and good luck with your move. Let me know if I can be of help."

Drake watched him all the way to the parking lot and felt very lucky indeed. The landscape of his future was definitely growing more picturesque. It occurred to him that the sheriff was the closest thing to family he had left, and he wondered what Rhonda would think of that. Too bad her love affair with the sheriff hadn't worked out—things would have been different for all of them. Nonetheless, he had spent the day with two terrific men and felt the heavy cloak of loss and loneliness slip from his shoulders.

Alice was polishing the tables, unfurling fresh tablecloths, filling salt shakers, preparing for the dinner crowd as he left the restaurant. "Don't be a stranger, Drake," she called out, giving him a taste of small town living where friends were as close as family.

A skyscape of cauliflower clouds had turned from white to gray as he climbed on his bike. Raindrops splashed onto his helmet. He hoped it wouldn't turn into a downpour—one of the negatives to traveling on two wheels. One more thing to think about—autumn would soon arrive and as a country boy he would need a different mode of transportation. It wasn't like he could hop a bus in bad weather.

The clouds dissipated as quickly as they had appeared—gliding away on the pre-autumn winds. His Harley caressed the curves and followed the undulating terrain without incident. To the hum of the motor, his mind revisited the day's events, bringing about a bit of ambiguity regarding his future. Quickly, he shook off the feeling— nothing was set in cement. He could always change his mind if things didn't work out. But he must not think like that—too much like the old Drake. Courage and grit were required now if he expected to make something of his life.

Success was not building a huge portfolio—it was creating something to enrich his life and hopefully the lives of others. Survival had taken on a greater significance now that he had come full circle. He refused to dwell on the past or the future. He had never felt more alive and would work toward becoming a decent man before the final curtain fell on his life's drama.

With the wind caressing his face, Drake vowed to pour his energies into becoming a man worthy of a decent future—in spite of his heritage. He would paint his new passions into an achievable goal—and not just for his own vain glory. It was time he let go of all those he had lost. He wouldn't wish to hold them back from their journey into the unknown—any more than he would wish to shy away from his own destiny.

He wondered if there really was an afterlife—if spirits lived on for eternity. He thought of those who had made up the tapestry of his past and wondered if they looked back to see how he was handling their passing, or what he was doing with his newly found knowledge of his early history? Would they have done anything differently? Could there really be a spiritual world where cares and worries were nonexistent? He hoped so.

Five

"You shall not fold your wings that you may pass through doors, nor bend your heads that they strike not against a ceiling, nor fear to breathe lest walls should crack and fall down."
Kahlil Gibran

Two weeks later, Drake surveyed his new living space, now furnished and organized. His belongings had fit in nicely. At the Porterville Hospice outlet where he had taken the sofa, he found a used, lightly paint-splattered professional easel. How else was an easel supposed to look? He hoped he would put it to more serious use than the previous owner who, for whatever reason, had obviously given up too easily. He vowed to give art his best try—to practice the patience of a peacock during the learning process, but then no artist stops learning. His father's masculine walnut, leather-topped desk fit nicely at right angles to the window with southern exposure.

Drake went to the desk and opened his laptop. He smiled as it come to life—the greater world once more at his fingertips. Perhaps he would participate in social media—Facebook, LinkedIn or Twitter—the most popular tools in networking. If his paintings were any good he might post them to see how the world responded. A personal website would be considered when and if his work showed a degree of talent or when he became comfortable with sharing his efforts with others. The only other desk accessory was an "Old Fisherman" lamp that suited his personality. In spite of his sofa and two side chairs the room did not appear crowded. His television and Bose stereo system looked as if they belonged. A small table and two chairs were snugly positioned beneath a small nearby window in the kitchen area.

A wooden wine rack on top of the refrigerator held a single bottle of Robert Mondovi Syrah, the neck pointing at him like the barrel of a gun. A lower shelf in the kitchen cabinet held unopened bottles of Jack Daniel's, Dewar's White Label, and a SKYY Vodka. The presence of the alcohol was an ongoing duel between his resolve and the bottles, but he had to prove to himself that he could face temptation and not succumb. Boxes of prized books waited to be unpacked.

Drake bought a new single bed for the bedroom/studio, first trying out the length for his six foot frame. Having room for the easel and painting supplies was more important than sleeping space. He was sure Mr. Tanner would permit him to build shelves for storage. All in all, the move had gone swiftly and smoothly. He laughed at his new mailing address, never dreaming he would live where his address was a numbered rural route.

After zapping a TV dinner in the microwave, Drake poured a mug of steaming dark roast, sprinkled a few grains of salt into it to cut the bitter taste, and moved to the deck which held a round redwood table, two chairs and two lounge chairs. As a lone bachelor he only had need for one of each but they were a good buy. He gave the unappetizing food a gentle stir on the toss-away plate, and vowed to never eat another one once he was settled. He also vowed to take better care of his body, do his own cooking, and leave the junk food in the grocery store. Liquor would never again be more enticing than a good meal. He ate quickly just to get it over with. Lifting the mug of coffee, he leaned back to survey the landscape, listen to the quiet and wait for the day to close down. Reflected pastel colors from a sunset tinted the few clouds in the eastern sky. They quickly disappeared as a diaphanous, soundless fog crept slowly into the lower valley, wrapping him in a blanket of contentment.

At the moment, it was enough to be a simple sheep, following his master into restful green pastures. Drake pondered the fact that his life appeared to be made up of tiny treasures strategically placed along his new pathway. New friendships—Mr. Tanner and Sheriff Webster—had appeared to accept him without reservation.

Would Oscar be equally receptive to his encroachment on what was once his private space? Time would tell. Happy thoughts played a lullaby in his mind, accompanied by chirps and peeps from nighttime creatures. Lying down in green pastures? Where did that come from? Perhaps he had heard it at the funeral of one of his parents. The green pastures that lay at the bottom of the incline on which the farm house sat soon disappeared in a cottony gray mist with fireflies mimicking the stars above.

Drake's life had been a tapestry woven with threads of different colors, some dark and foreboding, others bright and promising—all having their varied uses and lessons to be learned. All the stupid things he had done were indelibly woven into that tapestry, but Drake would no longer allow it to weight him down. What's done is done, he thought. He welcomed a new kind of life, and any challenges it was certain to bring.

The thought caused him pause. Oscar would be coming home soon, also to a new kind of life. Drake felt he had nothing to offer the soldier, certainly zero ability to deal with a psychological illness—unless alcohol abuse was classified as such. He made a mental note to have a more in-depth chat with Mr. Tanner and voice his feelings of inadequacy. He would also search the internet for further insight into Oscar's diagnosis. Surely the soldier would not be discharged if his condition was not at least manageable. "First do no harm" came to mind.

While night bugs partied around the post light at the corner of the garage apartment, Drake's eyelids grew heavy—partly due to the activities of the day—mostly due to the quiet and tranquil surroundings. He drank in the simplicity, the peacefulness, and felt no desire to be anywhere else. He picked up his dishes and entered his humble but comfortable nest, letting the screened door close quietly behind him. The wide screen HD Sony television sat dark and silent. Even the stereo held no appeal—the quiet was music enough.

Before turning in, Drake again stepped out onto the deck, not wanting the day to end. The fog had changed its contours and a cool wind fanned at his face and ruffled his hair. Funny, he never paid attention to the quality of the wind in the city. Here, it seemed every element of nature was marked with a yellow accent pen or exclamation points. Or perhaps it was because he was beginning to think, notice, and feel like an artist.

Later, lying in bed on his comfortable new mattress, he suddenly thought of Patricia. He regretted having treated her badly. What kind of man put the desire for booze before the happiness of a beautiful woman? He'd been an idiot and didn't blame her for taking off to God only knew where. Maybe someday fate would give him a chance to apologize.

His dreams brought no peace to the night. He saw only the reddened eyes of the grandfather of whom he held no waking memory—the staggering gait, the shaking wrinkled hands, the moment of recognition, the reluctant smile, and the voice—*"Come here, boy."* Drake awoke with a shudder, his forehead wet with perspiration.

Beams of sunlight crept through the slats of the vertical window shade, and Drake, disoriented, looked about for a familiar object to stabilize his sanity. Would his phantom-like past forever haunt him?

The objects in the room slowly took form—the easel in the corner by the north window, a supply of pre-primed canvases leaning against the wall, an antique table holding an array of used and unopened tubes of paint—ready and waiting for the muse to strike. An antique beer stein—another reminder of his earlier indulgences—held paint brushes of varying sizes. He hoped that, eventually visions of his earlier life would vanish, leaving no further impediment to the possibilities ahead of him.

Twice, he had been struck by a train—or so it seemed—first when he learned he was adopted, and again when he learned his entire biological family was lost to him. The news seemed to have come at him through a long, endless tunnel, growing more real and louder as it reached the mouth and struck him down. Would he ever be able to think of the events as trivial—something he could stash away and forget? He wondered if Oscar, after the horror he had experienced, was haunted by the same question.

Drake had thought his course had been set with little hope of alteration. Man, had he been wrong. Could he have continued to teach students, many of who showed little desire to learn? Had he been only a mediocre teacher at best? Hadn't it been his job to inspire the students, although lacking inspiration himself? With that kind of ambivalence, he felt certain he had made a wise choice. If the art world failed to embrace him, he would have, at least, given it a good try, and his failure would harm no one but himself.

Six

"And if you cannot work with love but only with distaste, it is better that you should leave your work and sit at the gate of the temple and take alms of those who work with joy."
Kahlil Gibran

Drake's new apartment—permanent or temporary—was not only sufficient but highly livable. He was settled in with time to spare before Oscar's homecoming. After a long talk with Mr. Tanner about the part he would be expected to play in his son's readjustment to civilian life, his mind had been put at ease.

"Let's not anticipate problems, Drake. He may be quiet or moody, but that's just part of his personality. I have not been told of any violent episodes. If anything disturbing should arise that we can't handle, his doctor will intervene. Just be yourself, listen when he needs an ear—that's all I ask. I'm hoping you two will become friends. I'll learn more when I talk to the doctors before bringing him home."

Autumn was approaching and Mr. Tanner agreed with him that the A/C could wait until hot weather. Drake was ready for the next item on his project list and that was to meet with Sheriff Charlie for a session on future plans for his vacant lot in Porterville.

They met for lunch in the back booth at Alice's Diner where coffee mugs were waiting to be filled by the perpetually smiling and efficient proprietor. After an update on Drake's move, his new digs, and two refills of coffee, the two men left the diner for a tour of the small town to ascertain the assets and liabilities. Drake had already voiced his desire to do something that would have a lasting benefit to not only the townspeople but to the surrounding community as well.

"As I see it, Drake, you have two choices. Rebuild on your vacant lot, or sell the lot and invest in another property, depending on your goals."

Drake learned the town had no library—only a weekly visit by a bookmobile. Second Avenue offered a bank with ATM, an attorney's office, a town museum, a card and gift shop, and the Sheriff's office, plus a movie theatre reminiscent of the 60's. Alice's Diner appeared to be the only eatery, although Charlie mentioned a McDonalds and a steak house north of town. A Home Depot had come to Kirkland, a short distance away. Elementary and High Schools were also located on the main highway to the north. In Drake's mind that meant there were a large number of school children, and no doubt rural adults who might benefit from what he planned to offer.

"There's no library, just a bookmobile?" Drake asked.

"That's right. There was much discussion of one a couple years ago but the town is too small to qualify in spite of the large drawing area from the surrounding county."

They traveled on, past the local high school. Drake noticed a large building on the left that seemed to be vacant. "What's that?" he asked Charlie.

"That is an example of what has happened to industry in this country. It used to be a linens factory— making towels and other dry goods—employed many of our local folks until it became cheaper to farm the work out to China or Bangladesh. Some of the employees moved away, others have stayed on and found other means of earning a living—truck farming and even sheep herding."

"Sheep herding—I thought sheep came from New Zealand or Sweden."

"I know, but it seems to be catching on around here. Fewer people are eating beef, so it may turn out to be a lucrative choice by the landowners. And, of course, they can sell the wool."

Charlie pulled into the vacant parking lot of the abandoned factory to turn the cruiser around. "This is an eyesore to the community. It's also a constant reminder of failed industry."

Drake asked him to stop—he wanted a closer look. They got out of the cruiser and Drake walked around the building that had held up well structurally. The windows were cracked and dirty. The parking lot was surrounded by weeds and miscellaneous debris. Undeterred, Drake turned back to the building and smiled. He saw it as a lady of the night, sitting there alone, saying, "Come and rescue me—you know you want me." But not like this, Drake's inner voice argued, and then why not like this—think what a fortnight of love could do. He could hear her saying "come on, use me—don't leave me with this ugly façade. Do with me as you will." He chuckled as he turned away to find Charlie leaning against the squad car, legs crossed at the ankles, looking like a nonchalant Clint Eastwood.

"So, will it just further deteriorate, or will it be sold now that the business is closed?"

"Who would have a need for it?" Charlie asked.

"Me?"

"You—what would you do with it?"

"Maybe nothing, but I'd sure like to see the interior."

Back on the highway, Drake and Charlie discussed what could be done with the property, if it could be bought, and at what price. Drake's mind was whirling. Mentally, he was thinking of a multi-purpose art center—a gallery, space for artisans to rent, conference room for teaching and lecturing on art to benefit adults as well as local children. Heck, in time perhaps the town could become an art colony like Taos, New Mexico. Those pioneering artists started out with nothing more than a dream. The more he thought about it, the more excited he became. His biological family certainly hadn't contributed much if anything to the town—perhaps he could make up for their lack—or go bankrupt trying.

"Do you have Boy Scouts, Kiwanis, or a place for AA meetings?"

"We do have a Boy Scout troupe. They meet at the school." He didn't know of an AA, although he was called out on occasion to settle spousal problems, often due to over-imbibing.

"People shouldn't have to travel thirty or forty miles for a little culture," he told Charlie.

Charlie listened with interest to Drake's ramblings, intrigued by how his mind worked. "I must say, you have some big ideas—not without merit mind you. You're talking big bucks with the cost of the property, the renovation, plus supporting such an endeavor. You're not that rich, are you, son?"

"I guess I'm getting a bit carried away. At least, it won't hurt to find out who owns it and go from there—right?"

Charlie knew who owned the property but kept mum for the moment. "That won't solve the problem of your vacant lot."

"Let's put that on hold until we know more about the factory, okay?"

"Have you thought of rebuilding? You're still young, but you'll need your own home at some point."

A silence filled the car and Charlie wondered if he'd hit a sore spot. Finally, he got an answer—one he hadn't expected.

"If it were possible to exorcise the ghosts, I might be interested in doing that."

"Rebuilding might do it. You don't want your life to remain as empty as that vacant lot, do you?" Then he really went out on a limb by adding, "A good woman might help."

"Look who's talking. You seem to do all right without a wife—your life a vacant lot?"

Charlie laughed as he glanced out at the familiar landscape.

DECENT DECEIT

"You got me, Drake—it does feel that way sometimes."

Two days later, Drake's phone jingled. "Want to see the property this afternoon?" Charlie asked. "Things are quiet here for a change."

"You bet—what time?"

"Three o'clock? Stop by my office first. If I'm out, I'll leave the keys with Ethel."

At some point he would inform Drake that a sheriff was an elected official with jurisdiction throughout the county. Charlie's job was to transport witnesses and prisoners for county courts in nearby towns, and even serve as tax collector. He could seize and sell property when taxes were in arrears, serve subpoenas and even divorce notices or eviction notices. He also decided on, and maintained, an operating budget. Every county must have a sheriff. In the meantime, he couldn't wait to see what Drake would come up with in his plan to repay his debt to Porterville. He didn't want to make it too easy—he wanted to see what the young man was made of.

In the meantime, Drake paced the floor, the Syrah bottle lying on its side in the wine rack, collecting dust, and aiming right at him. Instead of succumbing, he put on his running shoes and went for a jog down the country road, took the graceful curve to the right and on through a picturesque covered bridge he had viewed from his deck. He came back, showered, dressed for his visit with Charlie. None of it cured his anxiety. His mind was a whirling weathervane of ideas, but no longer on the unopened bottle in plain sight. He assembled a green salad of romaine and arugula, added shaved cheese, sliced almonds, a few drops of extra virgin olive oil and a dash of balsamic vinegar, grabbed a glass of water and went to the deck where a nice breeze welcomed him.

Fortified with food and finally breathing normally, he went to his computer to evaluate his finances one more time. He looked at the figures and not for the first time since their death, appreciated how his adopted parents had provided for him. It was not a fortune, but if he handled things wisely he just might be on the road to a happy and fulfilled future. If the factory idea worked out, his vacant lot could wait. The fire had left nothing living except some wild pink roses at the back edge of the plot. He would keep the grass mowed so the town would have no complaint. The rest he'd leave up to fate or to the Gods.

Seven

*"For what is it to die but to stand naked in
the wind and to melt into the sun."*
Kahlil Gibran

Drake, ten minutes early, again pulled his Harley in front of the sheriff's office, cut the engine, and reminded himself that he was only exploring possibilities regarding the factory. The knowledge that Charlie was becoming a good friend as well as mentor did much to quiet his unrest about his future. He was warmly greeted by Tom, the deputy, as well as the unsmiling Ethel. He wondered how much of his history had been revealed to them. Charlie was leaning back in his chair. One spit-shined boot rested on the corner of the desk amid scattered papers in spite of what appeared to be an updated Dell computer.

"Okay, let's get this field trip over with," he told Drake. He unfolded himself from his comfortable position and reached for his cruiser keys—a smile softening his usual strictly-business, tough guy persona.

The drive was short, thankfully—Drake was not yet comfortable riding in a cruiser. "I really appreciate all your help, Charlie. Hope I'm not taking up too much of your time."

"Happy to be of service," he responded.

Once again, Drake felt the uneasiness creep in as the enormity of the idea caused him to question his sanity. Charlie was strangely quiet as he unlocked the door to the building and stepped aside for Drake to enter. Typical of a sheriff, his first purpose was to observe, and second to assist if it became necessary.

Drake's first impression of the abandoned factory was positive. The interior was surprisingly large, previously used as a reception area with partitioned offices surrounding the central lobby. The space had been left intact and without discernible damage. He followed a hallway to the manufacturing work areas with long tables, rooms with sturdy racks on one side apparently used for materials as well as the same configuration on the opposite side for storage of finished merchandise, Drake surmised. Beyond that was another large room outfitted for packing and shipping. Making his way back to the front, he noted two large restrooms properly outfitted—one for the handicapped. It was in amazing condition. Other than the dirty, cobwebbed windows, the space was unexpectedly tidy. Too bad the enterprise had been unsuccessful, for the owners as well as the employees. The closing had to have been a blow to the residents of the friendly, picturesque town and county. Well, maybe he could do something about the eyesore.

He found Charlie waiting just where he had left him, his face devoid of expression. Drake was feeling strangely numb as the door was once again locked and they walked back to the cruiser without a word passing between them. The silence continued until Charlie pulled up beside the parked Harley. They shook hands and agreed to meet again on Saturday for further discussion. There was a time for talk and a time for silence.

On his way out of town, Drake's attention was drawn again to the cemetery. This time, he noticed the gravesites were in need of attention. The grass had been mowed but weeds were spreading at random near the modest grave markers. He knelt down and cleared some of them from his mother's grave, painfully aware of the necklace in his buttoned left shirt pocket—over his heart. His thoughts had grown kinder since he last visited her grave and most assuredly since finding the necklace. The simple piece of jewelry convinced him she had cared deeply for him, enough to trust another person to his care and upbringing— a promise of a better and safer life for him. Had she sacrificed her own chance for happiness for him? Overcome with emotion, a lifetime of unshed tears ran down his cheeks and seeped into the corners of his mouth as he thought of his childhood.

I didn't know you existed and yet, somehow, I was always aware of your absence. I understand now, and it's okay. You were the missing thread all those years. You always knew about me and your sense of loss had to be much greater than mine. I hope I can stay strong and make up for some of the heartache I caused you and the people to whom you gave your trust. He took the necklace with the silhouette of a child from his pocket and held it lovingly to his chest. *Thank you for this—I'll cherish it always—and I'll do my best to make you proud.*

He stood and wiped the dirt from his hands, the salty tears from his face, and all traces of resentment from his heart. Feeling an unexpected kinship to his past, he sighed deeply. On the next visit, he would tend her grave and perhaps adorn it with a bouquet of flowers, the loveliest he could find. Remembering the pink rose bush on the vacant lot, perhaps he could transplant it by her head marker, in case she missed the fragrance. The necklace would forever remind him that her releasing him was an act of love—not abandonment. As for his grandfather—he had nothing to say to him. His biological father required more thought.

After visiting the cemetery, Drake returned to his apartment feeling a definite shift in his sense of peace, plus a new resolve. He prepared his dinner, took his mug of coffee to his favorite spot—the deck. He welcomed the quiet but it was soon broken by a faraway whistle of a train. He thought of the passengers aboard on their way to another adventure, a soldier coming home, a young girl off to college, or someone called to the bedside of an ailing relative. Drake felt at peace, and not unlike the waning whistle, his anxiety slowly diminished into nothingness. Even his future, he left up to the universe.

That night, Drake slept soundly without the usual intrusive dreams. He awakened feeling invigorated but somewhat restless. He was alone on the farm. He could go to the main house and shoot some pool—Tanner had left him a key. He would be returning in less than two weeks with Oscar. After a breakfast of steel cut oatmeal with blueberries, he dressed in old Levi's and faded tee-shirt and left to tackle the lawn. Tanner had shown him the lawnmower and gas can in the garage, explained the mechanism in case he "felt a need to pay for his keep." Drake smiled at the memory— the man could still kid around in spite of his son's uncertain prognosis. "I promise not to cut off my toes," he had told him.

Drake had never had to cut grass but he had learned some aspects of gardening from watching old Ed, the family gardener, as well as his mother. As a youngster, she took him into the yard to rake leaves with his little yellow plastic rake, while she deadheaded her roses. The Garden Club was one of her most enjoyable activities. More and more Drake found himself remembering the way she had tried to stitch him into the quilt of her life. With shame, he recalled how that feeling of closeness had dissipated when he became a teenager and the rebellion and taste for alcohol took hold.

In retrospect, Drake regretted the anguish he had brought to his adoptive parents. With a little booze in him, he felt little compassion or concern for others. It was probably good that he could not recall the details of those periods—otherwise he might go mad. Now, the only thing he could do was try to make the rest of his life more meaningful, and provide some salve to the wounds of others. Somehow, he would become more understanding of the real world and the actions of mortal men. He wanted to remain sober, smell the fruit tree blossoms of spring, the chrysanthemums of autumn, the marigolds of summer, and the clean, pure aroma of the first snowfall. He didn't want to miss a thing of beauty in his newfound existence.

Two hours later, the lawn didn't exactly look like it was sheared with cuticle scissors, but much improved. The sidewalk leading to the front porch was edged, and a few weeds pulled away from what appeared to be budding chrysanthemums on the east side of the house. Drake remembered their strong fragrance—much less appealing than lilacs or roses. The time passed so quickly Drake didn't realize how tired or how dirty he had gotten. He was also surprised that he had enjoyed the workout as he breathed deeply of the clean pungent smell of freshly cut grass.

All his senses seemed sharper since the poison of alcohol had been washed from his system. Food tasted better and the smell of wind, rain and even thunderstorms made him feel healthy and vibrant. Each day that passed, he seemed to develop more respect for nature and the simple life, things to which he had given little thought in the past. He cleaned the residue of clippings from the lawnmower, returned it to its rightful place in the back of the garage, and climbed the stairs to his apartment for a cold tumbler of tea—and a much needed shower.

Eight

*"Should you really open your eyes and see, you
would behold your image in all images.
And should you open your ears and listen, you
would hear your own voice in all voices."*
Kahlil Gibran

On Saturday morning, Deputy Tom called saying Charlie would not be able to meet with him until late afternoon because he had to transport a man to Coopersville.

"That's fine. Tell him to buzz me when he returns."

With several empty hours ahead of him, Drake decided to check out the surrounding countryside for subject matter—if things ever settled down enough for him to start painting. He wanted to see what lay beyond the covered bridge he had viewed from his apartment.

He parked his Harley on the weeded and thistle-lined roadside to examine the structure more closely. He found a meandering creek beneath the surprisingly sturdy bridge with only a few missing vertical boards through which he could see readymade subjects for painting. The rippling, gurgling stream bed had washed the pebbles and stones smooth and bleached white by sunlight. He stood mesmerized by the steady, trickling water below. He didn't just look at the stream, he felt it—the coolness, the constancy of the flow, not unlike the blood flowing throughout his body. But the creek wouldn't stay that way. A heavy rain would send it scurrying to reach a safe place before succumbing to rushing smacking rapids. But for now, the water was clear and moved leisurely toward its God-only-knew-where destination—probably the Ohio River.

From his viewpoint the creek snaked through the bottomland of the Tanner property, and disappeared at the western foothills. Above the sound of rushing water varied songs of mockingbirds filled the air. The blue sky reflections in the water were disturbed only by shadows of a weeping willow tree turning the water a deep blue-green. The tree foliage danced and swayed in the breeze like a Viennese waltz, the long tendrils caressing the water while dragonflies hovered nearby. On the south side of the creek, Hereford cattle grazed on the tender grass amongst the nettles and wild roses.

Drake, back on his Harley, rounded a sharp curve to the northeast and came upon another isolated farmhouse. Black Angus cattle grazed beyond a barn in need of paint—Drake assumed they were Angus—they were black. A weathervane oscillated undecidedly in the gentle breeze. A mile or so further, he turned up a narrow meandering road with heavy foliage on both sides. He reduced his speed to a crawl to avoid being slapped in the face by arching tree branches. The road became steeper and steeper and, fearing the Harley's stability, he was about to turn back when he came out of the steep climb onto a plateau. He stopped to catch his breath. Before him sat a charming white framed country church, recognized as such only by a crudely built bell tower. The structure appeared in good condition—the surrounding land mowed and well cared for, no doubt by a dedicated parishioner. A sign indicated a Freewill Baptist Church open for Sunday services as well as prayer meeting on Wednesday nights. He questioned the definition of Freewill in the religious context. He wouldn't be attending, but he might seek it out again as subject matter for a painting. On further observation, he noted a newly paved road approaching the church from the opposite direction.

Not wishing to relive his previous experience, he continued on, not knowing where the road would lead. Taking his time, particularly on blind curves, he proceeded cautiously until he came upon a verdant valley. He continued on the road meandering through acres of farm land where sheep grazed contentedly. Children and dogs romped with each other in the yards of well maintained country homes. He smiled as he passed one house where a young lady lazed in a porch swing with a book in her hand. They raised a hand to each other—total strangers enjoying the country solitude. The pastoral views further whetted Drake's appetite for landscape painting. He certainly wouldn't lack for subject matter. The highway eventually led him to a wooden stop sign with an arrow directing him to Porterville. He slowed as he passed the old linen factory that just might play a big part in his future—if it was meant to be.

Drake passed the Bucket of Blood, the sheriff's office, the theatre, and pulled up in front of Alice's Diner. The parking lot was nearly full. Alice greeted him with a smile much brighter than the struggling late summer petunias in her window boxes. She brought him a mug of coffee while he waited for a table to be cleared. The usual air of friendliness was palpable throughout the diner - tables being shared by neighbors - lively chatter about the weeks news and weather. Drake sipped his coffee and marveled at how happy everyone seemed—with not a drop of booze in the place. How refreshing. The town might seem sleepy during the week but it was wide awake on Saturdays—more encouragement for pursuing his art center.

He ordered the daily special—homemade meatloaf sandwich and a slice of apple pie. He called the sheriff's office to determine if he should wait for Charlie or return home—his new home. Ethel informed him her boss would be available at 3:30 which meant he had time for lunch, and later perhaps a leisurely exploration of the town on foot. Drake tackled the warm meatloaf sandwich with gusto.

DECENT DECEIT

The apple pie was equally delicious, the crust light and flaky. Even Martha Stewart would approve.

Later, Drake left his wheels in the diner parking lot and took off on foot to get a better feel for the area, as well as walk off the excess calories from lunch. Complete strangers smiled as they passed—mothers with small children—men in work clothes exiting a hardware store with small tools, potting soil, and cans of paint. In front of the theatre, long legged girls in high heels and short dresses—the same as any other city—perused the movie posters, giggling as he passed, reminding him of his teaching days at the university. He was used to seeing girls with identical hairstyles and makeup, some with tattoos, dreadlocks—would-be thespians, each with personal stories to tell.

Drake was not surprised as he neared an antique shop to find a man who appeared to be the town character. Every town had one—this one wore a beret on his head, plus all the signs of eccentricity and alcoholism. He was sitting on the doorstep of Annie's Antiques, where a window was filled with R. S. Prussia chinaware. He remembered his adopted mother's collection proudly displayed in her lighted, glassed door china cabinet. He also remembered her kitchen, with a wooden coke bottle sample case, an antique coffee grinder and other assorted relics of the past intermixed with French Provincial and Early English. The disheveled man sat and stared at the sidewalk where pigeons strutted about like emperors. *There but for the grace of God go I,* Drake thought.

He also thought of the only mother he ever knew and a strange feeling of remorse stopped him cold. It seemed there were reminders everywhere —merging—in this small hometown of his biological mother. He didn't even have a picture of her, only the few facts from Charlie and the attorney. Perhaps Charlie had a picture of her—one he had carried to the war? He strolled past the man but stopped about half way of the block. He thought of the man's disheveled appearance and turned back. "Are you all right, mister?" he asked. "Can I help you?"

The man's head came up at a snail's pace, revealing bloodshot eyes and at least a three day beard. "Not unless you can find me a job—or spare a few bucks."

Drake squatted to his level. "What kind of work can you do?" he asked.

"Anything that needs doing—never thought it would come to this. Factory shuts down, work sent to China. Why do you ask—need something done?"

"I might. What's your name?"

"Roy Rubens—like the artist, except he was Peter Paul—you want me to spell it?"

"Where can I reach you—telephone number?"

"Do I look like I can afford an iPhone? You can find me here on the street most days."

The man gave Drake a studied look. "New around here?"

"Yes, I am, and I plan to be around awhile. I can't hire you though unless you're sober. Understand, pal?"

"Understand."

Drake looked back to see Roy's head had fallen again to his knees. A man who couldn't hold his head erect probably deserved a break. He wondered what the real story was. Maybe he could help. He made a mental note to ask Charlie about Roy Rubens. At least the man hadn't yet become a John Doe.

He cut through an alley to find another street with less Saturday activity than Main Street, but still alive with activity. Through the window of a Dollar Store he saw several shoppers, no doubt trying to save a few pennies on supplies. He passed a couple business offices—a CPA, two gift shops showing local crafts. A barbershop was next, with a single barber chair and a bench along the side with four men waiting their turn. Instead of reading a newspaper or magazine,

DECENT DECEIT

they all talked animatedly with each other —another example of small town camaraderie. The barber raised his hand in greeting. He was struck by the neatness of the town and the shopkeeper's obvious pride in their humble enterprises.

Drake returned to Alice's, retrieved his Harley and arrived at the Sheriff's office with ten minutes to spare. Ten minutes to work up an anxiety attack if he wasn't careful. He was learning to face potential problems head on, but still had a way to go. So far his day had been quite enjoyable. Now he must face the music like a man.

Charlie arrived, a little down at the mouth, but perked up when he greeted Drake, giving his usual slap on the shoulder and indicating the chair by his desk.

"I hope you have some good news for me," Drake said.

"Depends on how you look at it," Charlie responded, the old familiar smile back in place. Drake waited while the sheriff reached for his phone messages and tidied a few other papers on his desk.

"Sure you still want the property?"

"As sure as a man can be of anything, I guess. My interest hasn't diminished, if that's what you're asking."

"All right then. Here's the deal. The place is an eyesore to the community— screams of a failed enterprise—and a discouragement to prospective buyers. Members of the town council agree with me that it would cost a lot to tear the factory down. At first they were less than enthusiastic about your plans for the place, doubted you could make a go of it. They came around only after I explained your connection to our little town and the fact that you already owned a bit of land here. Plus, I convinced them your plan would be an asset to the young and old of our community. So, if you can purchase the land the factory sits on, you have carte blanche to develop the art center as you see fit. Also, you have to keep current with the taxes."

"Wow—I wasn't expecting an okay so soon."

Charlie gave him a figure that seemed reasonable for rural

property—and the yearly tax assessment. "I might add that these people are not always easy negotiators—they don't leave much room for dickering."

Drake squirmed in his chair, his heart pounding, while Ethel placed two mugs of coffee in front of them. Charlie pretended not to notice.

"Want to take some time to think about it?" he asked.

"No need—I can do it." If the renovation costs got out of hand he could always sell the now vacant lot he had inherited.

"Okay." Charlie said. We'll get the papers prepared right away." He extended his hand across the desk. "I can't wait to see you in action, and don't forget, I'm here for moral support any time you need me."

"Thank you, Sir. How good are you at pounding nails?"

"Terrible. I either bend them, or miss them altogether."

Drake, a bundle of nerves when he arrived back at his apartment, vacillated between excitement and acute fear of the commitment he had just made. The bottle of Mondovi Syrah, beaconed to him like the arms of an angel promising instant stress relief. He knew if he walked into the bottle's seductive arms his dreams for the future would become a nightmare—all would be lost. He wished Tanner was around—a distraction was what he needed. He shifted his gaze away from the bottle, picked up an apple from a basket on the table by the window. He reached for the Tanner house key and the mail he had picked up on his way in, and left the devil temptation behind.

He hurriedly unlocked the front door of the main house, placed the bills and junk mail on the entry hall table and looked around. Usually, he deposited the mail and returned to his own apartment. This time, he didn't feel safe there—the temptation was too great. Instead, he went into the family room, feeling strange in the house alone, but perhaps a game of pool would relax him. He took the last bite of his golden delicious, chose a cue stick from the rack on the wall and chalked the tip. He needed practice if he was going to compete against Oscar or Tanner.

The thought of Oscar gave him one more thing to fret about. Would or could he be of any help to a man recuperating from probably the worst experiences life could dole out. In comparison, he was just a wimp merely facing the possible danger of a failed business project. He broke the triangle of balls like they were his worst enemy, scattering them in every direction, breaking the silence of the house. One by one he pocketed the numbered balls until only the shooter was left. Only then did he pause in the onslaught to consider which hole he would aim for. After three attempts, the green felt tabletop was bare and the ball thundered down the hole and found its resting place. Feeling much better, Drake returned the cue stick to its rightful place in the rack, repositioned the balls in the triangle, picked up the apple core, and moved to the front door. Once again, he had slain his demon.

He re-entered his apartment just as the sun was painting a golden glow over the trees and farm buildings. Drake's attention was drawn to the nuance of tints the setting sun provided —another painting lesson from nature itself. The sheer beauty removed any further ambivalence about his future plans. He couldn't wait for Tanner's return to share his good news. He hoped that Tanner and Oscar would have good news as well. For sure, the future would bring changes for all three of them and Drake vowed to give those changes his best shot.

Unlike some, Drake attempted to keep abreast of what was happening in the world. He had not been directly connected to anyone involved in the war on terror, so in a sense it all seemed unreal. People being beheaded, countries fighting neighbors, so much hate in the name of religion, innocent children losing their chance for life before it really began—all beyond Drake's comprehension. He wanted to better understand at least a little of what Oscar had experienced before the man arrived home. Feeling inadequate was putting it mildly.

He went to the bookshelves Tanner had allowed him to build to accommodate his substantial, ever expanding library. Looking over the titles he came to a number of books by Ernest Hemingway. He had purchased the better known titles from the Hemingway home when on a trip with his Dad and Mom to Key West. He removed *A Farewell to Arms*, the story of an American ambulance driver in Italy during World War 1. He remembered it as an extremely vivid and personal account of the price one pays for peace—a story of love and pain, loyalty and desertion in a world gone mad. It was three hours later that he realized the time. The book had given him a better understanding of a soldier's life and the toll their experiences took on their physical, mental and emotional lives. Different eras and different fields of battle, but the consequences of war remained essentially the same. Drake also gained a better appreciation for Hemingway's gift to the world of literature. The intense love between Henry and Catherine caught up in the winds of war, living only for the moment —perhaps the only moments they would ever have—brought Patricia to mind. Unlike the book, his chance for true love had been lost because of his own weakness. The book, the memories, Oscar's imminent return to civilian life and the part he might be called upon to play, pushed aside concern about his own future. He then remembered that Charlie had been in the service and made a mental note to pick his mind on the subject of post traumatic stress.

Drake became aware of the eerie silence of the night. Much trouble could erupt from silence—it was not always golden. In his old apartment there were noises of people coming and going, car doors slamming, even occasional raised voices with undistinguishable words invading the night.

He had never considered himself to be an adrenalin addict but had to own his faults, fatalistic at times when he was drinking. His path in pursuit of happiness had been slippery—slithering between his fingers—particularly with women. He had been listless, immature, and had hurt and disappointed those who had cared for him. His past had been a flub-up, his path mostly an uphill plod. Now, here he was in a quiet rural setting, surrounded by lush meadows, and all the seductions of nature. He had learned that life was not so much about earning and deserving but about believing and receiving—and being grateful.

He remembered his expectations when he first considered answering the ad for the apartment. He envisioned a plot of land with cows, a horse named Winston, two goats, two dogs, an Irish setter named Whiskey, three cats and a peacock who thought it owned the place, a flock of Rhode Island Reds and an overbearing rooster blind in one eye to awaken him each morning at the crack of dawn. Instead, he had found a sense of peace and tranquility he hadn't known existed.

Drake often wondered if Patricia had found someone who was more capable than he of making her happy. He went to his computer, clicked on Google. Maybe she had a website or was on some social media where he might find her. He found nothing on Facebook, LinkedIn, or Twitter, or any other site he pulled up.

Disappointed, he went to the kitchen and got a pint of Edie's frozen yogurt and had himself a brief pity party before retiring to his lonely bedroom. At least there, he could be himself—surrounded by blank canvases, an empty easel, neglected paints and brushes. Tomorrow was another day—the beginning of a future of new experiences. Hopefully, it would bring a positive new friendship with Oscar. It would require all the strength within him to keep his old demons buried—deeply buried—if he was to be of some use to the returning soldier.

Nine

*"And in the sweetness of friendship let there
be laughter, and sharing of pleasures.
For in the dew of little things the heart finds
its morning and is refreshed."*
Kahlil Gibran

Drake had overslept after finishing *A FAREWELL TO ARMS* at one o'clock in the morning. Tanner's call came just as Drake was taking the last bite of breakfast.

"Drake, we'll be home around six this evening. How is everything?"

"Just fine—a bit lonely at times. Hope you don't mind, I tried out your pool table last night. What can I do for you?"

"Oscar's room is ready for him—took care of that before I left. But there is one thing you can do if you don't mind. The kitchen is stocked with supplies except fresh produce. If you could run into town and buy whatever you think looks good in that department, I'd appreciate it. Also, milk and eggs, then I won't need to stop for them. We're anxious to get home."

"I'll be happy to do it. In fact, why don't I have dinner waiting for you—that is, if you'll allow me the use of your kitchen? But first, how is your son?"

"He seems pretty good, his leg injury is healed and he even smiled a couple times. It will be an adjustment but I'll be so happy to have him home. About dinner—let's do that another time. We'll both be tired and he may want a little time to adjust to his old surroundings. Understand?"

"Of course—anything else I can do?"

"No, I just want ample food in the house. It's good to know you'll be nearby if I need you. Let's just take our time testing the water where Oscar is concerned—let him lead the way, if you know what I mean—give him time to heal emotionally. He's had enough pressure."

"I understand. I just hope I can be of help."

"Thanks for looking after the place, and I'll see you soon."

While Tanner was away, Drake had gone into Coopersville and bought a used van with low mileage—preparing for the winter months in the country. He couldn't quite part with the Harley and stored it in the back of the garage. He couldn't very well carry paintings and supplies around on a bike. The van would be necessary when he started work on his new adventure and he couldn't wait for Charlie to get back to him with the legal papers. His mind was in a whirl but he firmly believed in the old adage *"an idle mind is the Devil's workshop"* or was it idle hands?

He drove the van into town and purchased the items Tanner had requested. He also bought a big orange pumpkin for their front porch. He then went over to Alice's Diner and got one of her homemade apple pies. He felt if Oscar was any kind of a man he would enjoy an apple pie—probably years since he had eaten one. On the short drive back to the farm he tried to think of some other way to welcome the soldier back. He thought of painting a big welcome sign on one of his canvases, adding an Oscar Meyer hotdog with mustard as a joke, but changed his mind after recalling Tanner's advice. He would hang low and let Oscar make the first move toward friendship.

It was close to seven when they arrived—daylight quickly fading. Drake had gone down to the main house and turned on the porch light and a light in the living room. It was the least he could do. When the car pulled into the garage, he went to see if they needed help with luggage. The days were getting shorter and the automatic pole light at the corner of the garage had come on. Drake shook hands with Tanner before turning to Oscar with outstretched hand.

"I'm Drake. It's good to meet you." Their handclasp was firm.

"Good to meet you. Dad told me about you. Enjoying my old playpen?"

"Very much, thank you."

Tanner lifted two bags out of the trunk and suggested they leave the rest for later. They were obviously tired from the trip.

"I'll say goodnight," Drake said. "I got in the supplies you asked for, Tanner—hope they'll be satisfactory. Sleep well, both of you. Glad you're back, Oscar. After you've rested, come up and see what I've done to your space."

Drake went back upstairs, his heart both heavy and happy. He couldn't imagine what the father and son were feeling after so long a separation. The prodigal son came to mind, but Oscar had been through much more than laboring in a pen of swine—he had been through Hell itself.

Ten

"For without words, in friendship, all thoughts, all desires, all expectations born and shared, with joy that is unacclaimed."
Kahlil Gibran

Charlie called the next morning at nine sharp. "The transfer papers are ready for your signature—I'll need your check for the back taxes, of course. That is, unless you've changed your mind about the property. You can still do that, you know."

"No, I haven't changed my mind. In fact, I feel more certain than ever that this is worth a try. Besides, your town has made me an offer I can't refuse. I just hope you won't be sorry."

"All right, then. When do you want to apply the ink?"

"Why don't you bring the papers out here tonight and I'll grill you a steak? Tanner and Oscar got in last night and I can use a little of your wisdom, as well as company."

"Well, I've gambled on other things, so why not on your cooking? However, you have to promise if I'm a little late, you won't throw a fit or pout all night."

"You apparently have me mixed up with someone else. Six o'clock suit you?"

"Fine, I'll just drive out from the office. If something comes up, I'll call."

"Good idea, I won't cremate the steaks until you arrive."

Drake hung up with a chuckle. He really liked the man. Too bad the relationship with his Mom hadn't worked out. The man could have been his father. For the first time in his life he felt connected to other people and his former reluctance to trust was disappearing with each new friendship. It was a good feeling.

He spent the morning tidying up the apartment. Fresh candles were placed on the deck table in case he decided to eat out there. The summer mosquito season was almost over. He had all the ingredients for a Caesar salad, an apple pie from Alice's, and a couple beers were cooling in the refrigerator for Charlie—just in case. A lit match to the grill on the deck, and a little time would take care of the steak.

Drake hadn't seen or heard any activity from the main house. The night before, he had noticed for the first time that a light was burning in the upstairs southeast window—apparently Oscar's bedroom. The soldier was either too tired to sleep or memories were keeping him awake.

Somewhat apprehensive regarding his first attempt at entertaining a man of the law, Drake picked up a sketch pad, went to the deck to capture the view of the covered bridge in the late afternoon sun. It didn't take him long to get lost in the creative process. The hills beyond, lightly tinted with a hint of autumn, made a pleasing backdrop for the focal point—the red painted bridge faded by time and weather. The shadows of the bridge and weeping willow tree grew longer as the sun slowly descended, creating a realistic feeling of perspective to the drawing. It would need something in the foreground to lead the eye, perhaps a branch of the mulberry tree just a few feet off the deck.

Noting the time, he put the pad and charcoal pencil aside to prepare for his first dinner guest. The drawing had totally relaxed him and instead of freaking out over the life-changing event that was about to happen, he flipped on the Bose with the remote, and hummed along with George Strait to *All My Exes are in Texas* while he went about preparing the salad. Then he remembered Oscar. He dialed Tanner's number and filled him in on his dinner plans. "I didn't want you to freak out if you saw a sheriff's car up here," he told him.

"You're full of surprises. Not every man can befriend the local sheriff. Good for you."

"Remember the property I told you about? I'm signing the papers tonight. I'll give you the details later."

"Give the good Sheriff my regards, and try not to poison him."

Charlie appeared at his door just as Drake was checking the baked Idaho potatoes in the oven. He had rubbed them with olive oil and salt before placing them in the heated oven —a trick he had learned from some restaurant somewhere. Instead of sour cream and chives, he favored Greek yogurt and chives and hoped Charlie wouldn't notice the difference.

"You're my first dinner guest, so hope you're prepared for failure," Drake told him. "Throw your hat there on the desk."

"Sorry about the power suit—didn't have time to go home and change."

"That power suit might have made me nervous at one time, but now that I know you're a marshmallow deep down, I don't worry about it."

"Don't put me to the test, and please don't share that opinion with anyone else—I have an image to uphold, you know."

Charlie looked around the cozy, neat-as-a-pin space and thought of Rhonda. Like mother, like son, it appeared. She, too, had been a neat-freak. He couldn't believe he was having dinner with her son—a handsome specimen of DNA from a woman he once loved—and lost.

"Make yourself comfortable while I throw these chunks of cholesterol on the grill."

"Sure looks good." He couldn't help noticing the salad as well as the perfectly browned potatoes. He also noticed the similarities of personality and gestures between mother and son. Memories caught him unawares.

Drake came back inside. "Care for a beer?" he asked.

"Nope—just water. Have to watch my reputation, you know?"

Drake laughed. "I know what you mean. In case you noticed the wine—I keep it as a reminder of all I have to lose if I give in to temptation."

They took their glasses to the deck where a bowl of mixed nuts waited on the table already set with placemats and napkins. Charlie sat down and drew in a deep breath. "Man, you've got it made. Look at that view. In another week or so those hills will be brilliant with color." The sun in the west reflected peach and lavender tints onto the barely moving clouds floating above the distant hills. A yellowish orange wash highlighted the roof of the covered bridge.

"This is just what I need at the end of a day—peace and tranquility—less ugliness and more beauty," Charlie said.

"I know, never thought I'd live in the country, but this place is not only growing on me, it's thriving and I hope will one day bear fruit."

"I can see why. I need to pay more attention to nature—the only thing we can count on most of the time."

"You've never told me where you live?"

"I have a small house just west of town—big enough for my needs—but I don't have a view like this. As you can imagine, I don't spend much time there. Tom's a good deputy but is a bit shy about handling some issues on his own. I don't mind—I'm lucky to have him."

"Do your own cooking?"

"Occasionally, but Alice's Diner is handier, and the food considerably more palatable."

"You two should pair up. It's obvious she's smitten with you." He got up to check the steaks.

Charlie laughed and changed the subject. "Might as well get those papers signed, in case I have to leave in a hurry. They're inside by my hat."

"Alright, but these steaks are almost done if you like them medium rare?"

Drake quickly returned with the manila file, flipping on the deck light by the door and lighting the candle before sitting down.

"You're sure about this?"

"You keep asking me that. I know, I know, you don't want me to be sorry if it doesn't work out. I appreciate that, but I feel in my gut that I'm doing the right thing. Besides, if I fall flat on my face I won't be any worse off than I am now. So where do I sign?"

Charlie laughed. The boy had guts and Rhonda would be proud of him. He went over the terms of the agreement they had discussed before. Charlie handed him his pen. He was getting a deal that would not have been offered anyone else, but Drake didn't have to know that.

Drake signed his name with a hand that only slightly trembled, removed his checkbook from his back pocket and wrote a check for the back taxes, thereby sealing the deal.

The two men shook hands and Charlie wished Drake the best of luck.

"Now, let's eat," Drake said, taking a deep breath, relieved the first step was over. He brought out the salad and potatoes from the kitchen, forked the perfectly grilled steaks onto the plates, lifted his water glass to the Sheriff, smiled, sat down, and the two men dug in. The call of night creatures surrounded them with strange music—a whippoorwill gave Drake a thumbs-up from a distant hill. It felt like the beginning of something good.

After the satisfying meal, the two men sipped their dark roast

Columbian, discussed plans for the new Art and Culture Center. Charlie supplied Drake a list of people to contact regarding the reconstruction of the space, informed him of special permits needed to carry out the project. Drake jotted down the names on a legal pad.

"What do you know about a Roy Rubens, a skinny, scruffy looking man I've seen hanging around town?" Drake asked.

Charlie laughed and shook his head. "Poor old Roy— I know he enjoys his booze, never goes without his beret. Why do you ask?"

"I had a chat with him the other day. He says he needs work."

"He does that, particularly during the winter months. I guess he's harmless enough— knows how to use his smarts. Last winter, we had to lock him up for writing bad checks. When he can't find work to feed his wife and child, he writes a bad check so the county will feed and keep them warm while he keeps cozy in his jail cell. Can you fault a guy for making that kind of sacrifice for his wife and kid?"

"Think he could stay sober long enough to help me with the project? He promised me he could—also said he could do any kind of work."

"Can't promise, but it won't hurt to give him a chance. In a couple months the weather will be cold which should be an incentive for him to make some money."

"Charlie, I can't thank you enough for your advice, and for your encouragement."

"No problem. Beside, Rhonda may come back and haunt me if I don't do right by you. Let me add—I'm depending on you to not let our town councilmen down. They are taking a chance on you, and you need to be a good citizen, make a name for yourself. We hope you'll be around for a long time."

"I'll do my best, Sir. I have another question. You were in the service—how familiar are you with post traumatic stress—Oscar's illness? We're going to be thrown together a lot and I'm a bit nervous

DECENT DECEIT

about the situation—way out of my element. I've only met him briefly and he appeared to be all right. Tanner says his injuries have healed, but it's his mental state I'm concerned about."

"It's good that he's not left with a physical disability, but sometimes mental or emotional damage is even harder to overcome. It's a damn shame, and in spite of the sacrifices our men have made, the situation over there appears to be getting worse instead of better. We thought Baghdad was taken care of and now it's being threatened by those thugs. I'm no expert but I've seen men consumed by hate at the things they've seen and been forced to endure. My advice is to let Oscar lead the way. Just observe, be a good listener if and when he feels like talking. Watch for signs of temper and emotional outbursts. Every case is different—depends on their personal experiences and reactions to them. I have no doubt you'll be able to handle any situation that might arise. Just follow your instincts as well as your heart. I would avoid any confrontations until you have a better feel for his condition."

"That's what Tanner told me. Thanks."

"The peace and quiet around here should be good medicine for him—familiar territory—good family memories. The apple festival is next week. That should be a homecoming treat for him. Nothing like being out in the fresh air, doing ordinary things to renew the mind, I would think."

"Good advice. Maybe he'll go running with me. I'm sure he's had a lot of physical therapy in the hospital. And according to Tanner, his son is quite a musician and plays several instruments. This apartment was built as a place for him to practice his music without disturbing others. Of course, his grandparents as well as his mother are gone now. Those memories may be difficult to deal with. He and Tanner have that big house all to themselves. Tanner remodeled it for his wife and son when they moved back here. He added a large family room with a pool table, redid the kitchen, etc.

Instead of college, Oscar traveled the world for a period before joining the Army. That was a disappointment for Tanner, but father and son remained close."

"He'll need something to keep his mind occupied, I would think."

"Maybe I can get him involved with the development of the Art Center."

"Good thinking, Drake. He might even help you run the place if you can get him interested. Or he could offer music instruction classes, start his own band. That would be great for the young folks."

"You may be right. Nothing worse than being in an unfulfilling profession—I discovered that the hard way. I don't miss teaching at all. Oscar and I just might have a lot in common."

The two men sat in contented quietness until Charlie broke the silence. "I had to break up a family fight early this morning— apparently started the night before—but the anger was still there. It seems like the entire world is mad about something. It's like there's a contest on who can be the "maddest", particularly where politics and the state of the world are concerned. Guests on TV news and the talk shows scream at each other to get their share of a few minutes of fame. I switch the channel and find the same thing. Why are people so angry? When gas prices were over the moon, people went crazy. I advised them to relax and ride out the temporary set-back—everything is temporary. Sure enough, gas prices are down, and they find something else to be mad about. It's much healthier, like you, to channel anger into some positive action like your painting, or, better still, doing something to lighten the load of others. The only certainty in life is change, Drake, and we know that all too well, don't we?"

The air had become cool as the evening progressed. A breeze shook a nearby mulberry tree, blowing a few dried leaves onto the table in front of them, threatening the lighted candle that had burned low. Charlie reluctantly got to his feet. "This has been a delightful evening, but I must get my beauty sleep. Feels like a good night for that. I give you an A-plus for your cooking, and I can't wait to learn of your other talents."

The evening ended with a heart-felt handshake, Charlie went inside and got his hat, picked up the signed contract and took his leave. The war in the Middle East, and political unrest had been forgotten, at least for a little while.

Contented with the successful evening, Drake did the necessary KP duty, and went to the deck to make sure the charcoal had cooled before turning in. He turned out the lights and looked out on the peaceful night. The bedroom window in the main house was dark. Drake saluted the young soldier and wished him a restful night. Tomorrow was the beginning of the rest of their lives, and there was much to be done.

Eleven

*"The image of the morning sun in a
dewdrop is not less than the sun.
The reflection of life in your soul is not less than life. The
dewdrop mirrors the light because it is one with light,
and you reflect life because you and life are one."*
Kahlil Gibran

Drake awakened slowly. He stepped out on the deck, feeling good about the previous evening with Charlie. The air had gotten much cooler and smelled of autumn—including an occasional whiff of ripened apples from the tree near the road. He preferred even that to the gas fumes and staleness of the city air he had almost forgotten.

As the sun sneaked above the rim of the distant hill, Drake watched the curtain open on the vistas around him—the rail fence, the faded red of the barn, the stubble of corn stalks in the field below the barn. The light grew brighter. A deer crossed the road, gracefully jumped the rail fence and raced across the open field—to what? It reminded him of a teenager who had stayed out all night and was slipping home before being discovered. Storms were predicted for later in the day. It was Saturday, and he wanted to do a bit more in the yard of the main house before the curtain fell on the last act of autumn. He had noticed when he mowed the grass that more work needed to be done. Maybe his presence would entice Oscar out of the house to join him, but again reminded himself to give the man his space. When the rain came he would come back inside and work on the plans for the Art Center, and make some calls.

Oscar appeared from the back of the house shortly after eleven. "Good morning, Drake. Is gardening part of your agreement with Dad?"

"I need to earn my lodging, don't you think? I'm learning how refreshing it is to work outside—good exercise. You're probably better at this than I am. Hope I don't cut something down that I shouldn't. No harm in clipping these dead roses, is there?"

The sun had warmed the air considerably. He stopped and wiped at his forehead with his wrist. He noted that Oscar hadn't responded—seemed to be lost in thought.

Finally…"Those were Mom's favorite tea roses. That rambler along the fence appears to have retired for the winter."

"What are these?" Drake asked, indicating large leafed, straggling shrubs by the front porch.

"Hydrangea—these big dried clumps turn into blue blossoms during the summer."

"You seem to know your stuff. Thanks."

"I used to help my grandmother when I visited her during the summer."

Drake didn't know how to respond, so he remained quiet and hoped the man would continue to talk. Oscar then told him not to work too hard and returned to the house. Drake noted the debris around the chrysanthemums—the last blooms of autumn. Many buds were ready to open up and perfume the air with their strong essence. He started to clean around them with the rake but decided the leaves would supply a mulch to keep the roots protected during the winter. Sweaty and dirty, he returned to his apartment for a hot bath before the storms approached.

He spent the afternoon making notes and drawings for his new project. A thorough cleaning of the space would be first on the agenda. Roy Rubens didn't have a phone, so he would stake out the town to find and present him with his first assignment. A shopping trip was also on his agenda to purchase cleaning supplies, stepladders and other paraphernalia that would be useful in the coming weeks. The a/c and heating would need to be checked, as well as an inspection of the wiring—a major requirement of the town.

Drake took a break around four o'clock and again went to the deck, his favorite spot, with a glass of iced tea. The earlier clouds had passed over, but there was a big chance they would return. He watched as squirrels quarreled from the branches of the mulberry tree, gathering food for the winter—much like humans making sure they got their share.

Perhaps it was the peaceful atmosphere, or maybe he just needed someone to share his new project, but thoughts of Patricia sneaked in—a woman he had once scorned while in an inebriated state. Regret often haunted him where she was concerned. She was the only woman who had left a favorable impression on him. Not for the first time, he felt he had been unfair in his earlier, less than loving thoughts of her—unfairly linking her with other women he had known. He owed her an apology—more than one—if their paths crossed again. On the other hand, he wondered if he could give up his newfound peace to share his life with another person. For now, his new venture would demand all his energies.

Summer lightening flashed harmlessly in the distance, but it was not until late, around eleven, that the storm blasted its way into the valley with a vengeance. Brilliant flashes lit up the apartment while thunder frolicked overhead, one blast after another, like an ocean's surf, only louder. He remembered his adopted mother telling him the noise was from God's potato wagon.

The violence of the night reminded him of Oscar. From the south window, he looked toward the main house. Oscar's bedroom light was on and Drake wondered if the noise brought back memories of his war experiences— the sound of missiles and grenades exploding—lighting up the sky. How could any soldier forget or live a peaceful life after experiencing such destruction? How could he have been so uninvolved and self-absorbed? He poured himself a glass of milk and, with the intermittent flashes of lightening that lit up the room, waited for the storm to abate and another morning to awaken. He thought of other young men and women thousands of miles to the east who no doubt were dreaming of home. God help them.

Early the next morning, Drake felt the pride of ownership as he unlocked the door to his building. He look around to see if any cleaning supplies or equipment had been left behind, but he found nothing. They had done a clean sweep of everything that was not bolted or nailed down. At least he wouldn't have the chore of clearing out the prior owner's debris. He turned on the tap in a bathroom and at first water only spurted out, then a steady stream—probably another act of kindness by Charlie so the cleanup could be started immediately.

At the local hardware store, he loaded up on cleaning supplies, and then went in search of Roy Rubens—hopefully his first employee. He planned to advance him some pay before he was tempted to write another bad check and get himself locked up. Drake didn't have to look far. He found him sitting on a bench under a tree at Alice's Diner. If he had a hangover he was doing a good job of covering it up—seemingly alert—watching Alice's customers come and go.

"Good morning, Roy, remember me?"

This time he got to his feet without difficulty. "Sure do. You're the man I talked with about a job. I've wondered if you'd show up."

"Are you still interested?" Drake asked.

"What do you need done? I'm not particular."

"Remember me telling you I was buying the old linen factory? Well, it's a done deal, signed, sealed and delivered. Now, I need someone to help me clean up the place and turn it into an Art Center."

Roy looked him over, and smiled. "An art center—sounds ambitious—but interesting. I'll do what I can."

"Let's go inside here and have a cup of coffee and one of Alice's pecan rolls."

"If she'll let me inside the way I'm dressed."

Drake knew Alice—she wouldn't mind as long as he didn't smell up the place or cause a scene. The man seemed to have cleaned himself up since they last talked. He still wore the old black beret which he took off, folded and stuffed into his back pocket as Alice directed them to a booth.

"What's with the beret, Roy? You wear it like a badge of honor."

Roy laughed but his face quickly changed to a look of sadness. "It's like an old friend. My grandfather gave it to me—said I needed to think like an artist."

"Really? Are you one of these starving artists we hear about?"

"Maybe near starving, but not much of an artist. Not good enough to earn a living at it anyway."

"So you gave up? What if Rembrandt or Monet had given up?"

"Paint costs money and my wife and kid come first."

Drake learned more about the man, his struggles and his mistakes which led him to find solace in alcohol and eventual poverty. Drake offered encouragement and admitted that he, too, had a similar history except for the poverty. "You can turn your life around, Roy, but you have to want to change. If I could do it, so can you."

They discussed Drake's plans for the building. Roy's eyes were a little blood shot but he was sober enough to seriously consider everything they discussed. He thanked Drake for the coffee and pastry—as well as the advice. They agreed on an hourly wage that left Roy's eyes sparkling. The sparkle faded slightly when Drake reminded him of his promise to come to work sober or the deal was off. He would pay him a week's advance but made him promise not to spend it on alcohol. Alice was her usual friendly self but didn't impose herself on the unexpected friendship that appeared to be developing before her eyes.

"Come on. You need to see the place, and you can help me unload the supplies I just purchased. First, we need to scrub the place from top to bottom. I also bought some window glass to replace the broken panes—do you know how to do that?" Drake asked.

"I've done it before."

"Good. I think we're going to make a good team—as long as you stay sober."

Drake smiled when he said it. He didn't want to be too hard on the guy, but he knew from experience how easy it was to give into temptation. Maybe he could restore some self-confidence by keeping him too busy to think about booze. Physical exercise should help. After the interior was cleaned up, the windows repaired, he would put Roy to work on the outside to relieve some of the exterior eyesore. Landscaping would have to wait until spring, but the lot could be cleaned up to look presentable.

Drake arrived back at the farm that evening feeling relieved that the day had gone well. He would see how Roy worked out and proceed with other workmen, or a contractor, as needed. It was a little early for dinner so he set out for a walk in the cool autumn air to clear his mind. The autumn colors were becoming more vivid every day.

He was walking toward the barn between the main house and creek when he heard clinking sounds from inside the well maintained structure. The double wide doors were open and there was Oscar bent over the engine of an old model Jeep.

Drake approached cautiously. "Wow, that looks like it's been around awhile."

"It belonged to my Grandfather, but it's still in pretty fair shape. Battery's dead."

"Can you get it running?"

"I learned a lot about engines over there. Vehicles were always breaking down. Keeping them running was often a matter of life or death." *Oscar, while checking spark plugs and pistons, had difficulty erasing mental pictures of bullet-ridden jeeps and human body parts.*

A silence ensued and Drake was reluctant to comment further, since he had no idea what to add. Oscar slammed the hood down. "I'll ask Dad to pick up a battery. There's no point in letting it sit here and further deteriorate."

"Might be fun to use it to go fishing," Drake offered.

"Dad tells me you're a painter. If you paint on site, it might come in handy—take you places you can't go in a car."

"I hope to do some painting, but this new Art Center is going to take a lot of my time."

"I've never tried painting—music has always been my thing."

"I hear you're proficient with more than one instrument. I'd love to hear you play."

The compliment brought forth a brief smile. "Maybe sometime," Oscar said. *How can one make beautiful music in a world filled with death and dying?*

Drake sensed a bit of progress in their developing friendship and it felt good. He also sensed there were deeply embedded emotional scars in the soldier that might take a long time to heal.

"Oscar, I'd like to talk to you further about my new project sometime. It seems we have similar interests in the arts."

"I won't be going anywhere for a while—have to be available for follow-up at the VA." *There was nothing wrong with his mind except memories, and he doubted if even the VA could supply a big enough erasure to wipe away all of those.*

"Good luck with the Jeep," Drake said, sensing the brief bonding had come to an end.

Drake returned to his man cave, feeling good about the day—the first day of his new venture. He reheated some leftovers for dinner and watched the news while eating. People continued to blow each other up on the other side of the world. Baghdad was again in harm's way. Other cities were being taken over by ISIS, their citizens fleeing in droves—fearful they would be lined up and shot—or beheaded. No wonder Oscar had come home with nightmare memories.

Drake clicked the off button, reached for his sketch pad and forced himself to concentrate on the bowl of fruit on the counter until he had the proportions and shadows correctly placed. He went to bed early and immediately fell asleep.

However, his intended good night's sleep was interrupted at 2:15 by a loud crash, followed by a continuous blaring of a car horn piercing the night. His first thought was of Oscar—and if he had heard the noise. He quickly pulled on his jeans, ran to the deck and found a car had plowed into the electric pole at the corner of the garage. He ran back inside for his cell phone. When he reached the top step, Oscar passed below, the first to approach the wreckage. With the speed of a comet, he had the car door open and lifted a man out from beneath the steering wheel.

Seeing Drake, he yelled. "Call 911— and bring some clean towels."

Drake did as he was told, grabbed his phone from the bedside table and towels from the bathroom. He had 911 on the phone while rushing back down the steps to Oscar. Next, he asked to speak to the sheriff who responded immediately.

"Charlie, we need you; there's been an accident in front of my apartment."

When Drake returned to the scene with the arm load of towels, Oscar had the driver prone on a patch of grass, talking to the man and urging him to stay awake. Drake instantly saw that Oscar had removed the man's belt and was using it as a tourniquet around the upper left leg. Love for his fellow man had taken over.

"Roll up a towel and place it under his head," Oscar directed, as he reached for towels to apply to the profusely bleeding leg.

Drake lifted the man's head and carefully lowered it onto the rolled towel. Blood trickled over the left temple. Grabbing another towel, he pressed it over the wound. Thankfully, the towels were clean and new. But what difference did it make? The man was bleeding. The night had grown cooler. Drake ran back upstairs and returned with a couple blankets.

"Good thinking, man—we need to keep him warm to avoid shock." *How many times in the past had he done this? He had lost count—numbers and days had lost their meaning.*

The two continued to work together to keep the man awake—probably had a concussion. They continued the pressure on the bleeding wounds, and at the first sound of distant sirens, Drake looked at Oscar and their gaze clashed. "You should go into medicine, man—you're a healer—not a killer." They smiled briefly at each other in the light from the pole lamp and just like on the battlefield, both men knew a bond had formed. The rest of the world no longer existed. Oscar had the stranger's hand in his. "You're going to be all right, Buddy—try to stay awake—help is on the way."

"Must have dozed off," the man mumbled.

The voice was weak but there was no odor of alcohol. "Working a late shift or returning from a hot date?" Drake asked.

A deeply furrowed brow and a gritting of teeth was the only response.

The sound of sirens grew increasingly louder, breaking the stillness of the night and bringing a sense of relief to the good Samaritans.

"Oscar, the world can be cruel but it can also be incredibly beautiful, can't it? This man is injured, but he's going to make it. Nothing is ever all black or all white. The in-between gray is what matters, like in a painting—the grays can be relieved by adding colors that please. Whether in the battlefield, keeping the streets of a foreign country safe, or here at home, you're useful, man—giving all you have to make this time and this place safer for others. I'm proud of you." Oscar lowered his head—his attention focused on the injured stranger and the faces of women and children in the periphery of his memory.

Unnoticed by the two young men, Tanner, tears overflowing, watched from the shadows. He leaned against a post, heart bursting with pride at seeing his son handling the crisis like a pro. For the first time in months, optimism crept in and somehow he knew his son was going to heal. The paramedics and sheriff arrived and quickly took charge. Only then did the father step into the light. The patient was quickly prepped for traveling, the leg secured, and he was moved into the ambulance. The three men stood side by side and watched while the vehicle u-turned and headed back the way it had come. The sheriff continued forward in the night to inform a probably worried and sleepless wife. Charlie had found the injured man's ID and address—he lived only a couple miles down the country road, just beyond the covered bridge— but a telephone call would not suffice. He hurried on.

A new day would soon be dawning and the three weary men silently returned to their bunkers, Tanner's hand on his son's shoulder. Drake watched until they entered their home and closed the door. Somewhere in the dark forest to the north the call of a whippoorwill went on ceaselessly as if nothing of note had happened.

Too keyed up to sleep, Drake made a cup of coffee and returned to the deck to watch the sunrise. He sat down, raised his feet to the railing, and sipped the steaming brew while reliving the events of the day. He sat the empty mug aside and dozed until teased out of his slumber by bird song. The yellow light of dawn appeared cautiously at first and then with gusto as it changed to orange and red, and accented the tree line at the top of the eastern hill. Drake watched in awe as the brilliant colors splashed across the canvas below a robin's egg blue sky, gilding the cloud edges with gold. How could mere man ever hope to duplicate such beauty with paint?

From the southeast corner window of the main house Oscar, too, watched in silence. His thoughts drifted, as they often did, to where death and destruction continued as a way of life, obscuring any beauty that might be found. Through the glorious sunrise, he thought of those he had left behind to continue the fight, and felt sad that his presence was no longer needed. He turned away and saw his room just as he had left it so long ago. His clothing, some now out of date, were carefully arranged in his closet, his musical instruments free of dust and waiting to be reawakened from their long period of uselessness. Perhaps his father and Drake were right—he had served his time and maybe he didn't have the mental capacity for war after all. He felt a definite change in his perspective. The accident had made him feel useful again, and Drake's comments had done much to help him believe in himself again, but what was he to do with his persistent memories?

Drake had just left the shower when he heard a soft knock at the door. He pulled on a terry robe and found Tanner at the door showing obvious sleep deprivation. Drake invited him in for a cup of coffee and learned he had been called to Washington for another assignment. They discussed the previous night's activities. The injured man owned the farm just beyond the covered bridge, and was in the hospital recovering from his injuries. If the accident hadn't happened nearby, and if they hadn't acted quickly, he could have died from loss of blood.

Tanner said, "I was so proud of you two boys, the way you

handled everything. For the first time, I feel that Oscar is going to be healthy again—in mind and body."

I feel the same way," Drake said, "it was amazing how quickly he responded to the crash and plunged in with no other thought but to save the poor man."

"Thank you for helping my son."

"I'm not doing anything. After last night I think Oscar will feel useful again—his confidence restored."

"After this assignment is completed, I'm going to fully retire. Can I trust you two boys to behave while I'm away?"

"We'll do our best, Sir."

"Don't let him be alone too much. Go down and play some pool, cook up some great food, make yourself at home, okay? And don't forget the apple festival this weekend. You might enjoy seeing how these rural folks manage to have a good time."

"Okay. Thanks. Don't worry about us. Everything is going to be all right. You have a great son—one I hope to know better."

"See you in about two weeks, Drake—or sooner. Oh, in case you're wondering—you're more than earning you keep."

"Do you think I should check on the man's wife and see if she needs any help?" Drake asked.

"Great idea—I haven't met them but perhaps we should offer to be of service while her husband is confined. Can't hurt to be neighborly, can it?"

Still pumped from the previous night and two cups of coffee, Drake arrived at the Art Center site to find Roy gathering trash and debris from the parking lot—a sizeable pile at the corner of the building. His heart swelled as he rushed to unlock the door.

"Morning, Roy, ready to rumble?"

"I'm ready. Just killing time until you showed up."

They went inside. Drake showed him the cleaning supplies and the new panes of glass for the cracked windows. "And here's a box of large trash bags. You've got the lot looking better already." Roy seemed sober, alert, and ready to work.

Drake left him alone, partly to see what he could accomplish on his own, and partly because he wanted to go by the sheriff's office to check on his neighbor's condition.

Tanner was leaving in the cruiser just as Drake pulled in, but he reported that the patient was doing well and his wife was by his side. "Nice couple—you'll like them."

"I intend to visit her this evening. I see you've gotten a call, so have a good day."

Drake returned to find Roy on a ladder scrubbing away at the unbroken windows while whistling an unrecognized tune. They took time off for lunch at Alice's, and then back to the job until five o'clock. He had lasted the day in spite of the night's activity and very little sleep. He felt it might be wise to keep his employee on a steady schedule. He also meant to find out the real reason he wrote bad checks and why he became an alcoholic.

That evening as the light faded and the moon appeared above the hills, for the first time, Drake heard music coming from the main house. He saw Oscar's silhouette in the open window. A saxophone oozed notes as soft as melted butter—*Just a Closer Walk with Thee*—other ballads and blues as sweet as any coming from Preservation Hall in New Orleans. Drake pulled his desk chair to the south window, rested his arms on the sill and stayed there until the moon climbed high in the sky, obscuring Oscar's silhouette in darkness. And yet the music lingered on.

Before leaving the house the next morning, Drake called Oscar and asked if he would have dinner with him that evening. "I'll cook us a steak, up here or at your house". The response wasn't immediate, but then Oscar responded. "Dad told me you were a good cook. Come down here and we'll have a game of pool afterwards—if I survive your cooking."

Wow! Drake hung up, kicked his heels together, and headed for Porterville for another day of manual labor with his sidekick. On the short ride into town, he thought of the many projects that needed completion before his new venture became a reality. His goal was to have a grand opening in the spring to introduce himself and the new art center to the small town that was becoming more and more like home. If things went right, Oscar would become a part of his future. The man was a talented musician and had a wealth of ability to share with others. Drake reached inside his shirt and felt the charm that held his silhouette. He hoped with all his heart that Rhonda was resting in peace and somehow knew her son was finally becoming a responsible man.

Twelve

"What wound did ever heal but by degrees?—
William Shakespeare

Tanner warned Drake that Oscar might exhibit periods of moodiness and lack of participation at times but, so far, Drake had not found it a problem. He made an effort to not anticipate the man's behavior, but to stay sufficiently alert to back off when it seemed appropriate to do so.

At the market, Drake picked out two impressive rib eye steaks, a box of fresh mushrooms and a bunch of green onions. He would use the greens from his crisper for the salad. Anything he prepared would no doubt be an improvement over Oscar's previous Army cuisine. Although he didn't doubt that Tanner could put a decent meal together, he wanted the dinner to be a success. Out of respect, he would curb his enthusiasm over the path his own life appeared to be taking, and give Oscar his full attention. He wanted very much for them to be friends—a new experience for him.

Oscar greeted him at the door with a beer in his hand. "Come in—Dad says you know your way around our kitchen. Can I get you a beer?"

"No, thanks, alcohol is my personal enemy." *Oops, wrong choice of words.* "A glass of water will do fine."

Drake noted the pool table was set up and ready for a game. He had more confidence in his cooking than in pool playing—he was no Cool Hand Luke— and hoped he wouldn't come up short in either area.

In no time, he had the indoor grill heating in the kitchen island, while he gave the mushrooms a quick rinse and removed the moisture with a clean towel. He placed the chopped green onion and fresh minced garlic into a hot mixture of olive oil and butter, sautéed them until barely cooked and then added the mushrooms for a quick brown. Oscar entered the kitchen cautiously, commented on the aroma, and picked up the placemats, napkins, and silverware.

"Mind if we eat here in the kitchen?" he asked.

"Perfect. Keeping things simple is my motto. I enjoy eating outside but the evenings are getting a bit chilly." He turned the fan to high over the island grill and added the steaks, thoroughly enjoying the country kitchen's modern conveniences. Life was good and he began to relax.

"Did your Dad get a new battery for the Jeep?" Drake asked.

"I installed it today. Borrow it anytime you wish."

"I've never eaten mushrooms this good," Oscar later told Drake. "And the steak is just right. Hospital food was fair—better than what I was used to. Maybe you should open a restaurant in your building instead of an art gallery."

"No—wouldn't want to compete with Alice. But you just gave me an idea. I will need a small space for food preparation— refrigerator, stove, and coffee maker, at least. Eventually, we'll have art shows and events open to the public and that will require catering space."

"Man, you're on fire with this project, aren't you?"

"Oscar, this is the first time I've felt excited about my future. I've always leaned toward art and literature—barely tolerated my teaching career—and now I get to prove myself in a field I enjoy.

Hopefully, it will all work out and I can help others pursue their dreams."

They ate in silence until every morsel of food was devoured. Drake got up to pour a couple mugs of coffee. Oscar wiped his mouth and hands with his napkin, pushed his plate aside, turned and stared out the window. Drake observed the change in his demeanor, placed the coffee in front of him, sat down opposite—and observed. It was several minutes before Oscar found his voice. He was thinking of a young family in Iraq, and whether they had adequate food, if the children still played behind their high wall—safe from car bombs and stray bullets—instead of in the streets where danger was always present.

Finally, he turned away from the window. "I envy you, Drake—you've found a purpose. I have to get on with life in some manner. Afghanistan was beastly hot in summer and cold in winter. Our job was to secure the opium poppy fields—if you can believe that—and to protect the farmers from the Taliban—none of them strong or brave enough to fight off the enemy. We slept on the ground, we slept on roof tops, and we bunked together in camps." He paused while the memories continued.

"There were these large camel spiders—some as big as turtles—ugly creatures. It's good to smell air without inhaling sand. The silence gets to me, particularly at night. Over there, silence was not something you could relax in. The next instant a car bomb could go off or a missile could come screaming at you from a clear blue sky. The silence was worse than the sound of missiles, or bombardment. You were thankful the last shot missed you, but knew the next one might—that day or the next—but it would come. Or the next step might be your last. Camouflaged IEDs were hidden everywhere. Silence often meant everyone was dead, no cries of pain, no gun fire, no life—you alone—like a mollusk in its shell. Over there, we were close as brothers, each striving to stay alive. It hurt like hell to see buddies dismembered, spirits broken.

Before I enlisted, I wandered all over the place, even in other countries, often in dangerous places, and nothing bad happened. I was trying to *find myself.* I know— old cliché. Traveling the globe doesn't change things—you still have to live with yourself. During that time, I met all kinds of people and all remained strangers. Not true in war—you quickly become brothers, and you do what you can to protect each other. We constantly expected something to happen and knew that whatever that something was, it would not be good."

Drake forgot the coffee cooling in his mug and the steam from Oscar's had also dissipated. He searched for appropriate words, but none came.

"Maybe I should have let the guys with more grit than I fight the battles. I could have stayed here with my music, my globe-trotting to exotic places, moving through life like a robot with my naïve impression of what made a person happy. During short lulls in fighting, I often felt remorse that I hadn't spent more time with my mother—never dreaming her time on earth was limited."

"Why *did* you sign up?" Drake asked.

Returning to the insignificant mirage outside the window, Oscar answered. "The towers—I was furious when they fell. I wanted to kill the sons-of-bitches. They could blow up their own country, but how dare they have the audacity to attack America, to kill innocent people in such a horrible way. Yes, I wanted to kill them, but when I was in the midst of the fighting, I felt the futility of it all. There really is a thin line between good and evil. We try to obey God's teaching, try to keep His commandments, never knowing what evil deed we will be called on to commit in the next hour, the next minute.

In Iraq, anything of a Christian nature was not allowed to be printed or spoken. While on street patrol, I met one well-educated woman who had written books for children and was unable to get them published. She showed me the pages and her beautiful illustrations, but no publisher would accept them—they were *too Christian*. Packages arriving from America, particularly packages containing books or other literature were confiscated and destroyed. The only things safe were a person's thoughts.

She told me there was no one she could confide in. Even best friends couldn't be trusted. Children were encouraged to snitch on each other and teachers were tortured in front of children to teach them a lesson—a lesson in where their loyalty belonged. And now ISIS is recruiting women to spy on other women who might be disloyal to their cause, some are forced to become traitors to their own family and friends. How despicable can humanity become?"

Drake felt like a coward in front of this soldier, but it was not the time to make excuses for his earlier disinterest. He was fortunate to have survived his own self-absorption, his escape from the destructive world of alcohol. His story, too, could have been different. His life could have ended behind the wheel of his car or from a bullet from the gun of a drug dealer. Thank God he had never maimed or killed anyone—he would be wearing an orange jump suit in a room of cold gray steel—or worse. Oscar wasn't asking for pity and Drake wasn't about to insult the man by feebly offering it. He allowed him to ramble on as if he were alone—alone with the night sounds outside the window—and his memories—his awful memories."

Could the evening be a breakthrough for Oscar? Words were spewing out of him like a broken water main. Maybe his ability to talk of his experiences would push the horror he had suffered into the background of his mind—maybe he could build a new life.

"In war, you always expect the worst to happen—stepping on a land mine, grenades landing close enough to touch. We walked around the streets of Bagdad weighted down with armor—80 pounds of gear, an M240 or a 28 pound SAW machine gun plus ammo, grenades, water—wearing it all like a second skin, loaded and ready for another surprise confrontation from behind a crumbling building, an alley, an open window, or a car bomb exploding two feet away. People were blown to smithereens without warning—body parts strewn about like a disassembled picture puzzle. We were taught how to *cook* off grenades—pulling the pin and holding it longer than usual so the enemy couldn't throw it back at you—seconds counted."

Drake couldn't imagine how the man sitting across from him had been able to exhibit such bravery.

"It wasn't about being afraid to die—it was about dying before we'd lived— and whether or not our dying would change anything. Our worthy cause was to protect each other and the innocent people caught up in the despicable situation. Little children with missing limbs watched from doorways, listening and waiting to see what would happen next in the very real game of war—some showing excitement and others showing fear on their innocent faces—feeling the uncertainty of someone to protect them.

One mother came out on a balcony and before seeing I was an American, begged me not to harm her children—children I had just coaxed back into their compound for safety. I told the lady to keep her children inside and seconds later, a car bomb exploded in the street where they had been playing. She placed her hands over her heart and looked down at me with almost worshipful relief on her face. "You're an American. God bless you—and thank you." She said, and rushed back inside to her children—her eyes swimming in tears.

I'll never forget her, or the children. Our paths crossed often while I was on patrol duty. One day when the streets were a bit quieter, she invited me inside her compound and showed me a secret garden her father had planted before he was arrested and taken away because of his belief in God. She told me he was tortured, was a skeleton of a man when he was released two years later. 'He was well educated and had a library of books on different religions—a wonderful man—those devils threw his beloved books on the floor and stomped on them.' Tears filled her eyes and she couldn't go on. The garden was a precious thing to her. She kept it alive so her father could have fresh vegetables to eat and flowers on the table—to prevent him from going mad from his memories. The garden was like tulips in a trash can. She even gave me her address so I could let her know if I got back home safely.

I wrote her while in the hospital but she may or may not have received my letters. Many Christians feared for their lives, and now a new enemy is threatening them. The cowards concealed in their black garbs are planting even a worse terror than before. Children are probably having nightmares of their parents being beheaded. Such evil must be wiped off the face of the earth."

Their plates remained on the table in front of them, the grease from the steaks congealed on the surface, but it didn't matter. Oscar talked on. Drake listened.

"Some of my buddies joined up for what they thought would be excitement, others because there were no jobs available at home. And then there were those who genuinely believed in their country—believed there was merit in keeping it strong—believed it was worth saving in spite of the danger. We were thrown together in a common cause—a more peaceful and safe world. For the peaceful Christians, we did make it safer for them, at least for a time."

The night sounds continued as the two men were silent. "Depression is not so much a personal thing but a feeling of no hope for the entire world." Oscar continued. "Over there, you see little kids playing, giggling, with no hint of what they will face in the future or even if they will have a future. Back here, many of us come home to divorce papers, kids they haven't seen born, house mortgages—you know—the human condition? Huh! Over there, nothing seemed humane. We come home mangled and mauled and for what? Another generation with nothing changed? We come back to find people obsessed with social media, dot com's, I phones, I

DECENT DECEIT

pads, their ears plugged, oblivious to the ebb and flow of life around them. It seems so trivial and such a waste of time. Even the language has changed. The only thing I crave is relief from the memories—nightmares of seeing fear and disbelief mixed with determination in the eyes of a buddy. In all probability, the kids they rush home to will grow up to fight the same time-worn battles—battles to settle a score—real or imagined—with guns and grenades—or in cyberspace with more sophisticated technological weapons. Too bad if innocents suffer in the fallout."

Oscar's voice failed him and he reached out for his water glass. Some memories were too horrendous to put into words, like *the slick feel of a comrade's warm blood drying in the hot sun.*

Blake was unable to read Oscar's subsequent silence. One thing seemed clear: Osama bin Laden was gone but he had left a legacy of destruction behind in the minds of men like Oscar, and it would continue as long as evil existed.

Oscar continued his focus outside the window. "This is a Garden of Eden compared to other parts of the world where missiles strike homes without warning, where families once felt safe—just like us sitting here. So, how am I supposed to put it all behind me when our own country has become a dangerous place, and I'm doing nothing?" He turned in his chair to face Drake. "Of course, I'm depressed—there's very little to smile about. I still have all my extremities, but I can't forget those who don't."

Drake finally dared to comment. "Oscar, your usefulness is not over—your service might be on a smaller scale here in America—saving the life of a neighbor like the other night. You can help save our young people by getting them interested in music—show them how to enjoy beauty instead of the ugliness and nonsense of our present culture. Pair up with me in the art center and let's see what we can accomplish together. Lord knows I could use your help, and particularly your musical talent."

"How have you come to grips with all you've been through?" Oscar asked. "Yes, Dad told me some of your history."

"My troubled past seems petty compared to yours. I was a bit of a mess for awhile, but I've finally accepted life for what it is. I understand myself better. I've learned to be attentive to the now, putting the past behind me most of the time, calming my anger and blame toward those who meant me no harm. Forgiving them—none of us is perfect. Results are factors beyond our control. I've learned that to live in peace there can be no attachment to results. I have a new goal for my future and that's what I'm concentrating on—day by day. Results cannot be predicted. I resolve to not allow my enemy—a bottle of whiskey or any other crutch— to dictate my future or slow it down."

Oscar finally stood up and stretched as if he had fought another battle. Perhaps he had.

"Let's play some pool," he said. They took their utensils to the sink—Oscar insisted he would wash them later. Drake didn't argue—the man needed to feel useful, even if it was simply cleaning up a few dishes.

At the pool table, each chose a cue stick from the rack. While chalking up, the two men looked at each other across the green felt fabric of the table and felt a bond had formed.

"Sorry I rambled on so." Oscar said, shaking his head as if to clear his mind. "You know, I've never talked about my experiences that way to another human being—not even the psychiatrists. Guess they were right—it did feel good to open up. Thanks for listening—and for that you get to break first." Pretty soon the clack, clack, clack of billiard balls drowned out the silence of the night.

It was eleven when Drake returned to his apartment. Oscar had whipped his butt in pool, which wasn't surprising, but maybe with a little practice he'd do better. He turned on the late news. The war hadn't been personal before, but now it was. Oscar was a flesh and blood veteran. His personal story had made it real. The VA had healed his physical wounds but only time would tell if they would succeed in exorcising the restless demons inside his mind.

The breaking news was that another American had been beheaded by ISIS. Things couldn't get much worse than that. It was a selfish thought, but Drake was glad Oscar was safe at home in his own country where the sounds of nature diminished the thunder of war—at least for the moment.

Thirteen

*"Everybody needs beauty as well as bread,
places to play in and pray in, where nature may heal and cheer
and give strength to the body and soul."* John Muir

Drake awakened on Saturday morning, his mind on the previous evening with Oscar, not the pool playing but on the horror of the war on terror and the consequences. He felt a close friendship developing with Oscar. Inexperienced in matters of the mind, and particularly PTSD, he genuinely wanted to at least be available to lend an ear to the man. Oscar had responded like a true soldier when the accident happened in front of the apartment. That reminded him of the injured man's wife, Eloise, just down the road a ways. Drake got out of bed with the intention of calling on her to see if she needed anything—their car had been towed.

He showered, prepared a breakfast of extra crisp bacon, scrambled fresh farm eggs, and five grain toast. A steaming dark roast topped off the meal. Tom Henson was to be discharged on Tuesday, according to Charlie. Eloise might need some assistance in getting him home. The Art Center was still in the cleaning up stage and Roy could work alone. Drake suddenly smiled, still not used to his new resolve. When had he ever been concerned with neighbors? His regard for others was definitely changing—for the better. After the satisfying breakfast, he took his second cup of coffee out to the deck, looked around at the constantly changing colors of autumn before turning his attention to the main house.

The southeast window remained wide open. After breathing ceaseless sand for so long, and smelling the warm blood of fallen comrades, Drake could understand Oscar's need for fresh air. What would it take to rid him of the memories and the nightmares? Later he would call his new friend and hopefully divert his thoughts by inviting him to Alice's Café for dinner—and then checking out the Apple Festival. He couldn't imagine the Festival being terribly exciting, but he had been happily surprised at other aspects of country living. His gut told him that Oscar needed distraction—and what about old friends—or girl friends? Drake hadn't noticed that there had been visitors. Was that one more idiosyncrasy they shared—the seduction of solitude?

Drake had perused the internet to learn all he could about PTSD. Symptoms of insomnia, mental depression, and nightmares were common even years after a trauma had been suffered. Observing, first hand, the killing of others, friends and foe alike, left scars on the mind as well as heart and body. There was also the moral element of war—innocents killed in explosions, forced to kill or be killed, civilians caught in the cross-fires, all against their moral and ethical code of behavior. Although not physically on site, even drone operators who actually see the results of their attacks, are at risk. To them, it is not a video game—they actually see the body parts as do the men in the field. Yet, for security reasons, they are not allowed to talk about the experience, their risk will exculpate for moral injury. In Syria or Iraq where they target the al Qaida cells, the operators watch the carnage on screen and then go home to normal family lives. The shift of perspective leads to stress and a threat to their mental health. Harming others without being harmed—an improbable achievement—probably.

Later in the morning, Eloise Henson opened her door, dressed with a large purse hanging from her shoulder. Drake introduced himself and she motioned him inside. Tears pooled in her eyes as she took his hand. "I'm so glad to meet you, and to thank you for helping my husband the other night. If you hadn't been there, he might have bled to death." She dropped her purse on a chair to give him her full attention.

"Mrs. Henson, it was Mr. Tanner's son who saved your husband. He's just back from the war where he had plenty experience in that kind of injury. I helped, but Oscar is the one who deserves your thanks. I understand you are without a car and just came by to see if you needed anything."

"Thank you, but a friend is coming to take me to see Tom. She'll be my wheels until the car is fixed—and she will help me bring him home."

"Good. But if you need anything at all, please call." He gave her his phone number, and wished her the best. "I'm living in the Tanner garage apartment, and it's nice to meet a neighbor."

"Bless you, Drake, and please thank Oscar for me, until I can do it in person. I'm glad he came home safely."

Drake drove away with a smile and turned his thoughts to plans for the evening—another new experience—an Apple Festival, of all things. And he would be accompanied by a real hero.

The two men left for the festival in Drake's van. Oscar in civvies—clothes from his closet that hadn't been disturbed while he was away—his days of camouflage over. Drake was casually dressed also, appropriate for a country festival one would think. They were quiet for most of the drive into town, each with their own thoughts. Drake did venture to ask about Oscar's love life—or lack thereof.

"Before signing up, it was not easy to form a relationship, traveling the way I did. Over there, seeing the pain my buddies went through being away from family, I was actually glad I wasn't

DECENT DECEIT

attached—made it easier to concentrate on the job at hand. What about your love life, Drake?"

"Afraid I wasn't very good partner material because of my drinking. Closest I've been to *falling in love* was with a girl named Patricia, but she eventually gave up on me. I have no idea where she is, or if she found someone more deserving."

In Porterville, Drake pointed out the empty lot where his childhood home once stood. He told Oscar a little of the back story and that he hadn't decided what he would do about the property. They continued through town—bustling on a Saturday night—and passed the Bucket of Blood where the parking lot was filled with early boozers.

"Do you remember this, Oscar?" Drake asked.

"The building, yes, but Dad said it had changed hands."

At Alice's Cafe, the summer petunias had been replaced with pots of yellow and orange chrysanthemums—their pungent odor blending with the smell of country cooking. Alice's smile widened when she saw them enter the door. She led them to the only unoccupied booth. As usual, the smells were appetite whetting. The customers exuded a friendly atmosphere. Drake introduced her to Oscar to which she replied, "I heard you were back. Welcome home, and come visit me anytime. Free coffee to veterans."

"We're headed for the festival, Alice, and hungry for some of your excellent food." Drake said.

"You and everyone else in the county, it seems," she replied. "But I'm not complaining."

Both men ordered her meatloaf special although Drake had cut way back on red meat. After Alice left, he turned back to see Oscar scanning the place with quiet apprehension, and felt his own body grow tense—wondered how the evening would progress. He attempted to distract Oscar from the din surrounding them by talking about pool playing and fishing until their food arrived. The meatloaf, mashed potatoes and green beans distracted them from the crowd. They ate heartily. After coffee, Drake grabbed the check and dropped a generous tip for Alice. "My treat," he said to Oscar. After paying the check, they made a hasty exit. The food seemed to have calmed Oscar somewhat, or it could have been the happy, harmonious and safe atmosphere of the diner.

"Alice is quite a lady, you'll like her when you know her better," Drake offered as they returned to the van. "I told Charlie she would make him a good wife."

"So you're also a matchmaker," Oscar replied.

The Apple Festival was held at the Fair Grounds, a short distance out of town. Lights from the Ferris wheel lit up the sky as the two men approached. A man with a flashlight directed Drake into an open field where he lined up with a huge number of other vehicles. "I wasn't expecting this crowd," he told Oscar.

"This is typical. People come from miles around. This is country folk's rock concert. I can't remember when I last attended one of these, but it was fun when I was a youngster visiting my grandparents."

They left the van, carrying light jackets slung over their shoulders. They would be needed as the evening grew cooler.

"I don't particularly like crowds but we might as well check it out," Oscar said.

Drake felt more comfortable with Oscar than when they first met. Their evening of sharing food and pool at the main house had done much to reassure him of the man's state of mind. Nonetheless, he would remain cautious and observant. He didn't want to take on the role of a private eye, looking for signs of abnormal behavior when there might not be a need.

Charlie's cruiser was parked strategically at the entrance and Sheriff Charlie and Deputy Tom were on guard just inside the door—making their presence known. The four exchanged a few pleasantries before moving on. Drake and Oscar continued through the large building—normally used for livestock shows and auctions. Lined on each side were displays of apples and more apples, bushel baskets perfectly aligned. Young ladies offered smiles along with plates of apple slices for customers to sample. There were candied apples on a stick, long tables laden with apple pies, canned apple butter, apple jellies and jam, some with blue ribbons attached. Small paper cups of apple cider were also offered. The two young men ambled slowly through the displays until they came upon a large group of people with much laughing and frivolity.

"What's going on?" Drake asked.

Oscar explained they were bobbing for apples. A couple flirtatious young ladies approached, pulling them into the circle, urging them to join in the contest. How could they refuse? Looking at the apples swimming in a tub of water, they agreed to give it a good try. Finding it more difficult than it appeared they finally gave up with nothing more than drenched faces and humiliation. As they dried off with paper towels, for the first time Drake heard a hardy laugh from Oscar. But the laugh was short lived. After viewing the craft section where apples carved like pumpkins, painted note cards, small paintings displayed on miniature easels, apples painted on saw blades and shovels, indication to Drake that there was indeed an interest in creativity. Equally encouraging was the large crowd, old and young, teenagers more interested in each other than in the displays.

"I'm surprised at this crowd—where did they all come from?" Drake asked.

"Oh, they come from surrounding small towns, from Coopersville—thirty or so miles away."

"No kidding. When I lived in Coopersville, I heard no mention of it."

They walked silently out the back entrance of the building toward the sound of loud music and bright lights of the carnival.

Fearless young mothers pushed strollers, while young girls giggled and flirted, tossing their long straightened hair—people living lives without fear of being shot—a privilege no doubt taken for granted. Drake noted Oscar's preoccupation, or disinterest, the smile gone, probably back in memory mode. All of it must seem trivial to someone of his traumatic experiences.

Sensing a distraction was in order, Drake urged him toward a merry-go-round where music greeted them with *It's a Small World After All*. "Oscar, I've never been on one of these things, have you?"

"Of course—but that's for kids, man."

"Then let's be kids again." Drake bought tickets and the man with amusement sparkling in his eyes watched as they climbed aboard, and co-mingled with a swarm of excited children. Drake lost no time in choosing and straddling a smiling colorful giraffe. He motioned the obviously uncomfortable Oscar to a perky pink flamingo opposite him. The calliope music started up again and they were on their journey around and around, slowly at first, and then speeding up. Oscar looked as if he might die of embarrassment at any minute—Drake quickly snapped his picture.

Oscar yelled above the lively music, "I can't believe I let you talk me into this. You're a case of arrested development." In spite of his chagrin, he failed to hide the suggestion of a smile.

The ride slowed to a stop and they jumped off. It occurred to Drake that he wasn't clowning around for Oscar's sake—it felt good to discard the heavy thoughts that had used up most of his cerebral space the last several months.

Oscar had moved away from him and was talking to a woman with a small boy clinging and crying into her rumpled jeans. The next minute, Drake watched him remove some bills from his wallet and offer them to the woman. Drawing closer, he heard her protest before accepting the money. There was a time to speak and a time to keep silent, and this was the latter. The child was now smiling and wiping his nose on his sleeve, while he and his mother rushed toward the ticket booth. He approached Oscar from behind and the two continued through the crowd without comment.

As they approached the side-shows with provocative signs proclaiming the world's greatest whatever, barkers enticed the crowd with enthusiasm. It was obvious to Drake that Oscar saw no humor in any of it, his eyes constantly checking out his visual field, as if danger was hiding out behind the fun house. *All these people, young and old—how lucky they were. No children with leg braces or prosthesis, playing soldier, standing in doorways smiling as if violence was a game, pointing makeshift guns at passersby while a few blocks away children and parents were being blown to bits. School children forced to watch as teachers were tortured – the lesson of the day— to be loyal to barbaric leaders.*

"Such nonsensical exploitation," he finally said.

Drake turned back the way they had come, Oscar following, his sharp eye observing other fun-seekers. They soon heard arguing coming from the shadows between a couple tent-like structures. Oscar reached out his arm to caution Drake. Something was amiss. A man was acting aggressively toward a young girl trying to free her arms from his clutches. Drake paused, observed the altercation and Oscar's reaction to it—definite anger—an attempt at restraint. His heartbeat quickened. Would Oscar lose it or control it? And how should he respond if things got out of hand? He had little time to think—Oscar moved toward the couple.

"Is there a problem here?" he asked the obviously pissed-off male with dreadlocks and a ring attached to one eyebrow.

"Not your problem—beat it."

"I don't think so," Oscar said. "The lady isn't happy, so back away from her—now!" His voice left no doubt of his intentions.

The guy let go of her arms. Drake stepped between them to shield the trembling girl. "Leave," he told her quietly. "Let us handle it." She moved away without hesitation.

"I just came back from Afghanistan and Iraq," Oscar said to the young man, his voice authoritative, cold as steel, "Over there men don't know how to treat a lady either. Maybe you should sign up for duty and learn how to be a gentleman." Drake noticed Oscar's fists were more than prepared to proceed further.

"Oscar, let's go—the lady is safe." Drake said as he watched her at a distance.

But Oscar wasn't through. He took a step closer to the man, his stance threatening. "Look in my eyes and repeat after me," he said. "From now on, I will respect women and their rights."

The man—the no-longer-so-tough offender— raised trembling hands up in front of him and with squeaky voice repeated Oscar's words—verbatim.

Oscar demanded, "One more time."

The man repeated it again, his voice louder. Only then did Oscar step back.

He and Drake watched with disdain as the chastised man sauntered off in the opposite direction. Oscar loosened his fists and flexed his fingers. "Scumbag," he murmured.

Drake, high on adrenalin from the confrontation, put his hand on Oscar's shoulder as they walked away. "Good job, my friend."

"Sorry," Oscar said, with a hint of a smile. "I suffer from acute alertness, plus a temper I wasn't born with."

"I thought you handled the situation very well."

"We're not all ticking time bombs, you know, as some believe. Most of us didn't sign up because we were unskilled for civilian life. We wanted to do something meaningful, something specific, even life changing, but some people just don't get it. It's hard for us to understand how civilians can use their freedom so frivolously. There doesn't seem to be much effort, like in past wars, to aid the war effort, or support the troops. Unless they have a loved one embedded in the fight against terrorists, the effort seems impersonal. Soldiers often feel alone in their effort to solve the global dilemma."

Drake had no argument to offer. He, too, felt at times that humanity was going in the wrong direction. The media reported how even Christian children were being killed by ISIS for refusing to convert to Islam. Someone had to fight back to rid the world of such barbarianism.

"If America ever ceases to be good, America will cease to be great." Oscar quoted. After a quizzical look from Drake, he added, "de Tocqueville."

Drake shook his head. Oscar wasn't a college graduate, but he was apparently well-read.

Tanner had said that Oscar's period of hospitalization had been considered successful, according to the doctors, but Drake sensed that he had a way to go in re-acclimating himself to civilian life. As far as Drake was concerned, the man's anger was justified. Just spending time with Oscar was definitely wiping away some of his former complacency.

They retraced their steps, and found Charlie at the Sheriff's table just inside the main entrance to the Fairgrounds—Tom probably scouting the grounds for signs of trouble. Oscar and Drake reported what had happened with the young couple and gave him a description of the offending aggressor.

"Well—perhaps I should deputize you two," Charlie said. "In fact, the girl reported what happened and gave us his name. I'll keep an eye on him. She also told me about two men coming to her aid—helping a damsel in distress. It didn't occur to me that you two might be her angels of the night. She was still shaken—I asked Tom to take her home. You two go have a slice of Alice's apple pie—tell her to save a slice for me." He thanked them, shook hands and wished them a goodnight.

"I'll be sure to tell Alice you'll be by later," Drake called out as they left, lifting his eyebrows in a suggestive way.

Back at the van, the two men sighed deeply as they fastened their seat belts. "Well, that was an experience," Drake offered. "Not something I'd want to do every week, however."

"That's about the extent of the excitement around here. Sure you want to hang around permanently?"

Drake laughed. "I think we're just what this county needs—an asset, if you will." He drove out of the lot and headed to Alice's Diner for the apple pie and to deliver Charlie's message. Then he would take Oscar back to the peace and quiet of the farm, and hopefully to a night without dreams of car bombs and beheadings.

Fourteen

"I would rather never taste chickens' meat nor hens' eggs than never to see a hawk sailing through the upper air again." Thoreau

Sunday morning, Drake awakened to birdsong and a cool breeze from his slightly ajar window. He remembered the Festival of the night before and felt he had gained a better insight into Oscar's state of mind. After indulging at Alice's Diner and relaying the message from Charlie, they made their way home under the light of a full harvest moon. However, the beauty of it failed to elicit a comment from Oscar. Drake wondered if he was remembering seeing that same moon shine down over a very different landscape, a land of chaos and killing. *Where was the Iraqi family tonight? Were Miriam and her children safe? Was she able to get the diabetic medicine her daughter needed? If ISIS cut off the water supply, how would they survive? Were they still allowed only a few hours per day of electricity?*

Only when he parked the van under the garage overhang was the silence broken.

"What's on your agenda for Monday," Drake asked.

"No plans," Oscar replied.

"The cleanup is finished and the next step is buying materials for the construction of spaces for serious artists to rent. There are two separate rooms off the main gallery that I'll reserve for offices. I have drawn up tentative plans—now it's a matter of bringing it all altogether. Roy has remained sober, at least on the job, and has done good work so far. Before bringing in other help, I'll see what else he is capable of doing."

"I don't know how I could help—not much experience—but I'm willing to learn if you can trust me."

"Thanks, Oscar. If I took a chance on Roy, I most certainly can take a chance on you. But, surely you have more important plans."

"At the moment, I doubt if anyone would want to hire me with this so called *condition*. I've thought of trying for a college degree in music when and if I get a clean bill of health. I need something to do, and music interests me more than anything else at the moment."

"Excellent idea, I would think. In the meantime, I'm sure you can be of help. "

Sunday afternoon, Oscar called to ask if he'd like a lesson in pool playing which pleased Drake no end. His friend was like a chick pecking at the shell to get out into the world, and that was a good sign. He arrived at the main house with his construction plans in hand—anxious for another opinion. Two hours later he returned to his apartment, happy that he had came close to winning one game of pool, and looked forward to a week of progress on the Center. Oscar had agreed to accompany him on Monday to Kirkwood's Building Supply for the necessary material for the construction of booths etc. for his artists.

After Drake left, Oscar was alone with his own thoughts. His father had been correct in his analysis of their unexpected tenant. He admired the man for his tenacity in building a new kind of future for himself, for letting go of a profession that brought him little pleasure. Mostly he admired him for wanting to help others realize their dream. Oscar knew his feelings could not be encapsulated in red or black words printed on a piece of construction board and paraded before the news media. He didn't need accolades or publicity to know he had performed his job as long and as well as he could. His scars would heal in their own time. Many of his comrades had made —and were still making— far greater sacrifices. Too many had given their very lives. He had been brave in battle and now he must be brave in the reformation of his future—much as Drake was doing. No more dalliance. He would never forget his experiences but neither would he become a whiner. He would pull his cloak around him and plod through the upcoming icy winter of his discontent.

Drake had given him much to think about. He still had work to do, was well aware that many in his situation on returning to civilian life took to the bottle, others become non-communicative and combative, and the suicide number continued to rise. Oscar thought of the altercation at the Festival. He had shown better control than he would have six months ago. When he saw the young woman being traumatized—he had felt the anger in his entire being—for just a second he visualized her head wrapped in a burka, but he had curbed his aggressive tendency that had once served him well. He hoped in the future she would be more selective of her friends. He regretted that innocent people were dying all over the world and he was no longer allowed to participate in their rescue. His goal now was to better maintain control over his emotions while adjusting to being a civilian again. Helping Drake might be a temporary solution.

On Monday morning, Drake was enjoying his second cup of java when Oscar appeared on the deck, casually dressed and ready for a different form of recuperation. Within minutes, the two men were headed to Porterville, both in a good mood in spite of the gray sky obscuring the sunlight. Suddenly Oscar, riding shotgun, turned and looked at a farm gate they had just passed. "Did that sign say what I think it said? *Used cows for sale?*"

Drake laughed out loud. "That's been there for awhile. Some

of these farmers seem to have a good sense of humor. I assume it means cows that have given birth?"

"Heck, we've never figured out whether the chicken or the egg came first."

"I don't think the Bible says anything about God creating an egg, so the chicken must have come first." It felt good to see the change in Oscar, his willingness to converse, his increased moments of levity when they were together.

Drake slowed as they approached the small town, noting that it had taken on an atmosphere of the Christmas Season. The quaint coach style street lights were decorated with red bows—the poles wrapped to look like candy canes. Green wreaths with red crabapples—what else—and more red bows graced the windows and store fronts, adding color to the otherwise gray day. The local grocer was placing baskets of chestnuts, sacks of oranges—no doubt shipped in from Florida, and pecans from South Carolina, on the sidewalk in front of his store.

"This town looks like a Norman Rockwell painting." Drake offered.

"People here like tradition. I doubt if they will every change."

As they approached the Center the sky had become a dismal elephant gray, and soon the first snow of the season began to make an appearance. The flakes fell like a whisper, dancing *The Nutcracker* on the windshield. The sheriff cruiser pulled in next to them.

"Morning, boys," Charlie said, his window lowered half way. "Now this is winter. Pretty soon there will be little to talk about except the depth of the snow."

Other pleasantries were passed. Charlie complimented Drake on the exterior improvements. "It's no longer an eyesore, Drake, and the council members are impressed."

"Thanks. It needs a bit of architectural interest in the front to take away the factory look.

When spring comes, new landscaping will make a big difference. Roy has been a big help. Oscar and I are going inside to check on supplies, and then take a drive up to Kirkwood to spend some money."

"While you're up there you might visit the salvage yard just outside the city limits—people find all kinds of interesting and useful stuff there."

"Thanks, I appreciate the tip."

"Duty calls. Have a good day, boys. Stay out of trouble."

Roy arrived on his bicycle just as Drake unlocked the door. His ever constant beret was perched in a cocky manner atop his head, his neck draped in a bright red muffler. In spite of the weather, he seemed happy. The defeated expression was gone from his surprisingly clear eyes.

The three men spent the next hour or so discussing ways to build partitions for sectioning off work space for the individual artists. They would have to be on casters for easier mobility. Drake measured off the spaces, made some calculations, and a list of hardware they would need. The former linen factory's large work room was already equipped with ample shelving. Instead of towels and bed linens, Drake visualized canvases of all sizes, paintings in progress, and art supplies readily available. Leaving Roy to finish the woodwork painting in the front main gallery, Oscar and Drake left for Kirkwood. They trusted the snow would melt as fast as it fell. Surely the temperature would not allow for much accumulation. Too early in the season.

On the road again, Oscar looked over the drawings Drake had shown him on Sunday. One thing concerned Oscar. "With the folding partitions on casters, couldn't they tip over easily?"

"Good thinking. We can't afford to have an accident, although I plan to take out insurance before we open for business. How do you think we could stabilize them?"

By the time they reached Kirkwood, they had solved that problem plus a few others. Deciding that professional easels would be cost prohibitive, they agreed it would be quite easy to construct them, using Drake's easel back at his apartment as a template. "Serious artists will probably have their own easels. We'll make several and wait to see if there is a need for more."

In spite of the helpful orange apron-clad Home Depot salesman, Drake wasn't happy with the cost of lumber. Before committing, he decided to check out the salvage yard Charlie had suggested. An hour later the partition problem was solved. For half the money, they found almost new used doors, solid and uniform in size. They would be delivered the following day. Back at Home Depot, they purchased the hinges and casters and other hardware. If their work was satisfactory, they would tackle the easels next. Drake saw no reason, with three men on the job, why they couldn't also build a few turntables for sculpture students.

Pleased with their progress, both men were in a jovial mood as they left. The sun had broken through the gray clouds and the air ten degrees warmer. On the way back, they discussed a sign for the new center, coming up with several ideas for a possible logo. Drake thought of his birth mother, Rhonda, and how he might honor her with his new venture. "How about Rhonda's Second Chance Art Center?" he asked Oscar.

"Who's Rhonda?"

"Rhonda was my biological mother's name."

"I thought she abandoned you when you were a kid."

"She did, and for awhile I had some angry feelings about that. After getting to know Charlie—who knew her quite well—I realized she did it out of love, not because she didn't love me. She wanted me to have a better life. My anger is gone and this may be a way of honoring her."

"It would be a nice tribute, but a bit long. Second chance—where does that come from?

"Seems suitable to me, since I'm the owner, and this is a second chance to get things right. Last chance might be more realistic, however."

"The logo is very important, I would think."

It was past dinner time when they arrived back in Porterville. The Center was dark when they drove by. Thanksgiving was long gone—quickly forgotten, it seemed. At Alice's Café, the chrysanthemums had been replaced with poinsettias in the window boxes. Candles flickered on every table and in every window. The festive atmosphere reminded him of his adoptive parents, and the holidays they once shared. Memories of his old life were becoming more obscure with the excitement of his project and his friendship with Tanner, Charlie—and now Oscar. Seated across from him, Oscar appeared relaxed and at peace. They soon had the attention of a couple skin tight jeaned young ladies hanging out at the counter. After briefly sizing them up, both men quickly lost interest.

"Drake, you quizzed me about my love life—or lack thereof—what about you?"

Drake laughed and looked around the room before answering. "I thought I told you—I was too much in love with the bottle to maintain a relationship. Patricia was the only woman who came close to reforming me but I didn't treat her very well. I have no idea where she is now, or if her heart has softened toward me. She wasn't gorgeous by today's standards, but she was beautiful in a classic sort of way. With Botox, fake-tans and airbrushed makeup, women show only traces of the assets they were born with. One can no longer tell what's real and what isn't. Don't you agree?" He turned his attention back to what he really loved—Alice's apple pie.

"Haven't given it much thought, but can't say I disagree. You seem to have given women a lot of attention," Oscar replied, with a teasing grin.

"Seriously—since Patricia—I haven't met anyone who truly interested me—at least not enough to convince me that a relationship would be a good thing—particularly at this time. Besides, I have too many other things to deal with. My first goal is to get the gallery up and running."

The men were quiet on the drive home, only occasionally encountering another car. The earlier snow had dissipated, and once again the moon cast eerie shadows of trees, barns and other outbuildings along the way. Behind closed doors, country folks were settling in and calling it a day.

Oscar was thinking of their earlier conversation about regrets—a useless activity, a miserable way to live—a dampness of soul that penetrates every crack and crevice of memory. If he had regrets it was that he had been unable to intercept a bullet or a grenade to save his fellow soldiers. Like Drake, probably better to avoid any sense of entrapment, especially in his present circumstances. There were other destinations besides women to explore. Who needed extra baggage on a train that might lead to nowhere? He learned in his travels that place made not a bit of difference. He still felt cocooned in his own emptiness—better to be a solitary traveler or, like ships passing in the night, leaving behind only harmless echoes of a foghorn.

Prior to his deployment he had searched far and wide for new adventures, some fascinating and picturesque, but found most of them just a notch above boring. He passed through cities and countryside, often at night, the inhabitants unaware of his passing. Like an old photograph negative, he was never able to show his true colors—not until he found a purpose in Iraq and Afghanistan. His purpose had been that of protecting his fellow man, and mostly the innocent women and children living in fear—Sept.11 forever etched in his mind—making sure America would never again be the target of evil men. He did regret that he hadn't spent more time with his mother and grandparents when he had been free to do so.

"You're awfully quiet, Oscar. Still slaying dragons?" Drake asked.

"I was thinking of my grandparents, and visiting them here while I was growing up. It just dawned on me this is the only place I've felt truly at peace. It's what I thought of over there—when I wasn't concentrating on staying alive. Grandpa would take me into the woods to find May apples. The plants were like my father—their big leaves keeping the small apples under cover—keeping them safe. Now, I'm a big apple, and he's still doing it. Guess that comes with being a Dad. Grandpa called autumn leaves nature's confetti. I miss all of them, particularly my Mom. She was so vital—I never thought I'd be without her. At least I still have Dad."

"When will Tanner be home?"

"Monday—and he says he'll be home to stay. I don't think he's retiring because of my so-called illness—at least I hope not. He's done his part for his country—most of which will remain secret from the world. The big house is nice but every nook and cranny is filled with memories."

"He told me he was retiring. I've been thinking—all three of us are pretty much in the same boat—all reassessing our lives. Your dad surely will miss the excitement of his career, but perhaps not the pressure. We all need something worthwhile to occupy our time. Maybe we could cheer him up a bit when he gets home. The Holidays won't be easy for him either, you know, with your mother gone."

"He's a pretty steady guy, either that or a good actor."

"How about we decorate the house for Christmas—any lights in your attic? You said the jeep was in running condition, would it be possible to cut and bring in a real live tree? I've never done that."

Drake's enthusiasm was contagious, and Oscar quickly caught the germ. "Grandpa and I used to do just that. I can still smell the fragrance. There should be a tree stand and lights in the attic. I'll check it out. You're so busy—when can we do it?"

"This weekend—maybe sooner since the work at the Center is

progressing more quickly than I anticipated. I'll give Roy an afternoon off and we'll go—pretend we're kids again—deal?"

The moon had risen higher in the sky. Both men went to their own quarters with a sense of joy in their heart.

Before turning in around ten o'clock, Drake opened the living room window to take in the fresh air and relaxing sounds of the night. From the southeast window, he heard the strumming of a guitar and Oscar, for the first time, singing. The simple guitar chords and the words of *Where Have All the Flowers Gone* sobbed across the short distance and caught Drake by the throat. Oscar's voice was pure—every note clear and sharp—occasionally gliding from one note to another as smoothly as hot chocolate over ice cream. Only when the old Burl Ives tune ended did Drake lower the window. Oscar not only knew his music, it oozed from his very bones—he had not only found his voice, he had found his purpose. Drake was certain of it.

In his bedroom, the excitement of the day lingered. His easel sat neglected in the corner. *Soon, buddy, soon,* he promised. He propped himself up against the headboard and turned to the bedside table. He had been re-reading some of the classics and this time he picked up Steinbeck's *East of Eden* and was surprised to see what the man had written in the 1900's:

The world was changing. The sweetness was gone, and virtue too. Worry had crept on a corroding world and what was lost: good manners, ease and beauty. Ladies were not ladies anymore and you couldn't trust a gentleman's word. There was a time when people kept their fly buttons fastened. And man's freedom was boiling off. Even childhood was no good anymore—not the way it was." Drake smiled, remembering the conversation with Oscar. Not much had changed in the world after all.

Oscar was picking up his father on Monday which gave Drake an opportunity to visit Rhonda's grave. He left early, not to be late opening the Center for Roy. Spending time with Oscar had been more than just pleasant. A day alone was good for thinking—about a lot of things still to accomplish at the art center, his vacant lot, a springtime opening, and the most difficult—trying not to project the finished product prematurely.

The early morning air was clear and clean-smelling, decidedly much chillier than the night before—he realized as he left his van. An unusually late and silent fog lingered in the low places of the rolling terrain. He thought of *The Night Before Christmas* that was read to him as a young lad: *"Not a creature was stirring, not even a mouse."* As he approached the grave, a pair of cardinals called out from a leafless tree nearby, the silence too much for them, he supposed.

He knelt on one knee and his hand reached out to sweep the dead leaves from the grave marker until her name was spelled out before him. His left hand went to his neck. He had gotten a more substantial chain to wear the charm near his heart where it would be safer than in his shirt pocket. If he had only known her as he was growing up, he would at least have had memories in which to find solace. But he wouldn't allow feelings of blame or regret to overshadow the good feeling of knowing he was loved. No one else was around—only the cardinals welcoming a new day.

He quietly said her name—*Rhonda—Mom, are you listening? I know I've told you before that I understand why you gave me up, and I don't blame you anymore. You should see what is happening at the Art Center. I'm thinking of naming it Second Chance Art Center—what do you think? This was your home, your town, and I'm trying to make it mine. Charlie told me so much about you. He's a good man and I'm sorry things didn't work out for you two. He loved you, you know. Yes, he told me so. He respects you—had no use for the old man—and who can blame him? Charlie and I have become friends and I hope that pleases you.*

His hand reached down again and touched the damp, cold earth above where her heart would be. His eyes were moist. *Rest easy—I'm going to make you and this town proud of me. If by some miracle you are watching, please help me to never return to the person I used to be.*

When he stood to leave, the sun had burned off the valley fog but still too low in the sky to offer much warmth. He looked around at the rolling terrain. It wasn't a bad spot—serene was the word that came to mind. The trees had lost their leaves but, except for the graves, signs of life were all around. Other birds joined the cardinals and a couple gray squirrels dashed about, desperately hording food for the winter. Drake smiled at their ambitious and tireless gatherings. He could take a lesson from them. He brushed his knee and retrieved his keys from his pocket. Much work was waiting for him at the Center. He made a mental note to check on the heating system, so the construction could proceed throughout the winter.

Roy was waiting at the Art Center, dressed in the same outfit—jeans and jacket—to which he had added another brightly colored scarf—this one plaid. The stubble of beard was gone and his black hair beneath the beret shone in the sunlight. He did seem a bit antsy—a change from his usual quiet unassuming persona. Drake wondered briefly if the man had compromised his sobriety. They soon had Saturday's purchases inside. Drake told him about the doors he had found for the folding partitions and he could see that Roy was impressed when he told him they would be delivered later that day.

As if reading his mind, Roy said, "I really appreciate you giving me a job. I feel like a new man. When I leave here at the end of a day, I'm too tired to lift a bottle, much less drink from one. Long time since I've felt this good. I was pretty low when you found me on the street that day."

"I remember—you were as puny as a plucked pheasant and about as ugly."

DECENT DECEIT

Drake laughed, but he was touched and pleased. "Everyone deserves a chance, Roy—some of us more than one." *Second Chance* might be appropriate after all. "I'm happy to see the change in you. You're also a damn good worker. You have this front gallery space looking mighty impressive. I can't wait to see art on the wall, proper lighting, and an "Open" sign out front. Can't do without you now—still a lot to do—so don't let me, or yourself, down."

"I've done something you may not like, Boss. On Saturday, while you were gone, I took the liberty of painting a wall in the lounge area. Want to see?"

Drake was amused at Roy's excitement—he flitted about like a hummingbird on steroids—but not knowing what to expect, he followed him down the hall. What he saw left him momentarily speechless. On one wall in the small dining section of the lounge was a well-executed mural, a rural landscape typical of the surrounding area. Roy pranced about like a young colt in spring while waiting for a reaction.

"You painted this?" Drake asked.

Roy shyly nodded his head.

"I'm stunned—but where did you get the paints?

"The paint store gave me some samples of the primary colors and I mixed them myself."

"I had no idea you could do this. It reminds me of a Grant Wood—only more impressionistic."

"You exaggerate, but I didn't know I could do it either. It has been a long time since I painted. Guess I got carried away—I thought I could paint over it if you didn't like it."

The two men discussed painting for the next hour—not of door frames and baseboards, but of fine art painting, color harmony, perspective, and the all important—when to quit. Drake felt ashamed for having him do simple cleaning and industrial painting jobs. Learning of his life-long desire to be an artist, Drake realized by hiring the man, he had given him the courage to quit drinking and start creating again.

At quitting time, they were no longer boss and employee—they were kindred souls with the art spirit alive and well between them. Before leaving, they returned to the lounge for another appraisal of Roy's contribution. Drake turned to him with sage advice: "Painting is more intoxicating, more satisfying than the finest wine. Let's not ever forget that." At the door, Drake addressed Roy again. "Oh, yes, one more thing: You no longer look like a plucked pheasant—those few extra pounds have you looking pretty healthy—and it's good to see you smile."

Tanner and Oscar arrived late in the evening so Drake had no chance to welcome his landlord home. Just as well, they needed some space as father and son. The following day he went alone in search for outdoor shutters to add to the front windows of the Center. He found just what he needed at the Salvage Yard. A good coat of paint and new hinges would make them look like new. He also needed a few pieces of furniture for the main gallery—specifically a nice large desk and chair with a couple traditional upholstered chairs for guests. Benches for visitors to rest on would also be nice. He wanted the place to be welcoming, bright and cheerful, a gallery where people would not feel intimidated to enter. Art should be for everyone to enjoy, not just the elite or collegiate minded. He planned to visit the Hospice shop in Porterville before going to a regular furniture store. But that would have to wait for another day.

He arrived back at the farm to find a pick-up truck loaded with firewood at the back of the main house. The driver was passing the planks to father and the father to son in assembly line manner— and stacking it beneath the back deck of the house where it would stay dry. Drake hurried down, greeted Tanner and offered his help. They gladly accepted and reminded him that if his apartment became too cold he could share their fireplace on cold evenings.

Later in the evening, Tanner rapped on Drake's door. "I want to thank you again for helping with the firewood, but mainly for what you're doing for my son. He seems much more at peace than when he first came home, more open to conversation. He told me about all you two have been up to since I left. He's excited about your art center project. And you went to the Apple Festival. Your friendship is making a real difference in him, giving him hope, and easing his wounded heart. I know he can't delete all his memories like a line in a poem, but your keeping him busy is pushing those memories further into the background. Last night, he didn't once call out in his sleep. There is no way I can thank you properly."

I don't want any thanks, Tanner— I've enjoyed every minute of it. You know, I was pretty much a loner myself and I'm learning how important it is to have a close friend. You have quite a son, and I'm amazed at his talent."

"You've heard him play?"

"I've heard him play the sax, the guitar, and violin. He has been playing almost every evening with the window open in his room. I sit up here and marvel at his ability. His singing voice gave me goose bumps the other night when he sang an old Burl Ives ballad."

"He was singing?" Tanner asked, tears welling up.

"Yes, sir, he was singing."

Tanner turned his back, overcome with the news.

Drake put a hand on his shoulder. "I'm no doctor, but I think your son is going to be fine—as long as he can use the talents he's been given. His music, more than anything else, is going to play a big part in his healing. I would almost bet on it." Tanner walked to the door, too choked up to say more. He turned, shook Drake's hand, and went out into the night.

Fifteen

"Ah, the beauty of this last hour of the day—
when a power stills the air
and smoothes all waters and all minds—
that partakes of the light of the day
and the stillness of the night." Thoreau

Old Man Winter arrived, accompanied by snow in the forecast. Drake asked Roy to lock up so he and Oscar could scout for a Christmas tree. The Jeep had been cranked up the day before to make sure the new battery worked.

After lunch Oscar gave the old Jeep its first assignment in years, and the two men, padded in layered clothing, took off down the paved highway. Oscar knew just where to find a tree—having done the same thing as a boy with his grandfather. Drake was a bit alarmed when Oscar turned the jeep into the old gravel road leading to the church at the top of a hill. He remembered the rugged terrain, having barely navigated it previously on his Harley.

"I traveled this road on my Harley and almost didn't make it. Are you sure about this?" he asked Oscar.

"Relax. If you want a tree, I know where to find one."

The old Jeep coughed a couple times while Drake held his breath. Oscar switched to another gear; the wheels took hold and gained a second wind.

"You're pretty good at this," he told Oscar.

"I should be. Over there, you get pretty intimate with your vehicles when lives depend on them." *ISIS could not be allowed to confiscate the fighting equipment or all would be lost. A rifle with no ammunition was useless as was an armored vehicle no good without man power.* He secured himself more firmly in the seat and concentrated on making it to the top of the hill without overturning.

The old engine struggled on as the incline became steeper, more rutted. Leafless tree branches slapped at the windshield of the open vehicle, more threatening than on his previous trip up the treacherous road. Drake held on, ducked his head when necessary, and wondered if Oscar shouldn't take it a little slower. But perhaps it was necessary to keep up the momentum so the engine wouldn't die.

Eventually, they came out on the mesa Drake remembered from his prior trip. The quaint country church came into view, sitting alone in the cold—but on Sunday hymns would warm the old rafters and echo in the nearby woods. Oscar changed gears and drove the jeep along the edge of the woods until they came to a forest of evergreens.

Drake sighed audibly. He'd never ridden in a Jeep before—a bit more exciting than riding amusement park bumper cars when he was a kid. Conquering the steep, narrow, serpentine hill had given them both a natural high. Grabbing an ax and a handsaw from the back, they left the vehicle and wondered into the dense field of evergreens. "The tree—how big?" he asked Oscar.

"Five or six feet—the tree stand will make it another foot taller. Mom always said the shape and density were more important than the height."

"And this isn't private property—it's okay to cut them?"

"State owned property—nature will replace what we take out."

"I wouldn't want Charlie to have the embarrassment of locking us up for stealing a Christmas tree." They both laughed at the prospect.

They decided to separate in their search for the perfect specimen. "It's much like picking out a lady friend—not too fat, not too skinny, well proportioned, but most important—with a straight, sturdy spine. Whistle when you find one you like, or meet me back at the Jeep if you get lost," Oscar advised. He moved with purpose in the opposite direction.

Drake's head bobbed up and down like a yo-yo, not to stumble on a root and break a leg. He liked the feel of being surrounded by raw nature. Except for the occasional trill and chirp of birds, the quiet was awesome. A feeling of peace swept over him and he wondered if Oscar was experiencing the same feeling. The pungent fragrance of pine was almost overwhelming. After breathing sand for so many months, Oscar probably found it even more so.

It certainly wasn't like choosing a tree in the city where they were trucked in to local grocery parking lots—all sizes and species—ridiculous prices attached. Out here in nature, you had a choice of the good, the bad, and the ugly. It wasn't going to be easy. He kept looking but hadn't spotted a tree that looked the way he envisioned a Christmas tree. When he was young, they had a live tree, but his mother eventually succumbed to an artificial one with pre-attached lights—esthetically leaving much to be desired—in his estimation. It occurred to him that he no longer thought of her as his *adopted* mother.

Drake lost track of time, stopped and looked about for Oscar, without success. Where was he? He called out, but only the birds responded. He had a general idea of where the Jeep was left but where was Oscar? Playing a joke on him, perhaps? Trying to scare the city boy? He quickened his step back the way he had come—he hoped it was the way he had come. Perhaps Oscar had returned to the Jeep.

After some degree of apprehension, Drake finally came upon a clearing near the edge of the woods. There was Oscar—sitting on a fallen and decaying tree with his back to him— his head in his arms. Was he injured? Did he want to be left alone? Drake slowly moved closer until he saw the shoulders move and heard the sobs. He had never before seen or heard a grown man cry. What should he do? From somewhere in his subconscious mind came the question, *"Am I my brother's keeper?*

He leaned against a nearby tree and wondered how he should proceed. Leave the man to his grief? What had brought on the tears? Earlier he had seemed so *normal*, even happy? Perhaps he was thinking of his mother and other Christmases, or was he reliving the Holidays of the more recent past, in a land where Christians were treated with disrespect and hatred, bombed and beheaded? Another quote came to mind: *"Sadness is a solitary ailment—no one else can feel it exactly the same way."*

How true. There was no way he could relate to the trauma Oscar had suffered on the other side of the world. Like millions of other people, he saw the horror of war on TV and read much on the internet. Soldiers were being blown up in their military vehicles, suicide bombers with grenades hidden under their clothing, standing on a street corner, ready and willing to be blown to bits along with innocent bystanders. People were beheaded for no reason other than being of a different religion. He could visualize the horror of it all, but he couldn't feel the pain of the slain, or feel the broken hearts of mothers and fathers losing their sons and daughters in such a horrific way. No, he had watched as one watched a movie—albeit one of horror.

Had the world become immune to violence? The grown man sitting on the log crying his eyes out was not immune. Drake's heart ached for his new friend. Mere words seemed inadequate. Not knowing what else to do, he sat down on the same log, but at a non-intrusive distance. He looked out upon a peaceful valley and said nothing. *A time to speak and a time to be quiet.* He could be a friend without the oratory. A stately buck deer appeared in his left field of vision, stopped in mid-gait, his front right foot lifted as if assessing the situation. He then moved slowly to the tree line and disappeared.

"If someone won't let you in, eventually you stop knocking." Well, Drake wasn't about to stop knocking—even if all he had to offer was his presence. Overhead, a flock of snow geese surfed on the gently-moving winds in search of a safe place to land. After feeding, they would lift their wings as a family and soar the skies southward in search of warmer weather.

Eventually, Oscar became aware of Drake's presence. He looked about as if disoriented, wiped his eyes with the back of his gloves, pushed his hands deeper into his jacket pockets and shivered. "Sorry about that," he said, a sigh coming from deep within. He stood and brought his body to attention, a stance not unfamiliar to him.

"Want to talk about it?" Drake asked.

"It was weird," he said, "back there in the woods," nodding his head toward the pine forest— "frightening—as if a camouflaged sniper might be watching. The trees seemed to merge—into walls—the forest floor became a field of fighting debris." He paused and shook his head. "But then I remembered where I was and the fear disappeared. I felt safe and protected—an awesome feeling. But the feeling of safety comes with the guilt of leaving so many others in danger. A sense of uselessness and guilt is overshadowed by thankfulness that I survived. How selfish is that?"

"Oscar, I'm the selfish one—like all the others who don't have what it takes to put their lives on the line. We're the ones who should feel selfish and guilty—not you. We took the easy way out and stayed home to sleep in our comfortable beds and eat our rib eye steaks."

"Don't beat up on yourself, Drake. You were fighting your own battles—just as real to you."

Drake gave it some thought before responding. "Life is a series of stages, my friend. In all probability, you've just conquered the most difficult one of your life. Now, you have to let it go and start a new phase. Instead of fighting visible and invisible enemies, you can change the lives of others on a more individual level. Don't you think?"

"I know—you're right. First time I've broken down like that in a long time. Thanks for listening, and please don't tell Dad."

"I won't tell him. Besides, I have a feeling you're about cried out. I wouldn't give you two cents for a man who can't shed a tear once in a while. And now, we'd better get that tree before dark."

Another deep sigh from Oscar before he picked up the ax, jumped over the log and headed back toward the woods with determination in every step. "This way," he said.

Drake followed behind with the handsaw. He felt certain Oscar had discovered something more important than finding the perfect Christmas tree—he had found a way to at least temporarily disable his demons. It could be a new beginning.

The odor of wood smoke fogged the valley when Drake and Oscar arrived back at the foot of the challenging hill road. The tires of the old Jeep had skidded on occasion but, thankfully, the brakes had held firm. Oscar turned westward toward a crimson sky, where the setting sun had ignited a bonfire of color. With a seven foot near-perfect Christmas tree strapped to the Jeep they returned to the farmhouse, drove up to the back door just as the deck lights came on. Tanner was waiting in the family room with boxes of ornaments from the attic, a warm hearth and a welcoming heart for the two young men. It had been a long time since any of them had felt the true joy of Christmas. He already had the best possible gift—his son home from a seemingly endless war on terror and another young man fast becoming like a second son. He felt their meeting was more than serendipity—more like fate. Whatever it was, he was grateful.

The tree was dragged in by the two younger men and placed in the metal stand. It was a perfect height for the high-ceilinged room.

Layers of clothing were discarded and hung on antler hooks by the back door. The long screws were tightened to the trunk of the tree and Tanner went to the kitchen for a pitcher of water. The three sat down in front of a flickering fire with large mugs of hearty chicken soup prepared by Tanner in their absence. It was a man's world and if anyone felt the absence of the female touch he kept it to himself.

Later, ornaments collected over the years found their rightful place on the tree. Father and son were seen to pause occasionally, sharing wordless memories, and then continuing the age old custom.

"Have you checked on the Henson's while I was away?" Tanner asked.

Drake reported on Mr. Henson's convalescence, and reassured him that their needs were being met by a good family friend.

"If they're alone, why don't we invite them for Christmas dinner?" Tanner asked and quickly turned to Drake, adding "if you'll help with the cooking."

"You mean I'm invited?" Drake asked.

"Of course, you're invited—Old Tom Turkey will need your gourmet touch. Don't you agree, Oscar?"

"I agree, Dad. He's a better cook than pool player, for sure. You guys do the cooking—I'll take care of the KP."

There was an unexpected rap on the front door, an unusual occurrence at that time of night.

Oscar kept his dad in sight as he hurried to the door where the sheriff stood illuminated by the porch light.

Charlie was blowing warm breath onto his hands when Tanner opened the door. "Sorry to bother you, Mr. Tanner—I'm looking for Drake."

"Come in, please. He's here—helping trim the tree."

Drake came to his feet on seeing the sheriff. "Anything wrong?" he asked with visible apprehension. The afternoon activities immediately came to mind as did the partially dressed tree in the corner.

Oscar maintained the innocence of a choir boy.

"Relax—nothing wrong. I was just visiting Mr. Henson, wrapping up the accident report, and thought I'd stop by."

"You're welcome any time," Tanner said, insisting that he join them. "How is Mr. Henson?"

"Leg is healing well. He's diabetic, you know, and that caused his blackout the night of the accident. Nice couple."

They talked of the Art Center, Charlie reporting on the interest shown around town, the speculation about its future. He turned his attention to Oscar. "It's good to see you back, and looking well I might say. Injuries all healed?"

"Almost like new, thank you," Oscar responded.

"That's great. Just when things start to look better over there, something else happens."

Drake sensed Oscar's discomfort—not a subject he wanted to pursue. "How have you been, Charlie? Solved any interesting crimes, domestic disputes, stolen cattle, moonshiners?" he asked, attempting a little humor.

"Let's hope nothing more exciting than that happens over the holidays. It can be a stressful time for some. That reminds me, Roy may not have to be locked up this year—thanks to you for giving him a job. I haven't seen him hanging around town lately, and no calls from the bank."

Drake told him about the mural Roy had painted. "Don't sell the man short—he has hidden talent under that beret. I don't think he will be a problem in the future—not that he was a problem— except to himself."

"Glad to hear that," Charlie said. He stood and added, "Nice to see you're all doing well." Turning to Tanner, he added, "You home for the holidays, or for good?"

"I'm now officially retired and not the least unhappy about it. Going to spend some quality time with my son, here—and our good friend—and see what the New Year brings."

He turned to Drake and Oscar before continuing. "We were just discussing Christmas dinner. If you don't have other plans, you're welcome to join us."

Charlie seemed taken aback by the invitation. "That's mighty nice of you—four bachelors breaking bread? I'll see what I can work out and let you know."

After he left, Oscar turned to his Dad, "What's gotten into you, Dad? Inviting the sheriff for dinner? This is beginning to sound like feeding the multitude— and I volunteered for the cleanup!"

"Sorry, the invitation was spontaneous—Christmas spirit, I suppose. About time we became more neighborly, don't you think? It's not like any of us will be going anywhere for a while."

Drake and Oscar looked at each other, raised their eyebrows, turned and gave Tanner a high five.

It was almost midnight when Drake returned to his apartment, tired and elated at the same time. He was beginning to feel like a member of the Tanner family—a real family. While preparing for bed he remembered his first meeting with Tanner—sitting on the front porch in rocking chairs, sharing a pot of coffee, and admitting his past sins to a man he'd just met. Drake realized that morning of sharing and being accepted by Tanner had changed his life.

During the night, the blizzard made good on its promise. Drake awoke early to complete silence and a nose that felt like he had slept in a meat locker. Wrapping himself in the blanket, he hurried to the living room and turned the thermostat up a couple notches. The electric heat soon had the small apartment cozy warm—but Tanner had warned him it might not be sufficient if the temperature outside dropped to freezing. If the power failed, he could go to the main house and keep warm before an open fire with his friends.

The snow continued to seduce every branch and twig, softly swaddling them in a blanket of white. A male cardinal, feathers

DECENT DECEIT

ruffled and puffed, perched on a limb in the mulberry tree, providing a bright red focal point in the otherwise pristine winter wonderland. From the south window, no signs of life were evident at the main house. Hopefully, both men were getting some extra zees. No matter, Drake had plenty work to do.

After breakfast, he took a mug of his special dark to the desk. Waiting for the laptop to wake up, he thought of Roy and his only mode of transportation—a rickety bicycle—in such weather? Drake gave him a call and he answered on the second ring. "Are you up, Roy?"

"I am now, Boss. How's the weather out there?"

"Blizzard during the night and still snowing—what's it like in town?"

"Same."

"Take the day off, Roy. No sense in being out in this."

"Thanks. I'll find something to do around here."

"How about doing some painting? Not that you need practice."

Roy laughed, knowing the kind of painting his boss was referring to. "Afraid not—my paints are probably all dried up—what few I have left."

"We'll have to do something about that. I'll call you in the morning."

Drake spent the next two hours surfing the web for art-related sites, and information about traveling artist seminars. He finally opened Word and typed rough drafts for brochures, newsletters and posters to advertise the Center. He also jotted down some ideas for newspaper coverage, not just locally but also in Coopersville—and definitely Kirkwood, only a few miles away. He felt certain Alice would allow a notice in her café window. Hopefully, the Center would draw a few artists who could afford working space as well as those searching for summer retreats and seminars. The picturesque landscape surrounding the town would be a draw to pastoral painters. If his ideas panned out, the attendees would bring in revenue to subsidize lessons for those unable to pay.

His phone rang—Tanner—asking if he was warm and offering some leftover chicken soup from the evening before.

"Thanks, it was delicious, but I plan to hibernate for the rest of the day and get some work done. I called Roy and gave him the day off. Do you need anything?"

"No, we're fine. Thanks for all your help yesterday."

"I enjoyed it more than I can say."

"If you get bored, come down for a game of pool."

After lunch, Drake went back to his computer and checked his bank account. The good news was his investments were doing well in spite of the world financial situation, and the repairs to the Center were costing less than expected.

He tidied the apartment, dusted, ran the vacuum over the area rug in the living room, washed the few dishes in the sink and placed them in the rack to dry. He stretched out on the sofa, pulled an afghan over him and was soon in la-la land.

An hour later he awoke to more snow piled on the windowsills, and wind-carved drifts across the deck. Visibility was confined to the immediate surroundings—even the main house appeared shrouded in a cloak of white feathers. The odor of wood smoke rose from the chimney and no doubt penetrated the entire valley. He turned on the TV and learned not everyone in the area fared as well. Charlie was having a busy day with weather related accidents, and a house fire from an overheated stove. An expectant mother had been rushed to the hospital via fire truck—the only reliable vehicle in such a blizzard.

Tanner called again to ask if he was staying warm. Drake assured him he was comfortable, not divulging the fact that he had just put on a cardigan over his turtleneck sweater. He hoped the electricity remained on so he wouldn't be forced to seek warmth in the main house. He wanted to be alone, to luxuriate in his own space. He had a dinner of leftover shrimp Creole enhanced by an extra touch of filé, and basmati rice.

Later, he found comfort in a large bowl of popcorn and a movie he had previously seen more than once—*Shadows in the Sun*—great plot about a famous but reclusive writer finding refuge in a small Italian town. After losing his wife in an accident, the author had been unable to write until a young publishing agent found him, nagged him into writing again while, at the same time, falling in love with his daughter. The Italian countryside was a feast for the visual senses, the acting first class. The plot and snappy dialogue gave Drake encouragement in his personal endeavor. The movie sent a great message to never give up on creativity. Drake could relate to that. He could also relate to the love story—a young man coming close to losing the woman he loved due to his fear of change.

He added another of his mother's quilts to his bed, and soon his lids grew heavy as the immense quiet locked out the universe. He thought of Patricia and, like the movie, admitted he had lost her because he, too, had been unwilling to change.

He awakened the next morning to find over a foot of snow—even deeper in drifts. The only colors in the world of white was the red covered bridge in the distance, muted tints of a fading sunrise in the east, and a cardinal family playfully flipping snow from the feeder. Smoke arose from the chimney of the main house, indicating that more logs were being added to the fireplace.

Later in the morning, as the sun rose higher in the sky, the wind calmed, the air warmed, and the snow began to melt. Drake carried his easel from his bedroom to a window overlooking the valley. He wanted to capture the pastoral scene before the heat of the sun wiped the beauty from his memory forever. He quickly sketched in the main elements of the composition, squeezed onto his palette a large glob of white, cadmium red for the cardinals and covered bridge, purple for the shadows, a bit of yellow ochre to mix with white for the sunlit snow. He added a bit of cerulean blue for the narrow strip of sky visible above the distant hills. He mixed his colors and painted quickly with confidence and enthusiasm. He was aware only of the scene before him and watching it come alive on the canvas. Later he would remember it as a time of rare and total contentment—of being alive in the moment.

Sixteen

"The past is never dead. It's not even the past."
William Faulkner

Drake kept his promise to Oscar—he never told Tanner of his son's experience in the forest, the moment of confusion or flashback, or the copious tears he had shed. He saw no reason to cause further pain—for the father or son. Instead, he decided to keep a closer eye on Oscar, be there as a friend, plus find ways to help him feel useful—if he could.

The day after the blizzard, the snow melted on the highway sufficiently to allow safe travel. He borrowed Tanner tall ladder from the barn and Oscar helped him secure it on top of his van. The sun glistened on the residual snow in fields of corn stubble, roof tops, and hillsides. The outside shutters Drake had bought at the salvage store were painted black and waiting to be hung on the front windows. They stopped at the local hardware store and purchased the proper hinges.

On arrival, they found Roy in the shipping section of the old linen factory, now with his own key, busily sawing lumber for the assembly of easels—whistling as he worked. What a change from the man Drake had first encountered—broken, intoxicated, hope nearly gone—on the street in Porterville. Oscar also observed the difference and went immediately to the lounge to see the mural Drake had told him about. Once there, he unzipped his heavy jacket and poured a mug of coffee to enjoy while viewing the painting before him. He didn't recognize the scene—it could have been anywhere in rural Midwest. As he studied the distant hills and the foreground rolling terrain he recalled the lyrics of *America the Beautiful*. Drake had not exaggerated—the man had talent.

Drake appeared in the doorway. "Told you," he said to Oscar who was nodding his head in approval.

"Almost makes me want to try it," he said, draining the coffee mug.

"Okay, let's get those shutters hung," he told Drake.

Armed with the proper tools and Roy's help the men had them hung before noon and agreed they added just the right architectural accent to the otherwise nondescript building. Back inside, they warmed up with more coffee.

"You guys were so helpful, how about I treat you with a take-out lunch from Alice's?"

Drake left the two men to the inside tasks and headed for Alice's Diner. He felt full of life and on top of his game. He walked past the planters Alice had filled with red poinsettias and entered the front door. He gave Alice his take-out order, unzipped his jacket, and sat at a nearby table to wait. The lunch crowd was beginning to arrive—he would give up his chair if need be. Now a country boy, he still remembered his manners.

His mind was on the progress at the Center, not on the customers, when a woman entered the door and stopped in her tracks. Patricia? Her recovery was swift. She looked him over briefly, and without even a nod, moved to the back booth where she sat alone. At first, Drake wasn't positive it was her. The hair was the same—shimmering black as a raven's wing. The long legs and body were definitely familiar. She sat facing in his direction. Their eyes met. *Eyes don't change*. Her's were large, hazel and needed no enhancement. But once again she looked away.

Suddenly, Drake was a teenager again. Dare he approach her? He remembered his past mistakes. He couldn't fail again. He was a new man—the alcoholic Drake of before had been transformed. He had a new calling. He knew who he was and who he wanted to be in the future. Patricia was not only beautiful—she was real and she was good. It was he who had been undeserving—he who had been selfish and inconsiderate—and it was he who had acted like a total ass. He couldn't let her disappear again. Somehow his legs carried him the short distance to her booth.

"Patricia—is it really you?" he asked.

She looked up and uttered one word in acknowledgement—"Drake". It was an awkward moment to say the least. Their eyes locked. Finally Drake spoke. "I've been hoping to find you again, but didn't know how to contact you. What are you doing here in Porterville?"

"I came back to care for my mother." Drake remembered her mother had lived in Kirkwood, but he had never met her. He and Patricia had met in Coopersville, where she had her own apartment.

"How is she?" Drake asked.

"She died."

"I'm so sorry." He knew what it was like to lose people. "May I sit down?"

She shrugged her shoulders, and he eased onto the seat opposite her. "Where have you been since—?" He didn't know how to finish—so much had happened.

"New Mexico." She stared at her placemat, but finally lifted her eyes to his. "You seem different."

"Older, and wiser—I hope. I've missed you. I've lost my parents, too. More importantly, I'm sober now and have been hoping for a chance to apologize for the way I treated you."

Patricia looked at him without response. She studied him—searched for signs of authenticity. The small mole on his brow was still there, just a bit right of the three gray hairs at his temple. The left ear was marred only by a tiny mole on the lower lobe. It hadn't grown. His eyes were still the color of a robin egg, only clearer than she remembered—no evidence of red that had once been a dead giveaway. His sandy hair seemed thicker and well groomed. He looked healthy and fit.

"You look well. I didn't expect to see you again, and especially not here," she said. "Someone told me you were teaching in Coopersville. What are you doing here?"

"I'm opening up an art center—in the old linen factory building. I was teaching at the University, but after I lost my parents, I decided to change course. I didn't really enjoy teaching."

Alice arrived at the table and gave the take-out package to Drake. He handed over his credit card.

"What may I get you, Miss?" Alice's smile spread as she tactfully sized up the attractive stranger.

"Just black coffee, please," Patricia answered, glancing at Drake—obviously ill at ease.

Drake noticed her hair was worn a little shorter but still caressed the sides of her smooth, blemish-free cheeks. In spite of the sadness in her eyes, she was as lovely as he remembered.

Patricia was seeing Drake as the man she had first met—obviously sober, more mature, a man she once loved—until alcohol became his sneaky seductress. Here he was again, invading her tranquility, sitting there like a dignitary, a man with a mission. But she couldn't be drawn in again. She'd had enough heartache.

"Well, good luck with your gallery," she said, in a dismissive way.

Drake hesitated—didn't want to press his luck, but he also couldn't let her disappear again. "May I call you sometime?"

"I'll be busy settling up my mother's affairs. She left me her house and there's still a lot to do."

"So you no longer have your apartment in Coopersville?"

"Of course not," she said, perhaps a bit too sharply.

Her sad expression broke Drake's heart—he felt like an intruder and he didn't want to add to her present grief. He wanted to put his arms around her and adore her like a prized and rare orchid.

Alice returned with coffee for Patricia, and Drake's card. He signed his name and thanked her.

"Patricia?"

She knew what was coming. "Too much is going on right now, Drake. I don't know how I feel—maybe later. I know where you'll be. Good luck with the gallery." She had already said that.

With no other choice, he got up to leave. "Patricia, I know I don't deserve your forgiveness, but please give me a chance to make it up to you. I promise you won't be sorry when you hear all that has happened. I've missed you, and I want to hear more about you. Here's my number – please call me, or stop in at the Center. I'm there most every day preparing for an opening in the spring. Please don't disappear again."

That night, after his encounter with Patricia, Drake had a nightmare. A house was burning. He was leaving the scene, then saw a woman approaching from the rear of the building, clothing tattered, her face and arms blackened by smoke. He rushed to her aid but stopped abruptly when they came face to face. It was Patricia, and she had bruises on her face and neck. Her arms reached out to him, but before he could touch her, the dream ended.

Seventeen

"The face is the mirror of the mind, and eyes without speaking confess the secrets of the heart." Saint Jerome

The snow had melted when Patricia arrived back in Kirkwood. She sat in a white wicker porch chair, postponing the need to enter her mother's empty house—a house that now belonged to her. She shivered and pulled the yellow wool scarf more snugly around her throat. Her hand reached in her jacket pocket and came out with a tattered business card—a Taos, New Mexico attorney—a reminder of her past. He had been a good friend and boss, and had asked her to keep in touch regarding her mother's condition. She had enjoyed her job, had a small rented studio apartment in Taos. Life had taken on new meaning after her breakup with Drake—at least for a while.

But then she met Mike—big, macho Mike. He had promised her a bright future. He had sat on her camel-backed sofa, his masculinity in sharp contrast to the peach toned tapestry fabric. The feminine décor of the room only made him appear more virile, more indomitable, and, as it turned out, more threatening in her vulnerable state. After Drake, she had vowed to keep relationships casual, and for a long while it had worked—until it didn't work. She couldn't believe she had fallen for Mike's charming manipulations. But fall she did and getting up had not been easy.

She shivered and shook her head to regain some sense of her present reality. She hadn't expected to ever see Drake again. She stood up and entered her familiar childhood home. Without her mom, the emptiness was overwhelming. They had grown even closer as Patricia willingly and lovingly tended to her every need. She turned on the lights as she made her way to her old room, where she dropped the business card on the bedside table. A return to Taos was doubtful. She loved the quaint artist colony, the galleries and magnificent art work, the big sky, mountains and clean air, but she had left too many unhappy memories there.

Her image in the antique full length mirror became blurred by her tears. The long-sleeved red flannel blouse draped her thin upper body, the fabric only hinting at the swell of her breasts. Faded jeans rode low on her slim hips. The two-inch rhinestone-studded leather belt had lost its glitter as well as its appeal, and suggested only minimal support at the lowered waistline. She stood motionless with both thumbs caught in the vertically slanted pockets. Slowly her right hand moved upward to her neckline where it met the collar of her blouse and lingered briefly before freeing the top buttons. Her fingers read the discoloration just above her clavicle as if written in Braille.

Why had she left her nice apartment in Coopersville in the first place? She knew the answer—for no other reason than to remove any proximity to Drake. Her aim was to explore a different part of the country and forget about romance. The aim was challenged a few months later when she met a man who appeared to be mature, thoughtful, and successful. Harmless— she had thought. As it turned out, Mike eventually turned her trust into fear and loathing. What had she been thinking? How could she have been so gullible a second time? In comparison, he made Drake's drinking seem like a minor flaw.

Her thoughts continued to slither in and out of the past. Her mother was gone, but her essence lingered in every inch of the house—in every cookbook, knickknack, article of clothing, needlework—her touch was everywhere. She should have moved in with her instead of foolishly escaping to New Mexico after her breakup with Drake. Now, she had no one on which to tether her hopes and dreams. A cataract of salty tears flowed down her cheeks. She had been terribly naïve about men—there was no denying it. Well, she wouldn't make the same mistakes again. Her thoughts turned to the surprise encounter with Drake. He was the last person she expected to see in Porterville. The change in him was obvious —more handsome than she remembered. He appeared to have whipped his addiction—but how long would it last?

Eighteen

"When one tries to hide love, one gives the best evidence of its existence." Italian Proverb

When Drake awakened the next morning, he recalled bits and snippets of a dream, without much clarity. He felt certain that Patricia had been present. In the shower and all through breakfast, he tried to retrieve the details, but to no avail. Had their unexpected meeting been just a dream?

He poured another mug of coffee and stepped out on the deck to clear his mind. He lifted his head and flakes of snow, soft as silk, fell onto his upturned face and quickly melted. Patricia used to casually kiss him on the forehead as she swept behind his chair—when things were right between them. Seeing her again, although briefly, had made him realize the value of what he had lost. He ached to hold her again, not out of physical need but just to verify that she was real, that she still existed. She must have seen something worthy in him else she would not have tolerated his behavior as long as she had. She had been smart to avoid further enabling of his destructive addiction.

He had thought he was content in his new life, his plans for the future, but meeting her so unexpectedly had pulled him out of his comfort zone. Now, he feared she would disappear again. He worried about her unhappy expression, although it was understandable, having just lost her mother.

The snow continued to fall softly and unhurried, promising nothing spectacular in accumulation. The mug grew cold in his hands and a chill brought him back to the moment. He hurried inside, telling himself he would wait—give her time—and pray she would call or stop by the Center. Suddenly, it seemed imperative that he have Patricia by his side in his new adventure. She had to give him another chance, a chance to restore her belief in him. He dressed quickly, but carefully, for another day at the Center. It could be the day she showed up—out of curiosity if nothing else.

Somehow, the list of chores he and Ray worked on failed to offer the excitement he had become accustomed to. He couldn't seem to shake off a feeling of loss, but he got through the day and drove home. The sun had come out in the afternoon but he hadn't been aware. He sensed a difference in his enthusiasm as he opened the door to his apartment—it hadn't felt empty before he encountered Patricia at the diner. He hung his fleece-lined jacket on the rack by the door. The bottle of wine on top of the refrigerator grabbed his attention. He had forgotten it was there, or the liquor in the bottom cabinet. The thirst for booze had left him, but that was then and this was now. Now the problem was Patricia's absence and her capacity, or lack thereof, to give him another chance.

What to do? It was too cold for a run. He thought of Charlie's invitation to call anytime he needed to talk. What he needed most was a distraction from the bottle staring seductively back at him. Damn women. He had worked his way through to a new beginning, but now that Patricia had re-emerged his resolve was threatening to slip away.

Drake's gaze darted around the apartment like a squirrel in search of food. He looked out the window toward the main house. Not a creature was stirring—no musical notes escaped through

Oscar's window—only a slow, lazy lifting of smoke from the chimney. It occurred to him that this was not like before when he was tempted. He now had friends and they were close enough to hear his voice if he dared call out to them—men who were what men should be—honest, unpretentious, kind, helpful and genuine in every way that Drake could see—men who were closer than family had ever been. All he had to do was reach out. The bottle taunted him, but he turned away and lifted his phone. Oscar answered on the third ring—one ring before Drake would have ended the call—the call for help.

"What are you up to?" Oscar asked.

"Just got home and could use some company—if you're not busy."

"Come on down. Dad and I just finished a game of pool."

Warmth and the odor of homemade cooking greeted Drake as Tanner opened the door a few minutes later. Flames hissed and crackled in the fireplace where a log had just been added. An evening news anchor was reporting from the flat screen TV on the far wall, the sound muted, but pictures didn't lie. Tanner hit the off button as Oscar approached from upstairs, pulling a fresh T-shirt over his head and rushing to join the other two.

Tanner closed the door and reached to help Drake with his jacket. "Glad you called—Oscar and I needed someone to share a fresh pot of chili and cornbread."

At their welcome, Drake felt his previous unsettling mood slip away. "Smells delicious—I'd love to stay if you're sure you have enough. It's a perfect evening for chili."

After an evening of dinner—the best chili and cornbread he had ever tasted—followed by pool playing and popcorn—Drake felt it safe to return to his apartment. He hadn't thought to turn on a light before he went to the main house, his path now lit only by the pole light at the corner of the garage. Regardless, he took the steps two at a time, flipped on the inside light to find his space again welcoming and free of ghosts. The devil on the top of the refrigerator no longer threatened. He refused to allow a few weak moments to shake his resolve. Instead, he took a shower, brushed his teeth, and thanked God for putting him in his present position. He was thankful for friends—or were they angels— and for strength to overcome his diminished, partially disabled demon—for another day.

The following morning, Drake approached the day determined to allow nothing to slow down the progress at the Art Center, nor allow anyone to compromise his dream. Patricia would contact him when and if she was ready to face a possible future with him. As he drove into town, his thoughts returned to the previous evening with Oscar and Tanner. Oscar had appeared to be more quiet and thoughtful than usual and Drake wondered if the Holiday Season was going to be a difficult time for him—remembering past Christmases far from home, and thinking of the soldiers remaining in harm's way. Plus, the house was probably filled with echoes of his mother. He needed to find more projects to keep Oscar busy. Work was an excellent panacea—at least it had been for him.

A few minutes later, Roy arrived disheveled and unsmiling. Drake greeted him without additional comment, but with careful observation. He would share whatever was bothering him in due time—a lesson Drake had learned the hard way. He picked up the chore list and marked off the projects that had been completed the previous day. Seeing real progress, Drake felt a return of optimism.

It wasn't until lunch time that Roy broke his silence. His mood had not interfered with his morning performance—if anything, he showed more brawn than usual. Near noon, Drake noticed Roy had not brought his usual bag lunch. No problem—he had an extra ham and Swiss to share. He placed them on paper plates in the lunch room, along with a dill pickle and some sweet potato chips. Roy poured them each a mug of coffee and the two men sat across from each other, eating silently. Drake studied Roy's mural on the wall beside them—Roy studied the ham and cheese—and the tabletop—with little enthusiasm. After they had eaten, Drake threw their plates and napkins in the metal waste bin, closed the lid, refilled their coffee mugs and sat back down.

"Roy, my friend, do you want to talk about whatever is bothering you?"

All hesitation ceased. "Pauline has left me, and has taken Sophia with her." His voice broke when he spoke his daughter's name, his head dropped to his arms on the tabletop, and his shoulders shook.

Every curse word Drake had ever heard entered his mind but resulted only in tightly clinched teeth. Of all the rotten deals—just when the man was getting his act together. Drake had never met Pauline or the daughter, but Roy had never spoken one word of disrespect about either. However, he didn't recall many positive comments either. Roy's addiction was no doubt a source of unrest, but the man was in recovery—didn't he deserve another chance? Yet Patricia had given him more than one chance and he had rejected them all. Roy appeared to be an intelligent and kind man, at least while sober, and there was no doubt about his artistic abilities.

Taking a deep breath, Drake placed a hand briefly on the weeping man's shoulder. He needed to bring his sympathy under control and figure out what he could do to help without being intrusive. If Roy needed an excuse to break his sobriety, this would be the catalyst. What he needed was a friend, just as Oscar and Tanner had been there for him. He left the room, giving Roy privacy to work on his emotions.

Drake went to the loading section of the gallery he had reserved for the construction and other dirty work. He built two more easels before Roy appeared. The sawing, pounding and tightening of screws did much to ease the anxieties of both. They worked in tandem until they had built an adequate number to supply the need of the project.

Instead of parting ways at closing time, Drake suggested Roy join him for an early dinner at Alice's Diner. During dinner, the true nature of Roy's marriage was brought to light. It had been an imperfect union—Pauline had never supported his desire to be an artist—and during the last year his drinking had become a serious issue, leaving both unhappy and without hope.

"I can't blame her, really. I wasn't a proper provider, although during the early years I did my best to support the family with different occupations, even when my heart wasn't in it. I can see that now. I didn't do right by Sophia. She's a sweet girl and I miss her. I just hope she forgives me for failing her."

"I think children are more observant than we know. They're aware when a household isn't functioning properly. If Sophia has your artistic genes, she'll come around as she gets older. She'll understand your feeling of emptiness without art to sustain you."

"I hope so."

"Look—my biological mother gave me up and I've totally forgiven her because I know she did it out of love. Let's work on proving you've changed, and in time she'll understand. As for your wife, a short separation may be a good thing, but only you can determine that."

"I think you've saved me once again, Boss. If you hadn't given me that job, this turn of events would be the end of me. While I've been finding my way to health and happiness, Pauline has become less and less so—and I hadn't noticed. Our communication has died a slow death."

"Promise to call me—day or night—when temptation raises its ugly head. And it will—when you least expect it. We can support each other in our sobriety." Drake admitted his recent weak moments and how much his friendship with Tanner and Oscar's had helped him.

Drake drove him home and offered another suggestion. "Roy,

think about this. While they're away, the best thing you can do is make art. Lose yourself again in the creative process—the way you did on that mural. We've both wasted too much time in self-denial about what we really want to do with our lives. If you need art supplies, I'll see that you get them. Okay, pal?"

Roy's news haunted Drake throughout the evening. It stayed with him through chopping vegetables and stir-frying his dinner. He thought back on his recent solitary life, realizing it had been, for the most part, a carefree and happy time. He had learned how to accept what he couldn't change and, more importantly, he had found a positive direction for his life—a life of creative fulfillment as well as being of service to others. He had found contentment and friendships he had never before experienced. He hoped Roy would have a similar experience, now that fate had stepped in, and he would become reacquainted with his creative core.

Nineteen

"In the end, we will remember not the words of our enemies, but the silence of our friends." Martin Luther King, Jr.

The Holiday Season transformed the town of Porterville. People bravely left their heated homes to attend caroling at the churches, on street corners, and other locations including Alice's Diner. Smiles appeared on the faces of those without a whole lot to smile about—particularly those who had been effected by the linen factory shutdown. On the other hand, the more well-to-do landowners, sheep ranchers, and local store owners, appeared to open their hearts and purses to make sure no one in the town went without.

Drake and Charlie were having one of their leisurely dinners at Alice's—it had become a habit although Charlie was often interrupted by a call from someone in trouble—or causing trouble. Drake had learned much about the lives of the locals—the good, the bad, and the ugly. Every town had them. It was Charlie's job to maintain law and order as much as possible. "Most of our citizens behave respectfully during the season, but a few over indulge on merriment. Every man leaves a shadow—some darker than others—and it's not always easy to anticipate the ugly."

On that particular evening, Charlie's phone remained silent. Drake told him about Roy and his concern that he might again turn to booze.

"I'm sorry to hear that. There are worse things than being a bachelor, though I have to admit it's a bit lonely this time of year."

"You're right there," Drake replied, his thoughts going to Patricia—they didn't have far to go. He was having a hard time accepting that he had found her, perhaps to only lose her again.

"Drake, all couples go through periods of disenchantment. Don't allow the marital problems of others to discourage you. Roy and his wife may solve their differences in time—if not, probably not meant to be."

Alice arrived with a coffee refill. "You guys are too serious. How about trying my eggnog custard pie—might put you in a more Yule frame of mind?"

"Does it have rum or bourbon in it?" Drake asked.

"Not a drop. Your pal here would lock me up for serving liquor without a license."

"Then bring it on, Alice. Anything you bake is destined to be good."

"Well, Drake, at least you know how to make a woman happy—just brag on her cooking."

Drake was not in the best of mood. He hadn't told Charlie about Patricia's re-entrance on the scene. The phone remained quiet and Drake decided talking about it might help. Charlie had become as close as one could get to being a confidant. Half an hour later, Drake had opened his soul to a man who might have been his dad if circumstances had been different. Somehow, his anxiety concerning Patricia's forgiveness lessened and hope returned. He just needed to be patient—and stay busy.

Twenty

"We know what a person thinks not when he tells us what he thinks, but by his actions." Isaac B. Singer

Back in Kirkwood, Patricia sat in her mother's house alone with memories of Christmases past. Carolers arrived on the front porch singing of angels on high and little drummer boys, but she could not bring herself to go to the door and thank them. Their lovely voices soon faded as they continued on to another house—one where the occupants might be more receptive to their message of Peace and Good Will.

She reached for the iron poker and rearranged the logs in the fireplace causing multicolored sparks to light up the room. A soft snow turned the streets and sidewalks to white and covered the winter's residue on the window sills. She was lonely and wondered how long she could resist the temptation to contact Drake. Her mother's legal affairs were completed. The house was spruced up from stem to stern and turned over to a realtor. She had no excuses left.

Remaining in the town of her childhood was out of the question. The real problem was how did she reinvent herself? She definitely needed a job and she definitely didn't wish to return to New Mexico. In fact, she had no desire to seek out strange locales or exotic places as she had done when she and Drake had first parted company. She could return to Coopersville and try for a paralegal job but that also held scant interest. Her wanderlust was a thing of the past—running away had only brought more heartache.

Subconsciously, her hand went to her throat as it often did, and she thanked God for the hundredth time that her very life had been spared. One couldn't survive simply by wishing—eventually the future had to be met head on. She hoped the lesson had taught her well.

She pulled the afghan closer as the logs burned lower. The surprise encounter with Drake continued to trouble her. Did he deserve another chance? Did she dare believe in him again? The change in him was obvious—more like when they had first known each other. When he talked of his new venture, she hadn't been prepared to see the confidence and enthusiasm in his clear sparkling blue eyes. His hair, the color of a sunlit field of wheat was clean and well groomed. He even stood taller than she remembered—his body more virile—further proof that he was no longer drinking.

Drake had been kind and thoughtful when they first met, treated her with a gentle touch, was undeniably sexy without meaning to be—before alcohol changed him into a man she had refused to enable. Her dangerous thinking only made her melancholy more acute. She placed the screen in front of the fireplace, turned off the light at the end of the sofa and made her way upstairs. Like Scarlet O'Hara, she would think about Drake tomorrow—next week—or maybe never.

Twenty-one

*"Your friend is your needs answered.
He is your field which you sow with love
and reap with thanksgiving."*
Kahlil Gibran

Tanner called Drake to finalize plans for the Christmas Day feast. They had just returned from the VA Hospital for Oscar's re-evaluation. Tanner wasted no time giving Drake the good news. The soldier's recovery was remarkable, the prognosis excellent, and a return visit suggested in six months. "Whatever you're doing—keep it up" was the doctor's advice.

"That's great news. You've made my day."

"Much of his recovery is due to you, Drake, and I'll be forever grateful."

"No—his recovery is due to his own strength and need to be useful. Music, in one form or another, is where he will find his purpose. I'm convinced of it."

"On the way home, he told me he's considering going to college for a degree in music, and perhaps teach. My advice was to do whatever would make him happiest. I must admit both of us came home carrying a much lighter load. My boy is going to be fine."

"What a great Christmas gift. I'm happy for both of you." Drake offered his hand but a handshake didn't cut it—Tanner reached out and gave him a manly hug instead. "Now we have two things to celebrate: The Season and my son's recovery."

"Just tell me what I can do to help," Drake offered.

"The Hanson's will not be coming—other plans—so it's the three of us, and the sheriff if he can make it. Is there anyone you'd like to invite?"

Drake told Tanner about Roy's situation and the danger of him feeling even more alone during the Holidays—a time for family gatherings.

"By all means, invite him. But that means it will be a stag party—and I'm not referring to Rudolph and his reindeers. You young men should have some female companionship, don't you think? The pickings may not be great around here but kick the idea around, will you?"

Drake laughed but the gayety was short lived. He wouldn't be adding his name and photo to a website like eHarmony until his future with Patricia was resolved—perhaps not even then. Somehow, he felt Oscar was not quite ready either for a relationship, but he could be wrong. He, no doubt, was elated at his prognosis and finally giving thought to his future.

After Tanner left, Oscar texted him and asked if they could talk. The two young men ended up spending the evening together. They drove into town to celebrate Oscar's positive prognosis. Drake phoned Charlie and asked him to join them at Alice's. It was either there or Bucket of Blood—the latter appealing to neither of the three.

"You have a college degree, Drake. Do you think my going for a degree in music advisable?"

"I'm the wrong person to ask that question. The degree didn't work for me, as you know, but it was because I chose the wrong field. Depends on what you expect from the degree and how you plan to utilize it. If you want to teach music on an academic level, then you will need it. However, if you just want to make music, you can do that without a degree. Somehow, I can't see you in an academic setting, but you have time to sort it out before applying."

"Dad would probably be pleased."

"Don't do it solely to please your Dad—he is so happy to have you back home, it won't matter that much."

"How do you know that?"

"He told me so. Now, let's relax and enjoy the evening."

Oscar laughed. It seemed the spirit of Christmas had hitch-hiked a ride into town with them.

"Just had an idea," Drake added, "You could teach music at my gallery. Probably wouldn't put you in a high income bracket, but you'd be doing what you love."

"That's nice of you. I'll give it some thought. I don't know if I could teach kids—I have zero experience in that area."

Drake gave him some silence to mull it over. Finally, Oscar asked about the Veteran population in the area.

"I don't know, except there has been occasional news coverage about our returning men and women—just like you. Why do you ask?"

"Just thinking—wondering if music might help rehabilitate some of them. Many of my comrades spoke of their music and art interests—when we weren't preoccupied with grenades, car bombs and just staying alive."

"What a great idea, Oscar. Wow! Why didn't I think of that? Could you do some research and explore that need? We don't open until the spring, and you could help get it started, at least, in case you decide you want to go to college after all. See what you can do, and I'll work on another media announcement. Charlie and Alice probably know the locals better than anyone and we can also pick their brains."

"Whoa, slow down," Oscar said. "It was just a suggestion."

"And the best one I've heard so far."

They rode in silence until they reached the town limits. Drake's old enthusiasm returned threefold.

"Oscar, I haven't talked about it much, but I've had a guilt complex over not participating in the military, and especially after meeting you. If we could make your idea work, it would give me a sense of doing at least a smidgen of good—one way to show my appreciation."

"I understand—your heart's in the right place."

"By the way, would you mind if Roy had Christmas dinner with us? Your dad said it was okay." Drake filled him on the details and without hesitation he gave his consent. They both laughed when Drake told him about his father's suggestion that they needed to find some female companionship.

Oscar had begun to see a future of possibilities. He had dealt with terrorists, seen indescribable cruelty and contemptible acts, but now he had a different reality—the farm, the simple life and his music. It was not something to take lightly. The part he played in the tragedy of war seemed farther away, even some other lifetime in spite of the escalating threat of ISIS. Or did the peaceful valley only seem like an Eden in comparison. He had learned there could be no valleys without mountains.

He turned to Drake who had become a valued, non-judgmental listener. "Every time I pulled a trigger over there or threw a grenade, a part of me went with the projectile, leaving a deep emptiness. Visualizing the planes plowing into the towers gave me the courage to do what someone had to do—help eradicate the evil that caused it all. Now that the barbarianism is growing worse, I have to accept that others have that same need to do their part in making the world safe. All I want now is to live my music, and pass that sense of joy on to others—preferably other returning soldiers—so their hearts do not become hardened to the ways of the world. Like with your art, if I can put down a few notes of music, some meaningful lyric, I can begin to live again. You've encouraged me not to give up on my creative dreams, and I thank you."

Drake gave him a high-five. "What are big brothers for?" He realized for the first time that they had become brothers in every way except DNA.

He pulled into Alice's parking lot and killed the engine. "Oscar, you know what Harper Lee said in *'To Kill a Mockingbird?'* Mockingbirds don't do one thing but make music for us to enjoy. They don't eat up people's gardens, don't nest in corncribs, they don't do one thing but sing their hearts out. That's why it's a sin in kill a mockingbird, and it's why you should make music."

Snowflakes kissed the windshield and Drake thought of his old collection of poetry stashed away in a file. He wondered if Oscar could put some of his poems to music.

"Oscar, some things can't be rushed, like sunsets, the birth of animals, Christmas morning— even love."

Through the diner window, Drake noticed Charlie and Alice in a cozy conversation, and wondered again about their true relationship. He would definitely, at Tanner's request, offer an invitation for Christmas dinner. He had never played the role of cupid—too wrapped up in his own drama—but they were playing a positive role in his new life and he wanted them to be happy.

The evening, food and camaraderie continued for over an hour. Alice had accepted their invitation for Christmas—the only day of the year she closed the diner. They were just finishing a superb bread pudding when the call came—Charlie summoned to the Bucket of Blood.

"Sorry guys—sounds like trouble."

He gulped a last sip of coffee and was out the door before Drake or Oscar could react. Alice rushed to their table for information. Drake didn't miss her concerned look when he told her there was trouble at the Bucket of Blood. She slumped in the booth beside them, her few remaining customers forgotten. "That place is nothing but trouble. I hope Charlie can handle it—one more time."

Oscar grew antsy and looked at Drake with raised eyebrows. Reading his mind, Drake said,

"Let's go."

"Be careful, boys," Alice warned. From the frown lines on her forehead, they could have been her own sons.

At the Bucket of Blood, they spotted the cruiser immediately and pulled up alongside. People were rushing out the door of the tavern as if the Devil himself was pursuing them. Neither Drake nor Oscar uttered a word. Their car doors opened in tandem and they rushed forward with no thought of their own safety. Just as they reached the door, a shot rang out. Oscar touched Drake's arm, they paused a second not to be caught in a cross fire. Immediately, the door banged open, narrowly missing them. A man staggered onto the stoop, gun in hand. Oscar put out his foot just in time and the man fell, his gun landing a safe distance away. In seconds, Oscar had him pinned to the cement. The shooter was going nowhere. "Check on Charlie," he yelled. Drake was already entering the bar. No need to call the police—he was already there. Someone must have called Tom because the deputy arrived just behind Drake and Oscar. Drake found Charlie attempting to rise from the filthy, peanut shell carpeted floor, blood darkening the left arm and front of his uniform. He rushed toward him but Charlie motioned him aside. "Don't let him get away."

"Don't worry—Oscar has him under control. He's not going anywhere."

"Check the man behind the bar—he's shot, too."

Drake's main concern was for the man that might have been his father if circumstances had played out in a different way. He sat on the floor and held the near fainting Charlie against his chest. He needed Oscar there to assess the injury, but Oscar was busy with the gunman. "Hang in there" he told Charlie, "Help is coming—they'll have you fixed up in no time." Blood was becoming more obvious and he asked a lady customer to bring clean towels from the bar. Drake wished he were better at praying. He did his best.

Meanwhile, outside the Bucket of Blood, Deputy Tom had the gunman in cuffs and secured in the patrol car. From the slightly lowered cruiser window, obscenities polluted the night air. Seeing the situation was under control a few stragglers lingered to watch the drama further unfold. The gun was bagged. Tom rushed inside to check on his boss just as the emergency team pulled in—sirens slashing gashes into the stillness of the night.

Oscar was assessing Charlie's wound when the paramedics arrived. As soon as Charlie and the bar owner were under the care of the professionals, Drake called Alice before the news reached her from another source.

"I had a bad feeling about this one, Drake. You're sure he'll be all right?"

"I think so—the shot hit him in the left inner arm and outer left chest. There was a lot of bleeding but he was conscious. He was more concerned about the other victim and whether the shooter escaped."

"That sounds like Charlie. Did the shooter get away?"

"No way—Oscar tripped him as he ran out the door and had him disabled in seconds. Tom cuffed him and they got him in the patrol car while I was inside with Charlie."

Alice became quiet, her emotions barely under control. "Are you sure he'll be all right?"

"It was a close call—a few inches to the right and it would have hit his heart. Oscar and I are on our way to the hospital now. I'll call you as soon as I know more. Okay?"

"Give him my love, will you?"

Drake smiled for the first time since the drama unfolded. "I sure will, Alice. Talk to you later."

He turned to Oscar. "You'd better call your Dad before he hears this from someone else. Small town, you know."

"I've already called him."

"Man, that was quick thinking back there—an impressive tackle, I might add. I'm beginning to like having you around," Drake told him.

"It was nothing," Oscar responded. They rode in silence for a time—Oscar probably thinking of the constant danger he faced as a soldier—making the evening's activity seem like child's play. Neither of the men wished to consider the possible tragic outcome of the last few hours. It could have ended in a blood bath from which the small town would not have soon recovered.

Drake drove within the speed limit and the distance to Kirkwood General seemed endless. On this trip, he wasn't thinking of Patricia—so near and yet so far away. They finally arrived and rushed to the emergency room door. The night was as clear as a polished sheet of stainless steel. A field of platinum stars were putting on their best performance. The moon's razor-sharp edges appeared to be cut and pasted onto the sky. But the focus of the two young men was on one lone target—the condition of their good friend, the sheriff, beyond the double doors.

"Do you know your blood type, Drake? He lost a lot of blood and may need a transfusion."

"No, but I hope one of us is a match."

The nurse informed them Charlie was being taken care of and asked them to wait for further instruction. "I hear you men were a big help. Have some coffee and relax—the Sheriff's in good hands."

"We can give blood if needed," Oscar said, his hand on Drake's arm.

"I'll let them know—and thank you."

After half an hour—and a second helping of barely drinkable coffee—a nurse arrived and advised them that Charlie's condition was good, the bleeding had been stopped, and the wound was being repaired as she spoke.

"When can we see him?" Drake asked.

"As soon as he's stabilized and the doctor gives his okay."

Another hour and they were standing by Charlie's bed in a different wing, relieved to see him sitting up. The patient looked a bit pale and frustrated at the I.V. attached to his arm. "They insist I stay overnight, boys. I don't have time for this—Tom will be beside himself."

"Now, now," Drake said. "I just talked to Tom and everything at your office is under control. He says not to worry. I also talked to a very anxious Alice. She said to give you her love." Charlie didn't respond verbally but Drake could tell he was touched.

"You gave all of us a fright."

The sheriff turned his attention to Oscar. "I'm told you detained the shooter until Tom arrived. Good job—thank you."

"No problem," Oscar replied. "We'd better let you rest now."

Charlie moved his swaddled arm and winced. "I thought it would just be another drunken fist fight. The bartender refused to sell him another drink, and he pulls out a gun and starts shooting. We were lucky he was too drunk to aim straight."

"We're just glad you're going to be okay, you old rascal," Drake said in an attempt to cover his fragile emotions.

"What made you follow me to the bar?"

Drake and Oscar looked at each other and Drake replied, "Gut feeling, I guess—plus Alice was wearing some serious worry lines."

Charlie looked down at the sheet in a moment of embarrassment. "Well, I appreciate all you two did to help. I won't forget it."

"Okay, we're out of here. Get a good night's sleep and call when you're discharged. I'll come and deliver you back to Porterville where you belong."

"Maybe I should deputize you two—in case Tom needs some

DECENT DECEIT

help while I'm slightly out of commission."

Nurses paused in their duty as the two young men made their way down the hallway—a new spring in their step. It wasn't every day one observed two heroes at once.

News travels fast—good and bad. This time the news was good. As the two men stepped out under the eerie neon lights, their gait became brisk and determined. Drake looked at the sky, the moon now directly overhead—smiling down at them. God did seem to work in mysterious ways.

Twenty-two

"And let there be no purpose in friendship save the deepening of the spirit." Kalil Gibran

As Christmas Day approached, the sheriff was back on duty and the grateful town even more satiated with the spirit of the season. The shooting at the Bucket of Blood had made newspaper headlines as well as on television. The bar owner suffered only superficial wounds. The shooter remained behind bars at the county jail were Charlie and Tom kept a close eye on him. He would be transferred to Kirkwood later for his trial. He was known for his lack of control when drinking, was a frequent customer at the bar, and recently unemployed—none of which justified him carrying a gun.

In the news, much was made of Oscar, a recently returned soldier, disabling the shooter and perhaps saving the lives of innocent people. To Oscar, it was a small thing he had done, but knowing the shooter was incarcerated the town would sleep easier during the holidays.

Fat raindrops began to smack against the window as Drake found comfort in the aroma of frying bacon and brewing coffee. Having found his food supply nearly exhausted, he had come into town for breakfast and would visit the grocer on his way home. He listened to muted voices of parents with sleepy-eyed youngsters coaxed prematurely from their nocturnal slumber. How different was his attitude from his first visit to Porterville, when he had looked on the area as godforsaken, quaint, and uninteresting—offering him nothing of value. How wrong those first impressions had been. He had found a sense of belonging among these people, and unexpected hope for a worthwhile future. Looking back, he felt a disassociation from his former self—an alcohol abusing, lost and disenchanted young man with no understanding of happiness or life in general.

His thoughts were interrupted as Alice appeared with the source of those earlier aromas —two perfectly poached eggs—fresh daily from a local farmer—grits perfectly seasoned with butter and black pepper—an addition to his favorite food list—and a refill of coffee.

"Alice, you get a number of travelers in here, don't you?"

"Yes, I do. This is a convenient stopover for refueling of body and machine between Kirkwood and Coopersville—and destinations further on. Your gallery will, no doubt become an interesting side attraction. You've seen the Greyhound bus stop by the police station, and the new high school that was built before the linen factory closed—we get a lot of traffic through our little town. Porterville hasn't been orphaned by an interstate as have so many small towns.

"I hope you're right."

Alice appeared even more cheerful than usual as she mingled among her customers. Had the Tanner Christmas invitation enhanced her Holiday spirit? Every surface of the diner was scrubbed and sparkling, red candles on the tables, and flickering miniature lights framed the windows. Unlike Alice, Drake's usual cheerful countenance was barely discernible. Patricia's lovely face haunted him. He wondered where she would spend Christmas— undoubtedly it would be a difficult day for her—the first Christmas without her mother.

The atmosphere outside became chilled as he left the café. The raindrops turned to snow and fell softly like feathers of angel wings. Strange, he had never before thought of snow as anything but a nuisance—something to tolerate until the sun came out and dried the resulting slush and mud.

At the Second Chance Gallery, Drake placed a large wreath on the door. Newly activated security lights had been installed in the parking lot and at the front entrance. An opening date of April 1st. was posted in the front window. His announcements had already prompted phone calls and e-mails requests for further information. The future looked bright for the gallery but still no word from Patricia. He feared she might stop by and he would miss seeing her. He was tempted to place a sign on the door asking her to call him—a foolish thought—she would seek him out when she was ready. He had vowed to be patient if she gave him another chance.

Gifts had been chosen for his close friends—Oscar, Tanner, Charlie, Alice and, of course, Roy, who remained despondent but had not broken his sobriety—as far as Drake could tell. He had accepted Drake's Christmas invitation with his head lowered in humility. The guest list had grown to six for dinner at the Tanner household. The menu had been prepared and each given an assignment. Even Alice insisted on supplying the dessert and rolls.

Excitement filled the air and hearts were grateful that the county still had a sheriff. The shooting episode was a reminder that complacency could change into chaos in an instant, and that evil was ever present in all parts of the world—including small towns across America.

Oscar had gradually become more talkative and in greater depth about his war experiences. He often confided in Drake about his views of the worsening war on terror all over the world, his concern—particularly for the children—caught up in the devastation. He had shared with Drake an e-mail from Miriam, the Iraqi woman whose children he had saved from the car bomb. She wrote of her fears and uncertainty. She told Oscar about her ill father, a good righteous man who had been taken by Saddam's men, imprisoned and tortured by breaking his arm and neck. After two years he was released back to his family in an emaciated indescribable state of health. He continued to suffer the results of those two years and was now hospitalized.

Miriam had spent the night with him in a near-freezing room where no one offered her a blanket. *"There were so many people around I couldn't even say my night prayer—I prayed only in my heart. I want to take him home and see that he does nothing to hurt his health. He's an old retired general and every time he watches the news he feels bad about all that is happening in Iraq. After the American army kicked away those dirty men of Al-Qaeda from our zone in 2007, we lived in some peace. Now the wicked men of ISIS are attacking like vampires in their black attire, burning houses and stealing from shops. My son's girlfriend lived in another zone and she and her family were forced to run away in fear at three o'clock at night. Thousands of people are running away from the hell of war with ISIS. After all these hard years, I really feel tired. I am no longer scared or even care if I live or die. Near God I can find the peace I have been starved for."*

Drake worried that these communications might undo the progress Oscar had made in his recovery. Oscar felt otherwise. "My memories will never completely go away, and the least I can do now is to be a sounding board for her. I need to know they're all right. Bad news is better than no news. It's also a reminder that I did some good and can continue to help in some small way. Understand?"

"I think I do. Keep me posted, will you?"

"It's good of you to care, Drake—I appreciate it. By the way, I haven't gotten Dad a Christmas present. I'd like to do something special—he misses Mom a lot this time of year."

"How is he adjusting to retirement?"

"He spends a lot of time in his study. For a retired man, he gets a lot of calls, does some consulting. We've talked. He plans to stay on the farm, raise vegetables, plant more fruit trees, and do some writing."

"Sounds great to me—I like having him around. You know, I've been wondering why you don't have a dog out here. All this land just seems to cry out for a companion, a canine to run capers with the rabbits, the squirrels—and the occasional skunk."

"Oh, God, have you ever smelled a skunk?"

"Not that I'd remember."

"Believe me, you would remember."

"Then forget the skunk. A dog might be good for your Dad—something to look after besides you." He punched Oscar on the shoulder good naturedly.

Drake had never had a dog—his mother was allergic to animal hair—and his dad wouldn't have wanted the bother. Now Rhonda—his real mother—would she have wanted him to have a dog? His hand went to his throat and closed over the silhouette—a constant reminder. He made a mental note to put a poinsettia on her grave.

"A dog might be a good idea, Drake. If I go away to college, Dad will be alone. I'll think about it."

Twenty-three

*"And in the sweetness of friendship let there
be laughter, and sharing of pleasures.
For in the dew of little things the heart finds
its morning and is refreshed."*
Kahlil Gibran

Christmas morning floated in on a snowy white blanket but no dangerous accumulation was predicted. Drake was awakened by the gentle nudge of a brushed and groomed Irish setter named O'Toole. The beautiful, healthy sienna colored animal had been found in the classified section of the paper. His master had died and the dog needed a loving home. Drake had managed to keep him happy overnight in his apartment—after a bath and thorough brushing, of course. Thankfully, there had been no barking. Drake and Oscar couldn't wait to spring the surprise on his new master. He dressed quickly, and fastened the leash around the dog's neck—no roaming free this morning. Drake was careful not to walk where they could be seen from the main house. O'Toole's debut in the Tanner household would take place later in the day.

The cornbread and sage dressing had been prepared the day before at the main house. The three men worked in tandem to have everything prepared according to Mrs. Tanner's Southern Living cookbook. Oscar asked Drake to cook the mushrooms the way he had prepared them the night he had opened up to his new friend about his experiences. The two men had come a long way in their varied yet similar rehabilitation.

The good china and silverware came out of retirement to grace the dining room table. Tanner added a potted poinsettia as a centerpiece. The live Christmas tree held up well, blending its pine fragrance with the culinary odors from the kitchen. The guests arrived at the main house on time. Charlie had gathered Alice, as well as Roy, and they arrived spruced up for the occasion. Even Roy looked dapper in what appeared to be new trousers, a red shirt and the ever present black French beret sat at a cocky angle atop his head. Gifts were placed around the tree. Carols from an elaborate music system, added an authentic touch to the day—the true meaning of Christmas. In spite of the camaraderie and good will, the absence of Mrs. Tanner was felt, but not in a morbid way. Her china, her recipes, and the house itself were the gifts she continued to give.

In spite of being outnumbered, Alice pitched in and helped place the abundant food on the table, aware of the numerous glances Charlie cast her way. Were they just friends, or was there more? Did she dare hope? She smiled, thinking she should have put Charlie on her wish list? She had to admit it was fun riding in his patrol car. But what kind of life would they have, never knowing when he was called out if he would return? Of course that could be true of anyone in any profession.

Tanner raised his glass to the guests, thanking them for sharing the day. With a trembling voice, he lifted his glass to the portrait hanging over the fireplace. "And to Annabelle for the joy she brought to my life." He turned to Oscar. "I'm so thankful to have my son home—and healthy. We're thankful for new friendships—Peace on earth and good will to all—Merry Christmas. And now, let's eat."

He carved the bird with great skill while the others watched with great interest.

"Well done, Tanner," Drake said. "You should be a heart surgeon." Everyone applauded.

They devoured the food like a pack of hungry wolves. Alice congratulated the men on their culinary expertise, "Now I know who to call if I need an extra chef." She topped off the meal with her mincemeat pie.

Overfed and over stimulated, they gathered around the tree for exchange of gifts. Drake presented Alice with a signed copy of the New Orleans Famous Restaurant Cookbook wrapped in an apron imprinted with "Kiss the Cook". She modeled the apron, and each man rushed to give her a kiss on the cheek, causing her to blush like a debutante.

Alice caressed the book and turned to Drake. "Where did you ever find this?" Drake explained it was from his mother's collection, leaving her speechless. Oscar was amply pleased with a collection of CD's and Tanner was given the painting Drake had done of the snow scene with covered bridge. Roy, the quietest of the group, was visibly touched by Drake's gift of a set of Holland Oils and brushes. Charlie was taken aback by a gift of fishing rod and reel. "You need to do something besides break up bar fights," Drake told him.

Drake felt he got the best gift, a great surprise, from Oscar—a Christmas card with a sizeable check. "I'm going to take you up on your idea of teaching music at your Gallery. In order to do that, you're going to need sound-proofing for a separate room. We can't be disturbing the visual artists, can we? That check should cover the cost."

"Oscar, that's wonderful— but what about college?"

"I'm going to postpone that for awhile. I've contacted several veterans—five of them are interested in pursuing their music. I want to try to help them. We'll see how it goes."

Drake looked at Tanner who responded with a smile and nod of approval.

When the last gift had been unwrapped, Oscar signaled to Drake who quickly excused himself and returned to his apartment. A few minutes later he came onto the porch where a pacing Oscar awaited. He took the dog inside and bedlam erupted. "Merry Christmas, Dad," Oscar said to his startled and astonished father. "Meet O'Toole." The dog ran from one to the other as if he were Santa himself. He returned to Tanner and lifted a heavy paw—begging in no uncertain terms— his tail wagging. "I'm a good boy—now feed me."

The celebration had been a success. Spirits were high and hearts were filled with joy that fate had brought them together. Charlie had gotten through the day without an emergency call; however, the night before had not been so uneventful. The Holiday season was not a happy time for many. Frustrations and family squabbles were intensified by booze—the latter resulting in disorderly conduct and even auto accidents. Charlie hadn't gotten much sleep but was relieved that none of his calls resulted in tragedy.

Goodbyes were finally said, and O'Toole walked leisurely to a rug by the back door, settled down with his chin resting on his front paws. He eyeballed Oscar and Tanner one more time, yawned and closed his eyes. He had a new home and people to love—Santa had been good.

The men continued to nibble during the clean-up. Leftovers were divided for another day. Drake, with great humility, expressed his thanks for their generosity. At the door, he added an emotional adieu. "This is the best Christmas I've ever had, guys." He gave Tanner and Oscar a handshake and a hug. The glimmer in his eyes left no doubt of his heartfelt sincerity.

The excitement and emotion of the day left him drained. He returned to his apartment, put the leftovers in the refrigerator—rudely ignoring the ever present seductress on the top—and attempted to understand how he had become so lucky. When he turned into the road leading to the Tanner farm for the first time, he hadn't the faintest idea that one turn in the road could change his life—and his attitude about life in general. He remembered how they had sat on the front porch, how Tanner had so unabashedly sung *I Believe.* He shouldn't have been surprised when at Christmas dinner Tanner had asked them to hold hands while he said a brief prayer of thankfulness that Jesus had come into the world as a baby and later gave his life on a cross for the sins of mankind. He thanked God for bringing them all together in friendship. Drake felt that every person at the table believed they had been brought together for a reason, but only time would reveal the reason. How could he not believe there was a God when his path had opened up so seamlessly? He now had real friends, good people who treated him like a person of value— yet he felt undeserving.

Drake was overwhelmed not only by Oscar's contribution of money to the gallery, but his willingness to become a part of the dream—and his desire to help his fellow veterans with his gift of music. Five local veterans had already expressed a desire to join his classes and showed genuine enthusiasm in the project. Oscar's smiles were now more spontaneous, and their conversations more varied and frequent. To Drake, he was a true hero—not only for his service to his country, but how he fought back to regain and preserve his sanity. Oscar's check for soundproofing a music room was unexpected to say the least. He decided to turn the project over to him so his contribution would be used wisely. Also, staying busy would be a great panacea for his continued recovery.

Twenty-four

*"And what is your friend that you should
seek him with hours to kill?
Seek him always with hours to live."*
Kahlil Gibran

The following morning, Drake and Oscar left for the Gallery still on a high from their Christmas dinner and the delightful day they all enjoyed. Oscar reported that his dad was already in love with O'Toole, and he thanked Drake again for the suggestion. "That dog is going to make a huge difference in his retirement."

"Do you think he'll ever remarry? I mean your Dad—not O'Toole. And how would you feel about it if he did?

"I doubt it. He and Mom were joined at the hip. Another woman couldn't measure up—in his eyes. If it should happen, I wouldn't object. His happiness is the important thing."

"Since you were so generous with your gift yesterday, could I ask you to handle the soundproofing of the music room? After all, it will be your project. And we have to decide the best location. The shipping room in the back is huge and could easily be converted into two rooms. We don't need all of it for storage. And, it would be further removed from the main gallery."

"Good idea. Violin practice can sound like agitated alley cats."

"You can start your lessons as soon as the space is completed—no need to wait for the formal opening."

"That would be good. I don't want my recruits to grow impatient and change their mind. If I find they have true talent we might even form a band—help them reacquaint with civilian society. Two of them are PTSD—just like me."

"You've certainly made a good recovery, it seems to me. I've been wondering—was there a specific trigger point for you?"

"More like an accumulation of events. PTSD doesn't totally go away, you know. They say once the brain has been traumatized there is no cure. Even the drone operators, working behind a desk and going home to their kids at night often suffer a similar fate. The only difference is they are not physically watching as their buddies are blown to bits or feeling them die in their arms. How can any human survive that without being stressed to one degree or another? And no magical breakthrough is expected. Painting, music, writing—all help but won't cure it. It makes you a different person."

He signed deeply before continuing. "Well, *this* different person is going to make music. I plan to tell my students that the lessons are not only about personal battles, but the joy of playing music, feeling the beauty of it. The most I can hope for is that it will be enough to drown out the sounds of missiles and bombs."

Drake found no appropriate words in his vocabulary to respond. He wondered what his friend thought about when he was playing his violin or guitar late at night. Was he thinking of Miriam in far away Iraq—walking in her family's walled garden where roses bloomed and vegetables grew to keep them alive for another day. Did Oscar's music help muffle the sounds of his own personal war?

Drake pulled into the parking lot and as usual felt pleased with the progress. He couldn't wait for spring to see new landscaping and an *open* sign on the door. Roy had arrived before them, evidenced by the bicycle parked near the entrance. Drake prayed the man would get through the New Year in a sober state. A gift and card from his daughter appeared to have greatly improved his mood.

Once inside, Drake went immediately to his desk to check his e-mail—nothing from Patricia. By noon, he and Oscar had solved the problem of the music room. A section by the rear entrance previously used as the loading dock for the linen factory would be partitioned off and sound-proofed, and still leaving ample space for storage. It would be a cost Drake had not anticipated, but Oscar's check would more than cover the expense. The measurements were agreed upon and notes taken.

"Okay, buddy, the project is yours. The sooner you get to work the sooner you and your men can start making beautiful music."

Drake went to his personal studio with a north light. His easel now held a painting in progress, a table on wheels holding an array of paints and brushes. The temptation was strong to put aside the rest of the day and just paint, but other matters tempered the temptation. An art supply company had agreed to provide a display of painting materials that would bring the gallery extra income, as well as an extra convenience for his artists. The front gallery was just as he had envisioned it, thanks to Roy's assistance and perfectionism. Now was the time to increase publicity, solicit clients, and prepare for the opening. He hoped that running the gallery would not demand his full time—he needed more personal time in front of his easel.

He went in search of Roy to tell him about Oscar's plan for the music room. "I hate to ask you, but he'll probably need your help with the carpentry."

"No problem, boss. How could I refuse after your great Christmas gift?"

"I know you're dying to try those new brushes, so take the rest of the day off and paint. If the canvases are any good, we'll display them at the opening."

Roy lowered his head. "They won't be that good—I'm rusty."

"Let me be the judge of that. Now get out of here."

Drake returned to the back to find Oscar making more notes, completely absorbed in his new project. "Oscar, could we close up? I'd like to stop by the cemetery on the way home."

"Of course, be right with you."

They rode through town, barely below the speed limit, past Alice's Cafe, the theatre, and Drake's empty lot—the spot where his long mysterious life had begun. With no snow on the ground, it appeared as a lonely orphan amidst the other modest homes with wreaths on the door, and smoke rising from chimneys. He really needed to do something about it—maybe someday build a house on it. At least the lot was free of debris and spring would bring green grass and a leafing of the large maple tree in the front. Strange—humans bundle up in the winter but nature disrobes entirely, challenging the elements, so to speak. What kind of sense did that make?

Oscar continued to make notes—Drake drove on without comment. When he pulled into the church lot, Oscar placed his notes and pen on the dashboard. "Want me to come with you?"

"Only if you want to," Drake replied, opening his door. "I'll be brief."

The weather remained above freezing, and the potted poinsettia had stayed reasonably fresh. Drake brushed a bit of debris from the headstone and fished out the necklace from beneath his jacket and sweater. *"I'm hanging in, Mom. Charlie and I are getting along just fine and the Tanners have become like family. I'm in good hands."*

He touched the silhouette charm to his lips, replaced it beneath his shirt and turned to see Oscar approaching. They walked shoulder to shoulder back toward the van.

"Oscar, I don't think I told you—Charlie is my only connection to my mother. They were very close at one time and I think he still loves her—probably why he never married."

"No, you didn't tell me. Wow! No wonder you two are close."

"He might have been my dad, if things hadn't turned out the way they did."

"I don't mean to pry, but you never mention your biological father. Is he buried here also—and your grandfather?"

"Both of them, but to be honest—I've completely tuned them out. My grandfather was a no-good, mean, drunken, poor excuse for a man. He ruined my mother's life, interfered with Charlie's relationship with my mom, and turned my life into a work of fiction."

They leaned against the van and surveyed the surrounding countryside, each thinking their private thoughts.

"Strange, but I feel no connection whatever to my father. All I know about him is the little Charlie told me. Apparently, he was an okay guy—but he did abandon my mother at one point—and I was part of the package."

"My friend, hate is a destructive and dangerous emotion. When I went into the Army, I was filled with hate for the swine that attacked our country, and all that happened afterward. It's easy to hate those who hurt you or your loved ones. Forgiveness is difficult, but if we don't forgive them, they'll forever have a hold on us. Forgiveness can save your sanity—believe me. I learned that the hard way."

On the way home, Drake told Oscar more of his story. They discussed how Charlie had helped him acquire the gallery property and let him off the hook about the fire he had set.

"He would have been a great dad. Too bad he doesn't have a wife and kids—to drive him crazy." They both laughed.

"I can't imagine how it felt to be deceived the way you were. And you haven't allowed it to defeat you. Guess I've been pretty lucky in that department.

"Yes, you have. Tanner is a great guy. I'll never forget the day we first met. I had no idea what to expect when I answered that ad for the apartment. After ten minutes of sitting on your porch with him, I knew he was special. I kept calling him *Sir*—don't think I'd ever addressed anyone so formally before—his presence just seemed to demand it. We shared our stories like long lost brothers. I knew from the get go that I wanted to know him better. And I wanted to meet you—although that scared the pants off me."

Oscar laughed. "No one has ever said that to me." He put up a fist in jest. "Still scared of me?"

"Not the least. By the way, where is your Mom buried?"

"In Washington—that was her home—and ours for many years. As I told you, we visited my grandparents here as often as we could with Dad's work—and I spent time here every summer."

That evening, alone in his apartment, Drake reviewed his day with Oscar, their conversation at the cemetery, and Oscar's questions about his biological family. He turned on his Bose and stretched out on the sofa. The cemetery visits always left him a bit melancholy. Christmas Day had an unexpected impact on him—his once hardened heart had felt a change, and that change remained after the day ended. Whether it was the season, good friends gathered together like family, Tanner's toast or the holding of hands while he blessed the food. His heart in that one day mellowed and opened wide to accept the friendships that had been placed in his path. He learned what it felt like to be truly thankful.

However, the one area of his life he had locked away to deal with later, if ever, was his inability or reluctance to forgive both his biological father and grandfather. His mother was a different story—she had been a victim just as he had been. The necklace helped his heart to heal where she was concerned. He held her blameless, but found it difficult to forgive the other two. It had been easier to lock them out of the equation. He now realized to find total peace he would have to forgive them, and he was certain Rhonda would agree with him.

Twenty-five

*"Think not you can direct the course of love, for love,
if it finds you worthy, directs your course."*
Kahlil Gibran

The year was coming to an end on a chilly note, in more ways than one. Not only did Drake miss Oscar and Tanner—they were away for a brief vacation with friends—he still had not seen or heard from Patricia. He had been foolishly acting like a private eye in search of a felon on the lam—had barely stopped short of asking Alice if she had been in the Café.

He spent the day in the gallery, a place he was beginning to feel possessive and protective of, knowing it was all his—his idea and his accomplishment. His sense of pride was a nine and half, approaching the ten mark. Maybe at the opening he would reach that goal in his degree of satisfaction.

During the morning, he scrutinized the few paintings he had completed, now lined up along the wall beneath the window. *Were they good enough to introduce to the public?* He had given Roy the day off and was beginning to feel a bit antsy. He went to the lunch room and ate a container of Waldorf tuna salad he had brought from home. The landscape kept his visual senses alive—also reminding him never to overlook the talent of others. Roy, with his wife and daughter away, was adjusting fairly well to being a single man but he still needed occasional encouragement, as do all creative minds. Drake considered the feasibility of promising him a show if he continued painting—and stayed off the booze. At least his daughter was staying in contact with him and that made a huge difference.

After draining his mug of the last sip of dark roast, Drake returned to his work area beyond the screen in the front gallery. Looking over his book of plein-air sketches, he decided to paint a larger version of one he felt showed promise as a finished work. As was usual, he became wrapped up in the process. The outside world vanished—including thoughts of Patricia, beautiful Patricia—even the fact that it was New Year's Eve and he was alone.

Three hours later, a twinge in his right shoulder reminded him of the broader world. Light from the north window was fading. He might as well bring the day—as well as the year—to a close. For some reason, he didn't look forward to spending another New Year's Eve alone, although it had not been a problem in the past.

He swished his brushes in a can of odor-free turpentine and wiped them on paper towel. He took his palette of unused paint and the brushes to the kitchenette where he cleaned them more thoroughly with cake soap, placed them flat on the counter and left to dry. The palette was moved to the empty bottom shelf of the refrigerator—an acceptable way to keep the paint fresh between painting sessions. Paints were expensive and he had learned to be a frugal artist without compromising the integrity of the painting. Who knew when the gallery would be able to support itself?

The front doorbell pealed out in the silence just as he was finishing up. *Patricia?* Silly idea, it could only be Charlie, coming to check up on him and wish him a Happy New Year. He quickly washed his hands and ran his damp fingers through his hair—finger combing the best he could.

"Coming," he yelled as he approached the front gallery. "Who is it?" he asked, feeling a bit silly but one couldn't be too careful. A reply came only after he asked a second time.

"Patricia."

He wiped his still-damp hand on his pants leg and opened the door. She was standing on the stoop surrounded by gently falling snow, the collar of her red coat buttoned at her neck, her face turned slightly aside. She was trembling.

"I saw a light…am I bothering you?"

"No, no. Come inside where it's warm." The term *snow angel* immediately came to mind.

"I was on my way home and needed a break. You did ask me to stop in."

"That's fine. I was just closing up shop after three hours of painting. It's good to see you—let me take your coat."

"No, I'll only stay a minute." She looked around the space—no paintings on the walls, but an attractive French reception desk with matching chair sat in the back to the right with an oriental screen as a backdrop.

Drake temporarily lost his voice—and his mind—at the sight of her. The raven hair against the red of her coat collar was a sight to behold—no hallucination—no wishful thinking. He guided her back toward the desk and moved a visitor's chair closer. "Please sit down—can I get you something? I can make you a cup of coffee, or tea if you prefer."

"Nothing Drake," she answered with a slightly out of control smile, noting his dampened hair in need of a comb. "I'm impressed with what you've done here. Everything is freshly painted and ready to go—it seems."

"Would you like to see what else we've done?"

Flitting about like a swan with new babies, he guided her through the other rooms, explaining their purpose—even the original loading dock that would hold a separate music room for Oscar and his fellow veterans.

Finally, back in the front gallery, she turned to him. "Drake, this is a side of you I wouldn't have guessed. You're obviously pleased with your change in occupation—it seems to suit you. I wish you lots of luck."

She took another view of the room. "When do you open?"

Drake told her and quickly added, "You're invited."

"I'd like that. Have you ever been to Taos or Santa Fe?" Another nervous laugh, and "Sounds like a song title."

"No, I haven't, but I've read about the area—an artist paradise, I understand."

"You should go. The Santa Fe and Taos area are loaded with art galleries—openings, shows and festivals going on all the time. I couldn't get enough of the beautiful art work."

"Sounds wonderful—I didn't know you liked art that much."

"Spending time in that area teaches one to appreciate all genres of art."

Again she toyed with her coat collar. *Even her hands were lovely with long fingers—like a musician's hands.* "I really must go."

"Please—it's New Years Eve. Could we at least go to Alice's for a bite to eat—unless you've made other plans for the evening?" Afraid he was pushing his luck, he quickly added, "We can talk more about art."

"I should think you would have plans," *You're good looking, obviously sober, and have an exciting future mapped out for yourself.*

"No—I've been too busy for much social life—concentrating on the future," *waiting for you to show up.*

"All right, but then I have to get back to Kirkwood."

Drake wasn't sure Alice would be open, but luck was with him. Patricia insisted on driving her car and he hadn't argued. Even one car length between them seemed too far, but Drake counted his blessings. Alice greeted them with a wide smile—a hug for Drake and a surprised hello again for Patricia. Only two of the booths were occupied—they could have their choice—but Alice directed them to the back corner booth humbly equipped with an ambiance of intimacy. She took their orders and winked at Drake as she turned away.

They sat quietly for a moment, neither knowing how to proceed. Aware of her unease, Drake spoke—not believing she was sitting opposite him like a mirage—as if they had never parted. He didn't want their time to be about him. His previous years of self-absorption were over. He wanted to know everything about her—things he hadn't considered important before, being preoccupied with his own needs and desires. He wanted to rain kisses on her perfect ivory face, gaze into her dark, dreamy eyes and make them sparkle with some clever witticism.

"Patricia," *just saying her name was bliss,* "how are you coping? Has your house sold and have you made future plans?"

"The realtor has one interested buyer. She should have an answer next week. I almost took it off the market but decided it best to make another new start somewhere else. I always seem to be making a new start."

"I feel much the same way."

Their food was placed before them, the aromas tantalizing but, for once, Drake was more interested in the vision across from him than in Alice's cooking expertise. Patricia noticed he hardly took his eyes off her, his scrutiny a bit intimidating.

"Drake, you're staring at me like I'm the Mona Lisa."

"Sorry—I can't believe you're here—and more beautiful than I remembered." *Oops, time to return to safe territory. She really was gorgeous— a classic beauty and he was human after all. Her dark hazel eyes had flecks of green—most unusual—he desperately wanted to make them sparkle with happiness.*

The food calmed their nerves, and Patricia talked of the repairs she had made to the house and the difficulty of selling in mid winter—not the most attractive season of the year. Spring would have been better, but she was anxious to have the process over with.

Holding his breath, Drake asked, "Once it's sold, where will you go—any plans?"

"No definite plans. I know I don't want to return to New Mexico. I prefer this part of the country, but I'll eventually need to find a job. I've heard that idleness is the Devil's workshop—or something like that." She actually smiled at him. The ice appeared to be having an early thaw and Drake felt like doing cartwheels. Every word from her mouth was a melody. He realized that in his previous self-absorbed state he had not gotten to know her at all. This time, if given the chance, it would be a different story and he hoped with a much happier ending.

They talked on through coconut cream pie and two refills of coffee. "Tell me more about Santa Fe and Taos," Drake encouraged, knowing he was attempting to postpone another inevitable parting.

He sensed hesitancy in her response, as well as a graying of her mood as she again placed her hand on her neck.

"I'm sorry, Patricia, I'm being too inquisitive, and I have no right to be."

"I'd rather not talk about it—maybe some other time."

"Of course—whenever you're ready. I'm not going anywhere." *His hopes puffed up like a soufflé—she actually indicated there might be another time.*

"Tell me more about how you ended up in Porterville?"

He told her more of his story, how he had found his biological family, how he had been deceived all his life, and his coming to terms with that fact—how he had been able to finally forgive and move forward—the part Charlie had played in his early life and his help in acquiring the gallery property.

"When I first came here, I was so shocked and out of control I burned the old house—Charlie even ignored that I had committed a crime—he understood and believed I had turned over a new leaf. I still own the lot here on Main Street where the house was—haven't decided what to do with it. Getting the gallery up and running has absorbed all my thinking." He reached inside his shirt collar and his hand came out caressing the necklace before showing her the inscription. "This is all I have left of her," he told Patricia. "It was a loving kind of deceit, if there is such a thing. Charlie knew her well and assured me her choice was for my welfare—not one of neglect or abandonment."

He talked about how he met Tanner and eventually Oscar, and how they had become like family. He didn't elaborate on Oscar's history except he was a returned war veteran.

Alice appeared at their booth and Drake saw the place was otherwise empty. Time to face reality—the evening had to end sometime. "I'm sorry, Alice. You probably want to close up shop for the year. Can you believe?"

"If you don't mind, I would like to call it a day."

Drake gave her his card and when she returned, he introduced her to Patricia. "We go way back," he told her and turned back to Patricia.

"Alice is the brightest star in this little town. She and Charlie were the first residents I met."

He turned back to Alice, "Where is he, by the way? Keeping the town safe, as usual?"

"He'll be stopping by later unless there's an emergency." Her happy smile gave her away. Drake got up and gave her a tight hug and kiss on the forehead. "Happy New Year—and give Charlie my best. Looks like the new year might be a bright one."

"What a nice lady," Patricia said as they moved slowly to their vehicles. It was becoming more and more obvious to her that Drake had indeed changed. He had apparently won the hearts of Alice and the sheriff, as well as his Tanner and Oscar.

DECENT DECEIT

Patricia found him even more appealing than when they first became a couple so long ago. His radiant smile awakened something in her heart—he wasn't being pushy or obnoxious. She was seeing a new Drake, a man with a dream and the confidence to make it come true. He had the courage to leave a profession he felt unsuited for—she had to admire him for that—although the fact that he had no family responsibilities no doubt made it an easier decision. However, restraint was called for—she must remember her past mistakes and not be drawn into another situation that could bring her another punch in the gut. Caution had become her motto.

Drake held her car door open. "Patricia, do I dare ask to see you again? We still have a lot to talk about. Since you've become an art lover yourself, I could use your help in planning the opening. Another eye would be helpful in the gallery hanging, and I need to locate work by other artists. I've contacted the art department at Kaiser College and they invited me to come for their student show next week. I want to give promising young artists a chance to exhibit if their work merits it."

His enthusiasm was not lost on Patricia. *Could this be the man she used to know—the melancholy, confused man with little drive or interest in building a worthwhile future? A man more interested in what a bottle could offer than a strong and lasting relationship?*

"Patricia, I would like—*he even hesitated to use the word love*—you to go with me—a second pair of eyes, if you will. While there, we can visit our old stomping ground, have lunch at Mandy's—if it's still there—leave behind some flyers about my gallery opening. It's not that far away. What do you say? I promise to behave, and, besides, wouldn't it be a nice break for you?"

The lights went out in the restaurant behind them, leaving only the eerie glow from the pole lights in the parking lot. The town, what they could see of it, appeared to have closed up shop and called it a day. The most New Year's Eve excitement in Porterville would be random exploding of firecrackers. Even the movie theatre didn't appear to be doing a thriving business. Just as well, Charlie and Alice deserved a quiet, undisturbed evening.

"I don't know, Drake, things might get hectic if the couple makes an offer on the house. The furniture, most of which I'm keeping, will have to go in storage until I find a place to live."

"Kirkwood is not far, so let me know if I can help in any way. I have more muscles now," he added, flexing his biceps like a cocky teenager.

You certainly do, she thought, turning her head aside to hide her smile.

"Tell you what—you have my number—call me Tuesday night if you can go. The show opens on Wednesday. I really would like your company." *Okay stupid, don't overdo the sales pitch. Don't scare her away—and don't even think of a Happy New Year kiss.*

He watched until the tail lights disappeared into the night, and already he missed her. Only then did he remember O'Toole. In his excitement of being reunited with Patricia, he had completely forgotten the poor dog—left alone and ignored like an introverted child who made no demands. Patricia could make one forget his name or nationality. He rushed to his van, jerked on his seatbelt and burned rubber as reality hit him in the gut. What kind of man was he—couldn't even be trusted to properly care for a dog. No wonder he had never been gifted with one as a child.

He ignored the rural speed limit as he headed out of town, as he did the occasional rut or pothole. He had left food and water for him, but O'Toole's bladder could burst and he'd have a clean-up and deodorizing job when he got home. His remorse was such that even Patricia's face dimmed in his personal condemnation. O'Toole had brought a lot of pleasure to the Tanner household, and Drake was more than happy to dog-set occasionally. His apartment floor was wood, so he had no reservations about leaving the dog inside—no carpet stains to contend with. Only an ogre would leave a dog outside in the near freezing temperature. He really had to take better control of his emotions. When he left mid-morning, he only intended to be gone for a few hours—but then Patricia appeared and his normal sane reasoning went out the proverbial window.

Only the front porch light was on at the main house as he drove by. He pulled into the overhang and had just started up the stairs to his apartment when he heard O'Toole's welcoming bark. He hoped the dog would forgive his selfish neglect. Such happiness erupted at his return that he quickly grabbed the leash and the two were on a mad rush for terra firma. "Good dog," Drake declared. After a prolonged relief at a spot near the light pole, the two took off at a trot along the highway lit only by a half moon. They returned the best of pals, all sins forgiven, and tomorrow was another day. No encounters with skunks or other wild life, thank goodness. The apartment was as he had left it, no accidents, the food dish empty. Drake refilled the water bowl with cold fresh water that disappeared quickly with noisy laps and appreciative head shakes and beautiful long tail moving like a metronome. He laughed in relief, picked up the dog brush and within seconds they were languishing in a pleasure that could only be shared between a man and his dog—well, Tanner's dog, but his for the moment. Patricia was forgotten—at least for the moment.

After a thorough brushing, O'Toole moved contentedly to the throw rug Drake had placed by the door. He turned the TV on to see the New Years Eve celebrations in Times Square, but turned it off before the ball started its descent. It had been an unexpectedly eventful day and he was drained emotionally. Sleep came quickly as did visions of Patricia dancing in his head. Sometime during the night he awakened briefly when he felt the presence of O'Toole making himself quite at home at the side of his bed. He smiled, turned over, prepared for further dreams.

Twenty-six

*"Direct your eyes inward, and you'll find
a thousand regions in your mind yet undiscovered."*
Henry David Thoreau

The Tanners returned late afternoon on Saturday. With reluctance, Drake returned O'Toole to his rightful owner—their bonding had been swift and mutually pleasing. Tanner commented on Drake's upbeat mood, to which he responded, "Your hound dog kept me happy, but he missed you. When we went for walks he first looked toward your house as if seeking permission."

"I think he's beginning to think of us as family but, just in case, let's keep the leash on him. He might get the idea to run off in search of his original home." Tanner advised. "I know. I can't wait either to give him free rein to explore as he pleases. He could probably handle any animal he might come in contact with—except maybe a skunk—God forbid."

"It does seem a shame to tether him with all this land to enjoy," Drake agreed.

"We just bought T-bones from the butcher—an extra one for you—so join us for dinner."

"I'd be delighted. It's good to have you back.

As usual, the steaks were superb. Oscar seemed a bit pre-occupied, but perhaps he was just tired. Over coffee, Drake turned the conversation to the Art Center and asked about his recruits for music therapy—although he didn't use that term.

"I have four guys definitely interested—and one maybe. One will need transportation—unable to drive because of a visual problem. He lives just outside Porterville, so I'm thinking of purchasing a van. I can't continue depriving Dad of his wheels. I think I'll go into Kirkwood Monday to see what I can find." They continued to talk automotives until Drake bid them adieu. He hadn't mentioned Patricia and wouldn't until—or if—anything came of their re-connection.

They had eaten early, so a long evening stretched out before him. His apartment seemed empty with O'Toole now at the main house. He was surprised at how quickly one could bond with a pet. He wondered if Patricia liked animals—one more thing he had failed to learn about the woman who had stolen his heart.

He turned on the PBS classical music station and put his feet up for a bit of relaxation. His mind replayed his time with Patricia, looking for old familiar mannerisms, he supposed, but mostly for any sign of encouragement from her. She had seemed much quieter and reserved than he remembered, but that could be grief over losing her mother—and finding herself quite alone. She dressed more conservatively than he remembered, although she had never flaunted herself provocatively, that he recalled. During dinner at Alice's she had sat with her hand at her throat much of the time. She indicated no desire to be close to him when he had walked her to her car, and he was determined not to step out of line. He had much to make up for.

His reverie was interrupted by footsteps on the deck and a rap on the door. He opened it, surprised to see Oscar on the stoop so soon after they had bid each other goodnight.

"Mind if I come in?" Oscar asked, appearing a bit nervous.

"Of course not—come in. I was just doing a little wool-gathering." He clicked off the music.

Oscar looked toward the black TV screen. "You don't have the news on? Dad has a tendency to be over-protective—he switches it off when the news is bad—at least when I'm around."

"You seem upset. Has something happened?"

Oscar ran a hand through his black hair and then cracked his knuckles. Drake had not noticed that mannerism before. "Another blood bath in Baghdad—car bomb explosion in a marketplace with over a hundred lives lost, including women and children—ISIS taking responsibility."

Drake motioned him to a chair but he kept pacing. "And if that's not enough, there has been a shooting at a military base in Tennessee with five marines killed. Thank God the police killed the shooter before he could continue his barrage of hate—or whatever the shooter thought he was doing. Our men leave loved ones to go over there, fight and even win medals—some a Purple Heart—and return only to lose their lives on home soil—the one place where they should feel safe. What's the sense of it all?"

Drake, observing his state of turmoil, thought of Oscar's friend in Baghdad. "Have you heard anything from Miriam—if they are all right?"

"No, I hope she e-mails me soon. It happened about twenty miles outside Baghdad—I doubt if they would have been at the marketplace, they stay pretty close to home, in their own walled compound. She said in her last e-mail that Iraq is still a big mess, that no one in the government had a clean heart—those were her words—and that some of them are just loyal dogs and servants to Iran, and others to ISIS. She said Iraq was like a weak fat goat with wolves around it enjoying drinking its blood and eating its meat. Her English is not perfect but she manages to make her feelings known. Life is nothing like we have here. She has to go to Jordan to stock up on insulin for her diabetic daughter. The fighting has gone on so long she says they get used to it. How could that be possible? She's a strong woman, but how much more can they take?"

Oscar continued to pace, leaving Drake feeling helpless, without an intelligent word to offer.

"Someone has to stop this senseless killing of innocent women and children."

Oscar finally sat down and Drake asked if he wanted the news on—was relieved when the answer was no. They continued to discuss what had been reported so far. The news about both incidents was bound to become worse, as was usually the case. Drake went to the kitchenette and returned with a couple mugs of coffee. He was prepared to listen as long as his friend wanted to talk. It was inevitable that news such as this would continue to be upsetting to one who had firsthand knowledge of the carnage of war. He felt grateful that Oscar trusted him enough to express his emotions. Hopefully the telling would have a calming effect. He wondered how any soldier could completely forget and put aside the horrors they experienced.

"Most people don't understand how lives are restricted over there—afraid to go beyond their walls or compounds to visit a marketplace for food or supplies. Here, we have distractions of every kind, so much to divert our attention from unpleasantness. Our politicians are even reluctant to call them by their real name, or to acknowledge the extent of their destructive natures. Bombings and mass killing are treated like something we see on a movie screen. One has to see and experience war first hand to see the extent of its effect on the innocent as well as the not so innocent."

Drake could only imagine the thoughts buzzing around in Oscar's head—like a bee on steroids. Would his friend regress at this latest news, or could he once again put it all in perspective? Could merely being there as a friend and a sounding board make a difference? He hoped so.

They sat in silence until Oscar finished his coffee and got up. He thanked Drake for listening. "Guess I still have a ways to go before I can fully accept what's happening."

"You're doing fine, my friend. I find it deplorable myself, as do many Americans, but until the enemy is defeated we have to keep plugging along. Just concentrate on the good we can do here at home. Good luck with the car shopping and knock on my—your door—anytime."

That evening, Drake heard no music from the main house. He hoped Miriam and her family were safe. He looked around his small space and felt very fortunate indeed, but no one knew what tomorrow would bring—even in America.

Twenty-seven

"Only the heart knows how to find what is precious." Dostoyevsky

Drake had about given up on hearing from Patricia when the call came around nine on Tuesday evening. "Drake, do you still want me to go to Coopersville with you tomorrow?" she asked.

"I certainly do, if you can get away."

"Good news. I've had an acceptable offer on the house and signed the papers today."

"Wonderful. Then we have something to celebrate. Meet me at the gallery around nine-thirty? Or is that too early?"

"No problem—I'm an early riser. Just keep in mind this trip is just for old time's sake."

It's a problem but I can handle it. "Of course—whatever you say. See you in the morning."

Five minutes later another phone call—Oscar. "Want me to go to Coopersville with you in the morning?" He sounded less morose than before and Drake hated to decline his offer, but could hardly suppress his excitement. "Remember me telling you about Patricia some time ago? Well, you won't believe this, but she is going with me tomorrow."

"Wow. Aren't you the secretive one? When did this happen?"

Drake explained how she had surprised him at the gallery on

New Year's Eve, their having dinner at Alice's Diner.

"So, is the magic still there? You sound excited."

"I never thought I'd see her again. I just hope I don't blow it this time."

"Well, I guess your answer is no—I'd be a third wheel. Have a good time tomorrow—check in when you get back, okay? And, for God's sake, get a hold on yourself." he added with a chuckle.

The next morning Drake awakened early—too excited to sleep. When he first heard the music he thought he was dreaming. He grabbed his robe from the foot of the bed and rushed to the front window. Oscar's window was fully open to the forty-five degree temperature. The sound of the trumpet not only awakened Drake but probably the birds in the nude mulberry tree, the deer in the woods, and possibly the neighbors beyond the covered bridge. *What the heck—had Oscar lost it or had he found it? He'd never heard him play this early in the morning, but The Saints were marching in—no doubt about that.*

The phone summoned him. Tanner. "Don't be alarmed, this is how he deals with bad news as well as good. He heard from Marian and they're safe. He came down from your place last night much more relaxed than when he left."

"I only listened," Drake told him.

"That probably did it. Thank you for filling a void that I can't—we're too close. I've promised myself to stop trying to protect him."

"I've never heard anyone play like that. It's like he's spitting his guts into that trumpet."

"It's when we don't hear music from him that we need to be concerned. Go on with your day—we're going to be fine. In fact, we're going car shopping later. I hope you have a good day."

Patricia was late. Ten minutes late—enough time for Drake's imagination to slip into overdrive. He got out of the van and did a couple laps around the building, stopping only when he saw her car approaching. *Okay, this is no big deal. You're not an awkward teenager on his first date. Just play it cool, pretend she's your sister—not likely. As she said—it's just for old time's sake.*

He opened her car door—a late model Buick that probably had belonged to her mother—and accepted her immediate apology for being late. "No problem—you're here now." Her smile put him at ease. *Great, she's in a good mood.*

His heart chambers were rebelling. Instead of supporting each other they were battling for supremacy. If he didn't calm down he would require a pacemaker before he was thirty. *Was it love—infatuation? Or was he infatuated with the idea of love?*

"A call from the realtor held me up. I'm so glad the house sold—the delay was getting to me."

They moved to his van without discussion. She was dressed in an emerald green turtle neck sweater that contrasted nicely with her raven hair. They removed their coats and Drake placed them in the back seat, preparing for a cozy warm trip to Coopersville. Her jeans were neither too tight nor too loose. The temperature was predicted to be in the low 50's, promising a day filled with sunshine and, he hoped, a new beginning.

He drove through the town not yet fully awakened, pointed out the empty lot where his old home once stood. Patricia commented that it was a nice-sized lot and the neighboring homes well kept, but showed no interest in discussing it further.

As they left the quaint town—population of several—Drake encouraged her to talk about her house sale and future plans without being too personal. She seemed relaxed, no doubt relieved about the sale. They talked about the holidays—quiet for both of them—Oscar and Tanner, and Drake told her about O'Toole. He learned that she did like pets, but was allergic to dog hair. *So who needs a dog anyway?* The sun had quickly warmed the car and Drake turned the heater down and moved the CD player to Rachmaninoff's Rhapsody on a Theme of Paganini, leaned back to, at least, fake relaxation.

"You can change that, if you like," he told her, torn between watching the road and snatching glimpses of her.

"No, it's beautiful. I didn't know you liked classical music."

"Actually, I like almost all kinds of music—depends on my mood at the time."

"Same here, except hard core."

"Seriously, Patricia—I'm not the guy you used to know—thank goodness—I don't know who he was except he was a confused, obnoxious, immature jerk. My taste in music is not the only change in me. I no longer drink alcohol, I like good food and conversation, and am most happy when I'm painting, and I might add—I'm very happy to have you sitting here beside me." *Damn, I shouldn't have said that.*

She gazed out her window at the constantly changing raw umber and yellow ochre landscape, seemingly not to have heard his comment. *Just as well.*

"Tell me more about the galleries in New Mexico. What were their secrets of success?

I always thought New York was the center of the art world."

"I suppose it remains so in the East. Southwest art has always been popular, but is becoming more so and greatly desired among collectors. It's not all about cowboys and Indians, you know. The light is wonderful—blue skies you wouldn't believe. My favorite artist is Ramon Kelly— who has been around for a while, and has become quite famous. His canvases are expressive, ripe with color, alive with impressive brush and knife application. His portraits—especially of children—make you want to reach out and hug them."

"Gosh, I'd love to see some of his work."

"Google him—you'll be amazed."

Drake was not familiar with the artist but he intended to follow her advice. Knowing the kind of art she liked would be an asset in the future, if she chose to hang around.

She turned her head aside, and gazed out the window. After a few miles of silence, Drake was surprised to see she had fallen asleep—peacefully asleep—her thick hair pillowing the headrest, her hands at ease in her lap, her long legs listing to one side. Cloud shadows moved across her face but were quickly replaced by the sunlight's gleam, bringing out the warm flesh tones of her cheeks and forehead, moving across her feathery eye lashes, frosting her raven hair with bright highlights. Her sweater became a landscape of myriad greens, her shapely figure not lost to his admiring eyes.

Drake slowed down, to better take in the lovely sight, his heart filled with emotion for a woman he hadn't seen in months—it was almost like the first time they met. She was younger then, of course, but sweet, trusting, intelligent. Her beauty, with little artificial enhancement, was an added bonus to her other good qualities. His remorse at his treatment of her almost made him yell at the top of his lungs. How could she forgive or trust him again—how could he ever forgive himself?

He wanted to park the car and just look at her. She didn't need words or sexiness to make him fall in love with her all over again—because that was just what he was doing. His heart was dancing like a yo-yo. *Why had they been reunited? Was it a second chance to make things right?* His body relaxed somewhat and he was once again hopeful. *She seemed at peace in his presence, comfortable, unafraid, and trusting—a good sign. God help him if he ever did anything to hurt her again. He would have to earn her trust if given another chance.*

After a few miles the devil censor again took control—*she was just overly tired, or relaxed and relieved that her house had sold. Was he a fool to hope she still cared for him and felt safe in his company? Nonsense—it had nothing to do with him.*

While she lay sleeping, his mind meandered into their past.

He didn't remember ever seeing her asleep—no doubt too preoccupied with self to notice. They had met at The Last Page Café in Coopersville —a popular spot on campus for students as well as faculty. He wondered if it was still there. It had been their trysting place—just around the corner from where she worked as a legal assistant. They had huddled in a far back corner booth, surrounded by photographs of Mark Twain, Hemingway, Capote, Gertrude Stein, Georgia O'Keefe and other great men and women of literature and the arts. Shelves were filled with plaques of famous quotes, old and new books—some with original covers—protecting, like a sentry at his post, the words and phrases of history-making writers and artists. Those were the happy times—before he became complacent about their relationship, thinking only of himself, or his next dose of intoxicating poison.

The morning traffic picked up as they entered the hustle and bustle of the city. Patricia awakened, stretched and looked around as if disoriented. "Oh, gosh—have I slept all this way? I'm sorry, Drake. Some company I am." She ran her fingers through her gorgeous hair, sat upright and rearranged herself—as much as the seatbelt allowed. "I must have been more tired than I realized."

"No problem, Patricia. *I loved watching you sleep.* You're probably exhausted from all you've been through, plus feeling relief that your house has sold. No reason to apologize."

"Have you been back since you gave up teaching?" she asked.

"No, I've only been in contact with the university by phone. It will be interesting to see if anything has changed. I was just thinking of The Last Page Café where we used to hang out. Remember? You haven't been back since…"

"I didn't hang around very long—gave up the apartment, packed the car and took off for the Wild West—wide open skies—must have been out of my mind."

"I forgot to ask, did you have breakfast?"

"Just coffee and cereal," she replied.

"We have some time before my appointment at the gallery. Let's see if the Last Page Café is still here—have a little brunch. I'm starving. Okay?"

She didn't object, instead took a brush from her purse and tidied her hair, although he thought it unnecessary. Drake watched as she applied a bit of lip gloss—until his overactive imagination forced him to concentrate more fully on their destination.

Nothing appeared to have changed—the same buildings, a beauty salon next door. Patricia pointed out an office building that had been converted to a walk-in clinic half a block down.

Drake found a parking space nearby. They left their coats behind and hurried into the warmth of the café.

Drake was surprised when a familiar hostess quickly greeted them—all smiles. "Well, look who's here," she exclaimed. "Mr. Dawson, we've missed you around here." *That's a surprise. I doubted that anyone would remember me."*

"It's good to see you, Miss Hazel. You haven't changed a bit." Drake offered. Without asking, she led them toward the back of the café, and to a familiar corner booth.

"This one still has your name on it," she told him as she handed them menus.

Drake looked at Patricia for signs of discomfort, but none were evident. He noticed there were few customers—too late for breakfast, too early for lunch.

Patricia ordered coffee and whole wheat toast. Drake ordered bacon, two poached eggs and toast.

"I see why you're looking so fit."

"Food tastes much better since I've rid myself of alcohol. I even enjoy cooking, can you believe that?"

"I'm beginning to believe you are a changed man, Drake."

Hallelujah! "I'm glad, and to prove it, sometime I'll make you the best steak and sautéed mushrooms you've ever eaten."

"Okay, let's concentrate on why we're here. What can I do to help?"

"First, we'll meet with Ms. Cloud, chair of the art department, check out the gallery and see if we can recruit an artist or two ready to exhibit in a regular gallery, or need studio space. We'll leave some brochures there, in the student center, and, if we have time, distribute some at local businesses. I'd welcome any suggestions you might have."

"We can start right here. Let's ask Miss Hazel—she seems to be the manager now—if we can place brochures here. Lots of foot traffic—probably the busiest place in town," she observed.

Without being summoned, Hazel appeared at their table with a coffee carafe in hand. Drake told her about his move to Porterville and his plans for the Art Center, went out to the van and returned with a handful of brochures.

"Tell you what," she said. "How about if I staple one to each menu—customers would be more likely to read it?"

"You're a doll, Miss Hazel—great idea." He gallantly reached out and placed a kiss on her hand, causing her to blush. Recovering quickly, she turned to Patricia.

"What have you been feeding him, girl? He used to be so shy and studious."

After she left them, Patricia said, "That was sweet."

"I'm sweet?"

"Yes—the way you were when we first met."

Later, as they walked about campus, Drake was surprised at the friendly greetings including two girls who actually told him he was missed. It wasn't the cold, non-stimulating place he remembered. *Maybe I wasn't such a failure at teaching as I thought. Had alcohol damaged his brain to such an extent that he was unable to see life in its entirety—that among the negative aspects there were also the positive.* The students seemed more alert, more mannerly, more impressive than he recalled. As they neared the administration building, a couple faculty members greeted him warmly. *Had he been the one who was aloof and unresponsive to their offers of friendship? Wrapped up in his own low self esteem, had he failed to make an attempt to be civil?*

Drake felt buoyed up by Patricia's presence. It was a privilege just to breathe the same chilly air she breathed, to occupy the same space. Everything appeared different—a sharper image. Even the skeletal fingers of the campus elms seemed stately in their nakedness.

After the warm reception, plus the hardy brunch he's just devoured, they entered the university arts department with Drake feeling at the top of his game. There, too, they were greeted warmly by Ms. Cloud, the art professor and instructor—new since Drake had been on the faculty. She informed him of the changes she had made, her attempt to interest the students in a more conventional method of teaching, including study of the old masters.

"How can they learn to express themselves without the rudimentary rules of what makes good art? We need to learn the rules before we can break them. Agree?"

"I whole-heartedly agree, Ms. Cloud. When I was a student here, I felt the frustration of not being taught perspective, color harmony, etc. I was more comfortable as a literature instructor. He told her of his gallery opening in Porterville, and his need for promising art to display on his walls, as well as artists who might need studio space in which to work.

Drake turned the attention onto Patricia who had been gracious, interested, without interjecting views of her own. "Patricia has just returned from New Mexico, and has been telling me about the marvelous southwestern art in Taos and the Santa Fe area."

"I've read about it—in fact, I'm planning a vacation to that area this summer."

"I found it all very stimulating—although I'm not an artist," Patricia added. "The area is a Mecca for artists as well as art lovers and collectors."

They spent the next hour touring the gallery. Drake was impressed with the variety and level of talent in many of the pieces. He and Patricia agreed for the most part, leaning more toward impressionism, she a bit more diverse in her taste. Ms. Cloud recommended three students with outstanding ability and interested in pursuing a career in art. They agreed on a three o'clock session with the students, after their normal classes.

The schedule was working out perfectly for Drake. He and Patricia could have lunch as well as explore the rest of the small college town. Before parting, he had one more thought. "Ms. Cloud, would you be interested in coming to Porterville and give a lecture—or series of lectures—to the town residents—that is, if I could work it out?"

She gave it some thought before answering. "I might like that, but I'll be on my trip during July."

"Then perhaps after your return? I've also thought of offering workshops, if there is enough interest."

"Mr. Dawson, I'm truly impressed with your desire to bring art to your small town. I'm sure it is much needed. Please keep me informed about your progress. I'll help however I can."

"Wonderful, and let me know if you need more brochures. You have my card—call me at any time. Thanks for the student recommendations—we'll be back at three to meet with them."

Patricia offered her hand, "Enjoy your trip—I recommend the Taos Inn if you haven't made other plans."

Pleased at how the meeting went, Drake said, "Let's take a short drive around town before lunch—unless you're hungry?"

"That would be nice. Ms. Cloud seems like a good sort, don't you think?"

"Yes, and who knows where this will lead? Porterville may be in for a cultural treat if we can work in a few lectures and workshops. I hadn't even considered that possibility."

After driving a couple blocks, Drake pointed out the Dawson & Walker Law Firm, the plaque still there but not much sign of activity—only one car in the parking lot. He wondered if Brian was keeping the practice going, or if he had let it go to pot after buying out the Dawson shares. *Someday I may tell Patricia about Brian, but not now. He would not let unhappy memories spoil the day—a day he thought would never happen—a day he now didn't want to end.*

They took a short drive around the city park and observed a few people hanging out in spite of the chill. As in most other cities, there were young men and women showing their independence by displaying an excessive number of primary colors to the otherwise drab day—eyebrow and lip piercings, and, of course—tattoos.

"Drake, do you have tattoos?"

Drake laughed. "No way—I wouldn't like my body being devoured by dragons, snakes creeping up my biceps."

Patricia giggled—something he hadn't heard in a long time—a sound that caused his heart to perform cartwheels.

"Look, *Mandy's* is still here. Want to have lunch?"

"I've never eaten here, but I'm sure it's fine."

"I'm not very hungry, but we should eat. I don't want to be late meeting the art students."

"There were few people in the restaurant, unlike *The Last Page Café* it catered more to the dinner crowd. After being seated and ordering, Patricia appeared ill at ease, studying everyone and everything in the room except Drake, preoccupied with her own thoughts. Drake excused himself, went to the men's room to freshen up. When he returned, Patricia was sitting with her back to him, her head down, and again her hand at her throat. He watched her for a moment—reluctant to intrude on her thoughts—sensing something was amiss. She had seemed to enjoy their little jaunt, was pleasant and friendly—so what happened?

She didn't look up as he slid into the booth. Hot coffee had been served. He cautiously took a sip. "Um—good coffee," he said, eliciting no response.

"Patricia—everything okay? Is all this talk about art boring you?"

Only then did she lift her head. "Boring me? Of course not, why do you ask?"

"You seem guarded—did I say or do something—have you decided you still hate me?"

That brought a hint of a smile as she sat up straighter and reached for her coffee. "Let's just say I'm less mad at you than I was yesterday," reminding Drake of the movie *Shadows in the Sun.*

"You stole that from one of my favorite movies, didn't you?" I watched it again just the other night.

"It's one of my favorites, too. Another quote, "You don't choose art, it chooses you.""

"Her face was framed by the golden glow of honey light," Drake quoted.

Their food arrived just in time—before his heart outsmarted his mouth. *She smiled, so I must not be the cause of her occasional melancholy.*

"Patricia, this may not be the time, but I hope at some point you'll tell me about your life while we were apart. You've only talked about the art. I've already bored you with my story—at least a large part of it."

"Perhaps sometime—as you say—when the time is right? Let's concentrate on our food." *I can't tell him now, not when he's already had to deal with one act of deceit. She wasn't certain he could deal with another one. She would give it more time.*

Her mood became more cheerful, but Drake felt it was an act.

Only after their empty plates were taken away did she break the silence. "Drake, have you ever hated anyone?" she asked.

The question surprised him, his answer with the first thought that came to mind—only myself.

"Why do you ask?"

"I just wondered."

"Okay, I haven't given that question much thought, but there was one person I hated for quite awhile. I guess it was hate, or more like disgust." He tells her about Brian, his father's partner and their altercation when he was a teenager, and then added: "Patricia, for a long time I didn't care enough to feel any deep emotion like hate. Even in Brian's case, if it was hate it later became camouflaged by indifference."

"You seem so, I don't know—altogether."

"Maybe I'm just more grown up. I know I look at life differently. I have a purpose now, hope in the future. Coming to terms with my addiction has made all the difference. Knowing I had a real mother who loved me answered the questions I had been subconsciously asking all my life. I'm not sure how I feel about my biological father and grandfather. It's easier to just not think of them. I can't go back and change things. All I can do is try to build a better future."

The trip back to Porterville was more leisurely. Drake was pleased with the progress they made. He now had three student artists to consider for representation, plus the possibility of a series of lectures and workshops. Patricia remained rather subdued but understandably so—she had lost her mother and her own future was uncertain. Drake was so happy he didn't feel a need to immediately further their relationship. *I'll give her time to get her domestic life in order before proposing that she help run the gallery.* After spending the day together, he felt confident Patricia would find her niche in the arts—just as he had—but he could be wrong.

They approached Porterville much too soon—the wonderful day

with Patricia was coming to an end. The late afternoon landscape was painted in shades of gray and brown, no residual snow whitewashing the fields and hillsides, no snow in which to write their initials or to make snow angels with their bodies.

He didn't want the day to end, but he also didn't want Patricia driving home by herself after dark. He drove up to the gallery and parked next to her car. "Your chariot is waiting, I see."

"One more thing I'll need to dispose of. I prefer driving my own car."

He turned in the seat and thanked her for spending the day with him, for her input about the art, and "just for being you." *Careful—don't overdo it. She's not ready.*

"I enjoyed the day, Drake, and seeing your enthusiasm. I'm really happy for you, and wish you the best."

"Patricia, let me help you through this tough time, will you? I promise not to make a nuisance of myself—I just want to be available and help any way I can."

"Thanks, for the outing. It was just what I needed. And now, I better get on the highway." *Had she just ignored his offer to help?*

Drake got out, retrieved her coat from the back seat, rushed to open her door. He put the coat around her, his hands coming to rest lightly on the shoulders. "You'd better put this on until your car warms up."

"I'll be fine. Thanks again for including me."

"No, Patricia, thank you." He kissed her lightly on the forehead, his lips lingering until she turned away. "Call me when you get home, so I'll know you're safe, okay?"

She started the car, said "I will," and helped him close the door.

Drake watched until her car was out of sight. *Something is not right in her life, and it's more than the loss of her mother. But what could it be?*

Twenty-eight

"War talk by men who have been in a war is always interesting; whereas moon talk by a poet who has not been to the moon is likely to be dull."
Mark Twain

The front seat of Drake's van suddenly felt too roomy for one person. He placed his hand on the seat to feel any residual warmth. Patricia's absence was keenly felt, but there was nothing he could do about it. He hadn't swerved in his determination to allow her to lead the way, but the more he was with her the more he wanted her in his life. He couldn't help feeling that if she went away again, he would lead a very lonely life. He wanted to share everything with her.

He drove by the cemetery but it was too late to stop. At some point he wanted Patricia to know more about his mother—his real mother. He was now anxious to get home, to learn about Oscar's day and if he had found just the right vehicle. Drake was pleased that Oscar had put together a small group of musicians for study and fellowship. *I wonder if I could get him to provide the music for the gallery opening.* He knew it was a selfish thought, but Drake was glad Oscar had chosen to postpone college. He liked having the man around, not only as a friend but for what he and his music would contribute to the success of his Art Center.

He didn't expect to hear from Patricia right away, she would be involved in the final stages of emptying her mother's house, and finalizing the sale. He knew what that was like. He didn't have to be at the gallery every day and hoped she would solicit his help in some way. She hadn't discussed her future plans—another apartment—or whether or not she would stay in the area. This bothered Drake. Surely she wouldn't just disappear again. *I'll talk to Alice regarding rental space in Porterville—just in case—of course.*

Drake found everything in order at his apartment. He talked briefly on the phone to Oscar, learned he had bought a van that he would pick up later. It was white. "Any color but sand," he said. Drake informed him that his day in Coopersville with Patricia had been positive and promised him more details later on.

He turned in early, feeling emotionally drained. He needed to stay awake until Patricia called to assure him she had gotten home safely. He mentally planned the following day. He would go to the gallery and make his first try at portrait painting. Patricia's face, as she lay sleeping in his van, was sharply etched in his memory—the tranquility of her pose—the sunlight and shadows on her face.

The next morning at the gallery, as Drake painted, an unexpected snow fell languidly outside the studio window. By noon, as if awakening from a merely dosing state, the snow began falling and flailing as fast and frantically as a bungee jumper. Drake became so engrossed in the portrait of Patricia that he paid the weather no mind. By the time he arrived back at his apartment in late afternoon the roads were nearly impassible—even the mailman was forced to break his promise of delivery in spite of storm or peril.

Later that evening, the blizzard proved to be no match for Oscar. He arrived at Drake's doorstep, having shoveled a step at a time until he reached the deck and continuing on by clearing a narrow path to the door. Drake, preoccupied with his computer, was barely aware of the storm's fury outside his door. He was receiving a few e-mails every day from artist asking him to view their work, some through personal websites with samples of their work attached. He was more interested in those with websites since it indicated they were serious about their artistic future. The rap on the door startled him. He shut down the computer, opened the door to see Oscar with a shovel in his hand.

"What are you doing out in this weather?" Drake asked, his first thought that something had happened to Tanner. He rushed to take his friend's heavy fleece-lined jacket, shaking off the accumulated snow and hanging it on a peg. Oscar removed his boots and placed them, now dripping, on a rug by the door.

"I thought you could use some company," he said, vigorously rubbing his hands for warmth. "Dad's cocooned in his office—wrapped in memorabilia."

"Sure. I was on the computer and lost track of time." *Has he come up to quiz me about my day with Patricia—apparently not.*

"Drake, are you aware that the greatest things in life are invisible—or at least the most interesting things?" he asked. He pranced around like a frisky colt, attempting to rid himself of the chill. Finally, he moved to the sofa and made himself comfortable. If Drake didn't know better, he would think the man was high on some artificial stimuli. This was far from his usual subdued, often melancholy friend.

"For instance," Oscar continued, "Who has ever seen the wind? Not you, nor I," he quoted, his voice animated, higher pitched than usual. "We only see the *effects* of the wind, what it leaves in its wake—a quivering leaf, snapped tree branches, flapping shingles on a roof, or the lifting and dancing of a woman's hair. I find it fascinating how the wind can move one branch of a tree, leaving all the others motionless. Everything quiet, not even a squirrel or bird stirring—just that one limb or leaf showing a spark of life." He leaned forward as if to put more emphasis on his train of thought. "What if we humans were invisible and others could see only the damage or the good we do? Who would we blame or applaud?"

Without waiting for a response, he continued. "Oscar, last night I dreamed of a vast desert carpeted with the remains of young soldiers, civilians, mothers with their babies still in their arms, all huddled together like an extended family sleeping in the same bed. But—all around them there was quiet—a sense of peacefulness—a motionless moon in the sky—the only sign of life the silhouette of a bird flying across its brightness. There was no sign or hint of the cause of the carnage, as if the evil wind had never passed through. Bullets are like the wind, you know—unseen—you hear the blast, but you never know exactly where they will strike."

This was a side of Oscar that Drake had not previously observed—revealing thoughts most people would be unable to express—even to a best friend. Yet, he was speaking almost poetically, albeit on a subject that would seem dark and unfathomable to most. How could one respond without ever having experienced the horror of war? He only watched as Oscar sighed and turned his attention toward the deck—as if he could see beyond the window now covered with a coat of snow that obscured the outside world. What was his mind seeing?

Not knowing what to say or do, Drake went to the kitchen and sliced two servings of Alice's apple pie, placing them on plates. He removed a couple forks and napkins from the drawer. He looked back at Oscar, now sitting quietly. *Maybe the pie will release him from his troublesome thoughts.*

"Here, Oscar, have a piece of pie."

"Thanks, Bud— that looks good."

"You're in a philosophical mood tonight," Drake ventured.

"Sorry if I'm disturbing your evening—needed to get out of the house—sometimes I find it too confining."

Before Drake could comment further, his phone beeped. He sat his plate aside before answering. Not a number he recognized—a male voice asking if Oscar Tanner was there. Drake handed the phone to him. "It's for you."

Oscar's expression immediately changed. He listened to the caller, responded and asked questions, finally ended the call and turned to Drake with a smile. He took a bite of the pie. "That was one of the vets—Pete, the drummer. He wants to know if we have to wait until April to start the music sessions. What should I tell him?"

Drake was so relieved he would have agreed to anything. "The music room is finished. I see no reason why you can't start right away—and use it as often as you like. Roy and I will be the only people there—and you won't disturb us. I say—the sooner the better."

"That's great. I'll call him back in the morning. He's probably going a little star-crazy himself."

The two men finished their pie and Oscar asked for a second slice. "I hope you don't mind me giving Pete your number—to use only if he can't reach me, of course." He removed his own phone from his pocket and looked puzzled. "Guess I didn't hear it ring earlier."

"No problem. I can't wait to hear you guys play. You do want to proceed with your plan, don't you?"

"I sure do—can't let the others down now, can I?" He got up and reached for his coat. "Thanks for the pie—and the company. Sorry, I'm a bit keyed up tonight."

"No problem—anytime. And thanks for clearing my steps, although they're probably covered over again."

Oscar put on his boots, Drake walked out on the deck with him, handed him the shovel and thanked him again. He was now more certain than ever that music—and having a purpose would play a huge part in his ultimate recovery. "Oscar, I want you to feel free to use the Center however and whenever you like. It's the least I can do for you and Tanner for allowing me to live here. Your generous contributions and friendship have given me new life."

The snow had slowed to a few flurries. Oscar held up the shovel and said, "Looks like we won't need this tomorrow." As he reached the corner he called back, "Thanks for the pie."

Twenty-nine

"The purpose of art is washing the dust of daily life off our Souls."
Picasso

The next morning, Drake awakened to sunlight. The wind had calmed to a whisper, causing the temperature to rise. Icicles hung from the mulberry tree with chandelier brilliance—branches of the same tree he had heard scraping the window during the night. Every branch and twig now dressed in jewels, the light of the sun bringing out a rainbow of facets. The January blizzard was likely to be the last of Old Man Winter. Wishful thinking probably, but just the thought of spring, opening his gallery, the possibility of Patricia by his side, lifted his spirit. The smile quickly faded as he remembered Oscar's unexpected visit and wondered what his brief mood change meant. Only time would tell.

The repairs to the gallery were finished except for a few minor details. His project now was to prepare for the opening. Drake had given Roy extra time off, instructed him to use the time painting—he needed to produce a body of work for later evaluation. He had maintained contact with his daughter, Sophia, which had made him a happier man than the one who sat sobbing just a few months earlier. There was no question he wanted to continue his association with the Art Center. This gave Drake pause—he was uncomfortable using a man of his talents in a handyman capacity—one more thing to be worked out when the time was appropriate.

The road conditions were such that he felt no hurry to leave his safe little world. The rising temperature would melt the snow in no time. The portrait of Patricia wasn't going anywhere although he was anxious to see it in a new light. It was always good to take periodic breaks while painting, returning to the work with a fresh eye. He wondered what she would think when she saw it finished—a bit over the top—offended that he had taken such personal liberty with her likeness? Why was he fretting about something that may never happen?

Charlie—they hadn't talked in a while. Did that mean the sheriff no longer felt a need to keep an eye on him? Or did it mean his mind was preoccupied with Alice? Either way, it was a good thing. Why not call him anyway?

His call was directed to the sheriff's office. Ethel—Drake had not once seen her smile— answered in her no-nonsense way. "He's out on a call."

"But he's not answering his phone. My call was forwarded to you."

"Then keep trying."

"As soon as you hear from him, please tell him I called."

Drake's eyes squinted and a line deepened in his forehead. *Nonsense—Charlie was more than able to take care of himself.*

His next call was to Roy. "How's the weather in there?"

"Warming up—snow's melting fast. Are you coming to the gallery?"

"Around one o'clock. Do you have any new paintings to show me?

"A couple, but I'm not sure they're finished."

"I'd like to see them anyway."

"All right, see you soon."

Drake was proud of Roy—so far no obvious break in his sobriety—but he needed income for art supplies—his Christmas gift wouldn't last forever. Selling a few paintings would help.

Feeling antsy, the next call was to Tanner's house phone. No answer—and he hadn't heard the car leave the garage. He ran down the steps to check and saw the garage empty except for his own neglected Harley gathering dust in the back. *Probably gone to pick up Oscar's new auto—no cause to worry, but Oscar's impromptu visit and state of mind did concern him.*

What about my own frame of mind? Patricia's reappearance, their unpredictable future, the trip to Coopersville, the countdown to opening a business, his concern for Oscar—enough to bring on a psychotic event of his own. He needed to talk to Charlie who was good at putting things in proper perspective.

He did his few household chores, ate a chicken salad sandwich, pulled on a turtleneck sweater over his wool shirt and left his apartment. In the shade of the overhang, snow still clung to his windshield but went flying at the first swipe of the wipers.

At the gallery, Roy had already arrived. Each time Drake drove into the parking lot, he felt exhilarated at the progress made and the prospect of introducing a more cultural atmosphere to the small community. He walked into the gallery with empty walls that must be filled. He could not fail—himself—or the town.

Roy had five paintings lined up against the back wall. He was alert, his black hair combed and his mustache trimmed. The ever present beret peeked out from his hip pocket. *Drake smiled. Roy would have been a perfect subject for Franz Hals or John Singer Sargent. He was now a far cry from the lonely lost soul he had first met on the street.*

After the usual greetings, Drake went to the gallery reception desk to check for messages.

Two, with request for call back. Interest was picking up—the brochures and posters were beginning to pay off.

Drake then turned his full attention to Roy's work. The canvases were well executed—four out of five, in his opinion, were ready for public's scrutiny. Roy was taken aback by the critique. "I don't know if I'm ready to be ridiculed."

"Ridiculed? Are you kidding? I've seen worse in the Kaiser University gallery." He backed up to the middle of the room. "Roy, some critics say that a painting must stand out across a room in order to be considered gallery quality. Come and observe from this distance."

Roy joined him and they spent some time discussing the paintings. Drake suggested only a few minor alterations. "I'm glad you used the new gallery wrapped canvases. With no staples, you can paint the edges a neutral color and eliminate a need for framing—at least for now. It may not be possible to frame all of them before the opening. "And don't forget, your signature is an important part of the painting."

"I have a few traditional frames at home—appropriate for landscapes. Want me to see if any of them will work?"

"That would be a great help, however, better to leave them unframed than to display them with incompatible frames. The frame should never outperform the painting."

"I understand. I'm pretty good at making frames from stock molding you know, had some experience working in a frame shop."

"Bring in the ones you have, and I'd also like to see your own handiwork. Okay?"

"Boss, I never thought this would happen. You've changed my life, you know?"

"Are you saying the bottle no longer taunts you?"

"Not for some time." He laughed, "Now I'm drunk on paint."

"I know exactly how you feel. We're both very fortunate, aren't we?"

Roy left to make coffee. Drake returned to his own painting space behind the shoji screen. He picked up the painting of Patricia he had turned to the wall, sat it on his easel facing the window and away from prying eyes. He decided it wasn't half bad, but he was far from ready to share it with others. He had been reading John Howard Sanden's excellent book on portrait painting, but admitted it would not be easy or quick to advance to his degree of expertise in the field. After all, Sanden was a painter of presidents and kings.

He removed his sweater and put on an old paint-splattered shirt. He needed to work off some tension. Painting always brought him immense pleasure. God never ran out of subject matter when He created the world—a world filled with living art, ever changing skies and earth. Drake imagined Him with mighty brushes, constantly composing—a stronger red in the sunset, more pink and yellow in the sunrise, a field of multi-colored flowers accenting all the green. Sometimes He painted with excitement and other times—restfully.

Two hours later, a call came from Charlie, apologizing for not getting back to him sooner.

"I admit I was a bit concerned when you didn't take my call," Drake told him.

"Remember the young man you and Oscar tangled with at the Apple Festival—saving the young damsel in distress? Well, he's still stirring up trouble. It was a family dispute this time. I'll tell you more when I see you. How are you doing?"

"Fine—a bit apprehensive about the gallery opening in less than three months—still a lot of work to do."

Charlie laughed. "As long as it keeps you out of trouble," he teased.

"Thanks for returning my call. Stop by the gallery when you can, or maybe we could have lunch?"

"I'll see what I can do, son. Take it easy."

Drake breathed deeply when the call ended. *Did Charlie just call him "son"?*

He called out to Roy, "Time to call it a day."

Roy appeared from the back, looking very pleased if not downright cocky in his beret. It had been a good day for the artist, and Drake was happy to play a part in it. "Put your bike in my van and I'll drive you home."

Charlie called Drake that evening just as he was finishing dinner, stating he was nearby and asked to stop in. "Of course, Charlie." He arrived ten minutes later wearing a furrowed brow.

"What's going on, Charlie?"

"Had a call—first house beyond the Henson's—you know, the man who crashed into your light pole? An elderly man and woman living out here alone—someone broke in and relieved them of a flat screen TV and stereo, a shotgun, a shoebox full of coins..."

"That surprises me—out here in the country?"

"It happens, Drake, more than you'd think. I'm afraid drugs are destroying peace of mind for rural people as well as urban. Users will lie, cheat and steal to get a fix. It's getting to be a big problem—this is the second house invasion in less than three weeks. In this case, it may be an inside job—they have a grandson who has been in trouble before." He took off his hat, ran his hand through his hair and over his brow, fatigue written all over his face. Drake handed him a cup of fresh brewed coffee. "Here, drink this—and sit down and relax a bit."

"Thanks. I need it. Maybe I'm getting too old for this job. With our cyber age, the internet, social media, there's only a thin wall between town and country anymore."

Our young people follow the big city trends in clothing, hairstyles, drugs—everything. It seems the whole world has become homogenized."

"It must be frustrating having to deal with the worst of the worst. Wish I could help."

"That reminds me: Lady called me the other day asking about

you. She saw one of your gallery flyers. I've known her for a long time. She wondered if you thought art lessons might help her eleven year old son. He's been diagnosed with ADD—attention deficit disorder."

"I know what it is. I saw it in some of my students at the university. Parents have difficulty coping, particularly if the patient isn't medicated, it seems."

Charlie took out his pocket memo book. "I have her number if you wouldn't mind calling her."

"I'll be happy to talk with her—especially if she's a friend. I'll need to start giving lessons to keep the place going." He refilled Charlie's cup while thinking of a way to cheer him up.

"By the way, how are you and Alice doing? You seemed a bit "close" on Christmas day. And she blushed the other day when I mentioned you."

The sheriff sat his cup down before responding. "Don't read anything into that. We have been spending some time together—when I have time—but we're just friends."

"If you say so, but I sense she feels a bit more than friendship."

Charlie smiled and grabbed his hat. "I'm beat, so will run along. Be sure to keep your doors locked—*country ain't cool anymore.*"

Thirty

"Writing is not life, but I think that sometimes it can be a way back to life."
Stephen King

Two days passed before Drake had an opportunity to talk alone with Tanner. Oscar now had his own vehicle and had gone to visit one of the veteran musicians. It was early evening when Tanner called asking him to come down to the main house. At first they talked about writing and Tanner's current project. "I'm working on a short family history—Oscar's children may find it interesting—if he ever settles down to having a family. After that, I might try my hand at novel writing. What do you think—you're an English major—think I'd be wasting my time?"

"Not at all—with your background you wouldn't have trouble finding subject material."

"That's the problem—most of what I know, I'm not at liberty to divulge."

"Write your stories as fiction based on fact. Change names, locations, etc.—it's done all the time. Look at all the crime and legal novels—many of them are written by lawyers."

"You're right. Don't think I'm too old?"

"Of course not—writers need to have lived a life to have

something worthwhile to write about, don't you think? I'd give it a try and see where it leads. One good thing about writing is you don't have to get it right the first time."

"Okay—if you promise to be my editor."

"I'd be honored."

"One other thing—I want to talk to you about Oscar. Think he's doing the right thing with his music? I'm a bit concerned, not about the music part, but his association with vets who have serious injuries. Not only would it be depressing but a constant reminder of what went on over there. On the other hand, if the music helps them, it could make him feel useful again."

"I agree. From some of the things he's said, serving his country has and is very important to him. It has to be frustrating for him to be denied that privilege. Sharing with other vets the healing aspect of music could give him that purpose that he needs right now." Not wanting to alarm Tanner needlessly, Drake gave some thought to Oscar's visit to his apartment before responding further. "Have you noticed any changes in him lately?"

"Seems a bit hyper at times, but it could be his new wheels, plus his decision to help the veterans with their music. I don't know—perhaps I'm reading too much into it."

"When is he due another visit to the VA hospital?"

"He's been discharged, as you know, but told to return for a follow-up anytime he felt a need."

"A follow-up visit might be in order."

"I don't want to upset him by suggesting it. Besides, it could be a good sign—feeling enthusiastic about his future."

"Maybe that's all it is. We hope so. I would be up front about it—never a good idea to evade issues or ignore them. I'm a good example of that. Tell him a medical follow-up would make his old man feel better."

Tanner laughed. "He's come such a long way—much due to your influence."

"Nonsense—Oscar is a strong talented man, not one to let life defeat him. Besides, he has good genes. We have become good friends, but you're his Dad and he loves and respects you. That I know for sure."

"Thanks for coming down."

"No problem, call or come up anytime you want to chat."

Drake returned to his apartment, his mind in a whirl—so much to think about regarding the gallery. Licenses and permits had been handled without difficulty and he had the support of the town managers. His flyers and brochures were resulting in inquiries. The local school was supportive, as were other businesses locally. He'd contacted the Kirkwood newspaper, the closest TV station was in Coopersville and he would seek an interview with them nearer to the opening date.

January was almost gone and there remained much to do. To be honest with himself, the unresolved issue with Patricia was causing him the most anxiety. The bottle in the wine rack on top of the refrigerator caught his attention for a moment. Nope. No way would he jeopardize the gallery or a future with Patricia—now that he had found her again.

His thoughts returned to his talk with Tanner. Perhaps he should take his own advice and just be honest with her. She was in limbo, selling her home and apparently no definite plans for the near future. He looked at his watch—not too late to call. He took one more look at the bottle, turned his back and punched in her number.

Patricia's voice sounded somewhat deflated. "Hello—I hope I'm not calling too late. I wanted to thank you again for going to Coopersville with me, and for your help. How are things going?"

"Glad to stop packing for a minute. I had no idea it would be such a big job. It's not just Mom's stuff but a lifetime of memories."

"I wish I could help in some way."

"No one can help with the sorting—but I won't bore you with

all of that."

"Nothing about you bores me. Have you made plans for after you have vacated the house?"

"Been looking for apartment rentals, and also keeping an eye on the classifieds for a job."

Dare I bring this up now? "Patricia, I have a suggestion. Would you consider working for me—help me get the gallery up and running? I can't pay you what you'd earn in a better job, but until you find something you like, I'd really like your help. Would you, at least, give it some thought?"

"Give me a few days to think about it, okay? I've only checked on apartments here in Kirkwood. Do you think I could find something there, if not an apartment, perhaps a small house?

"I'll inquire around and let you know." *This means she's not rejecting my proposal. Thank you, God.*

Thirty-one

"Destiny is not a matter of chance, it is a matter of choices; it is not a thing to be waited for, it is a thing to be achieved."
William Jennings Bryan

Strange, until Patricia reappeared on the scene, Drake hadn't known he was lonely. The drab winter weather was bringing him down—a place he didn't want to be. Fewer people were out and about as he drove to and from the gallery every day. Farmers, no doubt, were feeling claustrophobic. Winter was not a time for planting or harvesting—the fields lay barren and infertile.

On some mornings the rural highway forced him to follow a school bus, stopping when it stopped, no passing allowed even if he could. He watched as sleepy-eyed and bored-appearing nursery to high school students reluctantly made their way from front doors. The big yellow monster would take them to another world—a world of learning—without the faintest idea of what it would all mean to their future.

On this morning the procession took longer. Five children seemingly of evenly spaced ages, made their way at a snail's pace, donning jackets as they walked or skidded down the steep bank from their unkempt small house at the edge of the road—no porch swing—not even a porch. Drake wondered what life was like for them in such close quarters, and in the bad economy. Would his life have been different had he been brought up in similar circumstances—sharing a room with a sibling? Would they have had twin beds or bunks? Would he have been a pest or a prankster? He would never know. If he and Patricia married, would they want children? Loving someone was a serious matter, not something to enter into lightly.

Finally, the stop warning sign swung back flat against the side of the bus and Drake moved his foot to the gas pedal. The bus turned off on a graveled side road, leaving him to his mental musings all the way to Porterville.

Alice's Diner was a cheerful place to be on a winter day. In spite of that, he turned his thoughts to spring when her window boxes would be filled once again with multi-colored petunias or other annuals. His mood lifted without effort as he stepped inside, his nostrils responding to the odor of coffee, bacon, eggs and homemade buttermilk biscuits. Her warm greeting raised him to an even higher level of mental clarity.

He hung his heavy coat on the corner of his usual booth—the one he and Patricia shared on an earlier day—a day when a modicum of hope had returned. There was nothing wrong with his appetite: a cream cheese and chive omelet with two crisp bacon slices—he never allowed himself more than two—and one biscuit with black raspberry jam. Too easy to gain weight during the winter months when jogging was unpleasant, if not downright hazardous. The only gym was miles away.

During a lull in business, Alice, with her own mug of coffee, slipped in opposite him. Drake decided not to tease her about Charlie. They talked about the weather and the gallery for a few minutes before Drake changed the topic to what was more pressing.

"Alice, do you know of any rental property here in town?"

"Why do you ask—you leaving the Tanner's?"

"No, I'm happy with my apartment—and the Tanners have

become like family. I'm asking for a friend who might want to move here."

"A friend, huh—any chance of it being that pretty girl you introduced me to?"

"As a matter of fact, it is." He told her about Patricia's need for a house or apartment.

"Short or long term?" she asked.

"Undetermined at the moment—I've asked her to work for me at the gallery and if she accepts my offer, it may be long term."

"No apartment houses that I know of, but some of our townspeople rent out a portion of their homes. As a last resort, she could check out Bea's Bed and Breakfast over on Third Street. I understand it's very nice—and Beatrice is a lovely person. I'll keep my eyes and ears open."

Drake added the name and number on his phone. "Thanks, I'll tell her next time we talk."

Not wanting to encourage further talk of his personal life—or lack thereof—he was saved by another customer entering the door. He gave Alice a kiss on the cheek, patted his abs, bringing a smile to her friendly face.

Good—he now had a legitimate excuse to call Patricia. She picked up on the third ring. After the usual greetings, he gave her his news without first inquiring about her working for him—he knew when not to exert pressure.

"I have some information for you about rentals here in Porterville." He gave her the data he had gotten from Alice. "I thought you'd like to know—just in case."

"I appreciate it, Drake. This house is beginning to feel spooky empty. I've had the things I want to keep put in storage, gave a lot to Goodwill. At least I still have a bed to sleep in and a kitchen that still works, and a couple weeks before I have to vacate."

"That's good. Alice told me to say hello. She knows the lady who owns the bed and breakfast and vouches for her and her establishment."

"I really like Alice—she's one of a kind."

"Well, I have to go—a lady is coming to discuss art lessons for her son who has ADD. Keep in touch, okay?" *I have lots more to say but I promised not to pressure you.*

Her voice lingered in his ear like a favorite song. Her personality would be a definite asset in the gallery. He wanted visitors and students to feel comfortable—their insecurities or lack of artistic knowledge left outside the door. A gallery should be a cohesive part of the community. Patricia was a good people person as he witnessed when they visited the gallery in Coopersville. Yet, when they were alone, he sensed a reservation in her demeanor. Not for the first time, he wondered about her life in New Mexico. He sensed she was suffering from more than the usual grieving process.

Thirty-two

"It's a sad day when you find out that it's not accident or time or fortune, but yourself that kept things from you." Lillian Hellman

That night, after the call from Drake, Patricia lay in bed and wept. Eventually, the tears stopped, leaving her exhausted and drained. The house gave her an eerie feeling—empty except the bare minimum of furniture. As a teenager, she had slept in the very same bed and dreamed of a Prince Charming coming into her life, and them creating a home with picket fence and a botanical garden of all things beautiful. A teenager's dream—where had she gone wrong?

It wasn't rebellion—her mistakes were the grown-up kind when she let her heart lead the way. Even the pillow beneath her head now felt limp and unsubstantial. She thought of her childhood and her mother coming to her room for a private talk about her school day—and later about her friendships—how important her teen years were, and how they could make or break her future. She had been a good mother, her advice not given in a lecturing way, but with kindness and caring. Patricia felt she had been a good daughter and although she had moved away she had kept in touch.

She thought of all that came in the aftermath of her Mom's illness—her death—disposal of the house. She could have made the house her home, but to what end? The town was old—the last new addition a Home Depot on the outskirts. Like Porterville, the interstate system had pushed the town aside like a junk car. Likewise, she had felt pushed aside by people she once believed in, and somehow she had to build a new future for herself. Money would not be an immediate problem since she had the proceeds from the house sale. She didn't know if she even wanted another relationship—with Drake or any other man.

Her mother had been a woman of faith and always, when things went wrong, reassured her that God would take care of her—all she needed to do was ask. But her mother hadn't known of her disappointing experience in New Mexico, or about Mike's abuse. She had been too ashamed to tell her. So what was she to do, walk through the rest of her life with resigned rigidity? She thought of a quote from her school days—the author long forgotten—*"sooner or later we all sit down to a banquet of consequences."* Her hand automatically went to her throat as it always did when her mind wondered into the past.

Patricia got out of bed and entered the sparsely equipped kitchen. A cup of tea might help. Only a few items were left in the cabinets but she found a box of green tea bags, set the teakettle on the burner and turned it to high. The small table and chairs had been moved to the storage unit along with other furniture and items she felt might be useful in the future. She sat on a barstool with a yellow marker and once again scanned the classified—not quite a full page. She found nothing of interest. The teakettle whistled. She took the mug of tea back to her room and placed it on the bedside table to cool. The television was on—she flipped through the channels and finding no relief from her frustration, turned it off. She wasn't the only person with an undecided future—the whole world seemed to be in a state of indecision.

The tea was delicious and her mind soon calmed to the healing powers of the added honey. Was she being unfair in not giving Drake a second chance? From all she had observed, he was a changed and sober man, more mature than she remembered. Even when drinking, he had never physically harmed her—had not even come close. What did she have to lose—a few weeks or months of her life—at the moment a directionless life? His progress at the gallery was impressive, he appeared clear headed and had positive plans for the future. He was not pressuring her into a renewal of their relationship. So why not accept his offer? It might be interesting to watch his dream come to fruition. It would be a new challenge for her, something different. Looking back, she had enjoyed learning more about art when she was in New Mexico. Her new appreciation of art was the only positive thing she had brought away from that sojourn.

She took the last sip of tea, turned out the light and said a silent prayer: *God, please guide me in the right direction, help me to find purpose in my life.*

The tea must have induced pleasant dreams. She dreamed of meeting an exceptionally handsome man. It was one of those moments when eyes meet and cling like gold leaf—leaving you feeling like a priceless masterpiece in a museum—a feeling that things will never again be dull. He was a Rhett Butler kind of guy with hair as black as her own, intoxicating eyes that see right through you—exposing all your secrets—a face that refuses to disappear after your eyes turn away—a life-altering experience, knowing that you will be changed and perhaps not for the better. You're helpless to care, leaving you as irresponsible as hot fudge hardening on ice cream.

The next morning Patricia awoke with a start, recalling her dream—not even close to a nightmare, for a change—wonderful while it lasted. For once, it wasn't about Mike. The Clarke Gable look-alike bore no resemblance to anyone she knew. *At least I'm still young enough to dream.*

She thought of Alice and her diner in Portersville. She had liked the lady at their first meeting—and for some reason felt an affinity to her. She decided a drive would do her good and a nice brunch at Alice's Café couldn't hurt. She could also pick the lady's brain regarding the B&B Drake had mentioned. A long-term living arrangement would not be feasible until she decided if she would remain in the area.

She dressed in record time, grabbed her purse and keys, and rushed out the door that no longer belonged to her. For the first time in days, she felt a spark of excitement. Maybe she just needed another woman to talk with—or perhaps it was the dream?

Alice greeted her with a warm smile. Patricia removed her coat and folded it on the seat beside her. After ordering, she gazed out the window at a playground across the street. School would soon be out and the now abandoned park would come alive with happy children, picnics, and birthday parties—if it was anything like the playgrounds of her youth—oh, so long ago.

Alice snapped her out of her reverie by serving a plate of perfectly fried over-easy eggs, three slices of bacon, and a side order of whole wheat toast. Only then did Patricia realize she was ravishingly hungry. Alice left and returned with a coffee refill. The homey, warm feel of the place gave Patricia a sense of ease she hadn't felt in a long time. The Café was quiet—only one elderly couple lingered over coffee. "Do you have a minute?" she asked Alice. "I could use your advice."

"I'll be right back. My assistant can handle things for a few minutes. Besides, it'll feel good to sit down."

She soon returned with a mug of her own, and joined Patricia with a deep sigh. "I'm glad to see you're still in the area. How can I help you, dear?"

Touched by her words, Patricia sipped her coffee before responding. "First, I'd like to know more about you. Drake thinks the world of you, I know. How long have you had this charming restaurant?"

"Going on six years—the property was left to me by my

grandmother, Delilah—a saint if there ever was one. She's the one who taught me the love of cooking—or more importantly—the love of satisfying the hunger of other people. She guided me as a child and throughout my earlier years—her sage advice serves me well even to this day."

"How very lucky for you—my grandmother died when I was ten, so I don't remember much about her."

"And you've just lost your mother—I'm so sorry. Is there anything I can do?"

"Maybe you can. I've sold my family home in Kirkwood and I need a temporary rental until I decide what next to do with my life."

"Aw, yes. Drake mentioned that. So he told you about Bea's B&B here in town? I've know the lovely lady for some time. I haven't seen her accommodations lately, but I understand they are quite nice. She's not a young woman, but young in mind. How soon do you need a place?"

"Like yesterday," she answered with a laugh. "No, seriously, I don't have to vacate for another two weeks, but I'm finding it very depressing to be there with the bare minimum of furniture and childhood memories. I've stored most everything until I find a permanent location."

"Why don't I give Bea a call and see if she has an opening. It just might solve your problem." She took her phone from her apron pocket and almost immediately connected with Beatrice. After a few niceties, she glanced at Patricia. "I have a young lady here who needs something furnished. She's a friend of Drake from our new gallery." She listened carefully and then continued, "So, you have only one vacancy? You can show her the space at 4:00? That's great—I'm sure you will like her. Just a minute..." She looked to Patricia for approval. "That will be perfect, Bea. Thanks so much."

"Well, young lady, that was easy."

"Thank you, but can I ask you another question?"

DECENT DECEIT

"Of course—you may ask me anything. I have no secrets."

"How well do you know Drake, and has he talked to you about me?"

"That's two questions. I've known him since he first arrived in town and bought that property. Our local sheriff, Charlie Webster, is a very close friend. Being a friend of the sheriff should be an excellent recommendation, don't you think?" They both laughed. "As to your second question—Drake only told me that you knew each other in the past—otherwise, he was rather close-mouthed. But, if I read the young man correctly, he's very fond of you."

"He has asked me to work for him at the Art Center—help with the opening to make sure it gets off to a good start."

"That sounds wonderful—I'd like to see you hang around. I'm sure you couldn't find a better boss—or friend, I might add."

"We used to be close, some time ago, and I'm a bit apprehensive about accepting his offer."

"Patricia, I think I understand. With losing your Mom, life is not going to feel quite right for a while. It's an adjustment. Losing a loved one is the most traumatic happening in a person's life, you know, so you shouldn't even try to sort everything out at once. Give yourself time to heal."

Patricia's lowered her head and swallowed hard before responding. "I know you're right—I'm just feeling like a ship with no rudder at the moment—too much has happened. Meeting Drake again—so unexpectedly—has only added to my dilemma."

Alice sensed, without a doubt, that the girl was in love with Drake, and that whatever had separated them in the past must be resolved if either of them were to find happiness. She leaned forward and placed a hand over that of the troubled young lady.

"Patricia, Drake has made a big impression on people of this town. Did you know that he and his friend saved our sheriff's life—in an act of genuine courage? He also has taken under his wing what we thought of as our town's misfit—a man almost destroyed by alcohol—gave him a job at his gallery. Now the man is sober and has turned out to be an excellent artist. Our town is very proud of Drake and his desire to improve the community. Frankly, I haven't met a finer young man in a long time."

Patricia calmed at the warm hand over hers. "I did learn of the shooting at the Bucket of Blood, but Drake hasn't mentioned it to me."

"Well, that's Drake for you—he's an extremely humble man. I wish I had a son like him."

Both became silent, deep in personal thoughts. Alice wondered what more she could say to the troubled woman. Patricia, torn between the past and the possibility of a bright future with Drake, gave Alice the only thing she had to give at the moment—a smile.

"Life is good at throwing curve balls, but it doesn't have to end the game. Leave the past behind you, my child—look to the future. Maybe you and Drake have met again because your story isn't finished? Perhaps he had to find himself before he had anything to offer someone else? If you feel you would like to share in his adventure then go for it—you both deserve another chance at happiness." She waited for her advice to sink in or be rejected before continuing.

"You know, I lost my husband after being married only thirty months, but I had those months and I'm so thankful for them. I hesitated to marry him because I was young and feared of failing to be a good wife. If I hadn't put aside my fears, we would have shared nothing. Life is about taking chances and listening to your heart. Even a short time of happiness is worth more than a lifetime of regret."

Patricia lifted her head. "What happened, Alice?"

"He was killed in an auto accident that was not his fault."

Words were insufficient. Patricia could only allow her tearing eyes and expression to say what she couldn't verbalize. *Thank you, Alice, from the bottom of my heart.*

Customers arrived for an early lunch. Alice arose and Patricia reached for her purse.

"Don't bother, brunch is on me."

Patricia got up and the two shared a warm embrace. A new friendship was born and they both knew exactly where they were going.

Thirty-three

"You gain strength, courage and confidence by every experience in which you really stop to look fear in the face." Eleanor Roosevelt

Touched by Alice's council, Patricia checked her appearance in the restroom mirror, and left the Café with a new sense of hope in her heart. The future couldn't possibly hurt more than had her past. Determined to put the latter behind her, she wasted no time driving to the Second Chance Art Center.

She opened the door to the sound of musical instruments being tuned somewhere in the background. Drake emerged from his studio beyond the screen and reception desk. He wore an old white shirt badly stained by every hue on the color wheel. His mussed hair indicated frustration. He held three paint brushes in his hand and an unreadable expression on his face. In spite of it all, Patricia liked what she saw.

"What a nice surprise," he said, after he found his voice. Suddenly aware of his appearance, he quickly shed the smock and threw it and his brushes across a table laden with paint tubes and palette knives.

"Don't let me disturb an artist at work," she said, amused at catching him unawares. "I've just had brunch and a long talk with Alice and decided to stop in to see how things are progressing."

"As you can see, right now I'm playing—and you can disturb me

DECENT DECEIT

any time you like. This is a good time for a visit."

Both acted like they were walking on frozen pavement, placing each step precisely. Sensing his unease, Patricia asked about the background music that had progressed from the tuning-up stage to a rather nice song she didn't recognize.

"That's Oscar—my landlord's son. I told you about him. He's building a music group of veterans with disabilities. You'll like him. But first, how are you doing?"

"Better. I have an appointment later at the B&B you mentioned. I've also decided to accept your offer of a job if we can work out the details—and, of course, if you still want me."

Want her? Is she kidding? I want her in any or whatever capacity possible. She fits me like a well-designed prosthesis, and I'll wear her like my natural skin. I've built a moat around my heart and only Patricia can build a bridge to set me free. If she offers nothing other than her presence, I'll be content. I just want her in my life.

"Want you? You'll be perfect. I can't wait to get this place up and running—we'll make a good team." *Okay, don't oversell—the gallery or yourself.*

Patricia walked around him to the far wall where his and Roy's paintings were lined up. "Are these your paintings?"

He pointed out Roy's canvases first and explained his surprise to find he was a good artist. "You'll see a mural he did in our lunch room later."

Drake, feeling like a magpie, zipped his lips and watched as she moved his works about— silently studying each with interest. Finally she turned to him, studying his face as studiously as she had his paintings. "Drake, your work is excellent. I can hardly believe you're the—uh, same person. You've truly found your calling, haven't you?" She moved toward his work area and only then did he remember her portrait on an easel by the window.

"Excuse me," he said, as he rushed to hide it from view, but it was too late.

"Drake—wait, I want to see that."

He looked out the window and gritted his teeth—it wasn't ready for exhibit—especially not to her. All he could do was pause for her response. *Maybe she won't recognize herself.*

Her gasp startled him into action. He tidied up his work table and waited. He moved a chair behind her and watched as she lowered herself—without a word.

"I wasn't ready for you to see that, Patricia."

"You did a painting of me sleeping in your van? But how—did you take a picture of me?"

"No, I did it from memory."

"You painted that from memory? Drake, that's amazing." She touched a finger beneath her eyes, turned and faced him, her hand automatically moving to her throat. "I can't believe you painted me. I'm touched." She giggled slightly. "I don't know what I look like, but the painting is beautiful."

"You're not angry at me for taking the liberty?"

"No, I'm not angry."

"Patricia," he dared not touch her, "I'm just so sorry for ever treating you badly. Maybe you could forgive me in stages—not all at once—that would be too much to ask."

She got up and gave him a hug. "I do forgive you, Drake. I've made mistakes, too, but I can only blame myself for them. Alcohol kept you from being your true self—I understand that now. I also see you were born to be an artist and I'd love to help you with your gallery. When do you want me to start?"

"Whenever you're ready—we'll work out the details when you're settled. Thank you, Patricia."

Drake felt like he had just won the lottery although Patricia was much more precious than money.

Roy was having a mug of coffee in the lounge when they walked in to see the mural. He welcomed her like any polished gentleman, offered her coffee, and blushed when she praised his painting technique. Drake told him she would be a member of their staff and his eyes gleamed as he offered her a welcoming hand. It was a good day for all three of them.

Patricia left for her appointment at Bea's B&B, promising to call Drake regarding her progress. She left behind two men, one who found it difficult to hide his overwhelming joy, and another with renewed hope for the future happiness of a first class boss.

Thirty-four

"Let your future ride on the winds—it knows where to go." Anon

Drake rushed to his apartment to shower before dinner at the Tanner's. He saw Oscar at work, but they no longer shared a ride. One of his musicians had no transportation and Oscar was happy to share his wheels.

Drake was moved almost to tears when he met the veterans Oscar had recruited, but he managed to hide his emotions as much as possible. He'd learned from Oscar that the veterans didn't want sympathy. Two were amputees. Dan, the drummer, wore a lower left arm and hand prosthesis. Eddie had a prosthetic leg but that didn't prevent him from playing a clarinet, and Steven, legally blind, could play keyboard by ear as well as anyone with 20/20 vision. Oscar, of course, could fill any vacancy with any instrument. Two students would be coming from Kirkwood by bus twice weekly for violin lessons, in response to the Gallery flyers. Oscar's previous hyper episode was fixed with a slight change in his medication. He was happy with his fellow vets and their project and there was no longer a need to tread lightly in his presence. Drake was proud as a peacock of all of them. Oscar was learning he still had a lot to offer—just not on a far-flung battlefield.

Drake was anxious to tell Tanner and Oscar about Patricia. So many positive things were happening that he was near a state of euphoria. In addition, spring was coming—another thing to celebrate. Soon the cumbersome coats, flannel-lined pants and wool shirts would be replaced by jeans and cotton tee shirts. The more daring would be showing off tattoos—suntans and sandaled feet would follow.

Heeding Charlie's warning about break-ins, he locked his apartment door and carefully carried a carrot cake he had picked up from Alice's. He returned home each evening to his solitude but no longer felt the "aloneness". He felt a part of the greater household. Tanner and Oscar had taken him into their lives and he was thankful. They had needed each other. No longer a loner, he cherished these occasional family type get-togethers. Sharing a meal and a couple hours of pool playing were always uplifting. Although the Art Center activities had recently monopolized most of he and Oscar's time it had been time well spent. He couldn't help feeling that God had been producer and director of their drama and deserved his own Oscar, for sure.

After the usual backslaps, shoulder punches, and happy frolicking with O'Toole, the three men settled down to a snack of colorful sweet mini-peppers and peach mango salsa—straight from the super market. "Not very original," Tanner explained, "we're having a baked picnic pork shoulder and sweet potato casserole later."

"Smells marvelous," Drake said. "I haven't concentrated much on food lately."

"It doesn't show—you look well nourished to me," Oscar said, eyeing Drake's enviable physique. "Better not neglect the abs though," he teased. *A far cry from the somber returning vet he had first met.*

"I have news to share. Remember, I told you about Patricia? Well, she came into the Center today and accepted my request to help with the opening. She has sold her home in Kirkwood, and will temporarily live at Bea's B&B until she finds a more permanent place."

"You son-of-a-gun," said Tanner. "I thought you looked especially chipper."

Drake answered their questions about Patricia's knowledge of art—and her experience while living in the Santa Fe and Taos area. "That's an art Mecca probably second to New York City. I'm sure she'll be a great asset. She's a geek with the computer, and can even build a website—an important part of running a present day gallery."

"I've wondered how you would handle management and still have time to pursue your own painting," Tanner said, before they were interrupted by the oven timer.

"I just hope she'll stay on after the opening."

O'Toole showed off his good manners throughout dinner—no begging at the table or whining to go out. The men talked of galleries they had visited around the world. Tanner was well versed about the art scene in Washington and New York, and Oscar had visited many galleries in Europe. Drake told of his visit to Mexico City, and an artist's studio in the Zona Rosa. "The artist painted in a courtyard and used a brush with a long extension so he didn't have to back off to view his canvas. The Museum of Modern Art in Chapultepec Park was outstanding. I've never forgotten the landscapes by Jose Marie Velasco. I searched every book store to find more about him and his work, and finally found one hidden in a neglected upstairs room."

"When were you there?" Oscar asked.

Drake laughed. "My mom gave me the trip as a graduation gift from college. She knew I loved art—she just wanted me to seek a more traditional and promising career. Of course, Dad wanted me to be a lawyer." His expression left nothing to supposition regarding that possibility.

"Then you've always been interested in painting," Oscar noted.

"Guess so. I feel like my authentic self when painting—it gives me a feeling of accomplishment. I try to capture the vitality and rich diversity of a scene as well as the emotional aspect. That's crucial to me but it's not easy to capture emotion in a landscape painting. It's always a challenge. When I'm painting, I never feel like I should be doing something else."

"Then it's a good think Patricia is willing to help out with the management of your gallery— give you more time at the easel."

They finished the meal and each carried their dishes to the kitchen where Drake continued the conversation.

"I don't want this gallery to be pretentious in any way. I want it to be a place where artists at any stage of learning can try, fail, and start again. No one visiting a gallery should feel intimidated to seek out and find enjoyment in art. Mine will be a working gallery where students can get something they don't get in an academic setting. Of course, learning the basics of drawing, composition, perspective, and color harmony are crucial. After that, they should trust their own instincts. Many successful artists, like Robert Bateman had little formal training—mostly self-taught. Many beginners are discouraged in art school, as was I for a while. Some people are born to paint—just as some are born to play music," he added, looking at Oscar.

"But galleries are supposed to be quiet, aren't they? A place to rest and meditate?" asked Oscar.

"Why can't they be both, Drake?" Tanner asked.

"Of course—that's what I'm striving toward. The large front area will be the more traditional gallery, reserved for shows, etc. and it will be more typically quiet, as you say, Oscar."

Realizing he was a bit wired with enthusiasm, Drake added. "It's going to be a work in progress, so your ideas and input are always welcome."

After sharing the KP duty, they went to the family room, each carrying a piece of Drake's cake, and coffee. O'Toole followed closely at Tanner's heels, hoping for a dropped crumb. When it didn't happen, he left his master's feet to seek more sympathetic attention from Drake.

Oscar seemed to be absorbed in memories—probably the ongoing chaos in other parts of the world—the Taliban or ISIS's destruction of ancient art and artifacts as well as humans. The recent news had not been encouraging. Oscar finished his cake and turned to Drake.

"What if you had a second, small gallery in one of the front spaces you've set aside for studio rentals—maybe a room to the left of the main gallery? Make it into a meditation room with just three or four special paintings, a sofa or bench to sit on—like an oriental type room with minimum furnishings? You could call it Secret Garden, or Oasis, a place to visit alone to re-nourish the Soul."

So he had been thinking of Miriam and her hidden garden, Drake thought.

Drake and Tanner looked at each other, trying not to show their amazement at Oscar's comment. They shouldn't have been surprised. After all, Oscar was a true artist himself and appreciated the need to be alone with his music.

Moved to keep the conversation going, Drake offered: "But we have the entire rural countryside all around us on which to meditate. "I might add you have some beautiful vistas in this part of the county."

"Perhaps that's the problem," Tanner offered. "Living in the country is such a part of us that we don't always notice its beauty. Oscar's idea would help people focus and meditate on that beauty in one painting at a time."

"You're right, Tanner. We artists can't expect to compete with God," Drake said, "only bring attention to what He has already created. Georgia O'Keefe said she painted large flowers because people didn't really look at a flower. She opened eyes to the minutia in nature, even saw beauty in sun bleached skulls of animals." He reached down to scratch O'Toole's massive head and was rewarded by a tongue wash of his fingers.

After another comfortable silence, Drake continued. "Some people ridicule modern art—color field paintings etc. and some find enjoyment in the obscure—or are drawn to a specific color or composition."

"I agree—art should fill a need for anyone who shows an interest," Tanner added.

The conversation continued over coffee. The three discussed a name for Oscar's group— Oscar emphasizing the name should have nothing to do with disabilities or their veteran status.

Thinking of the compassion felt for Oscar and his buddies, Drake suggested, "How does *The Key of C Players* sound—the *C* for caring?"

"I like that," Tanner said, looking at his son who had turned aside and lowered his head.

Oscar agreed. "Good thinking, Drake. I like it, too."

Drake said his goodnights and thanked the men for their input. "Great dinner, Tanner—you should publish a cookbook—in your spare time."

"We can't wait to meet your Patricia,"

Drake laughed. "She's not mine—yet. I'll run your ideas by her and see what she thinks. And don't read anything into this—we're just friends—and I'd like you to treat her as such—okay? She's just lost her mother and is a bit fragile at the moment. And Oscar, make sure your men practice a lot—I'll need you to supply the music for the grand opening."

"Let me know if you need any help from me," Tanner offered before bidding him a good night.

The moon illuminated his path back to the apartment. At his

deck, he paused to drink in the beauty of the night. Harmless clouds moved about, driven by a playful wind, causing the light to fade and reappear like from a lighthouse beam. He wondered how Patricia would respond to the peace and tranquility of his little piece of Eden. With his hand going to the medallion around his neck, he also wondered how Rhonda would have reacted to his present project. Some might label him a lunatic—or "that man's brain is distorted by drink." He chuckled to himself—he had never been more clear-headed in his life.

Drake shivered and turned to unlock his door. He paused and smiled before going in. A violin sobbed from across the way and merged with the nocturnal music of the countryside.

Thirty-five

"Human beings, by changing the inner attitude of their minds, can change the outer aspects of their lives."
William James

Patricia returned to her temporary abode in Kirkwood. In her mother's absence, the house no longer felt like home, but she was in a much better frame of mind than when she left that morning. Alice's comments gave her a much brighter mental attitude regarding her future. After her experience in Santa Fe, she often felt that other women were peacocks and she was a barnyard hen.

Now, she was angry at herself for allowing Mike to destroy her self-esteem, giving her a cloudy forecast for the future. Merely kicking oneself over past mistakes was not very productive—it required action to overcome, as she was learning. Alice's comments about Drake gave her hope that he really was a changed man. The abuse of alcohol—a stigma of his past—was a stigma he seemed to have erased. Like many others, he had kept stumbling over the same stone. She had to admit that his addiction had been the only serious flaw in their previous relationship.

In Alice, she felt she had gained a sister—or at least the beginning of a good friendship. Without her words of wisdom, and in spite of her own interest in the gallery project, she might not have found the courage to accept Drake's offer. On the drive home, she admitted to herself that part of her decision was to prove she was made of more than fluff and feathers. She had the skills to be an independent woman—her happiness did not depend on a love relationship.

Bea's B&B was a pleasant surprise, as was Bea—a woman in her 70's, but alert and quick on her feet, and possessing a warm heart. It couldn't be an easy job for a woman her age. Expecting shabby-chic, Patricia found the lovely old home much more chic than shabby. No flocked wallpaper or lace doilies. No pink flamingos on the lawn.

Bea had converted the B&B from a large home previously owned by an elderly much-loved female doctor who had served the county for years—delivering babies, sewing up wounds, and caring for the ills of young and old alike. The available space was large and well appointed, walls painted a pale sage, chintz padded window seats and private bath—charming and welcoming to one in Patricia's state of mind. A garden outside the window showed promise of a lovely spring view, pruned rose bushes waiting for spring to awaken new growth—a cobblestone path throughout. What was not to like? It would certainly be a nice roof over her head until she determined how to put the proceeds from her mother's house to good use.

Would working with Drake be a gift of something new and wonderful or would it excavate old hurts? Only time would tell. She was now ready to explore a new, different, and challenging occupation. Would she have felt differently if the challenge had been offered by someone other than Drake?

That night, as she readied herself for bed, the mirror reflected none of the past trauma to her physical body. The neck bruises were gone but the underlying memory remained. Her heart softened further when she thought of the portrait Drake had painted. Nothing could have surprised her more. Was it a sign that he cared deeply for her—more evident now that liquor no longer called the shots? He was much more like the man she had known in the beginning of the relationship. Was she once again gambling with her heart, and would the stakes prove to be too high? More importantly, did she dare gamble with his heart, with the secret she had carried with her since their parting? How would he handle one more act of deceit?

In bed with the lights out, her thoughts returned to the gallery and the commitment she had made. She had not promised a long-term association—keeping her options open if either of them became unhappy with the arrangement. After exploring the many galleries in New Mexico, plus her general business sense and her heightened appreciation for art, she felt qualified to take on the role Drake had assigned to her.

First, an eye-catching website would need to be built—one the search engines would have no trouble finding. She would include a bio of the owner—his image—certain to catch an eye or two, his intentions for the gallery, photos of the paintings available, cost of lessons, etc. An appealing newsletter must be written announcing the Grand Opening. She had her work cut out for her. If she was to ward off thoughts of a more personal nature, the distraction would be a good thing. Drake's new maturity, his enthusiasm for life, and his natural manly appeal would not be easy to ignore. Memories of their unhappy past was beginning to fade—taking second place to the more recent tender and true.

The next day she made arrangements for her few remaining items, including the bed she slept in, to be moved to the storage rental unit. She had only to move her clothing and toiletries to the B&B. That she could do by herself. Bea was not a young woman and she hoped they would become friends. Patricia was impressed with the friendliness of the small town—if that feeling grew, she may never want to leave.

Feeling relief that a decision had been made, she finally fell asleep. Along with her material trappings, she was locking her past in storage as well. Time would tell when and if it was safe to throw away the key.

A week later all ties to her childhood home were severed. Her clothes were in a spacious closet at the B&B, her toiletries organized in the private bath drawers. She heard no street noises—only blessed quietness. Exhausted from the move, she took a leisurely bath and climbed into bed. Her eyes were heavy as she reached for the bedside lamp, but sleep did not come. Instead of drifting off to dreamland, her thoughts went helter-skelter, first to Drake, the gallery and what lay ahead—to Alice, Bea, the local sheriff whom she had finally met, and the flamboyant Roy with his jaunty French beret. Hard to believe he was once the town drunk. Her mind was a jumble of new faces and new challenges.

Her hand moved from under the pillow to her throat as images of Mike also intruded. At some point, would she have to tell Drake all that had happened while they were apart? And was that why she felt a need to proceed cautiously where they were concerned? Fatigue won out eventually and smothered her concerns—at least for a few hours.

She awakened the next morning to the sound of singing. Bea apparently started each day with song—her own form of reveille. Patricia was treated to a breakfast of orange juice, French toast, bacon and coffee—served at the dining room table along with four other guests of the B&B. The table was set with linen place mats and napkins, and a round antique platter of pastries. She was enchanted with her new quarters. It felt like a new beginning. One of the guests suggested she explore the pathway from the house to a lovely secluded lake and natural area behind the B&B. She had every intention of doing just that before going on the clock at the Art Center.

Before returning to her room, Patricia complimented Bea on the breakfast, and added "it was lovely being awakened by your singing."

"I'm afraid my voice has gone raspy from overuse—and old age." she said, somewhat embarrassed at the compliment. "I have arthritis, and I sing to make my pain so angry it will go away."

"Does it work?" Patricia asked. "It wouldn't make me angry." They both laughed.

"Sometimes it works, other times it just helps me to ignore it."

"My mother was a sweet, kind woman, but I never heard her sing. She told or read me stories, but I don't remember any lullabies."

Thirty-six

"Sow a seed and the earth will yield you a flower.
Dream your dream to the sky and it will bring you your beloved."
Kahlil Gibran

Drake was as nervous as a tabby cat on a hot tin roof the morning Patricia was to arrive for work. His sleep had been restless. Thought of them spending six days a week in such close proximity kept him awake and aware of what he was facing. With no inkling of how it would all work out, one thing was certain—he wanted her in his life. When he almost put bacterial ointment instead of toothpaste on his toothbrush he knew he had to get his act together.

He keyed in Charlie's number, knowing the sheriff would be up and at it. Crime had increased in the county—some of it probably due to the long cold winter, too much time indoors, or just plain boredom.

"Drake, what's on your mind so early in the morning?"

"I'm in the mood for a man to man talk." Drake said.

"Sure—but not until around one—meet me at Alice's unless I need to call and cancel?"

"Perfect. See you then."

Good old Charlie—a man to be counted on. Drake worried about him dealing day and night with domestic and drug problems.

Meth labs were springing up in remote areas on highways seldom traveled. The lives of many young people were out of hand, a cause for concern for families and community alike. Charlie had been shot once and Drake hoped it never happened again. He looked forward to their talk.

Drake left his apartment earlier than usual. He planned to stop by the cemetery—hadn't visited for a while. He had no idea if the woman who gave him birth was aware of his presence but the visits had a calming effect on him anyway. Amazing—a mother he couldn't even remember having made such an impression on him, all due to Charlie's high regard for her. Without their connection, he would have gone to his grave knowing nothing about her, and consequently blaming her for giving him up. He no longer gave much thought to his mysterious past, nor should he—the future was what counted. However, he would always wear the charm around his neck as a reminder of her sacrifice in his behalf. He gave little thought to his biological father, but did lean toward giving him the benefit of the doubt. His mother must have seen some good in the man.

Patricia arrived on the dot at her new job, dressed appropriately—turtle neck sweater and skirt—no low cut jeans or tees—she knew how to present herself in a business-like way. Drake had lost some of his anxiety and welcomed her without suffering a panic attack. They made small talk until Roy and Oscar showed up and welcomed her warmly. Oscar smiled and raised his eyebrows at Drake before continuing on to his sound-proof music room to await a violin student. Roy twisted his French beret into a pretzel while prancing like a yearling at Churchill Downs before going to his chores of the day. Patricia assured Drake she was comfortable at the B&B, but seemed anxious to get started on the project—or was it nerves? They agreed the website was an important first step.

"You can build it?" he asked, incredulously. He knew his way around the internet but had no desire to learn URL.

"It's not that hard after a few basic lessons."

"Patricia, I'm so impressed. I'm lucky to have you on board."

"I'll do my best—but remember—no long term expectations by either of us."

"I promise to treat you with respect and dignity," he said, bowing low. She couldn't restrain a giggle at his antics—a part of his pre-boozing personality she had almost forgotten.

"I see you have a Dell—that's good—lots of memory. So shall I start work on the website?"

"Will this desk work okay for you or would you rather have a space in the back? No customers expected yet so you won't be disturbed."

"This is fine. Nice thing about computers— you need little or no space for physical storage." She put her coat and purse in the guest chair. "After I get things set up, we'll need a photo for the home page, plus the paintings you want to present to the public."

"I have an excellent camera, and I've already sorted out the best work. The three artists we selected from the Kaiser U. Gallery have already delivered their canvases."

Drake laughed and continued. "They were so excited and grateful for the chance to exhibit, you'd have thought we were the Tate."

"I assume you want to use *Second Chance Art Center* as the domain name?"

"I would assume so, but you know best."

"Drake, this is your project—I'll need your approval on everything I do."

"Will it bother you if I paint here behind the screen while you work? Not much noise in painting unless I knock my easel over."

Her laugh eased the tension but he questioned whether or not he would be able to concentrate with her so near. In spite of her attempt at gaiety, Drake continued to wonder about her sojourn to New Mexico and what had transpired there to cause her unease. After their trip to Coopersville—and since—he concluded it had nothing to do with him. He renewed his vow to not apply undue pressure. He owed her that much.

Drake spent the morning priming canvases with gesso. With Patricia only a few feet from him, he was too distracted to concentrate on the more creative aspects of painting. She consulted him on several occasions regarding his wishes and asked him to read what she had prepared for the home page of the website. He found no misspelled words or dangling participles—was impressed with her expertise in such matters. He yielded, for the most part, to her concepts.

The morning had gone well and he was in a good mood when he left to meet Charlie.

As usual, their lunch was a treat and Alice her usual cheerful self—patted his shoulder as she walked away.

"When are you two going to tie the knot?" Drake teasingly asked Charlie.

"Who says we are?" He sighed deeply and relaxed his shoulders. "The crime statistics would have to improve or she would never see me."

"That reminds me, what's the latest with the young man Oscar put the fear of God into at the Apple Festival?"

"Burt Adams. Since the altercation with his family that I told you about, I've been summoned twice more. That young man won't stop until he's behind bars. I've gotten tips that he is dealing in meth and who knows what else. I'm keeping an eye on him. For the parent's sake, I hope *using* is his worst crime—users are capable of anything. The county has had three drug overdoses in the last two months. Two died and one girl is recuperating in the hospital in Coopersville. We shut one lab down and another springs up—sad situation. This job is no longer simply keeping the peace."

"I didn't realize it was that bad."

"I never thought our country would become a scary place, but it's happening—mass killings in schools and churches. Drugs and mental health are much to blame—in my estimation. If the urge to do evil is there and a gun is not available they will find another means to carry out their plan. It's not that we don't have laws—we have them but they're not always implemented. Our small town is not immune. We have to be continually vigilant."

"I worry about you, Charlie. I hope Tom is competent as a backup."

"He's competent, hasn't had much experience in dealing with today's crimes. Let's talk about something else—*your* love life, for instance."

"That's one reason I wanted to see you. Patricia has agreed to work for me at the gallery—to help prepare for the opening. She's moved into Bea's B&B temporarily. Today, she's building a website for the gallery, can you believe? The girl is much more talented than I realized."

"Sure it's her talent you're interested in?" Charlie teased. "Sorry—she's a lovely young lady—I've been wondering why you allowed her to get away in the first place."

"Truthfully, she couldn't put up with my drinking. She's been living in New Mexico and has developed a good eye for art."

"That should come in handy."

"Charlie, I'm crazy about her, but trying not to act on it. She says she has forgiven me for the past, but something is keeping her at arm's length. I'm so afraid of losing her again I'm losing all perspective. At least the job will keep her in the area for a time—I hope. Something is bothering her and I don't think it has anything to do with me."

"You sound like a man in love."

"All I know right now is I want her in my life—in any capacity—and I'm afraid I'll blow my chances again."

"Drake, take a deep breath—now relax your shoulders." They laughed as Drake obeyed. "A sheriff is not usually consulted about affairs of the heart, but how can I help?"

"I guess I just needed someone to talk to about her. Right now, I think the best thing I can do is proceed cautiously—agree?"

"Most certainly I agree. She may have had a bad experience—other than with you—and needs to deal with it before moving on. I would be there if and when she's ready to open up. Practice patience and, in the meantime, work your butt off. Do the right thing, and it will work out."

"If I get a second chance, our story will read like a Jane Austin novel. If the plot works, I may even drop on bended knee."

"Now, you're talking, son. This time, you may just get it right."

As they left the diner, Charlie asked, "How is Tanner adjusting to retirement?"

"He seems happy, best I can tell. He's started writing his memoir and thinking about a novel."

"The reason I ask is our city manager is retiring soon and we need a replacement. I thought of Tanner and his family connection in our area—that he might be interested—although overqualified, I'm sure."

"Want me to say anything to him?"

"No—not yet—not before I run his name by the committee. It's not a huge job but a responsible one."

"He would probably make a good one."

Drake returned to the gallery to find Patricia at rapt attention in front of the computer screen. She looked up briefly and then ran her hand through her thick hair—oblivious of the damage she was doing to its usual neatness. His heart rhythm paused briefly before hitting him with a double beat. He vaguely recalled her doing the same thing with her hair when they first met. She had no idea how her presence affected him—or how much he wanted to feel her tresses between his fingers and breathe in their fragrance. *Tread softly—love should have friendship as its base.* He was aware of her presence—as close as his thoughts—yet accepted that she was not yet approachable.

"It looks like a break is indicated," he said. "Let me fix you a cup of tea."

She looked at her watch, and stretched like a feline. "That would be lovely. I'm mentally depleted."

"I suggest you put it on hold until tomorrow."

Without argument, she hit "save" and closed down the computer. On the way to the lunch room she suggested he needed a new printer.

"That won't be a problem. Just order one on line, and any other office supplies you need."

While she drank her tea they, including Roy, discussed the items left to be done before the opening. Roy had spent the day opening and organizing cartons of painting supplies to be kept in stock for future students, saving them a trip to Kirkwood. He had become a jack-of-all-trades in addition to his own painting, and Drake had accepted his willingness to do anything needed to get the project up and running. They had come a long way since their encounter on the street and both had benefitted from the meeting. Roy showed his appreciation in any way he could. Drake sent them home early with a thank you for a rewarding day.

On his way home, Drake did much wool gathering. He wandered if Tanner would accept the job of town manager—if it were offered. He had much admiration for the man and his abilities, and his appraisal had not diminished since they first met. But, would he be content to stay at home, rock on his front porch and smoke his pipe? Probably not. Would the job interfere with his writing and his solitude? Only time would tell.

His thoughts, as usual, drifted to Patricia. Having her in his world again was exciting—and frustrating. How long could they maintain the *strictly business* agreement? His mind wondered to old fashioned wooing—he could do that. She deserved a proper courtship, not the selfish attentions of an alcoholic seeking his own desires. He was no longer that man and he vowed to behave like a gentleman. Now, his heart led him to thoughts of picnics, movies, dinners and holding hands when they were doing nothing at all. Just the thought brought a smile to his face.

Oscar had arrived before him, his van pulled to the side to make room for him. The Key of C Players was sounding more and more professional and Oscar was wearing the persona of a man if not yet fulfilled, was well on his way.

Tanner came out of the shadows with a manila folder in his hand—O'Toole faithfully at his heels. Drake greeted them both—hard to say who showed the most enthusiasm. "You're home a bit earlier than usual."

Drake unlocked his door and the three entered. O'Toole panted with excitement, circling the room before settling down near the couch—his front paws crossed in relaxation. "Patricia and Roy worked extra hard today, so I sent them home early."

"Patricia's first day, right?"

"Right—I'm blown away by her expertise. She worked all day on a website for the gallery. I would have needed to hire a professional web designer—had no idea she could build one."

"I know the geeks charge a fortune. Glad to know she has become an asset on her first day."

Drake flipped on a light. The days were yet to grow longer. "That file folder looks official. Hope it's not my eviction notice."

"Now why would I do that? You're the best tenant I've ever had. In fact, you're the only one I've ever had. As you requested, it's a bit of writing for you to critique. No hurry, you're a busy man—whenever you can."

Drake took the folder and was surprised at how much Tanner had accomplished in a short time. "I can't wait to read it. Won't keep me awake at night or give me nightmares, will it?"

"Not that exciting, I'm afraid."

"Seriously, Tanner, how do you feel about your retirement? Still enjoying your solitude or are you lonely here with Oscar occupied most days with his musicians?"

"Do I miss the pressure of my former job? No. I'm happy to be here with my son—you, and O'Toole. The writing is a big help—never thought I would enjoy it this much. Letting my mind roam about without a leash is a new experience for sure. Spring will be here soon and there will be plenty chores to do. I'm feeling a need for outside exercise. Anxious to get a garden started, and Annabelle's yard back in shape."

Drake went to his bookshelves and turned with a volume of quotes in his hand. He thumbed through the pages. "Ah haw—maybe this will help with your writing—an old quote by Robert Louis Stevenson." He began to read.

"Writers should recognize and understand joy, and 'give it a voice'. Every bright word or picture is a piece of pleasure set afloat. The reader catches it and goes on his way rejoicing. It's the business of art to send hints that way as often as possible. I have to believe that every heart that has beat strongly and cheerfully has left a hopeful impulse behind it in the world. If I cannot believe that, then why should I go on? Why should anyone go on?"

Tanner was quiet for a moment before reaching out his hand. "Could I borrow that book?"

Drake handed it to him. "Take it—I've practically memorized it. Anything we create and leave behind is a source of joy—for the creator as well as those who find it." He sat back down and pursued another concern.

"Tanner, I'm really proud of Oscar for what he's doing at the Center, but how do *you* think he's doing?"

"More focused, for sure, now that he has a project. It seems the guys are good for each other—their music and similar experiences bonding them in a common cause."

"I don't hear him playing as much at night since he's been working with the Key of C Players. Is that's a good thing?"

"You've probably noticed that he's much calmer. His nightmares are less frequent—at least I haven't heard him lately. No way of knowing how his mind works when he's alone. Having a specific goal is good and he seems more concerned about the other vets than himself. I just thank God I have him back home. He certainly communicates more easily now, and your friendship has been a God-send."

"Then we're all making progress—that's good. I'm usually painting or doing something else when they are in session, but from what I have observed, the guys really like him."

"By the way, I had lunch with Charlie, and he says drugs are a big problem now with the young people—overdoses, drug related thievery—keeps him, as well as Tom, on the alert. He and Alice remain close, it seems, but he scoffed about her never seeing him when I teased him about tying the knot."

"That's too bad. Recreational drugs have never been a problem with Oscar. He doesn't even like taking his med although it's a minimum dose. With his music as a diversion as well as a challenge, he may be able to stop it altogether at some point. We hope so."

Tanner got up and O'Toole immediately leaped to his feet. "Thanks for looking at my writing, but take your time—no more deadlines for me."

Drake went to the cupboard and gave O'Toole a doggie treat. "Someday, I'm going to have my own dog," he told Tanner.

Thirty-seven

On falling in Love: "If it is right, it happens.
The main thing is not to hurry. Nothing good gets away."
John Steinbeck

*B*eware the Ides of March, Drake thought, as cauliflower clouds appeared in the sky, moving about like over-stuffed pillows. The wind twisted and rattled the dried heads of thistle and milkweed, flattened the dormant grasses along the rural road, and swirled the dry bare earth into pinwheels.

Like a piano out of tune, his body needed attention and refused to postpone another day the jogging he had missed during the long winter. March was defying the calendar and making its presence known a week earlier than expected. Drake pulled the zipper of his jacket tighter around his throat and fought nature's onslaught by increasing his gait. Clouds continued to move about like fighter jets swooping up and down, first evading and then aggressively pursuing the angry wind. It was a Saturday morning and Drake was a mile from home, but he was exhilarated and felt no fear.

The last three weeks had been a beehive of activity. The website was up and running, the main gallery walls were arrayed with landscapes, still life and experimental works in various degrees of expertise—all chosen for their artistic credibility and promise of continued growth. Proper lighting had been installed with Tanner's generous contribution.

The *Secret Garden* meditation room—Oscar's suggestion—was arranged for private viewings. The small room needed only seating and one or two paintings on display. Oscar and Tanner had found at the local antique store a small Queen Ann loveseat for the room and surprised Drake with the donation. He added an end table and lamp, and an area rug to soften the space. The new *Second Chance Art Center* sign had been built and installed, visible to all north and southbound travelers, the logo's meaning left for personal interpretation. Food and drink for the opening reception had been chosen by Patricia and Alice.

He and Roy had made a trip to Kirkwood to purchase landscaping shrubs for the front entrance, and he hoped the weather warmed enough for planting before the big day. If not, they would be placed in decorative pots to suffice until a more suitable time. The entire crew had been so involved there was no time for frivolous thinking. He couldn't have been more proud of them, or more thankful for their support. Patricia's anxiety dissipated as she became more and more involved in the gallery. Drake rejoiced to see the girl he once knew—and now loved—becoming more relaxed in his presence. It was enough for now.

Tanner and O'Toole were taking care of business—their early morning chore—when Drake arrived back at his apartment, breathless and sweating.

"Drake, you're running in this weather—and so early in the morning?"

"Yeah—crazy, I know." He managed to say, between gasping breaths. "You can see, I'm out of shape—difficult running in this wind, and March yet a few days away. Running is a good way to alleviate anxiety."

"You should relax today and tomorrow. Oscar has told me how

hard you've been working."

"Oscar has been a huge help—as has everyone else—including you. I really appreciate all you've done."

"You need to get inside. If you don't have a Saturday night date, come down and join us for dinner."

"That would be great. Thanks."

Drake hurried up the steps, anxious for a hot shower and a glass of iced coffee. He felt good. Anticipating an evening with Tanner and Oscar made him feel even better.

The weekend went well—nothing like good food, conversation, and downtime to feed the soul. Winning a couple games of pool also helped. On Sunday afternoon, the wind calmed and bright sunlight gifted them with spring-like weather. On Monday, Oscar left his van behind—no music rehearsals until Wednesday—and joined Drake in the morning commute to the gallery.

In far-off Iraq, Afghanistan and Syria, people continued to kill each other. In America's Midwest, at an early morning hour, the two young men traveled the country roads in comfortable silence. Hereford milk cows with udders not yet swollen to maximum fullness dotted the bottoms and banks of the landscape as if they were planted there. Black Angus beef cattle fed on bales of hay tossed in feed-lots by ranchers. Other mixed herds roamed about in search of the first green blades of grass. Horses stood with heads down as if they, too, had grown bored with the long winter. Spring would revive the "frisky" in them—again they would feel their oats, especially if there were new foals prancing about. Breezes awakened nearby trees, ruffled leaves and offered promises they might not be able to keep. March was fast approaching—would it roar in like a lion or meek as a lamb? Would spring bring peace or peril, pain or passion?

Drake broke the silence. "Oscar, are you happy with your work with the other veterans? Feel like you're making a difference in their

DECENT DECEIT

lives—their adjustment as civilians?"

"I'm happy because they're happy. After a good session, their excitement is almost palpable. It's not easy for them, you know. Dan, the drummer with the lower left arm prosthesis, is often in pain during practice, but the music drives him onward. I don't know how he does it. Steven is amazing on the keyboard—can't see the music—but after hearing the melody a few times is able to improvise like a pro. Without sight, his hearing and memory seem even more acute. I'm proud of them. The two violin students don't seem to mind the commute from Kirkwood for lessons and have signed up for another month. To answer your question, I'm happy with the way it's all working out for them. That's the most important thing. I'm happy I can give them an escape from their lingering memories."

"Heard from Miriam lately?"

"Had an e-mail last week, and the situation is not improving. She's concerned the sons of friends are joining ISIS—being brainwashed. ISIS is now controlling a large part of Baghdad. Who knows how it will end—or if it will ever end?"

Their pleasant early morning was not meant to last the day. Drake turned into the gallery parking lot. The first shock was the attractive new sign, now marred by debris of some kind. Drake slammed on the brakes, and the two men exited the van in a state of disbelief. On closer inspection they agreed it was smashed eggs—not paint, thank goodness—and what appeared to be dried catsup. They turned to the gallery entrance to find more smudges of what looked like catsup on the front door and newly installed side shutters. Stuck beneath the door was a note, *"mine y r own bizness"* scribbled on a paper towel—a Twitter message, without a hashtag? Or was it written by a person of limited education? Both men fought their dismay. Drake punched in Charlie's number and waited. Oscar pranced about, anger building like volcanic lava.

"He'll be right here," Drake said—more concerned about his

friend's reaction than the damage they had found. "Oscar, it's not that bad—soap and water will take care of it." His words seemed not to register—and Drake stood helpless to find words that did.

Charlie pulled into the lot, the wheels of the patrol car throwing gravel in every direction. He approached them with hands facing downward. Oscar's pacing, his clinched fist and facial expression didn't go undetected. "First, let's calm down and see what we have here."

Drake didn't speak—this sort of vandalism was a new experience for him. He certainly hadn't expected it in quiet, laid-back Porterville. Charlie went to the newly installed sign, rubbed a finger over the damage to ascertain the probable time it had happened, took out his phone and snapped photos. He went through the same routine at the front door before turning his attention back to the men. "Let's go inside."

The interior was as they had left it the previous night. "Do you have any idea who might have done this?" Charlie asked, looking from one to the other.

Neither replied, but Drake handed him the note. Charlie studied it, placed it in a plastic evidence bag. "Have you checked out back—doors and windows?"

"No, I called you immediately." Charlie and Drake made their way through the work spaces to find the back entrance intact. They went outside, circled the building and found nothing amiss. The sheriff looked for any evidence left in the parking lot, found nothing of interest.

Oscar paced the main gallery with hands deep in his pockets, his mind alert and searching for motivation. Drake and Charlie returned through the front door.

"All right," Charlie said, "now let's talk." Drake led them into the kitchen/lounge where they sat at the small table.

Charlie, in full sheriff mode, asked, "Have you guys been

ruffling any feathers recently?"

The guys looked at each other, shrugged their shoulders.

Oscar, now in better control of his emotions, broke his silence. "Not since the Apple Festival. I was plenty rough on the young man taking advantage of his girlfriend—you remember—your deputy took the girl home. The punk may have been humiliated, but he deserved it. The "mind your own business note" indicates it might be him."

"Burt Adams," Charlie said, "and the girl was Tammy Thornton—her parents have sent her away to a private school. Burt has gotten to know *me* quite well lately due to drugs and other trouble-making."

Drake agreed there had been no other altercations. "But Oscar, how would he know who we were or our connection to the gallery? We didn't exactly shake hands and introduce ourselves."

"You forget this is a small town—nothing remains a secret for very long—and neither do newcomers remain strangers. Afraid to tackle me personally, Burt—or whoever did this—might have sent me a message through my friends." Charlie closed his notepad and placed it in his shirt pocket. "He will be the first suspect, since neither of you can think of anyone else who might want to take revenge. On the other hand, it could be just teenagers out for an evening of tomfoolery after a few beers."

The door opened and Patricia walked in, her eyes wide at seeing the patrol car in the lot. "What has happened here?" she asked, looking from one to the other.

The situation was explained to her—Charlie asked her a question. "You're fairly new in town, but do you know of anyone who might have done this in retaliation for some real or perceived injustice?"

"I know no one except you guys—Alice, at the Diner, and my landlady." She looked so sad that Drake thought she was going to cry. "This is crazy—who would want to damage something as innocuous as an art gallery?" She looked at Drake with what—sorrow, love, or both?

Charlie picked up his hat and the three followed him to the door. "Don't try to solve this yourself," his attention first on Oscar and then the others. "Leave this to me. In the meantime, clean up the mess and get on with your plans for the opening. Don't allow this incident to dampen your enthusiasm. If you do, then the culprit—whoever it is—wins. Concentrate on what you do best—art and music. He shook hands with Drake and Oscar, and planted a gentle kiss on Patricia's cheek, causing her to blush like a teenager.

The door closed and Patricia did the unexpected. She turned to Drake—they stood face to face for more than a moment before she moved forward and wrapped her arms around him. "I'm so sorry." It was another step toward bridging the ambiguous gap between them—one more step to reconciliation. How many more would it take to obliterate their troubled pasts?

Thirty-eight

"But let there be spaces in your togetherness,
and let the winds of the heavens dance between you.
Kahlil Gibran

Roy arrived on the scene as the sheriff was leaving the parking lot. A brief discussion and an empty pot of dark roast later, the four remained puzzled, frustrated, and angry. Any abilities to create or concentrate were understandably absent. Drake was the first to take action. He went to a closet and brought out a bucket and brush, while the others—without comment—followed suit with other cleaning supplies and plastic gloves. As a small army they marched forward, and silently worked side by side like good little soldiers until every trace of the misdeed was wiped away.

Drake stood back. "There—good as new. The rest—we'll let Charlie handle—everyone agree?"

"Agreed," was the unanimous reply.

"And now, let's freshen up and go to Alice's for lunch. My treat," Drake said, feeling their bond of friendship had just grown stronger.

Lunching at Alice's was a treat, as usual. The morning's drama was not mentioned—heeding Charlie's advice—the conversation was limited to gallery business. Even Oscar put aside his earlier feelings of anger—a positive sign in his continuing recovery. His mind, instead of focusing on far-flung evil, was more and more often on what he could do to help his local fellow compatriots. Seeing their frown lines disappear while making music was a panacea for most of his ills. That, and his unexpected friendship with Drake and the others, were crucial elements in helping him feel whole again.

Drake closed up shop early. Before they left, he asked Patricia if she was pleased with the B & B. Her response was, "In every way except it is a bit confining."

Did he dare hope? Why not go for it?

"I have a solution to that. How about coming out to the farm on Saturday? You can see how a bachelor lives. I'll cook up a brunch and, if the weather permits, we'll take a long walk. Be good for you."

"You know—that sounds wonderful. What time?"

"Eleven?"

"Fine—what can I bring?"

"Two things—a huge appetite and a pair of walking shoes."

He and Oscar talked little on their way back to the farm, secure in their friendship, and a feeling of genuine brotherly love which neither of them had before experienced. Drake was elated Patricia had accepted his invitation without hesitation. He still felt the warmth in her earlier morning hug—a hug that he hoped was a breakthrough for both of them. Regardless, it had given him new hope and reaffirmed his belief that they were destined to be together.

He glanced across at Oscar who seemed relaxed and enjoying the familiar landscape. Although tempted, he refrained from telling him that Patricia would be spending Saturday on the farm. It would only have brought on additional friendly teasing, for sure.

It was Wednesday before Charlie contacted Drake about the gallery caper. Burt, the prime suspect, was interrogated by the sheriff. He named a friend as an alibi. The alibi didn't pan out. The parents reported their son had continued his drug use following his last altercation. Charlie took him outside for a private talk, where

Burt confessed he and the so-called friend were just funning around and meant no harm. Charlie's response was a lecture that left no choice for the young man: enter into a drug treatment program in Kirkwood—or go to jail. The leniency was due more to sympathy for the parents than to any favor to the perpetrator.

"It appears they picked the gallery just because it was there and near the Bucket of Blood where they had been booted from earlier. It didn't appear to be personal," Charlie added.

"That's a relief."

"I've given him a week to volunteer for treatment. If he doesn't show, I'll follow up by taking him into custody."

"Thanks, Charlie. I'm sure Oscar and the others will be relieved. I hope he will follow your advice and put an end to his shenanigans. After his run-in with Oscar at the Apple Festival, and the way he treated the girl, I fear he's headed for a heap more trouble. It's a shame."

For Drake, the remainder of the week passed at a snail's pace. The atmosphere at their workplace was much more relaxed. Patricia spent most of her time at the desk, addressing invitations for the opening—including the town officials, all business owners, and teachers from the local schools. Notices were sent to school and business personal in Kirkwood and Coopersville as a follow-up to the posters they had strategically placed earlier.

The weather warmed sufficiently for Roy to plant the previously bought evergreen shrubs along the front entrance, and boxwood at the base of the gallery sign—feeling that a possible cold snap in March would not damage them. Drake took before and after photos and wondered what Rhonda would think of their accomplishments. He was proud of the gallery and he was proud of his excellent crew.

Through Charlie, Drake learned that a group from Kirkwood had been inquiring about available property in Porterville for building a small out-patient clinic.

"I thought of your vacant lot, and also the extra space next to your gallery. You probably will never need it for additional parking since you already have a sizeable area. Would you be interested in selling it? You couldn't ask for a better business neighbor, and would save you the upkeep."

"I hadn't even thought of that. Wow! It would give me extra cash for maintaining the gallery until it supports itself."

"Exactly—would you like to discuss it with them?"

"A new building would be nice—if I have some say in the architecture. Wouldn't want it to clash with or detract from my gallery. Okay Charlie—won't hurt to discuss it."

"What about your other lot? Have any future plans for that?"

"None other than the upkeep when spring arrives."

"Well, you'll know when the time is right. That lovely administrative assistant you have might be interested. You think?"

"Charlie, if you keep this up, I'll have to recommend you for Porterville's chief matchmaker." *Gosh it was nice to have something to smile about.*

"I'll be in touch regarding your lot. In the meantime, stay cool."

"I keep forgetting to ask, Charlie—anything new regarding the Town Manager vacancy?"

"Nothing definite as far as I know—why do you ask?"

"Just curious, I guess. Do you think the present manager would agree to make a brief talk at my gallery opening? Would it be appropriate to ask?"

"I'm sure he would be pleased and flattered. I do know, he's impressed with what you're doing—considers you a definite asset to our town. He won't be leaving right away, not until a replacement has been hired. "

"Nice. Okay, go nab a few felons—but be careful."

Thirty-nine

*"And think not you can direct the course of love,
for love, if it finds you worthy, directs your course."*
Kahlil Gibran

Drake chose his Saturday brunch menu carefully. Everything in his apartment was polished and free of dust in anticipation of his very special visitor. The weather had warmed considerably on Friday, and during the night brought on an early season thunderstorm. Thunder rolling over the small mountain north of the highway awakened him. It sounded more like a tunneling through the hillside—filling the valley with sounds not unlike that of a bowling alley. Drake returned to his slumber resigned to his inability to control the weather. On the bright side, the rain would scrub the cedar deck—a chore he had left for last.

In spite of the earlier storm, he awoke to bright sunshine illuminating his room. His first thought was of Patricia—at least one dream was about to come true. His spirit lifted and banked like swallows in a March wind. As he sprang to his feet, he vowed to reign in his enthusiasm, treat her like a cherished friend instead of an object of desire. It was imperative that he further restore her faith in him. At least he felt capable in his culinary expertise.

His pulse quickened when he heard her car pull in behind his van. He took another quick look in the mirror, smoothed his thick hair, and rushed to the deck. A sight to behold was leaning against the car door, her eyes fixed on the panoramic view. He gloried in the moment before clearing his throat to get her attention.

"Good morning." *My love, gorgeous, sweetness—but he could say none of those things. It was too soon.*

"What a nice view," she said. "And that's the covered bridge you put in your painting—good job. I've never been out in this area."

"Come on up, the view isn't going anywhere." *That was a dumb comment by a person of my intelligence, he thought, grinning like a chipmunk.*

She was dressed in jeans—no silver belt this time—the collar of a cobalt blue blouse protruding from a light jacket. In her hand was a matching floral scarf.

"Something smells good," she said as they entered the apartment.

"Hollandaise sauce I just made for the eggs Benedict."

"You're kidding. I don't remember you ever cooking," she said, as he took her jacket.

"Hey, a man's gotta eat. I've ruined a few meals, but now that I'm old enough to read, it's no problem."

"I'm impressed."

Drake handed her a fresh brewed cup of dark roast. "Make yourself comfortable—it's humble but home."

Patricia moved to the south window. "That's a beautiful old house—large for a country home. I assume Tanner and Oscar live there?"

"You should see the inside—not at all what one would expect in a farmhouse."

"I like your apartment—small but more space than in my B&B. Nice light, and the view is great—peaceful. I can see why you like it here."

Drake sat two stem glasses of fresh squeezed orange juice on the already prepared table by the window.

"Can I help?" she asked, continuing to study the space and his belongings—the book shelves and his CD collection.

"Play some music, if you like, while I concentrate on the eggs."

Soon, they were seated at the small table sharing the well presented brunch like two best friends. The eggs Benedict were a hit. She was surprised to learn he had found Canadian bacon at their rural supermarket. The conversation was light and unhurried—food, country living, and art. No mention was made of their earlier involvement—what more was there to discuss? Neither had forgotten the cause of their breakup, and neither cared to rehash old hurts and mistakes. Drake preferred to concentrate on the future—painting, a successful gallery, and helping others realize their artistic dreams. Patricia remained ambivalent about her future—she had learned one couldn't always count on intentions.

With no conscious thought, her hand moved to her neck. The gesture happened less often now that the physical scars had healed. Instead of her usual turtlenecks, this morning she had chosen the blue front-buttoned blouse and felt unrestricted for the first time in months. Would she at some point tell Drake what had happened in New Mexico, and would she tell all or soft-soap the story of her past? What would be the benefit anyway?

Drake waited on her like an honored guest, insisting he needed no help with the cleanup— moved the plates to the sink, refilled their coffee cups, and sat back down.

"Drake, I believed you when you said you no longer drink and had no desire to do so, but I notice you still have a bottle," directing her gaze to the top of the refrigerator.

He explained that he kept it as a reminder of what he had lost and could still lose if he succumbed to the temptation. "It was put there as a challenge—so far, I'm winning." He gazed out the window to the covered bridge for some moments before turning back to her.

"Patricia, I signed a contract with myself when I stopped drinking—a contract to build something worthwhile of my life. I felt I owed it to the woman who sacrificed so much on my behalf. I don't think I've shown you this."

He took the charm from beneath the neck of his shirt. "This is a charm I found in the ashes on my lot in Porterville. It proves to me that my biological mother loved me and sacrificed herself in my behalf—so I could have a better life. I was out of my mind that morning, but if I had not set that fire, I would never have found this token of her love. And, I probably would never have been able to understand or forgive her for abandoning me."

Patricia fingered the charm and read the inscription. "I no longer believe in irony or serendipity when these things happen. I'm glad you found it. She must have been a very special lady."

He stood and reached out his hand. Although she had no idea of his intention, she stood and followed him. He removed the bottle from the rack and carried it to the counter. He let go of her hand, attached the opener, removed the cork, and turned back to her.

"Patricia, I no longer need this bottle to remind me to stay sober—you and the mother I never knew are my incentives—the only ones I need." He held the bottle over the sink and began to pour. Their gaze didn't waver until every drop of the wine gurgled down the drain until only the aroma remained. Even that held no appeal to him.

"It's just a bottle of wine," he said. "Never again will I jeopardize my future with alcohol. I need you to believe that."

The gesture and the sincerity in his eyes deeply moved her. He loved her that much? She lowered her gaze and hesitated—too touched to respond. She raised her eyes back to his and saw they contained his whole heart—waiting, and pleading.

"Yes, Drake, I do believe your intentions are true. I've seen your dedication to the gallery and to Oscar and the veterans, other artists

DECENT DECEIT

who haven't been given a chance to succeed—how could I not believe you? I also believe you won't fail this time. Life is no longer just about you. I see that—I'm proud of you."

"Could I have a hug?" he asked.

She laughed and walked into his arms, feeling safer in the moment than she had in a very long time. She soon pulled away as doubt slowly sneaked in. Could she trust her feelings? Could sweet words and even sweeter kisses obliterate the bad memories or would they re-open old wounds? She watched as he reluctantly moved away. He rinsed the empty bottle and dropped it into a recycle container, and placed their coffee cups in the sink. How could she gamble with his future happiness when her own remained so tentative?

Drake faced her again with a smile—a small one—but it was a smile. "Ready for that walk I promised?"

The sun was high in the sky, the winds were at rest and outside the window, birds were singing. He stepped out on the deck to check the temperature. "Still a bit chilly—you might want this."

He held her jacket but made no attempt to embrace her. He placed the scarf loosely around her neck but did not touch her. It was a perfect setting for a kiss but he sensed the timing was not ideal. A kiss wasn't imperative—her presence, however, was essential. *Give her time—give her time.*

Heeding Charlie's advice, Drake locked the door as they left although it seemed silly to do so in the tranquil setting. As they began their walk, his heart kept tune with the song of a mockingbird in the naked mulberry tree. Side by side they walked eastwardly, following the rural highway at the base of the heavily wooded low mountain terrain. On the right, the land sloped down to and beyond a meandering creek that flowed beneath the picturesque covered bridge. Their silence was broken only by their footsteps on the blacktop pavement. They were two lonely people who had met, loved briefly and parted, only to find each other again. At the moment, neither felt the need to rush into the future. The present was sufficient unto itself.

As they entered the bridge, they paused to watch and listen to the gurgling rushing stream beneath. They rested, leaning their arms on a horizontal board, their elbows touching. Three missing vertical boards provided them a perfect viewing spot to study the water waltzing over smooth pebbles below, and the naked graceful branches of a weeping willow tree.

"So, how do you like this little piece of Eden?" Drake asked.

"It's so lovely I have no other words to describe it. You were right—I did need this. It's as if the rest of the world doesn't exist." She thought of the New Mexico terrain but quickly put it out of her mind. "The world is such a mess—so many, like Oscar, are caught up in the senseless atrocities. By the way, how is he doing?" she asked.

"Great improvement from when I first met him. The Key of C combo has given him a new purpose. I think he's going to be okay. You don't get over PTSD easily—it takes time, but his buddies and their music are proving to be good medicine. Neither of us have siblings, so we've become almost like brothers. He needed a purpose and I believe he has found the perfect one."

A lone car approached the bridge and they moved closer to the side until it passed—whistles and hoots followed. "Shall we head back?" he asked.

As they stepped again into the sunshine, Patricia's foot slipped on loose gravel. Drake instantly reached out to steady her—moved his hand down her arm until their fingers entwined. Her small hand fit snugly within his—she didn't jerk away. He smiled. Assured she was okay, they continued on their way—not another person in sight—only cattle grazing in the meadow and the forlorn whistle of a distant train.

"So what do you do for entertainment out here?" she asked. "I'd probably just sit on the deck and enjoy the view."

"I did that a lot when I first moved here. Choices are limited, but you get used to it. The Tanners are great neighbors. We have meals together occasionally—and play a lot of pool. I paint when I can—sure don't miss the city life." He stopped and faced her. "You bored already?"

"Oh no, this is wonderful. I was thinking how beautiful it must be in the spring with everything green and wild flowers in bloom." She reached down and snapped off the head of a dried thistle.

He pointed to a stand of trees in the meadow near the house. "Another month or so those fruit trees will be in bloom with pink and white blossoms. You'll have to come back out then—and also in the autumn—to pick apples."

He told her about the Apple Festival and, in answer to her question, more details about the Bucket of Blood altercation. He also told her about Charlie's relationship with his mother and how she had asked him to keep tabs on him after his adoption.

"No wonder you two are close."

"And during all those years, I never knew it was taking place just a few miles away."

As they neared the apartment, Drake told her about the car accident when Oscar had first come home, and how his training had taken over to save the life of the driver. "It hasn't been dull around here, for sure."

They re-entered the apartment and Drake hung her jacket and scarf by the door, went to the refrigerator for iced raspberry tea he had made earlier. They settled on the sofa, slightly breathless from the long walk. "Do I hear music?" she asked.

Drake went to the south window and lifted it a few inches. "Come here—Oscar, playing his saxophone. He used to play almost every evening. He's amazingly talented. At first, his music was haunting—sad, yet beautiful—as if he was house-cleaning his heart. Knowing him has made me feel guilty for not enlisting and doing my part.

He's quite a guy, and his father is a fine man, too. Meeting them and moving out here has actually changed my life. They and Charlie have become family. I'm very lucky."

"His music is heart-felt, for sure." She moved back to the sofa. A passing cloud dimmed the sunlight and Drake lowered the window against the slight chill.

"How about watching an old movie?" Drake asked—not wanting her to leave.

"Didn't you tell me you have *Shadows in the Sun?*"

"I do. Good choice and one of my favorites." He handed the DVD to her and went to the kitchen cabinet for bags of chips which he seldom opened—and popcorn. Soon they were relaxed and laughing as if the past had been but a figment of their imagination. They laughed at the comical parts and held their breath at the end when the priest took the bird with the pretend broken leg out of the cage and released it through the train window. The movie ended with the lovers riding off through the Tuscan countryside atop two beautiful thoroughbred horses—into an undisclosed future—the stuff movies were made of.

Patricia was the first to move from the comfort of the sofa, gathered their empty glasses and snack bags—taking them the few steps to Drake's efficiency kitchen. "I must be going," she said, "unless I can help clean up? I didn't intend to stay this long."

"I'll do it later. Would you like to go down and say hello to Oscar and Tanner?"

"Not this time. I told Bea I would be back for dinner."

"You could call her."

"She has probably already started dinner. I really enjoyed the day, Drake—your brunch—you get an A in cooking—the walk and the movie."

"It has been a good day. Thank you for sharing it with me." He reached for her jacket, not wanting her to go but thankful for their time together. She allowed him to help with her jacket but not the scarf. She took it from him. "I don't think I'll need that—and realized it was true."

He walked her down the steps to her car, and with hands safely secured in his pockets, kissed her lightly on the forehead.

"I'll see you on Monday, then." He watched her car until it disappeared around a curve, leaving him with a feeling of emptiness. He climbed the steps but stopped on the deck to drink in the view—seeing it through Patricia's eyes—a view that had taken on even greater significance than before. A quote by Steinbeck came to mind, *"If it's right it happens. The main thing is not to hurry. Nothing good gets away."* He smiled and took out his phone, keyed in Oscar's number. A few games of pool to fill the evening were in order.

Forty

"Time flies over us but leaves its shadow behind." Nathaniel Hawthorne

Patricia was unaware of the countryside as she drove leisurely back to Porterville and her small private world at the B&B. The memory of Drake—his touch, the tender kiss on her forehead— unnerved her. Was she walking precariously along a narrow ledge of heartbreak or disaster? Was she placing him in a similar position by renewing their association? Was he, too, wearing a mask, as she had grown accustomed to doing? Laughing masks, tear-streaked masks, evil masks of feathers or beaks—masks of any kind—doesn't everyone, at one time or another, wear the one that suits them best? Would there come a time when she would be compelled to take off her mask and reveal all?

She didn't question Drake's promise as he disposed of the wine— another bottle was easily obtainable—nor did she doubt his sincerity. She believed this new Drake really loved her. She wanted to be free to love him back but could she gamble on his newfound strength and sobriety? Could she destroy his optimism for the future by emptying her heart to him, revealing a secret she had vowed to keep to herself? How strong would he remain if she told him the truth? He had lost everyone, two sets of parents, and herself—a woman he had counted on but who turned her back on him at his weakest moment. Could he handle one more deceit—a deceit of omission? Would he be able to understand and forgive as he had with his biological mother? Could she live with the possible consequences? She thought of John Kennedy's comment about truth. *"The greatest enemy of truth is very often not the lie—deliberate, contrived, and dishonest—but the myth—persistent, persuasive, and unrealistic."*

Her jumbled thoughts continued throughout dinner—the other lone guest had little to say.

"You're unusually quiet, Patricia," Bea said after they had finished dinner and the guest had retired to her room. "You didn't enjoy your day?"

"It was a beautiful day. I guess I'm just tired—and a bit concerned about the upcoming gallery opening. For Drake's sake, I hope all goes well. He's worked so hard to make it a success."

"I wouldn't worry. It's like a wedding, the bridal party is always apprehensive—yet I've never been to a wedding that wasn't beautiful." Patricia wasn't sure that was a good analogy but didn't wish to discuss it further. She wished she could share what really concerned her, but she would continue to keep her own council. As for the gallery opening, she would do her best not to disappoint Drake. Afterwards—she had no idea in what direction she would go.

Decisions needed to be made and they couldn't be postponed forever. Her rooms were pleasant and served her present purpose, but she must find a place of her own and build a life for herself. Her few earthly goods could not remain in public storage forever.

On Sunday, the walls of her room seemed to shrink to closet size—her thoughts as cluttered and crowded. She left the B&B and walked down an alee of trees to the lake beyond, accompanied only by nature sounds and the playfulness of a family of red squirrels. The breadth of the lake surprised her—what a lovely spot—totally unspoiled by human intrusion. On the far bank, a stag deer stood at attention as if the sound of her footsteps had called to him across the placid water. She sat down to rest on a nearby boulder, clearing her mind of everything but the magnificence of nature. Thoughts of Drake and their past sneaked in, but she deleted them quickly, focusing her attention on the peaceful surroundings. The whistles and peeps of birds, the pecking sound of a woodpecker foraging for an entrée of bugs or worms—just the emotional nourishment she needed.

She envied Bea and her ownership of such a special property. She hoped it would never be disturbed at the hands of greedy developers. The house and grounds were a perfect example of the disappearing rural landscape. She understood why Drake found his quiet lifestyle so appealing—free of city noises, pollution, crime, and lack of privacy. Had she been hungry for this all along?

When she returned to her room her mind was clearer and her heart lighter. She opened the window a few inches, and settled with her laptop into a comfortable chintz-covered wingback chair. Many inquiries had been made of the services Drake offered the public. If they followed through, Drake may not find time to pursue his own personal creativity. She hoped that wouldn't happen—his work was too promising for him to take a back seat to teaching and administrative duties.

With some reluctance, she had given him permission to display her portrait at the opening, but not on the website. Three of the private studio spaces had been rented by practicing artists, living obscurely in the local area. Ms. Cloud from the university art department had promised a series of lectures in autumn, after she returned from her vacation in Taos, giving Drake added encouragement.

An impressive portrait of Roy would also be on view. His flamboyant persona never failed to amuse her. He, too, had been able to turn his life around, not be a slave to addiction, and Drake had been his savior. He was now turning out paintings that impressed not only

Drake but others as well. This was in spite of his wife finalizing a divorce, ending a marriage that shouldn't have happened in the first place. He and his daughter, Sophia, remained close. She and his art kept him in a happy and creative frame of mind. When not painting he performed any chore around the gallery that needed to be done. He, Drake and Oscar worked together like a well-oiled clock. They had accepted her into their fold but she continued to keep her emotional luggage packed. Her heart urged her to store it away permanently, but could she do it?

Forty-one

*"When I die and go to Heaven, I want to spend
the first million years painting so I can get to
the bottom of the subject."* W. Churchill

On Monday morning, as Drake neared Porterville, he lowered his window to the fast approaching warmth of spring. He drove by the church and cemetery as he did every morning, hoping to spend some quiet time at his easel. His personal painting time was limited, of necessity, until after the gallery opening—as would romantic thoughts and daydreams of Patricia. He found the latter two most difficult. Their Saturday time together had been wonderful although he continued to feel she was holding some part of herself within. He sensed that anything more intimate than what they had already shared remained off limits.

What is it you're hiding, Patricia? Are you afraid I'll start drinking again? Between us, there's a web I don't dare walk into—it might contain spiders. Tell me—whatever it is, I'll understand.

Preparing for the upcoming opening was a good diversion—otherwise his time would be spent—day and night—thinking of a girl he had previously seen through a lens of alcohol, never seeing her as she truly was—kind, warm, and willing to love with her whole being. No doubt his weakness had held her true feelings at bay. He had been indifferent to her custom of running her fingers through his hair or letting her hand caress his cheek as she moved behind his chair—the way she had looked at him with adoration in the beginning. He had been as blind as one born without sight. Now, he felt only tenderness for her, every touch, every smile was a precious gift. He was impatient, but a successful opening of his gallery had to take priority over his personal dilemma.

He had already failed as a collegiate—at least he hadn't given it a fighting chance. He didn't want to fail in his pursuit of the arts. It was imperative that he become a success in at least one aspect of his life. Even more important, he didn't want to fail as a human being or disappoint those who had befriended him when he most needed support. Had that been his main fear all along—was that a part of what he had struggled with? How could others have understood him when he hadn't understood himself?

All of that was now in the past. He would become a decent person or die in the attempt. The good part—he was no longer alone in his efforts. New friends were now family. He had no more excuses. If Patricia failed to become a star in his universe he would give his all to his art, the establishment of the gallery, guiding others in their search for artistic fulfillment. He wanted to believe that the Gods would smile on his efforts to become a decent man, and make Patricia a part of his life. Having her would be the icing on the cake.

Drake drove into the parking lot as the warm March wind swept away the leaves and last fragments of winter. The newly planted shrubbery was thriving in the warmth and sunshine. He was now a business owner and he felt as proud as a peacock.

He had a free hour before the others arrived at ten. All the important steps had been put into motion. Almost all the invitations were accepted. A microphone had been obtained. The Town Manager was to give a short talk, as was Ms. Cloud from Kaiser College in Coopersville, outlining a series of lectures in the autumn. The three college students would be on hand for their first gallery showing of their art. He could only imagine their excitement—and that of the parents. Oscar had chosen the music for the evening and his Key of C players were excited that they once again had a purpose. Charlie and Tom would be on hand as guests but also to assure there would be no mischief making. It was shaping up to be an exciting evening for not only Drake but for everyone involved.

Other exciting changes were taking place—the least of which was Tanner's agreement to accept the job of Town Manager—his term to begin later in the year. Drake had sold his Harley and was comfortable with the outlay of money for what would no doubt be the most exciting evening of his life.

His team arrived on time, refreshed and excited. Patricia joined the three men with a yellow legal pad on which to list the steps left to be taken to assure a successful *grande* opening. In spite of their remote setting, the website was beginning to accumulate followers and inquiries about what they had to offer: workshops, lessons, atelier space, gallery shows for lesser known artists, and a special welcome to wounded warriors. With Oscar on board, they would find encouragement and help in pursuing their creative dreams.

Modern technology made it possible to reach the world at the click of a button. However, the people of Porterville and surrounding area who had welcomed him so warmly were Drake's primary foci. It was where he felt he could make a difference, where artistic study opportunity had been neglected or less than ideal. Everything was falling into place—almost as if a divine presence was calling the shots—and Patricia was completing the circle. He was a fortunate man.

Forty-two

"When you work you are a flute through whose heart the whispering of the hours turns to music. Which of you would be a reed, dumb and silent, when all else sings together in unison?
Kahlil Gibran

The day before the opening, Drake watched Patricia—wearing her legal pad like a fashion accessory—walk through the gallery, her focus on every detail. He saw her much as Gibran (The Prophet) said when he spoke of beauty: *she shall come with the spring leaping upon the hills.* For Drake, she had arrived *like a garden forever in bloom and a flock of angels forever in flight.* She had become a valuable asset in his adventure, putting aside any personal ambition to focus entirely on making his dream come true. It saddened him that he couldn't possibly reciprocate until she revealed her own dreams. Did he dare believe they could ever be one and the same? He gently removed the pad she held against her chest. "Patricia, please try to relax. Everything is perfect and you have made it so. I've sent Oscar and Roy home and now I'm taking you to lunch."

"Are you sure we haven't forgotten anything?" she asked.

"If we have, so be it. You've helped make this a much more impressive occasion than I ever imagined. Let's have lunch and do whatever else you'd like the rest of the day. Okay?"

She hesitated only a moment. "I could use a break, I guess. I have a tendency to over-think a new project."

Drake laughed. "I've noticed," he said, his eyes teasing.

At the cafe, Alice greeted them warmly. She, too, was excited and a wee bit nervous about the role she and her food would play in the Art Center Open House. Consequently, Drake and Patricia endured another period of reassurances before they could talk of other things.

"Do you think Alice and Charlie will get married," Patricia asked, after they had finished a bowl of homemade chicken chili and the best cornbread in the county.

"There's no question they're much taken with each other. Charlie doesn't see how they would have much time for each other if they did marry. I think they may have gotten used to their singular existence and hesitate to take the plunge—or they could be happy with things the way they are. Too much togetherness is not always a good thing either. Haven't you heard about the man in Florida who shot and killed his wife for nagging him to death?"

"I'm not surprised. I've known women and an occasional man who talk as if their tongues are attached in the middle—loose on both ends," she responded, beginning to relax.

"I don't think we have to worry about that."

Patricia decided to change the subject. "Drake, do you know about the lake behind the B&B?

"Heard about it—been meaning to check it out for fishing."

"How would you like to go now? It's a great place to unwind."

"Let's go." With a wave to Alice, they were on their way, pausing to admire the new pansy plants Alice had added to her window boxes. Petunias would appear next, for sure.

They stopped briefly at the B&B to inform Bea of their trespassing plan. She didn't own the lake—it belonged to the State, although both properties merged. She informed Drake that fishing was allowed if he had a license. The buds of azaleas were bursting forth with bloom, framing the wrap-around porch with color.

They continued on, walking quietly and unhurriedly along the natural pathway between the trees—now clothed in pea-green raiment of the season. On the shaded floor beneath the trees young ferns peeped through the mulch like baby chicks escaping their shell. It was a bit early for May-apples, but red-breasted robins waltzed about in search of food. Overhead, squirrels chased each other among the tree branches. Ah! Spring!—*when a young man's fancy turned to thoughts of love*—also true of squirrels apparently.

The lake came into view, the size surprising Drake—definitely more impressive than a farm pond—and not a house in sight. "Lovely," he said. "Let's hope it stays this way. A developer would have a field day with this property."

They soon found comfortable seating on the large fallen tree trunk—casting a single shadow from the mid-afternoon sun. Drake, his mind on Patricia more than the flora and fauna, asked, "Isn't your room at the B&B becoming a bit confining?"

"Somewhat, but aside from breakfast, Bea invites me for dinner occasionally. I think she's lonely. She's such a permanent fixture her image could easily merge with the Peace roses and Queen Ann's lace in the wallpaper. I sense she would welcome retirement."

"It's a lovely old house. The previous owner—a lady doctor—probably had servants. I can see a butler greeting guests dressed in a waistcoat."

Patricia laughed. "More likely her patients paid her with farm produce, chickens and fresh eggs."

After another peaceful silence, "Actually, I've enjoyed the simple living with minimal belongings, although I would like to update some of the décor to the present century."

"Why don't you buy the place from her?"

"You must be kidding."

"Speaking of which—have you given any thought to the future—a place of your own?"

He held his breath waiting for her response. The answer didn't come—only silence—encouraging him to speak further. "I've been hoping you'd stay on as my assistant after the opening."

"I have to admit my interest in the town and your gallery is growing. I like being surrounded by art, now that I know more about it. The people are nice and friendly—I like Oscar and Roy, Alice, and now Bea—she treats me like a daughter."

"Porterville might be a good place to settle down. It's showing signs of growth. We'll have a new medical clinic next door to the gallery, and you've probably noticed that some of the merchants are already sprucing up for spring."

"You sold the lot?"

"Sure did. A new building will be an improvement over the empty eyesore. I sold it with the provision that I'd have a say in the architecture. I still have my lot further down the street, but I'm not anxious to dispose of it—for some reason—too much else on my mind."

"Could it be because of its past history?

Drake looked at her—surprised at her question—and leaving him struggling for an honest answer. Actually, he hadn't thought of it that way. Did her question indicate she still cared about him and his state of mind?

"It's not easy," she continued, "to dispose of a past like an out-of-style dress. I miss Mom, but it was time to shed my coat of many colors—so to speak."

"Better than me—trying to dispose of my past with a cigarette lighter—can't believe I did that. I also can't believe Charlie came to my defense in the way he did. Instead of managing my own gallery, I could have butt calluses from sitting in a jail cell. I've learned it's wise to go slowly instead of trying to force things before the time is right."

"You mean practicing patience leaves space for good things to happen."

She took her time before continuing. "To answer your question, I should find an apartment, at least temporarily. I appreciate the job and you wanting me to stay on, but let's first see how the opening goes. I tend to think of only one thing at a time—I do want it to be a success. If I do leave, I'll give you plenty of notice—the least I can do."

"I've come to depend on you and your acumen. Oscar will have no time to assist in running the place if his music project continues to expand. And Roy, of course, has no business experience—he's a born painter."

They reluctantly left the tranquil spot—Patricia to her solitary room for a nap before dinner with Bea, and Drake to his apartment and an even later dinner with the Tanners.

Drake drove home under a graphite sky, pulling to the berm of the road to allow an occasional car or farm truck to pass. Sheep and spring lambs dotted the landscape—fruit trees now pregnant with buds—promising new life and new beginnings. He felt more relaxed about Patricia and their future. He now owned a gallery—a dream coming to fruition—but he didn't fool himself. It wouldn't be a success overnight but it was already showing positive signs for the future. He felt good about the community. Porterville was taking on a new face—next door a new medical facility for the body—and his gallery for the soul. The thought made him smile. Other merchants were taking pride in the town, painting and refurbishing. The ice cream shop welcomed customers with a new sign and multicolored balloons.

At Alice's Diner, over breakfast, lunch and dinner, citizens discussed and debated the state of the world, the latest terrorist activity—or the never-ending political scene. They had reasons to doubt the future but, for the most part, they remained optimistic. According to Alice, there was also much talk and excitement about his new art center and his plans for the future.

Drake's mish-mash of thoughts went to Alex, his ADHD student. The boy's mother reported that he appeared more focused since starting painting lessons. Drake had seen a gradual improvement in his attention span. He seemed to have a natural desire to create art. One day, he had shown up at the gallery unannounced after school with a package wrapped in what appeared to be butcher paper from the corner grocery. Drake watched from his easel as the boy entered timidly, clutching the small bundle under his arm. He browsed the gallery, prancing on one foot and then the other before each painting, and then started for the door. Drake caught up to him before he disappeared.

"What do you have there?" Drake asked.

"Nothing—I just wanted to see the show."

Drake had gotten to know the boy pretty well. "Looks like you have a painting—want to show me?"

"No, I guess not. It's just something I did on my own. You wouldn't like it—looks like it was painted by a goat."

Drake turned his back because his ribs were about to split from holding back a laugh— he didn't dare allow it to grow in momentum. A straight face was required or the boy's self confidence would be further shattered. He cleared his throat and turned back. "I have time. Let's see what you have."

It wasn't bad—much better than a goat could create. The 8 x 10 canvas depicted an amateurish rendition of an empty rocking chair, beside it a dog lying with head resting on its paws."

"Is this your dog, Alex?"

"Now it is—it was Grandpa's—before he died."

An empty rocking chair and the comment drained Drake of all

mirth. His heart turned to putty in the boy's hand. There was only one thing to do.

"Alex, I think your painting should be included in our show. Will you allow me to hang it?"

The young artist pulled his shoulders higher as his eyes brightened. "Grandpa would like that. Buddy was his pal."

"Come with me," he said. Drake led him to his work space, and asked him to sign the painting. He obeyed without comment—printing his name in the lower right corner. Drake then went in the back and returned with a hammer and nail. He found a prominent spot near the front of the gallery. "How about here—where everyone can see it?"

Seeing his little painting hanging with other nicely framed canvases, his young eyes glistened—his grin grew wider. "Mr. Drake, you're the best man I ever met—except for Grandpa."

Later, as Drake approached the farm, he saw Tanner rocking on the front porch—much like at their first meeting—only this time O'Toole lay on the floor beside him. He was smoking his pipe and the tobacco odor was no doubt blending with nature's spring eau-d-cologne of freshly mowed grass and apple blossoms.

Tanner and Oscar had been restoring Annabelle's garden to a semblance of order. Tender shoots of hydrangea and peonies were already peeping through the soil. Crocus and daffodils first planted by Tanner's mother and continued by Annabelle, added accents of yellow and blue. He and Oscar had tilled and planted the garden, including herbs at Drake's request. Marigold seeds were planted in a row surrounding the vegetables to discourage bugs. Drake recalled Oscar's return home, how they had made small talk—neither of them knowing quite what to say. Now all tension was gone and they were like brothers.

Drake tooted his horn and gave Tanner a wave before parking under the garage overhang. Leaves appeared on the mulberry tree by the deck, the creek in the meadow ran freely from fresh spring rain while billowy clouds moved about—obscuring a cerulean sky. March slid into April as smoothly as strawberry jam. He drank in the view as if it were fine wine.

Forty-three

"Every day one ought to hear a little song, read a good poem, and view a fine picture and, if possible, speak a few reasonable words." Goethe

The Opening
SECOND CHANCE ART CENTER

Drake's first thought on Patricia's arrival was the transformation from a few hours earlier. He was used to seeing her in jeans and t-shirt—skirts and blouses when on the job—but he'd never seen her look more lovely. She wore an emerald green dress that could have been especially designed for her. A rare gem herself, the color suited her, at least to Drake's eyes. She had swept her raven hair up off her neck with soft tendrils escaping over her cameo tinted forehead. Her cheeks were a blushing pink, her lips a matching gloss—makeup subtle and appropriate for the evening. She looked stunning. More importantly—she looked happy. Temptation was in full swing, causing Drake to clasp his hands tightly behind his back.

The day had been a whirl of activity for all of them. In addition to the special invitations, the public was invited as well. As Drake often said, "Art should be for everyone." And this included parents with children—never too early to introduce them to art. A three hour opening was long but he wanted to accommodate everyone, young and old. The city manager had requested a few minutes to speak to the guests and Drake was grateful for his offer. Members of the staff from Kaiser College, including Ms. Cloud from the art department, local business owners, and many throughout the countryside who had never attended an Art Center opening were expected.

The doors were closed at four, giving Oscar, Patricia, Alice, and Roy as well as Drake time to go home and spruce up for the big night. Adrenalin was working overtime. They were high on accomplishment yet apprehensive about the evening—perfectly normal. It would not be the usual gallery opening with wine and cheese and a sprinkling of art enthusiasts with nothing more interesting to do. Drake was offering a bit of culture for the masses plus an evening of fun, fine art, and music. It would not be dull, and it was a perfect venue to also introduce Oscar and his band to the community.

Drake's second thought on seeing his co-host was that everything about her was new and unexpected. He observed how absolutely perfect her ears were. He knew her lips—if he were privileged to kiss them—would be as soft as a peony petal, lush as a ripened peach. His senses were keen as a laser beam—he missed nothing. There was no doubt he was experiencing genuine love. He ached to feel those lips again and kiss the eyelids each morning to awaken her. During the brief moments of eye contact nothing else mattered—they were alone in the cosmos. Concerns of the world, the opening, even his past, disappeared like a meteorite.

She paused briefly when their eyes met—then came toward him without hesitation. This was not only his night of celebration but a night of accomplishment for Patricia. It had been a new adventure and possibly an introduction to her future. She not only wanted it to be a success for herself but also for Drake. He deserved it.

"Patricia, you're bubbly and beautiful—like champagne, and I'm root beer," he told her when he finally managed to make his mouth work, "but you're not playing fair—coming in here looking irresistible."

Reminding herself to keep it light, she said, "You clean up pretty well yourself." His sandy hair was groomed to perfection, no four o'clock shadow, and his dark suit suggestive of Brook's Brothers. She had never seen him look more handsome or self-confident. He was a young Robert Redford with thick hair the color of wheat, a sprinkling of gray at the temples—his blue-gray eyes sparkling. How much longer would she be able to resist him?

Boundaries be dammed! His lips first found the softness of her cheek and moved briefly to her lips. The wall that had kept them apart for so long began to crumble—and not a moment too soon.

Their private moments were soon interrupted by the arrival of the crew. Oscar and his Key of C Players appeared in full uniform—with shiny medals and ribbons—as a tribute to those still fighting for a safe world. In uniform their injuries were less evident. Dan, the drummer, wore a lower left arm and hand prosthesis, only the hand visible. Eddie, with a partial prosthetic leg walked with a barely distinguishable limp. Oscar guided Steven—legally blind and wearing dark glasses—to the stage Roy had constructed for the occasion—and guided him to the keyboard. They were making a statement and Drake applauded them.

The musicians showed surprise on seeing an easel holding a poster with their name and logo. Oscar was speechless and the others stood a little taller. "A surprise from Tanner," Drake told them. They took their places and began fine-tuning their instruments for their debut public appearance. Oscar showed no sign of nervousness or frustration—his focus on the music and his buddies. His future was being realized. He had come a long way from the battled and discouraged soldier Drake first met at the farm. He was the closest thing to a brother a man could have, and he felt proud that he had played a small part in his recovery. The Key of C Players had found a future and a purpose. At the end of the evening they would realize how much joy their purpose could bring to others.

Roy arrived looking very European in a dark suit and multi-colored bow tie as striking as his art. As usual, the black beret added to his debonair persona. Sophia—now a lovely young lady—proudly held her father's arm close as she admired his canvases.

Alice arrived through the back entrance, laden with more last-minute finger food. Drake gave her a hug when she appeared at the long serving table, making sure everything was ready. "Alice. I hope we have sufficient hungry people to eat all this food."

"If the grapevine can be believed, there won't be leftovers."

Charlie, spit-shined and polished in his dress uniform, congratulated Drake, giving him a man hug. "Well, you've done it, son—now relax and enjoy yourself. I knew..." His comments were cut short when a red-haired lady at the buffet table caught his attention. For once, she was without her apron, but wearing her familiar smile.

Drake didn't miss the change in the sheriff's demeanor. "Looking good—don't you think?" he asked with a teasing grin and lifted eyebrow.

"And your Patricia is a vision," he said, turning away as he muttered, "God help us." He gave Drake a thumbs-up and added, "I'd better start performing my duty. Tom is on duty so I'm at your service. Give me a signal if you need me."

With that, he made his way through the mostly familiar guests to the front entrance. Drake laughed and reminded himself of how lucky he was to have found such a friend. His fingers touched the charm beneath his starched white shirt. His thoughts had often gone to Rhonda while preparing for this night. He hoped her spirit was with them and that he'd finally make her proud.

For the first hour, mostly students and parents arrived, including Alex and his mother. Drake watched as he showed her his painting hanging among the others—hands in pockets and hopping from one foot to the other. Later, while Alex, still skinny as a plucked pullet, joined other school children, his mother approached Drake. Her emotions were obvious. "May I hug you?" she asked. "I can never thank you enough for what you are doing for Alex. He can't stop talking about you." Drake hugged her in return. "His little painting of the empty rocking chair and dog was too powerful not to include in the show. I was quite touched by it. A story I may someday want to tell my own son."

"You should know that what you have done for our little town is touching a lot of people in the community. God bless you. I hope your lovely gallery will be a huge success."

People came and went, including a few uniformed soldiers—no doubt friends of the Key of C Players. They hung around the band like every note played was manna from Heaven. A couple of them wore civilian clothes with visible scars—others wore undetectable scars—buried deep in their sub-conscious.

Drake's eyes seldom left Patricia for long. She interacted with the guests like a pro, answering questions about the paintings and making them feel welcome. Her laughter caught his attention on occasion, warming his heart. Drake also didn't fail to notice when the men sought her expertise regarding a still life or landscape. *Sorry, hands off—she's mine.* Alongside each painting, she had placed a card with the artist name, genre of painting, and price—knowledge she had gained from Santa Fe galleries.

Drake received many compliments about his work as well as those by other artists—particularly Roy's landscapes. The three artists chosen from the university brought friends and family—as did faculty members—to support their debut showing. As the evening progressed, Patricia added red dots to a number of paintings to indicate they were sold, each time with a nod to Drake. Her smile said it all. Roy stood a bit taller with each positive comment or red dot, and Drake was happy for him.

Mr. Davis, the town manager, arrived along with his office entourage. The main gallery was almost filled with well-wishers. Food and punch were being devoured, and guests were not only greeting friends and neighbors, they showed real interest in the art and often applauded the Key of C. The music played on with short breaks between songs.

Oscar geared the music to the crowd—light classics from Andrew Lloyd Weber for the more mature guests. Early arrivers were treated to country ballads and hymns. Some asked for favorites like *Danny Boy* and Burl Ives *Little Bitty Tear.* When guests entered the meditation room where Drake's portraits were hung, Oscar switched to a soft rendition of *Starry, Starry Night* and *Claire de Lune.* Guests gathered around when he pulled a stool closer to the mike and began *Amazing Grace* on his saxophone. Drake remembered the first time he heard Oscar play the song after his return home and how it had touched his heart. The song now touched the many guests—indicated by the hush in the room as the former soldier, his eyes closed, made the saxophone sob.

Mr. Davis took the mike, tapped his glass for silence. Everyone gathered around as he placed his hand on Drake's shoulder.

"Drake, I want to congratulate you and your crew, and thank you for all you're doing for Porterville and our county. You came to us as a stranger during a weak economy, established a business, and gave us renewed hope in the future. You've taken this abandoned eyesore and transformed it into a place of and for beauty."

Turning to the crowd, he continued. "Next door, we'll have a badly needed new medical facility with visiting specialists on the staff. It will be dedicated to the memory of our own late but beloved Dr. Ella, and her influence in the community. With people like you, Drake, and Dr. Ella, the blood of Porterville will continue to flow freely."

Following a loud applause, he directed more comments to the

guests. "I have more good news: Our former antique row and flea market at the other end of town is being refurbished and will open in May on weekends. This will entice the many who pass through our town to stop and do business with us. The spaces are already reserved for summer. I want to thank all our business owners for sprucing up your establishments with fresh paint and flowers—presenting smiley faces to our residents and visitors alike."

He hesitated before continuing. "And now, for the hard part: Some of you may already know that after a long and happy ten years, I'm resigning as your town manager. However, I'm leaving you in good hands. Mr. Tanner—where are you?" Tanner stepped up to another round of applause. He gave the people a run-down on Tanner's accomplishments and qualifications for the job.

After a hand shake, he added. "Treat him well—he'll do a great job."

"If I could have your attention, I'd like to share a few thoughts before I take my leave. With a new Art Center, and a new town manager, Porterville will grow and thrive as an example of small town America, continuing our tradition of friendship and love of neighbor. Terrorists are attempting to wipe away the smiles of many people around the civilized world, including our own country. In Porterville, with people like Drake, Oscar and our veterans, friendship, decency and beauty will thrive. Our troubled youth are gaining self-respect through art and music. Oscar and the Key of C Players—the C is for Caring, by the way—are examples of how physical and emotional scars can be healed through the arts. I'm told that music lessons will be available to our disabled veterans—and at a reduced rate. We all appreciate your sacrifice. Let's give our talented musicians a big hand."

Drake took the mike, thanked Mr. Davis for his comments and encouragement, and wished him a happy retirement. He next introduced Patricia and thanked her for her contribution, "I doubt if I could have done it without you. We hope you'll be around indefinitely to assure the success of this new undertaking."

He then turned to a startled Roy. "And to Roy, who has been indispensible in helping me establish this gallery, but mostly, we all want to congratulate you on your return to the art world as a talented contributor—evidenced by the canvases shown here tonight.

And, Oscar, words can't express how grateful I am for your friendship and for the hours of beautiful music you've given me—through your window to mine—and especially for tonight. I predict it won't be long before the Key of C Players and their music will be known far and wide. I'm proud to have you on my team."

Drake turned back to the guests. "I've opened this gallery so that everyone, young and old, rich and poor, can have access to the arts—not only for viewing but for learning as well. The pamphlets will spell out what we are offering in lessons. In addition there will be lectures from Dr. Cloud from Kaiser University, work-shops, and I hope to also sponsor an artist retreat in the near future. Please visit often. I appreciate your generous gift of welcome to your town, and now—back to Oscar and his Key of C Players."

After the speech, an elderly gentleman—a man who impressed on first sight—approached Drake. Dressed in a dark suit and tie, he also wore a gray, well trimmed beard that complimented his silver hair. His head leaned permanently toward his left shoulder, his blue eyes friendly and clear. "I'm Rev. Stevens from the Presbyterian Church. I've seen you visit the cemetery on several occasions and am pleased to finally meet you."

Drake shook his hand and welcomed him to the gallery, instantly impressed with the minister's kindly manner and stately stance.

"I knew your mother well," the Pastor continued. "She was a fine lady and would be proud of what you have accomplished here in our town."

Drake's mind went blank before realizing the entire town

probably knew of his history. It was a small town after all.

"Thank you, Sir. I wish I had known her."

"The next time you visit, stop in my office and we'll have a chat."

It was an awkward moment, but the minister's smile eased the tension. "Your paintings are beautiful. We need more people to bring attention to God's creativity—the beauty all around us—don't you think?"

"That's what I'm trying to do, in my small way."

"We seldom know the good we do—the point is to keep trying." He reached out his hand once more before taking his leave.

Patricia and Charlie watched the exchange with interest and both joined Drake as he watched the minister depart. "That man is worth knowing, Drake. You can learn a lot from him," Charlie said.

"He knew my mother. I wasn't expecting that."

"He's been here almost as long as the church—no, he's not quite that old. He's a wise and respected man regardless of religious leanings."

"I'll have to stop in and get to know him better."

The conversation ended abruptly when another visitor entered the door—a man Drake hadn't ever expected to see again. In fact, he had almost succeeded in erasing the man from his memory.

"Do you know that man?" Charlie asked, seeing Drake's smile change to concern.

"Yes, but I wish I didn't. He was my father's law partner—Brian—a sensationally uninteresting man." After a moment of pause, he added, "An ignoramus who bought a helicopter with no place to land it. What's he doing here? I certainly didn't send him an invitation."

Patricia, too, sensed Drake's discomfort. She came closer and placed her hand on his arm.

They watched closely as the somewhat bedraggled looking man, sheepishly walked about the paintings while sending furtive glances in Drake's direction. The crowd had thinned. The music stopped and Oscar turned to Drake. What he saw was a look of dismay on his friend's face. Charlie, too, saw his *could have been son's* expression change from pure contentment to misery. Oscar immediately got in his face. "What, Drake? What's wrong?"

"It's Brian—I told you about him—I don't want him here," Drake said, looking from Oscar to Charlie. "Don't let him interfere or make a scene."

"Do you want me to oust him?" Charlie asked.

"I don't want trouble. Just keep your eye on him. He appears to be intoxicated."

Patricia, her hand still on Drake's arm, said, "Let's go into the lounge for a minute."

He went along after another quick glance in Brian's direction. Alice, sensing they needed privacy, returned to the gallery.

Patricia put a glass of punch in Drake's hand. "Here, drink this and try to relax. Charlie and Oscar will keep an eye on him."

Drake took a sip of the punch. "I told you about him, didn't I?" he asked.

"Yes, and I can understand how you feel, but don't allow him to bring you down. He can't do that unless you let him."

Drake shook his head. "I can't imagine how he would have the nerve to show up. *I thought I was over the past—happy and optimistic about my future. I hadn't seen him or heard anything about him since my dad's funeral. I've never seen him so disheveled. He always dressed like a Brook's Brothers model. I never saw him drunk or out of control. I wonder if he's still practicing law.*"

Patricia rubbed his shoulder without interrupting his random thoughts. Minutes passed.

"Maybe guilt has turned him to drink."

"Drake, if he came here to put a damper on your opening, are you going to let him succeed? People can bring their garbage to your doorstep but you don't have to take it inside."

Her vehement comment elicited a small grin as he adjusted his focus to her. "You're right. When did you get so smart?"

"Maybe when you weren't looking?"

"You know, I've questioned whether what happened between him and my dad led to the heart attack. I thought I was past it, but apparently not. From the looks of him tonight, he has issues of his own. Guess I need to practice a little more forgiveness."

He looked at Patricia with such wordless thanks that she kissed him lightly on the lips.

"Let's go back in and see if Oscar and Charlie have things under control—okay?"

Both Charlie and Oscar were aware of Drakes animosity toward Brian but neither anticipated further contact between the two. After Patricia and Drake left the room, Charlie walked up to Brian who was staring at Alex's painting of the empty rocking chair with the dog lying nearby.

"I'm Sheriff Webster, and you are?"

Brian looked him over before responding. "Oh, Drake and I go back a long way."

"Did you receive an invitation?"

"Invitation—didn't know I needed one."

"You don't—the show is open to everyone as long as they don't cause trouble. Are you driving?"

"How else would I have gotten here?"

Oscar inched closer to the two while pretending to view a painting, his attention zoning in on the conversation.

"So it's going to be like that, huh?" Charlie said, taking another step forward.

"I wanna see Drake." His speech was slurred, eyes avoiding contact.

"Drake is unavailable. The show's over—I'll walk you to your car."

Oscar moved in closer—two uniforms usually got more attention than one.

"Who says I need an escort?" With a sneer, he turned and moved awkwardly toward the door. Balancing with his hand on the doorknob, he turned and looked around at the three walls of paintings. "What a bunch of shit—typical."

With that, the two large men blocked his view of the gallery. Charlie gently edged him to the outside where he immediately cuffed him and led him to the patrol car.

"Where's your car?"

"Over there," he said, looking around the lot before nodding toward a late model Mercedes. "Let go of me."

"Sorry, can't do that. You're going to lock-up until you're sober enough to drive."

Charlie turned to Oscar. "Would you check to be sure this man's car is locked? And tell Drake I'll be back shortly." After securing Brian in the back seat, he called out to Oscar, "Also, tell him I'm booking a D.U.I."

The crowd thinned to a trickle and at exactly ten, Drake locked the door and turned to his crew. What he saw were faces wrapped in happy smiles in a sea of upturned thumbs. Drake was so filled with emotion, he could hardly speak. What followed was a friendship tapestry fit to hang in any museum. Proud, yet feeling humbly blessed, he reached out his arms to each of them and felt acceptance, love, and a sense of accomplishment he would never forget.

The musicians were on a creative high they never thought they would experience again. Instruments were carefully placed in their cases. Oscar wore an expression Drake hoped would last forever. He and his compatriots had learned what it meant to live with weapons in their hands and it had nearly destroyed them. Tonight, those instruments of destruction had been exchanged for instruments of joy, not only for the brave men but for everyone who shared their story.

DECENT DECEIT

Tanner's heart was to the point of bursting to see his son again smiling and happy. Music had been the elixir to restore him and he had Drake to thank for that. He had no doubt that fate had brought all of them together.

Goodnights were expressed as each drifted to the door and toward their individual futures, leaving Drake and Patricia finally alone. Later, Drake lovingly placed her wrap across her shoulders—his hands lingering. The unspoken words between them required no embellishment. He walked her to her car, made certain she was comfortable. He leaned in and emptied his heart into hers with a kiss that was beyond mere passion.

He stood in the cool spring air and watched until the tail lights disappeared. Only then did he loosen his tie and unbutton the stiff, white collar. The necklace felt warm in his hand as his thumb caressed the silhouette. He raised a finger to wipe away tears of happiness intermixed with a feeling of thanksgiving. He would remember the night forever—of that he was certain.

Emotionally and physically exhausted, he turned his dampened eyes toward the night sky—a sky filled with a million stars. He wondered if stars were really holes through which loved ones from their celestial realm spied on those left on earth. "Thank you, God."

Forty-five

> *"Love gives naught but itself and takes naught but from itself.*
> *Love possesses not nor would it be pos-*
> *sessed; for love is sufficient unto love."*
> Kahlil Gibran

Following the stress—and the relief—of the gallery opening, Drake felt he could sleep a week. However, that wasn't the case the next morning when he awoke early—actually shortly before dawn. Once awake, excitement kept him that way. He got up, planted his feet into slippers, and donned a terry robe. He always prepared the coffee maker the night before. As soon as the drip slowed to a stop, he filled a large mug and greeted the dawn from the deck.

Cumulous clouds climbed from the horizon while wispy ones followed and frolicked behind like spring lambs—a promising start of a new day. Drake watched them waltz in concert but leaving spaces for the glorious colors of a sunrise. Narrow ribbons of gold haloed the cloud edges. They appeared to slow down as if to pick up passengers before moving higher and westward, leaving Drake in a state of awe. No two sunrises are ever the same, but this one reminded him of the one he welcomed the morning he held a lighted match to the remnants of his past. As he did on that morning, Drake felt liberated and believed more firmly in a creativity filled future.

DECENT DECEIT

From the mulberry tree now silhouetted against the brightening sky, a mocking bird chirped for attention. Swallows sliced the air nearby, dueling recklessly back and forth while a frisky squirrel taunted a mourning dove playing along the deck railing. In the distance, more tiny birds soared on the wings of a gentle wind. Ah, paradise.

Idleness was not on Drake's agenda on that morning. After downing his coffee, he went back inside, changed into jeans and sweat-shirt, went down the steps and began walking—alone. He liked walking alone, particularly after being confined indoors for a period of time.

Caught up in the beauty and peacefulness of the morning, Drake deleted thoughts of his schizophrenic past. Instead, he thought of Patricia and all desire for solitude left him. From out of the blue, Stevenson's poem to Fanny came to mind—a poem he had memorized for some reason. *"I will make you brooches and toys for your delight, of bird-song at morning and star-shine at night. I will make a palace fit for you and me, of green days in forest and blue days at sea. And this shall be for music where no one else is near, the fine song for singing, the rare song to hear. That only I remember, that only you admire, of the broad road that stretches and the roadside fire."* He may not be able to give her palaces but, given the chance, he could give her days of devotion and delight.

Another poem from his literary teaching days he had almost forgotten: *"I wish a companion to lie near me in the starlight, silent and not moving, but ever within touch, for there is a fellowship more quiet even than solitude, and which rightly understood, is solitude made perfect. And to live out of doors with the woman a man loves is of all lives the most complete and free."*

Why had he memorized those words—more importantly, why was he remembering them now? Was this what he had been seeking his entire life? He had the greatest of respect for literature—he just didn't enjoy teaching. Had romanticism resurfaced with the return of Patricia? Could one woman dictate a future, a destiny? Had all roads led to fulfilling his predestination—if there was such a thing?

He needed to hear her voice but found he had left his phone behind. At the gaping mouth of the bridge he did a rapid u-turn, his gait increasing to a spirited jog that slowed not a twit until he reached his deck. He grasped the phone with sweaty hands while beads of perspiration ran down his body. Her murmured hello was as manna from heaven. "Patricia, I'm sorry, have I awakened you?"

"Drake—what time is it? Is something wrong?"

"No, no," he said, with quickened breath. "It's a beautiful morning and I didn't look at the time. Go back to sleep and I'll call you later."

"Never mind—I'm awake now. Why are you calling?"

"Just thinking about how great you looked last night and what a terrific job you did with the opening."

"That's why you're calling?"

"I'd like to cook dinner for you. Go back to sleep and come out later. It's a beautiful day— we can take a walk—and talk."

An ensuing pause caused him to prance like a pony. "Are you there?"

"All right, I'll call you after lunch." She hung up.

His ego deflated by her lack of enthusiasm, he refilled his mug and went back to the deck—to think and cool off. She probably needed more sleep, or maybe she wasn't a morning person. Why hadn't he already known that—another example of his earlier self-absorption? He needed to learn more—the little things that made her unique. His hands hugged the hot mug, his feet propped on the deck railing. He relaxed his shoulders and looked about. His smile returned. *Okay, stupid, let's not over think this. There comes a time when even the wind must rest*—when birds sigh in relief, the tree leaves cease their flipping about—when nary an insect stirs and the earth whispers as if to a sleeping child.

The world is like a restless wind, he thought—never stopping to take a deep breath—rushing and gushing like rapids in a stream. He had been like a restless wind while preparing for the opening. Had he forgotten how to relax? He downed the last sip of coffee, went back inside and removed a couple rib-eyes from the freezer—just in case—and headed for the shower.

Patricia kept her word—called later to say she would be out at three. At ten after three, Drake heard her car pull into the carport and rushed to the deck. As she exited her car and called up to him, her greeting stopped him in his tracks.

"Drake, would you mind if I walk by myself? I need some quiet personal time to think."

It felt like a fist to the gut, but he remembered his vow not to pressure her.

"Take all the time you need. I'll start the prep for dinner." No welcoming hug, not even a kiss on the cheek. What was going on?

Dinner needed no further prep. He sat on the deck and attempted to analyze her change in demeanor. He watched her walk down the country road at a leisurely pace, head down, thumbs in the pockets of her jeans. In sharp contrast to her raven hair, a yellow scarf was loosely thrown around her neck—a *walking, living impressionistic painting.* He wondered how Monet would have interpreted the scene. Drake's mind switched to artist mode, first taking into account the time of day. The sun, on its approach to the west, cast shadows ahead of Patricia, and highlighted the Naples yellow of her scarf. The roof of the covered bridge—sun painted with pure cadmium red—with perhaps a touch of orange where the sun struck it most directly. Pea-green foliage of the willow tree suggested the early spring season.

His mind, dancing like a yo-yo, switched back to Patricia. Why did she pause? What was she thinking? Was she reassessing their relationship, fighting doubts about his character, his sobriety? Or was she struggling, as was he, with love's powerful force? Or was it something else? The successful gallery opening was behind them and another chapter in their life's drama awaited—why couldn't she just go with the flow?

She leisurely followed the creek bank beyond the bridge, stopping occasionally to pick a wildflower, *another painting,* or to tuck a strand of hair behind her ear. Apple blossoms fell from the branches, saturating the air with fragrance, but she seemed unaware—her gaze on the stones beneath her feet. Had she decided to leave the area? She had made no promises beyond the opening—she hadn't misled him. They had shared the gallery opening triumph, but she had claimed no credit for the success. Had it been only a moment in time for her—an interlude until she decided on her future? For some reason she was not allowing herself to shine. What could it be? Surely, she wouldn't allow their future to slip away like an evening sun over the horizon.

Drake couldn't force his gaze away from her. If he couldn't have her, he knew he would never again love the same way. But he would always have the memory of her, his once-in-a-lifetime love—the one that got away. Good title for a love song. He would have to run it by Oscar who could set the alphabet to music. There might be other women if he couldn't have her, but they would not touch him in such a profound way. He would continue to paint but the canvases would contain more shadows than light. A life with Patricia would be painted with bold strokes of color—perhaps with a few soft edges to rest the eye.

His early existence had been one of ambivalence, with no specific goals or thoughtful commitments. It had taken a tsunami of surprises to bring him out of his self-absorption, and into a life of acceptance and reaching out to help others. Patricia, he felt, was going through that same chapter of her life. He wanted to be there when she found her purpose, and he wanted to be the man who shared her awakening.

DECENT DECEIT

Drake finally refocused his gaze toward the main house where daffodils, the color of Patricia's scarf, warmed in the sunlight. The first roses of spring rambled over everything that didn't fight back. In the side yard, Tanner had planted sweet-peas in memory of Annabelle and they now climbed the wire fence behind a carpet of peonies. In the garden, strawberry plants bloomed. The house was quiet—Oscar and Tanner probably resting from the excitement of the previous night.

At the opening, Oscar had outdone himself with the music. He showed no apprehension while performing, but how much of an effort had it been for him to maintain a normal mental façade? Drake felt certain the effort had been little—the music finally replacing his anxiety and harsh memories. He marveled at the change in Oscar since their first meeting—all for the good—but how could anyone delve the depths of the mind of another, particularly the trauma experienced by men in service of their country? He wondered if Tanner was able to let down his guard where his son's future was concerned. It certainly appeared that he had.

Feeling blessed by their friendship, Drake turned his gaze back to the eastern meadow. At first he didn't see her—then she burst from the mouth of the bridge. Her hand lifted in a wave as her gait increased on her return journey. She took a shortcut across the field, her body blending into the long shadows of the sycamores. *What would he do if he lost her again?* She came out of the shadows into the sunlight and waved again. He stored the vision in his mind as another painting. Hope once again soared. *God, please be merciful and help me to get it right this time.*

As she approached the steps something caused her to pause. It was then that Drake heard the startling noise—like the cry of a child or animal. Patricia looked about frantically for the source. He ran down the steps and they moved forward onto the rural highway. A wire fence separated the hill and woods beyond from the road. At the fence, they found a young lamb caught up in the wire and emitting a pitiful cry. Drake took out his phone and called the Tanner house. In seconds, both Tanner and Oscar were there, observed the obviously lost lamb and the predicament it had gotten into.

Seeing Patricia's distress, Drake reached for her hand. The lamb was first soothed and quieted. Tanner held it close in his arms while Oscar gently removed the foreleg of the lamb from the sharp entangled wires of the fence. He examined the leg carefully, made sure it was not broken, and then took it from his father. The four rescuers felt the same unspoken need. *We have to find its family.*

Tanner was the first to speak. "There's a sheep farm on the other side of this hill—let's take this baby home."

Drake and Patricia crossed the fence to join them, Drake holding one strand of wire down with his foot while lifting the top one so Patricia could climb through. The lamb's cry was now a whimper of relief in being rescued. The four—now five—made their way through the dense outcropping of trees and brambles, climbing carefully over exposed roots and fallen debris, and avoiding low hanging branches. They came upon a stream trickling over rocks where they stopped and allowed the lamb to quench its thirst. Oscar carried the lost sheep, and Drake, still holding onto Patricia's hand, guided her onward over the rough terrain. Words were superfluous. The wild flowers, mosses and ferns were ignored on that day—the lamb needed its mother before nightfall.

The little lamb had strayed from the fold. Sheep usually roam and huddle close together, so why did this one stray? Tanner began to sing: "There were ninety and nine that safely lay in the shelter of the fold, but one was out in the fields away, far off from the gates of gold – away from the tender shepherd's care." Oscar had come by his musical talent naturally. Tanner's voice was a true baritone, strong and on perfect pitch. Drake recalled the first time he heard him sing—on the morning of their first meeting, sitting on Tanner's porch drinking coffee like old friends.

As the panting and sweaty crew drew near the apex of the hill, the lamb began bleating and squirming— demanding freedom from Oscar's confining arms. Out of the darkness of the forest and into the light, they observed a large hillside meadow dotted with sheep and newborn lambs. Some were huddled together like football players planning the next move.

"Wait, we may have a problem," Tanner told the others. "The mother may reject the offspring if she senses the odor of human hands. That's why the shepherds of old carried a staff—not as a walking stick as you might think—it was used to move the sheep around, through rough terrain, or onto a new path in search of fresh grass. The touch of the staff reassured them of the shepherd's care.

The huddling sheep turned in unison and rushed toward the cries of the little lost lamb. Oscar gently lowered it to the ground, made sure the leg was stable, and tenderly released it to a fast approaching mother ewe. Patricia, reminded of her own earlier traumatic experience, was now unashamedly blubbering. Drake arm moved to pull her closer as the lamb wavered slightly on the traumatized leg before sprinting happily toward the fold.

The four watched in awe as the mother ewe approached her child. Would she reject it? They all waited, silently except for Patricia's occasional sniff as she clung to Drake's arm. After a few moments of hesitation, the lamb was welcomed by the mother and the rest of the herd with much bleating and jumping about. The prodigal child had returned.

Assured that everything was as it should be, the four rescuers turned in unison, their hearts full. No words were spoken or necessary as they re-entered the woods, made their way back down the hill and across the wire fence—to home. With a mere lift of the hand, Tanner and Oscar moved toward the main house, Drake and Patricia toward the apartment, each feeling they had been changed in some mystical way by the experience they shared. Patricia's tears had further assured Drake of her compassionate heart. The tentative smiles they exchanged said it all.

Drake was reluctant to speak when he and Patricia entered his apartment—he wanted nothing to spoil the moment. He sensed a definite change in Patricia—a far cry from the melancholy girl who had arrived earlier. In spite of the long walk, including the small mountain climb, her expression was now calm and, he thought, almost as if a difficult decision had been reached. He took a couple bottles of water from the refrigerator, opened and handed her one. She threw aside her scarf and thanked him. He turned to his tiny kitchen to prepare dinner. She followed and offered to make the salad. "I'm starving," she said.

"Me, too," he said, realizing it was true. He went to the deck to light the grill, returned and switched on the Bose to Brahms's Intermezzo Sonata #3 and lowered the volume. While she prepared the salad, he rubbed the Idaho's with olive oil and salt, put them in the microwave to pre-cook while the grill heated. While he cleansed his oily hands at the sink, Patricia moved closer and stood on tiptoe. Surprised, he leaned down to her and felt her breath on his cheek. She kissed him near the corner of his mouth.

Before he could return the kiss, she skedaddled to set the table for two. He thought of how her head fit perfectly under his chin. His earlier doubts disappeared like fast melting snow. No longer did he feel like he was living on a fault line, or at the foot of a volcano—waiting for the top to blow. Still feeling the impact of the lamb rescue, and Patricia holding onto his arm through it all, made him feel more like Galahad than a humble small town artist. He wasn't on a search for the Holy Grail, for goodness sake—just a simple man who wanted to paint pictures and lead others to pursue their creative dreams.

They ate the superb dinner with gusto, with never a lull in

conversation. They talked about the successful opening, how Oscar's music added a special touch to the evening, and surprise at the number of paintings sold, and how Roy's excitement mounted as the evening progressed.

"I keep wondering what my mother's response would have been."

"I think she would have been filled with pride to know that her son was becoming the man she always wanted him to be."

Touched by her words, Drake stood and moved their empty plates to the sink. "Sorry, no desert," he told her.

"I couldn't eat another bite anyway—that steak was perfect."

"We make a good team, don't you think?" he asked. *Oops! Let her take the lead.*

Night had crept in while they were eating. Through the kitchen window and above the eastern hill, a near full moon slowly made its presence known. "Come, Patricia, let's look to the sky for our dessert."

She followed him to the deck with a refilled coffee mug in hand. Without city lights to obscure the sky, the moon shone in all its glory. As it drifted higher, bright sparkling reflections appeared on the creek water flowing through the meadow below them. A wide canopy of stars escorted the man in the moon on his slow journey across the celestial landscape.

"It's a strange feeling to know the earth is orbiting rather than the moon climbing, don't you think? Drake asked.

"I'd rather think about dessert," she said—giggling. "I like this dessert—so, what would you name it?" Patricia asked, giggling like a school girl.

"Moon Pie might be appropriate." They both laughed. "Or angel food cake with a million candles? He placed a forefinger under her chin and turned her face toward him. "I could no more give it an appropriate name than I could capture with paint the beauty of your face in this light."

"My, you're poetic tonight. Speaking of painting, I saw you had put a NFS sign on the portrait you did of me."

"I'll never sell that painting, Patricia. It means too much to me—one of those rare moments in time that I want to preserve. Maybe it'll hang in a museum someday—like the Mona Lisa. Seeing you sleeping in the car that day made me feel protective. I've never felt that way about another woman. *I started loving you all over again that day.*"

She turned aside. Once again she questioned their relationship. Did she dare trust her heart to him—or any other man? She thought of the words by Jimi Hendrix. *"Don't be reckless with other people's hearts and don't put up with people who are reckless with yours."* Yes, Drake had been reckless and had hurt her—in the past. Would he be equally as hurt to learn she had kept something from him—something so personal he had the right to know? She shivered and rubbed her arms for warmth. He had to be told before they could face a future together. She now knew that a future with him was what she wanted—with all her heart.

"You're cold—let's go inside."

As they turned to go, they heard slow, soulful music coming from the main house—Oscar—playing his saxophone. They went inside, Drake turned off the Bose, and they moved to the south window and opened it to the music of the night. Shoulders touching, they leaned on the sill and gave in to the wonder of it all.

"What is that song?" she whispered.

"It's from Paint Your Wagon. *I Talk to the Trees.* Beautiful, isn't it?" Hard to believe Clint Eastwood sang it in the movie when he was a young man—prior to his "make my day" period.

As if on request, Oscar began *Moon River*, and played with such feeling that the two at the window were utterly speechless. Seeing a sparkling of unshed tears, Drake gently drew her close. Almost without pause, Oscar began a classical piece neither of them recognized.

It was hauntingly beautiful and they lingered until the last note faded and the light in Oscar's room went dark. Drake closed the window against the chill of the night—a night he didn't want to end.

Although relaxed and upbeat throughout dinner, Patricia again became emotional, as she had earlier, over the lost lamb. He supposed it was the music, but feared it could be more. Her tears were too close to the surface, and that bothered Drake no end. He took her hand and led her to the sofa—the room now lighted only by moonlight. She sat beneath his arm, neither of them speaking until Patricia finally broke the silence. "Drake, we need to talk."

Not knowing what to expect, he moved to the end of the sofa. "You must be exhausted—lie down here and rest. Without hesitation, she stretched out and placed her head in his lap. "Talk whenever you're ready—I'm listening."

For awhile, she didn't speak, her eyes closed. Drake could hardly breathe—fearing what might be coming.

One deep sigh and she began. "This thing between us—before we can go any further, I need to tell you more about my life while we were apart. I should have told you sooner but so much was happening, including Mom's death, and the opening of your gallery. I didn't want to upset you at such a happy time in your life. On my earlier walk, I finally made the decision to be honest with you. When I finish, I'll understand if you need some time to think about it further.

First, I want you to know that I have fallen deeply in love with the new you—with the man you've become." She freed a button on his shirt, laid her lips on the bare skin of his chest, felt the strong beat of his heart, the warmth, and kissed him gently. At that moment, Drake was so moved by her touch, he wanted to give her the stars and the moon—in fact he wanted to give her the entire galaxy.

Patricia had already told him about her job with the attorney in Santa Fe, and a little about the abusive relationship she was in for a brief time, but this appeared far more important.

"After you walked out my door that last time, and I later moved to New Mexico—I discovered I was pregnant."

"What?" It was the last thing he had expected.

"Please, Drake—please let me finish."

"I'm sorry—go on."

"For a month, I agonized over your not knowing— questioning—because of your drinking—whether you could handle being a father and whether I could bring up a child in an alcoholic home. So, I hesitated. I carried the baby for five months when an ultrasound was done. Two weeks later the decision was made for me." Her hands covered her face and Drake held his breath waiting for her to continue.

"I miscarried—it was a little girl." More tears. "When I came back here and learned of all your personal losses, I couldn't bring myself to add one more. I was also afraid you'd start drinking again and I didn't want to be the cause of that. You've made such great progress, and I'm so proud of you. Rather than face my dilemma, I was tempted to run again. On the night of the opening, when you walked me to my car and kissed me, I knew I could never find peace until you knew."

Drake sat as still as stone as he tried to absorb her words. *And she had been all alone.* His chest heaved as he choked back sobs. His hand cradled her cheek—his thumb wiped away her tears as they merged with his own. They would never share the life of their child but they now traveled in the same bubbling stream of grief. All the pent up emotions of the past and hopes of the future came to a boiling point and spewed out in a flood of emotions.

"I'm so sorry, Drake. You gave me something beautiful, but I couldn't keep it."

He pulled her to him with such anguish it broke her heart. "No, my darling—I'm the one to be sorry, for so many things, but mostly for letting you down when you needed my love and support. I should have been there. I can't blame you for not telling me—I didn't deserve to know. Can you ever forgive me?"

"I already have. At first, I was angry, hurt, and frightened. Later, after finding you again, I realized I had loved you all along—what I hated was the alcohol and what it did to you and our relationship. I was so proud of you and the way you had turned your life around. Even if I lost you again, I knew I couldn't keep this secret any longer—you deserved the truth. Now you know, and I hope you can forgive me as you have forgiven the family who betrayed you. If you can't, I'll understand. Don't let this betrayal make you doubt my love—please?"

"Of course, I forgive you, but I doubt I can forgive myself for causing you to go through that alone. I can't go back and fix things, but we love each other and that's what counts now, isn't it? If you're willing, we can start over and build a better future for ourselves."

Forty-six

"Whatever is true, whatever is noble, whatever is right, whatever is pure, whatever is lovely, whatever is admirable—if anything is excellent or praiseworthy—think about such things."
Philippians 4:8

After Patricia left, Drake had difficulty wrapping his mind around the unexpected happenings of the day—the rescue of the lamb—and especially Patricia's shocking and emotional recount of the child they had lost. On the other hand, he felt blessed in the knowledge that she truly loved him. Of course, he forgave her—he had been the culprit who brought the heartbreak on and Patricia had suffered the greatest heartbreak of all.

His thoughts too fragmented for sleep, he turned on the evening news. Outside his small speck of earth, life went on as usual. Politics continued to monopolize every conversation. Would-be presidential candidates spouted their disdain for each other. Talking heads regurgitated every word and action, leaving viewers with frayed nerves and challenged anger management. Retirees worried about their Social Security, their medical coverage, and lessons of history were being forgotten. Social media didn't allow one to escape the ills of the world—even in a small town like Porterville.

In other countries, people continued to be slaughtered in the

DECENT DECEIT

name of religion and ancient beliefs. Lives were being taken and families ruined by ISIS and corrupt governments. Children were being killed or left as orphans in a world gone crazy. North Korea bragged about their hydrogen bomb—even the horrible mustard gas threatening mankind. Guns were being taken away from the innocent, and drugs were destroying the minds of weak individuals incapable of saying no. Where would it all end—a nuclear war too horrible to contemplate?

He thought of the child Patricia had lost and hoped they would have other children. But into what kind of world would they be born? What would it be like in ten years? When Patricia told him about the baby, his loss of emotional control surprised him. He now wondered—had he cried because of the lost baby or had it been for the sins of his past—his turning away—or both? Could his tainted sperm have had any effect on a child in the womb? What an ass he had been. Would it have made a difference if he had known and stayed by her side during the pregnancy?

In the past, he hadn't given much thought to kids. It was a shock to him. A part of his DNA was now lost forever, not given a chance at life. But his concern was not for himself—he had brought it on himself. His concern now was for Patricia. She had carried the baby inside her. Her feeling of loss had to be much greater than his own.

He turned off the TV. What few clips he had heard through his preoccupation certainly had not been encouraging. In spite of it all, Drake vowed to continue to be hopeful. In his small world, he would promote as much beauty as he could through the arts, music, and simple human kindness. No one would be turned away from his Art Center as long as he could pay the bills. If lucky, his paintings, and those of other struggling artists would find more buyers, not only through the gallery but through the internet. He would continue to take student who showed even a glimmer of talent under his wing—whether or not they could pay.

How had he become so lucky? Patricia loved him. He had more friends than he ever had in his life. Oscar was like a brother, Tanner like a father, Charlie and Alice as close as any relative could be. He felt blessed beyond measure—and all of it had happened in a small world of his own making. Something good had come from many of his ideas for the gallery. He smiled when he thought of Roy, how they met, and the amazing artist he had become. Somehow, he had to at least attempt to repair the hurt he had caused Patricia. In his heart though, he knew she would never—and neither would he—ever forget the child they had lost.

The following evening, Drake closed the gallery early and drove Patricia to Lake Ivan, about thirty miles from Porterville. Charlie had told him about the lake with a rustic lodge restaurant offering excellent cuisine. Unlike before, this time around he wanted to woo her as she deserved—this time, he was determined to give more than he took from the relationship.

They were seated at a table overlooking a sizeable lake surrounded by pale green growth of spring. Grasses and cattails dried from the winter cold graced the edges. While waiting for dinner, he surprised her with a gift of pearl earrings. "These belonged to my adopted mother, and I want you to have them—because I love you, and I know she would approve. The gift is also for forgiving me for past mistakes—although nothing can make up for them.

She sniffed again, her eyes glistening. "Thank you, Drake. I love them."

"I have just one question, Patricia. Are you going to cry every time I'm nice to you?"

"Probably," she answered.

After a relaxing dinner of Caesar salad, chicken cordon bleu, roasted new potatoes and snow peas—they declined the coconut cream pie. They walked out under a warm orange tinted sky, followed a path around the lake, lingered in a romantic gazebo, leaned on a railing and watched a pair of graceful swans glide over the water.

"You know they mate for life, don't you?" Drake asked.

"Yes, I did know that. Drake, do artists view life differently than the rest of us?"

"I guess we do in some respects. We probably learn to be more observing, otherwise we would be unable to draw and paint the shapes and colors needed for a painting, or write about any subject. We take in the nuances of nature as well as life in general. You know, we can't teach anyone how to paint, or write, or sculpt. We can only teach them how to see. Most people can learn composition, perspective, color harmony—the most difficult to master. Artists learn how to listen to and remember sounds, how to analyze taste and odors and compare them with others, how to own your feelings and remember them again like the first time—even if you laugh and cry at the memory—all important for writers, maybe less so for visual artists.

They were silent for some time, contented and relieved they were back where they were supposed to be in their relationship. Drake looked around at the early evening landscape and visualized artists, with pochade boxes and French easels, spotting the landscape—each attempting to record what God had wrought—knowing they were attempting the impossible. It was a perfect spot for writers and artists to find peace and beauty in a world of endless distractions. Even he feared it might all disappear before he could express his full appreciation in paint. He could only imagine his Art Center in five years, if his dreams fully materialized.

The evening was still young when they arrived back in Porterville. As they approached the diner, Drake reached for Patricia's hand. "Let's stop and see Alice. I haven't talked with her since the opening."

"I'd love to. She's a sweet lady. Charlie may be lingering somewhere nearby."

"I worry about Charlie and the long hours he puts in, but mostly about the danger he faces every day. It's not what I expected in such a rural area. Law enforcement is not appreciated the way it should be. What would the world be like without them?"

"Much scarier than now, I would think."

As usual, Alice greeted them warmly, obviously pleased to see them together. She and Charlie were both convinced the young couple was meant to be together. The evening crowd had dispersed and the three chatted over coffee until Alice flipped the sign on the front door. Minutes later, Charlie joined them. Before they called it a night, Drake drove Patricia back to Bea's B & B, escorted her to the door, kissed her tenderly and said, "Thank God, I have you in my life again."

Patricia responded by placing a forefinger on his lips. "Drake—shut up and kiss me."

"Yes ma'am." When he walked away he felt so much a gentleman it made him laugh.

While the town slept, he drove by the church and cemetery where a part of his past now slept, a constant reminder of where he had begun and how far he had come. He would visit Rhonda's grave in the morning before opening the Gallery.

The next morning, Drake was surprised to see someone had arrived at the cemetery before him. As he turned into the driveway, the sun was attempting to break through a dense fog. On the front seat beside him lay a fresh bouquet of lilacs still damp with dew, and a bottle of water. The Tanner household was asleep when he left. He had cut the blossoms and smiled as he made his getaway. The man turned as he shut the car door. Drake saw that it was Rev. Stevens, easily recognized by the tilt of his head toward his left shoulder, a full head of silver hair, and well groomed beard. Drake had felt drawn to the man during their conversation at the gallery opening. He now walked among the tombstones, pausing at times to read the inscriptions, or to say a prayer for the departed.

Not to disturb the pastor, Drake proceeded quietly to Rhonda's grave site. He removed the dead flowers, filled the vase with fresh water, and arranged the lilacs in a pleasing bouquet. His heart spoke, "Mom, I'm in love with a delightful woman and miraculously she loves me. That means I'll be nearby to visit you often—probably for the rest of my life—if she'll marry me."

Drake didn't hear the pastor's approach until he was by his side. "I was hoping to see you again, young man. Lovely morning isn't it?"

"Yes, it is—a very special morning."

"I knew your mother quite well," the pastor said as he looked at the humble marker. "She was a lovely woman who was determined that you would have a better life than the one she could give you."

"I know—Charlie has told me a lot about her. I can hardly believe how my past has come to the forefront. I now have an identity I would never otherwise have known about."

"Son, we all have to own the things of our past and then let them go. Think of this: If those things hadn't happened, would you have the life you have now? Everything in life leads us to our ultimate understanding of God and the universe. He has taken away your old life and family and has given you another—one more fitting for His purposes. He always wants the best for his children but too often we thwart His wishes. Would you care to share what is so special about this day?"

Drake told him about Patricia and how he had almost lost her, and then added. "But, now, she has forgiven me of past mistakes—she loves me and I'm a happy man."

"And why shouldn't you be happy? God put the red on the flicker's head, and purple on the martin's wing. He instilled the coo in the mourning dove and taught the mocking bird to sing. He placed the air beneath their wings and taught them all how to fly. Things of the world have scant appeal while things of nature bring beauty to the eye and music to the heart. Why wouldn't He do the same for you?"

"But, Sir, I'm so undeserving."

"We are all undeserving and come short, my boy. His dying on the cross paved the way for our redemption. Finding purpose, reason, and understanding is a matter of giving up control—giving your earthly life over to God so He can carry out His plan for your life. It seems to me He is already guiding you in the right direction. All you have to do is follow where He leads."

Drake felt the hand on his arm and knew he was right.

"Thank you, Reverend."

"Now, I must go and prepare my Sunday sermon, but first a bit of advice: Go tell that lovely lady how much you love her, and the two of you make a new life together. I hope to see you in church Sunday. And promise me one thing. If she accepts, let me be the one to make it official."

"I would be honored, and I'm sure Patricia would feel the same. It may be a while—I don't want to rush her."

Drake drove away from the cemetery with an eye in the rearview mirror. The pastor stood watching his departure as if in deep thought. The sun broke through the dense fog, highlighting flower boxes of petunias on porches, and pink and purple phlox blanketing the sloping edges of lawns. The town was coming to life—courageously facing another season. Drake passed his own vacant lot and shook his head—another decision to make. If Patricia agreed to marry him would she want a new house and would she want to live on that street? Did he dare believe they would be saying their vows in front of Rev. Stevens as he had offered?

His dream of an art center had come true, the grand opening was a great success, and now came the daunting task of making it a successful venture. He was now a business owner, academics were behind him, but teaching art in his own gallery was a whole different ball game. He thought of Alex and his painting of the empty rocking chair and dog, and how hanging it in the opening show had encouraged the lad. His mother had signed him up for weekly lessons and Drake looked forward to teaching and watching him grow in his love of art.

He glanced down at the way he was dressed—tastefully—in a crisp button-down blue shirt and casual dress pants—he would do. Visitors to his gallery would not take a cursory glance around and escape before anyone could welcome them. No, art would be the star of his gallery— learning and enjoying art and music. He made a mental note to move the reception desk to the front of the gallery—front, friendly and fearless— a more welcoming arrangement. It would be a place where one could feel free to talk about art, learn the real purpose of art and appreciation of the same. He was sure Patricia would agree.

As Drake approached the gallery he felt an excitement of another kind. A crew of construction workers were gathered at the site next door—the first stages of the Dr. Ella Memorial Clinic. It was really going to happen and what a boost it would be to the community, and hopefully a boost to his gallery. After giving them a thumbs-up he entered his parking lot, noting that the new landscaping was thriving. He entered the gallery to find Roy already at work in his makeshift studio in the back room, wearing his usual beret and neck scarf, looking debonair in spite of his paint smeared apron. He stood at the easel with a mug of coffee contemplating a large work of art in progress. Drake smiled as he remembered the broken, downtrodden man he had first met.

"Good morning Drake, coffee's ready."

Drake lingered, observing the painting, still amazed at his talent and the way art had transformed the man. "You get better and better, my friend. That one will sell quickly."

"Why do you say that?"

"Because your composition is good and you've captured the light and mood of the scene."

With that, he left the artist to prepare for his own day, and for Patricia's appearance at ten. The grand opening was over, but she had agreed to come in and manage the website part of the business—at least temporarily. His thoughts shifted to her confession about their lost child. Because of him she had gone through the heartbreak alone. How could a man forgive himself for that?

Forty-seven

"Be not afraid of life.
Believe that life is worth living and your belief will create the fact."
William James

Drake and Roy were lost in the creative process. Oscar and his fellow vets were jamming in their sound-proof music room when the call came from Patricia.

Drake's smile faded quickly when he heard the panic in her voice. "Drake, Bea has had an attack of some sort and the paramedics have just taken her to Kirkwood General."

"Are you there alone?"

"Yes, at the moment. Her only guests were just leaving when she had the attack."

"Hang tight, I'll be right there."

Drake asked Roy to hold down the fort until he returned, leaving him with the brief information from Patricia. On his way to her, he called Charlie's office and was told they already knew about it. He also called Alice, knowing they were well acquainted. That's how it worked in a small town—neighbors just doing the right and thoughtful thing.

Patricia, dwarfed by the long Victorian porch, was waiting on the front step, looking anxious—in stark contrast to the cheerful daffodils blooming on both sides of her—although a few were nearing their last leg. He took her in his arms, feeling her concern spread all through him. "It's going to be all right," he said, moving her toward the porch swing. "Just tell me what happened, Patricia."

"She seemed okay at breakfast—although I thought a bit distracted. The guests were leaving and I had just gone upstairs to get my purse when I heard a loud noise. I ran back to the kitchen and found her slumped at the counter with broken dishes and spilled orange juice around her. She appeared dazed and reached out for me to help her. I got her onto a chair and called 911."

"Did she show signs of a stroke or heart attack? Could she talk?"

"She just said, 'help me'. I got her a glass of water and she drank a little. She wasn't clutching her chest or anything—just seemed disoriented and frightened. Oh, I hope she'll be all right. She's such a dear lady."

Patricia fought back sobs and Drake pulled her closer. "It's a good sign that she didn't lose consciousness. You must have been so scared."

"I wanted to get her to a sofa or more comfortable chair but I couldn't lift her. I just pulled a chair close by and kept her from falling again. She held my hand so tight, Drake, and looked at me pleadingly as if trying to tell or ask me something."

"You did the right thing, my dear."

"A few minutes later and I would have left for the gallery. She would have been alone."

"She probably had a mini-stroke and will be all right. Let's not think the worst, okay? She's now in good hands."

"Oh, and Charlie was here, too. He told me to call you," she said, with her first smile of the day.

"Maybe we should clean up the broken glass in the kitchen—it's the least we can do for her right now."

Patricia led him inside and the two worked side by side, Drake carefully removing the broken glass from the counter and floor. Patricia got a mop and bucket and they soon had the kitchen looking pristine—as if nothing unusual had happened. They locked the lovely old home, walked down the steps, past the daffodils nodding in the breeze. Hoping to cheer her up, a poem came to mind and he broke off a stem and gave it to her. "*I wondered lonely as a cloud that floats on high o'er vale and hills, when all at once I saw a crowd—a host of golden daffodils; beside the lake, beneath the trees, fluttering and dancing in the breeze.*"

"Wordsworth—right?"

"Quite a poetic soul, wouldn't you say? Do you like poetry?"

"I like hearing you quote it. Does this mean you miss teaching?"

"Not as much as I would miss painting—if I had to give it up."

"Then you're secure in your role as a gallery owner."

"I'm quite secure and even more so now that you're back in my life."

It worked. She could no longer contain a smile. "Drake, I can still hardly believe the change in you. You always seem to know what I need to hear."

"Patricia, look at me." She turned. "I promise you. What you see now is the real me. I'll never let you down again."

"I believe you, Drake. Now we need to concentrate on Bea and her future."

They continued on to the gallery. Before leaving the house, Patricia had checked Bea's calendar and noted there were no guests scheduled until the weekend. There was also an instruction notice on her desk of who to call in case of an emergency—a sister—Elizabeth, with a telephone number and address in Florida.

Back at the gallery, the whole crew waited for further news. Two hours later, Charlie called from the hospital to say that Bea had been admitted and was resting quietly in bed. It would be awhile before the cause of her attack would be known.

Later, Drake and Patricia went to lunch at Alice's, leaving Roy and Oscar to man the gallery. Drake didn't want the doors locked to anyone passing by. Patricia had calmed down with Drake nearby.

"You and Bea have become quite close, haven't you?"

"You know, we have, and for the most part I've loved living there. I wonder what will happen with the place if she's not able to manage it as a B&B."

"Let's not worry about that now."

Alice arrived to take their order—she hadn't heard any more news about Bea, but did inform them that Charlie had returned to his office.

"Shouldn't her family or someone be informed about her hospitalization?" Drake asked.

Patricia told them of the note. "I didn't call, not knowing if Bea would want her sister to know if it turned out not to be serious. I don't think she has any other family."

"You're probably right. Tell you what, let's drive to the hospital after work to check on her and maybe learn what her wishes are."

"Oh, Drake, that would be great. I'm really worried about her."

They left the gallery immediately after closing and arriving in Kirkwood, found Bea sitting up, a partially eaten dinner on a tray table. She reached out her hands and tears filled her eyes.

"I see you didn't eat much of your dinner," Drake offered, "Can't say I blame you."

"So what do the doctors say?" Patricia asked.

"T.I.A. transient something or other."

"Transient ischemic attack," Drake offered. "It means a mini-stroke. How do you feel now?"

"I feel tired but otherwise okay. I want out of here." She looked around at all the medical paraphernalia, including a heart monitor, and shook her head. Drake and Patricia looked at each other and shared an amused smile.

"Bea you don't have any guests scheduled until the weekend. I'll look after things until you feel better—okay?"

"I think it would be wise to call and cancel the couple for next weekend. Will you do that for me?"

Patricia patted her hand. "Of course, we don't want this to happen again. By the way, shouldn't your sister in Florida be notified? Would you like me to call her?"

"No, let's not worry her—unless this happens again. She has been urging me to sell out, move to Florida and live with her. Guess I should give it some serious thought—not getting any younger for sure—but I would surely miss it, the town and lovely people." A deep sigh prompted them to end their visit and let her rest. The visit had reassured all three of them that she would be home soon.

After leaving the hospital, they drove by Patricia's former home to find no changes had been made by the new owner.

"Are you sorry you sold it?" Drake asked.

"No, it was time to move on—to the next best thing, as they say."

They stopped at Appleby's for dinner, so it was after dark when they returned to the highway. Drake reached for Patricia's hand. "Patricia, are we okay now?"

She placed her hand on his knee and smiled. "We're okay now."

"So where do we go from here?" He had vowed not to rush her, but their future was foremost on his mind—had been ever since she admitted she loved him.

"I'm so busy with the now that I'm afraid to think beyond it."

"Then let's talk of practical things—like what should I do with my empty lot? Sell it or build a house on it…"

"It isn't going anywhere, so what's the rush?"

"The conversation returned to Bea and the possibilities now open to her. "The lovely old home has become an important landmark in Porterville. If it closed down it would be a real shame," Drake said. They were of one mind on that matter—the legacy of Dr. Ella should live on in the town she loved.

"Other than being a woman doctor, what made her so special?"

"Well, according to Charlie, she spent her entire life of ninety-two years unselfishly serving the people of the entire county. She never married and seldom took a vacation."

They discussed the new medical clinic now under construction next door to the gallery, but again the conversation returned to Bea and her future. They arrived back at the B&B to find only darkness, the moonlight now obscured by cloud cover. They found their way to the front door by the van headlights. Patricia disengaged the security alarm. Drake lingered nearby until lamps illuminated the charming, welcoming old home.

"Patricia, if you're afraid to be here by yourself, we can go to my place, or I'll stay here with you—your call." *No pressure. This time he was doing it right.*

"Drake, are you forgetting this is a small town? I will be fine—now that I know Bea will be all right."

He didn't like leaving her alone and went from room to room to be sure everything was as it should be. The alarm was reassuring.

"Thank you for taking me to visit Bea—and for dinner. It was a nice evening." No invitation to stay longer. He understood—the day had been a stressful one.

She walked him to the door where they exchanged a long and ardent kiss. He looked into her eyes unwaveringly, but it wasn't going to work. He noticed the smile on her mouth didn't quite extend to her eyes. He lightly kissed both eyelids before turning aside with a groan.

"Okay, home to my lonely bed. Will you be at the gallery in the morning or will you have things to do here?"

"I'll be in around noon—how's that?"

"You know I want you with me all the time, but for now we have to think of Bea's needs first."

"Goodnight, Drake. Thanks again."

It was a lonely drive back to the farm. He watched the clouds play cat and mouse with the waning moon until his van swerved to the curb, forcing him back to reality. His thoughts were a recap of the happenings of the day—he couldn't shake an uneasy feeling. Did her rather hasty good night indicate concern for Bea, or reluctance on her part to move forward in their relationship? He reminded himself once again not to be too hasty in his desire to win her over completely.

Shortly after he entered his apartment, Tanner called to inquire about Bea's condition. After hearing the good news they talked further about their lack of quality time together.

"Even O'Toole is grumpy and spends most of his time under the pool table," Tanner said.

"Oscar is kept busy with his students and performance gigs with his veteran buddies—but I'm not complaining," he quickly added.

"I've never seen him happier," Drake said.

"I agree. He's feeling useful again. Music seems to have set him free of his nightmares and I'm so relieved. I just hope he doesn't overdo." Tanner closed the conversation with an invitation to dinner on Sunday night. "And you can bring along the lovely Patricia," he added with a chuckle before ending the call.

Tanner's new job as town manager was requiring more of his time than he had anticipated, leaving only the weekends for his writing. Drake was feeling guilty for accepting free rent with little effort on his part. Each time he mentioned it, Tanner just shrugged it off. He wondered how his life would have progressed had he not answered the apartment ad so long ago.

Back at the boarding house, Patricia was having an argument with herself. She had been so tempted to ask Drake to stay, but her insecurity continued to hold a tight rein on her actions. Yet, she felt more at peace when with him than at any other time. In fact, Drake and his friends were responsible for the comfort she was finding in the small town of Porterville. Without them, she would have no one. Unless she gave love another chance, she would have to start all over. Too much love—or what one thought was love—might not be a good thing either. She had given too much in the past, and while doing so had lost herself.

She would no longer chase after happiness—she would let it happen in its proper time. Thank goodness, she had lost much of her naiveté. All of nature was flawed in some way—nothing or no one was perfect. Accepting life and all it offered, including the rough edges was a sign of maturity. Without imperfections, happiness would not seem so sweet. If she accepted the imperfections in herself, she would need to accept the same in Drake. Although in his obvious sobriety she found near perfection in him. What one chases flees and that included happiness.

That night, before sleep overtook her, Patricia remembered something her mother had taught her long ago but somewhere along the way she had forgotten: "There are four things a person needs to be happy—the need to belong, the need to believe in something, the need to be loved and valued, and the need to be seen—that is, having someone who says you are important to them and you have a place in their heart." Patricia realized she had everything she needed right there in Porterville. The last thing she heard was the faraway call of a whippoorwill assuring her that all would be well.

Early the next morning, Bea called from the hospital stating she was being discharged around noon, and could Patricia or someone else escort her "out of this place."

Patricia called Drake at home to report her assignment for the day. "I won't be in. I want to change her bed and make sure everything is perfect for her homecoming."

"That's great news. Of course, I can handle things here. The stroke must have been a minor one if they are discharging her so soon.

"She didn't elaborate about that—she just wanted "out of that place."

"Sure you don't want me to go with you?" he asked.

"Drake, you have a business to run. We'll be fine. I'll call you when we get home, okay?"

"Drive carefully. I'll miss you."

An hour later, Patricia, relieved that her landlady was coming home, was on the highway headed for Kirkland. Once more, Drake had not let her down. She smiled at the memory of him helping her through another traumatic event. When and how had he become a take charge kind of guy? It didn't matter—she had buried her insecurities and was ready for whatever the future handed out. They had a lot in common—both alone with no siblings or other relatives. Now it seemed their past was leading them into a less lonely future. Both had suffered losses—her miscarriage had been her most traumatic one. An innocent child should be allowed to live. If she and Drake married and she was able to conceive, they would be starting a whole new generation. She wondered, not for the first time, if all lives were pre-determined.

Unlike Drake, she had known the love of a woman who had given her life. She had felt a connection. She hadn't felt like the only apple on the tree. With her thoughts going awry, she suddenly knew one more thing. She wanted to give Drake a connection—a sense of continuity. A child would do that. She had to take a chance—a chance for happiness for both of them.

Forty-seven

*"Your mind is a garden. Your thoughts are seeds.
You can grow flowers, or you can grow weeds."*
The Hope Handbook

Drake's mood immediately improved after Patricia's call. Strange, how much of his happiness now depended on hers—her comfort, her contentment, her sense of self-worth and accomplishment. Where before he had been stripped bare emotionally, he now felt clothed in a cozy cloak of connections—good friends, the love of a good woman, and a vocation he loved. He thought of Alex, a hyperactive little boy who missed his grandpa—who drew pictures of a lonely dog lying beside an empty rocking chair. With his art, Alex was learning how to live in an often jumbled world, how to find peace and calm in doing what he loved. With each lesson the boy was becoming more focused. It did Drake's heart good.

He rushed to dress for another day at the gallery, but first he made a quick call to the main house. Oscar answered, happy to hear Bea was being discharged. Drake offered his help including his culinary expertise for the upcoming dinner party.

"Dad has already left for the office but I'm sure he will accept your offer. I'm inviting my Key of C guys also—just so you know—we'll need lots of food."

"Sounds like a celebration. Want to ride into town with me?" Drake asked.

"Thanks, but I won't be coming home at five today," Oscar said. After an awkward hesitation, he added, "I'm meeting Dan's sister for dinner."

"You sneaky son-of-a-gun—how long has this been going on?"

"Don't get excited—first date."

Drake noted the excitement in Oscar's voice—almost palpable. "Well, I wish you the best, my friend, keep me posted." *One more step in his friend's healing process.*

Before leaving his apartment, Drake glanced briefly at the empty wine rack on top of the refrigerator and remembered the spontaneous kiss from Patricia after he had poured the contents down the sink. He no longer needed the reminder. *Who needed booze when love was in the air?* His smile grew wider. It was starting out to be a good day.

At the gallery, he opened the door to the aroma of dark roast. As usual, Roy had preceded him. Two cars pulled into the parking lot and lost no time unloading canvases and fishing tackle boxes of paints and brushes. The two ladies had rented studio space for three months. Business was already picking up and Drake had a fleeting image of his new venture leaving him with no time for his own creativity. He would worry about that when it happened.

It was after two when Patricia called to say they were on their way back to Porterville. Bea was feeling fine. "Drake, we have a lot to talk about after I get her settled."

"You mean you and Bea or the two of us?" he asked.

"Maybe all three of us," she replied. "Call me when you get home, okay? Or stop by the boarding house after you close and we'll take a walk to the lake."

Drake shook his head, wondering what that was all about. It had been quite a day.

Patricia was on the porch waiting when Drake drove up shortly after five. After hugs, Patricia said, "Let's walk." Hand in hand they walked silently across the wide lawn, past the hedge of pink azaleas now in full bloom. The aroma of lilacs was heavy in the fresh air—a perfect invitation to romance but holding hands and communicating with an occasional smile was enough at the moment. Patricia wore a white tunic blouse with lace sleeves, against which her raven hair appeared even more striking. Drake would guess she was a perfect size ten, or maybe twelve at the most, but what did he know? To him, she was perfect inside and out.

Only when they reached the lake did Drake break the silence. He couldn't hold back any longer. He had gone over every possibility since receiving her call.

"So, Patricia, what do we need to talk about?"

She waited until they were seated on the trunk of a fallen tree before responding. "Bea has decided to take her sister's advice and move to Florida. Her arthritis has gotten worse and having had the health scare she thinks the time has come to retire."

"Which means she will sell this place and you'll need someplace to live?"

"Promise not to laugh—she wants to sell it to me."

That possibility had not occurred to him. He gave it some thought before answering, at the same time watching a suggestion of a smile play around her lips.

"And—are you considering it?"

"I don't know. I've grown to love the place, but it's so big—what would I do with it? All I know about running a place like this is what I've learned the short time I've lived here." She toyed with a silver chain around her neck—her other hand grasped his a bit tighter. "I can't believe I'm saying this—it is tempting. Am I an idiot?

"No, you're not an idiot. I think you're a woman who enjoys a challenge. You sound like me when I found the old linen factory—excited, scared, a bit out of touch with reality."

They both observed the surroundings as if seeing the property for the first time. "I have no idea what this place is worth," she said, "Do you?"

"I don't know—it being a landmark and all. Charlie could probably give you an idea. Or why not discuss it with Bea? She surely has a figure in mind."

"The money from the sale of Mom's house may not be adequate."

Lost in thought, they were unaware of the birds holding choir practice in the surrounding trees, or the sun moving lower and lower in the western sky—well, the sun wasn't actually moving, but her world was definitely not standing still. Drake squirmed, cleared his throat while his arm crept around her waist. He leaned in with a kiss just above her left eye.

"What should I do, Drake?"

"I have a perfect solution for our future—just a suggestion, mind you—something to think about. It's something that's been on my mind recently."

"Okay, let's hear it."

"This is assuming you'll marry me." Not waiting for a reply, he continued. "Even if I built a house on my vacant lot, I don't think I'd be happy living there—too many ghosts. I could sell my lot, and we could combine our savings and buy this place. We could live here, you could run the B&B and I'll run the gallery. Artists signing up for our summer painting retreats would fill up the rooms—at least during the summer months—and bring in income for both of us. What do you think?

Giving her no time to respond, he continued as he gazed out over the lake. "And, if the stars are aligned properly, a couple kids with hazel eyes and black hair could grow up here. I could teach them how to fish."

Patricia's heart did a flip at his mention of children, but refused to allow the past to spoil the present. She leaned in closer. "And we would be preserving the place in honor of Dr. Ella. That should make all of Porterville happy, especially Bea."

"As well as Dr. Ella, wherever she is," Drake added.

Unable to curb his enthusiasm a minute longer, he knelt in front of Patricia and lifted both her hands to his lips. "Does this mean you'll marry me?"

"Yes, yes, yes—I'll marry you."

With an audible sigh of relief, he lifted her up and into his arms—arms too long empty. They laughed and cried, well on their way to feeling whole again.

Forty-nine

*"You may forget the one with whom you have laughed,
But never the one with whom you have wept."*
Kahlil Gibran

Happiness soared into Porterville and environs on the wings of spring robins, fruit tree blossoms, roses, and lilacs. Love and new beginnings arrived with April showers and May flowers.

News of a wedding would be made known at a dinner party at the Tanner farm. Father and son went all out in their preparations. Tanner looked forward to meeting Oscar's date—the first and only, to his knowledge, since his son's homecoming. It would be one more step on his ladder of recovery. That alone was reason for rejoicing—but not the only one. New friendships had been born and new beginnings established for all of them.

Tanner found his new job as town manager challenging but enjoyable. It was a small town, but just as in other towns and cities across America, people ate, drank, made love, and probably committed adultery. Illegal drugs were a problem but Charlie was doing a splendid job in handling, and often curtailing, the illegal activity. For the most part, Porterville residents clung closely to family values and treated neighbors with respect. It was a town where civilian and soldier met and found a common cause. Drake had become like a son to Tanner, as well as a brother to Oscar. They had come a long way since that first meeting—when the young man had arrived on his motorcycle in search of a more meaningful life in rural America. It appeared they were all finding just what they had been searching for.

Drake was the first to arrive at the party, carrying a tray of appetizing tidbits. He had offered to do more but was assured by Tanner that everything was in order.

Oscar opened the door and took the tray. "Thanks—but where is the lovely Patricia?" he asked.

"She'll be here soon. She's making sure Bea is settled in for the night."

Just inside the door, they were distracted by a young lady wearing a smile as pretty as her floral palazzo pants. A red rose was pinned above her left ear. Oscar quickly introduced them before escaping to the kitchen.

"It's nice to meet you, Kitty," Drake said—swiftly taking in the blue eyes and blonde hair, but was even more impressed by her smile and overall persona. She and Oscar made a striking couple. A smiling Oscar quickly returned, but Drake sensed a bit of uneasiness, probably concerning everyone's approval of Kitty. Drake liked what he saw and gave his friend an encouraging fist to the shoulder.

Charlie and Alice were next to arrive—Alice without food for a change. If they were not lovers, they certainly were a close and happy couple. A horn tooted outside and Oscar left to greet his fellow musicians and offer navigational aid as needed. Eddie had adjusted well to his prosthetic leg but might need a hand with the steps. Stephen, legally blind, handled himself quite well with the aid of his red-tipped cane. And Dan, his drummer, was a great fan—in spite of Oscar's obvious interest in his only sister.

Tanner joined them in the living room to greet the men who had given their best for the Country, but had also helped bring meaning and purpose to the life of his son. Patricia arrived a short time later to find the Tanner household filled with laughter, the clacking of pool balls—and music—always music.

The house oozed a potpourri of aromas from the kitchen. A centerpiece of fresh lilacs graced the extended dining table that seated the nine comfortably. Tanner and Oscar had done themselves proud with the food, served from a nearby buffet. Annabelle's beautiful china and silver were once again put to good use. Her memory maintained a welcome presence in the Tanner household.

The highlight of the evening came after hardy appetites had become satiated. Drake stood, lifted a slightly shaky glass of iced tea to the others with a special announcement. "Patricia and I want to share some happy news with all of you. This beautiful, wonderful woman has finally agreed to marry me."

The room erupted in wolf calls and applause. Patricia lifted her napkin as tears of happiness pooled and sparkled as brightly as her smile. The guests rushed to the happy couple with congratulations, hugs and kisses for the bride-to-be. O'Toole went crazy, joined in with loud barking while twirling like a top. His tail whipped about like a windmill in a March mistral.

Drake and Patricia had agreed earlier to make the announcement, but refrained from mentioning possible plans for the future—too early in the game. Negotiations with Bea about the property, and the sale of Drake's vacant lot remained to be worked out. One thing was certain—they wanted to wed as soon as possible.

The following two weeks were unbelievably busy. The gallery space was nearly filled to capacity by students and artists who had rented space to pursue their own love of art. Even the meditation room was beginning to draw customers searching for a peaceful oasis. In spite of the demand on their time, Drake and Charlie met often at Alice's to catch up on news and to discuss future plans. With the proliferation of illegal drug use, being a sheriff was often challenging. As a result, lives were being ruined and often lost as a result.

"Are Burt Adams and Tommy Thornton staying out of trouble now, or do you know?" Drake asked.

"You didn't hear? Last week, I was called and found they were operating a meth lab in Tommy' house. A fire started, destroyed the bedroom before firemen could get there. The parents were away at the time. Meth labs are becoming a problem, often requiring Tom to leave the office unattended—except for Ethel. I've talked with Tanner about hiring another deputy if we can't break up the trafficking soon. Between heroin use and now meth, we need more help to stop the dealers. By the way, Tanner is doing a great job so far—and he's well liked."

Charlie was delighted at Drake's choice of a wife, and to watch the jigsaw pieces of their future falling into place as if pre-ordained. Drake's vacant lot was put on the market and a week later a staff doctor at the new clinic purchased it with the intention of building a home and moving his full-time practice to Porterville.

Patricia and Bea had long discussions about the home purchase, and the joys, perils, and pitfalls of managing a Bed and Breakfast business.

"You already love this place, Patricia," Alice said. "Instead of living in one room and bath, the house and grounds would be yours to do with as you please. I don't doubt for a minute that you would be an excellent hostess, and you won't be alone—Drake will support you all the way. Nothing would make me happier than to know you were living here and loving it as much as I have."

"What about all the furniture?" Patricia asked. "Won't you want to take some of the beautiful objects with you?"

"My sister's house is not large, so I'd want only my personal items—the rest can remain here if you want. Most of it can be included in the cost of the property."

"You're making it difficult for me to decline."

"While I'm basking in Florida sunshine with other retirees pushing stuff around - you know, the little carts with baskets - if they aren't in wheelchairs or leaning on canes, I'd like to think of you and Drake making a home here with kids fishing in the lake and - well you know - I'm just an old romantic at heart."

Moved to tears, Patricia got up and embraced the dear lady.

"Let me discuss it all with Drake and we'll give you an answer very soon."

Drake rarely saw Oscar except at the Gallery. He was either spending his evenings with Kitty or his Key of C Players. He was surprised when a phone call came from the main house on Sunday afternoon.

"Drake, would you mind if I came up for a chat?" Oscar asked.

"Not at all—could use some company."

Drake's mind was immediately on the alert. Was it imagination or did Oscar sound a bit depressed? He hoped not, since he had been doing so well. Five minutes later he heard footsteps on the deck.

"Come in. It's a beautiful afternoon—shall we sit on the deck? First, would you like some fresh lemonade—or something else?

"Lemonade sounds good."

Drake brought the drinks along with a dish of mixed nuts. "What's on your mind? Don't tell me Kitty has broken your heart already."

Oscar had yet to settle in a chair—prancing like a man with something heavy on his mind. Drake waited for his friend to speak. Oscar finally settled in a chair and looked out at the peaceful valley fanned out before them, and sipped the lemonade. "Good."

"As a matter of fact, it does have to do with Kitty. I got a disturbing e-mail from Miriam—you know, my friend in Baghdad. ISIS is again invading the capitol in Baghdad, near where she and her family live. There have been several attacks in the last week, targeting market places as well as a gas plant. Several suicide bombers and militants broke in and clashed with the security forces. They killed a large number of people including civilians. Other bomb attacks have left many dead or wounded. They seem to be stirring up more chaos than usual and won't stop until the Iraqi government collapses."

"But Miriam and her family are all right?"

"At the moment—but who knows for how long? Her son lost a good friend. Those animals show no mercy, even target market places where families go for food and supplies. No safe place for the innocents."

"Oscar, what can I say except I'm sorry?"

"Drake, her message brought back the dreams. I thought they were over, but I've had two this week. You might as well know—I think I am in love with Kitty—her real name is Katherine, by the way. Everyone calls her Kitty. What do I have to offer her? A husband who can't put his past behind him? Waking up in the middle of the night drenched in sweat from visions of unimaginable evil? What's she supposed to do—kiss me on the forehead and tell me there is no such thing as a boogie man? I can't do that to her—or any woman."

"Oscar, if Kitty really loves you, she will want to help you through this, the same as if you had any other disease. That's what love is all about. You're lucky to have found her—and she's obviously nuts about you."

"Yeah, how did we get so lucky? Two beautiful women right here in Porterville."

"Are you still seeing your V.A. doctor?"

"I haven't felt the need to see him again—until now."

"Might be a good idea to discuss all this with him, don't you think? The letter from Iraq obviously prompted this temporary setback. And talk to Kitty about your concerns—you'll both feel better."

Oscar smiled unexpectedly. "When did you get to be an expert in matters of the heart?"

"Beats me—perhaps because I'm madly in love myself? Patricia and I have promised to be open and honest about our feelings."

"Good advice—as usual. Thanks, I'll call my doctor tomorrow."

"About Miriam—you have to trust that some kind of stability will return to her country eventually. I can't imagine living with that constant fear, but you've experienced it firsthand. You wouldn't be normal if it didn't depress you. As I've said before, you have done your part. Building a new life with Kitty should be your first priority. She can help you make those nightmares disappear. Before you know it they will be replaced with sweet dreams—you can bet on it."

Oscar's silence told Drake his suggestions were being taken seriously. They finished their lemonade while cool breezes moved in, quieting the mockingbirds in the nearby mulberry tree. The two men had come a long way in their mutual journey toward fulfillment and purpose. Now that they had found it, would they be able to keep it alive and well? Only time would tell, but with true love and friendships, how could it not thrive?

Before Oscar left, Drake shared another thought. "Oscar, our problems are somewhat similar, you know. My former alcoholism nearly destroyed my relationship with Patricia. I have promised never to hurt her again by drinking, but who knows what the future holds? She's willing to take a chance with me, the same as Kitty will stay by your side if she loves you. We have to give the future a chance—for everyone's sake—for love's sake. Okay, pal?"

"Okay, and thanks for the pep talk—I feel much better."

Later that evening, from Oscar's window, happy jazz music flowed from a well-seasoned saxophone. Drake called Patricia—the last voice he wanted to hear before going to sleep. Later still, both men slept and no dreams disturbed their slumber.

The next morning Drake met Patricia at the Diner. She filled him in on her conversation with Bea, giving him the details regarding the B&B purchase. "Wow," Drake said, "that price is much lower than I expected."

"I know, but she will be saved a realtor's fee. I think she just wants us to have it."

Drake reached out and grasped both her hands. "It's really going to happen, isn't it?"

Their combined finances were discussed and both agreed it was a chance they couldn't pass up. To the chagrin of a few early morning diners, they sealed it with a kiss. A couple giggling kids whose presence had been previously ignored reminded them they were in a public place. Alice approached cautiously to refill their cups and was the first to learn of their plans.

"I couldn't be happier for you two," she said, giving Patricia a hug. "If I can be of any help, please just ask."

"Alice, you've already been a tremendous help in making Porterville feel like home—thank you for being my friend. I'm sure to need some of your business savvy."

Drake and Patricia returned to the B&B, found Bea rocking on the front porch with a basket of green beans in her lap, half already strung. She put them aside as soon as they entered the porch, anxious to see what their answer would be. Drake shook her hand and Patricia leaned down and placed a gentle kiss on her forehead.

"Do you two lovebirds have an answer for me?"

They sat down on the swing, hands entwined, before responding. Drake nodded to Patricia to give Bea the news.

"Bea, our answer is YES, we want to buy this place but under one condition—you will consider it home anytime you want to visit. I understand Florida can be pretty hot during the summer months."

Bea drew a deep breath and closed her eyes, causing Patricia to ask, "Are you all right?"

"I don't know how I feel. This is going to be such a drastic change in my life—but it's time—and I'm so relieved that I don't have to sell it to strangers or some land developer."

She looked around at the yard, the flowers and trees as if storing the images in her mind for the future. When she turned back to them, a smile appeared along with a tiny tear on her cheek. She arose from the rocker and reached out to both of them for a hug.

"Okay, kids, have an attorney draw up the papers and I'll sign them—and the sooner the better. And now, if you'll excuse me, I need to prepare dinner."

Following her hospitalization, Patricia had sensed a degree of sadness in Bea. In fact, not once had she heard Bea singing in the morning while preparing breakfast.

"Drake, we need to be cautious about Bea's feeling during this transformation. It must be tearing her heart out to leave this place. We must be gentle with her."

"You're right. This is exciting for us because we're just beginning a life together, but she is facing the ending phase of her life. It can't be easy."

"If you don't need me at the gallery, I'd like to spend as much time with her as possible."

"By all means—involve her in our plans so she doesn't feel alone."

"You're a good man, Drake Dawson," she said as she lifted her lips to his.

They left the swing twisting wildly behind them, crossed the porch and headed toward the lake—both feeling the impact of the decision they had just made. Patricia danced backwards in front of Drake, her hands and arms reaching toward the sky.

"Drake, these birds in the trees, the wisteria, the wild flowers, the lake—all of it is going to be ours. I must be dreaming." The earth was alive but no more so than the two lovers.

"What is this, the Sound of Music?" he asked her, his heart ready to burst at seeing her so happy.

She moved into his arms. "No, but like Julie Andrews in the movie, I think we must be doing something good."

As they approached the fallen tree by the lake, Drake asked, "Patricia, are you sure…"

"Yes, I'm sure," she interrupted. "Are you?"

"Absolutely—absolutely I love you, absolutely I want us to own this beautiful place, and absolutely I want to marry you as soon as possible." He lifted her in his arms and swung her around while she held on tight and squealed with delight.

The long kiss ended and they sat down, Drake's long legs straddling the fallen tree trunk. He hand went to her chin to turn her happy face toward him. He studied her as if trying to memorize her every feature—as if he might go blind at some point. He gently moved a strand of hair behind her ear; his thumb caressed her eyebrows, her nose and her full lips still soft and moist from their kiss.

Patricia tried to read his expression. He was so different from the young man she had first known. In fact, the memory of the old Drake had almost vanished. The man looking at her so lovingly was a total transformation. She liked what she saw, but there was a serious note in the way he studied her.

"You have no idea how beautiful you are. I love everything about you—inside and out." His hand went again to her hair, "I wonder if this hair will be as beautiful when we're old, and if you'll try to cover every strand of gray."

She ran her fingers through his equally thick sandy hair. "And will we still be living here, and walking with our canes in the evenings to sit on this very log—and will we remember today?"

"You paint a nice picture, my lovely and, yes, we will remember. Speaking of the future, I want you to make me a promise, okay?"

"You look troubled, Drake. What is it?"

"I want you to promise that if I ever break my sobriety, you'll divorce me."

"What? We're not even married and you're talking about divorce?"

"The thought of ever again causing you unhappiness is scaring me."

"I'll make you this promise: Should you ever choose alcohol over me—your wife—I'll let you go, but I can't promise to stop loving you."

"I don't deserve you."

"I know - but you can work on it," she teased.

"Okay, I have another problem. I want to get you a ring—like the Hope diamond—but that's out of the question. I have my mother's engagement and wedding rings. Would it be appropriate for me to have the diamonds placed in a setting of your choice, or would you prefer I not do that—because—you know..."

"Drake, I would be honored, and a new setting is a great idea. I didn't know her, but I happen to think she did a great job raising you. Stop fretting—I don't need baubles and beads to be happy."

"I know, but I want more than anything to make you happy. Now that's settled—how soon can you marry me?"

"Is Memorial Day weekend too soon?"

"Tomorrow would not be too soon for me. I'm crazy in love with you, you know."

"I know. Now, kiss me again and then go home so I can make plans."

"Yes ma'am."

Drake didn't just drive back to the farm—he floated—his hands barely touching the steering wheel, he was drunk on happiness.

Later, in the apartment, he thought of Oscar's last visit and became even more restless—too restless to sleep. Things were going so well for all of them, he hoped nothing would interfere. His friend had come a long way in his search for a meaningful life as a civilian. His music and connection with those who had similar war experiences had done wonders for the man. His feelings of uselessness were no longer apparent—his smiles more spontaneous—particularly since

Kitty had come into his life. Drake met her only once but intuitively he knew she would be the final catalyst in his friend's recovery.

He went to his book shelves and removed *The Moon and Sixpence* by Somerset Maugham. He no longer taught literature, but his love of books had not waned. He respectfully thumbed through the aged book—one of the favorites in his library. Most were the classics and he had read some of them more than once, each time learning something new. Reading relaxed him. He turned on the lamp at the end of the sofa and began. He soon came upon a passage he had forgotten—remembered it had made an impression on him—not understanding why at the time.

"I have an idea that some men are born out of their due place. Accident has cast them amid strangers in their birthplace. They may spend their whole lives aliens among their kindred and remain aloof among the only scenes they have ever known. Perhaps it is this sense of strangeness that sends men far and wide in search for something permanent, to which they may attach themselves." Wow—the man could have been describing him. *"Perhaps some deep-rooted atavism urges the wanderer back to lands which his ancestors left in the dim beginnings of history."* Drake couldn't believe what he was reading and eagerly wanted to learn more of the author's amazing insight. *"Sometimes a man hits upon a place to which he mysteriously feels that he belongs. Here is the home he sought, and he will settle amid scenes that he has never seen before, among men he had never known, as though they were familiar to him from his birth. Here at last he finds rest."*

How could an author nearly a hundred years before have described his own life so perfectly? He read it again, absorbing every word, and inserted a bookmark. Suddenly it became imperative that he share Mr. Maugham's message with Tanner, Oscar and Charlie—but most of all with Patricia—his soon-to-be bride. If there had been any doubt before that they were destined to be together, what he just

DECENT DECEIT

read erased any ambiguity. There was no question in his mind that Porterville was where he belonged, and he felt certain the words would have an equally strong impact on Oscar and his future.

Seeing the lights were on at the main house, Drake could wait no longer to spread the news. As soon as Oscar answered, he just blurted it out: "Patricia and I are getting married over the Memorial weekend."

"I have a concert gig on Memorial Day—Monday—in Coopersville—Vets coming from all over."

"The wedding will be on Saturday or Sunday. Patricia is working on the details, and she will want you to supply the music."

"Then I guess there is no way I can miss your wedding. I'm flattered you're including me—couldn't be happier for you."

"Thanks, my friend. It'll be good practice for you."

Drake's next call was to Charlie—the man who could have been his father if things had worked out differently. Without his understanding and help when he first arrived in Porterville, he may not have the life he now had—a business of his own, a real home, and more importantly, a lovely young woman willing to share the rest of his life.

"What's up, Drake? I'm on an emergency call—will get back to you ASAP." Charlie's urgency was palpable in his voice. Drake worried about him—a good man who had done his part for his country and continued to fight on the home front. He prayed he would come to no harm in his present line of duty. Disappointed, Drake could do nothing but wait—and call Patricia just to hear her voice.

Charlie returned the call near eleven and apologized for the time—another heroin addict out of control had to be taken to Coopersville for medical treatment.

"I'm calling with good news—think you can handle it?" Drake asked. "It will only take a minute—then you can get some rest."

"It's always good news to hear from you. What can I do for you?"

"I need a best man for my wedding and you're my first choice." Silence followed while Charlie found his voice—a voice that he seldom allowed him to show emotion.

"Drake, I would be honored."

"Thank you— and thank you for all you've done for me. I owe a great deal of my happiness to you. Who knows where I might have ended up without your help and understanding? With that said— now go get some rest. I can't have a wedding without you."

Fifty

*"Love gives naught but itself and takes naught but from itself.
Love possesses not nor would it be possessed; for
love is sufficient unto love."* Kahlil Gibran

Drake approached his mother's burial site and not for the first time wondered if the spirit of the dead could look down on loved ones left behind. And why did he feel so close to a woman he did not remember as a mother. All he had were the impressions expressed by others who had known her—all positive. As he had done many times before, he arrived with fresh flowers.

As a child, Drake had been denied the chance to express his love by running to her with a few dandelions or daisies in his little hand. But that was in the past—he was free of all animosity or recrimination toward her. By all accounts, she had been a mother who had the courage to sacrifice her son for his own good. She did what she felt compelled to do. Caring for an alcoholic father was a huge burden. Drake carried the same genes but was determined he would neither allow alcohol to further dictate his life nor would he allow his weakness to interfere with the happiness of others.

He placed the flowers at the head of her grave alongside the rose bush he had transplanted from her garden. It had not only survived but thrived in the warm sunshine—numerous buds were opening to a new season. Drake, as usual, caressed the necklace in his hand and whispered of his upcoming wedding, his sorrow that she couldn't be there to share the happy day with him—to sit on the front row and smile as Charlie stood by him—knowing he had not broken his promise to her. Lost in the moment, he didn't hear the approaching footsteps of Rev. Stevens.

"Good morning, Drake. Sharing your good news this morning?" he asked, indicating the gravesite, as his smile grew a bit wider.

"Good morning to you, Sir." Drake reached out to shake his hand. "How did you know I had good news?"

"Your lovely fiancé called to ask if I would preside over your nuptials."

Wow, Patricia was wasting no time in her preparations for the big day. "Could you spare a few minutes, Pastor?" he asked.

"Of course—but let's go to my office where we can sit—these old legs tire easily."

They walked side by side to the church. The front door opened to a bright interior with white pews and lectern. A rainbow of colors beamed from a beautiful stained-glass window behind the choir loft, extending almost to the ceiling. Amid the colors, the artist had created a trailing vine with the words, *"I am the vine, ye are the branches."*

Noting Drakes startled reaction to the art work, Rev. Stevens asked, "Lovely, isn't it? Do you understand what it means?"

"I think I do. God is the artist and we are His apprentices?" Drake tentatively asked. The old man smiled. "I've never heard it explained more beautifully."

"Lovely church," Drake said, "so peaceful. I never expected to see that kind of art work in a country church this old."

"Yes, we're about the same age. We've grown old together." They continued on to his office and faced each other on opposite sides of his desk. The pastor knew about his past so Drake didn't hesitate to discuss his alcoholic history and his determination to be a good husband to Patricia. They discussed the joys and pleasures, plus the often difficult moments in every marriage. The conversation continued with Drake confessing a faith he hadn't practiced since his childhood.

"I came into this small town disillusioned by life—carrying the remnants of a deceitful past and a lost love. Porterville has changed my life, given me wonderful new friends, a new business and the love of a beautiful woman. My life now has meaning and purpose. Who else but God could have made all of that happen?"

"Who else, indeed?"

"Mr. Tanner, my landlord, once told me that a man has to believe in something or someone bigger than himself, or else be destroyed by what the world offers." Drake told him.

"Mr. Tanner is very wise. You're fortunate to have him as a friend." The pastor accompanied Drake back to his vehicle where he posed another question.

"Drake, tell me, what is your ultimate goal for your gallery?"

Drake gave it some thought before answering. "I want to help people—particularly veterans and young people—to find their true calling—to further the creative spirit that God instilled in all of us. I want others to feel the joy that I feel—to recognize their talents and put them to good use, not only for their own fulfillment and wellbeing, but for the enjoyment of others."

"Then I give you my blessing, son—on your career and on your marriage. Now, relax and be happy. The first great Creator will take you through any storm you might encounter. You only have to stay out of His way and let him do His work."

Drake put his key into the ignition but then removed it. He had another visit to make—time to acknowledge the rest of his family. He stood before graves he had ignored before—a man who had given him life, for which he was thankful, but had lost his own. He turned to the other grave, his grandfather—a man who had been responsible for changing the lives of many, and not for the better. He, too, needed forgiveness for his weakness and Drake was ready to forgive as he had been forgiven.

He returned to his van with a lighter heart, filled with love for life, for friends, and mostly for Patricia. He was ready to give his heart completely to her and it needed to be as pure as the driven snow—without malice toward anyone.

Drake drove on to the Art Center, anticipating a fruitful day with his young students— including Alex who never missed a class. His drawing and use of materials had improved but more importantly, his concentration was keener, his restlessness no longer a problem. Alex was happy, his mother much less concerned with his attention deficit disorder. Since Patricia's news of their own lost child, Drake found an increasing affinity toward the younger students.

As the work day came to an end, he couldn't wait to close shop since he would be having dinner at the B&B. Patricia would be cooking her first meal for him.

Bea had vacated the home and gone to her sister in Florida. The closing on the purchase would be handled electronically so there was no need to postpone her departure. Drake and Patricia had surprised her with their decision—with her permission—to retain her logo for the B& B. Tears were shed—happy tears. "It will stay Bea's B&B as long as we own it, and you will always be welcome in this house," they told her. Bea left Porterville a much happier woman.

Drake drove up to the entrance of the B&B, still in disbelief that he and Patricia would soon be living there as husband and wife. He tooted the horn and she came running out the front door to greet him. He was unconcerned about the dinner. She seemed to excel in whatever project she chose. He had no doubt about her abilities—in the kitchen or elsewhere.

They met on the porch and after a long hug and even longer kiss, they followed the covered porch to the west side of the large home, relishing in the excitement of ownership.

Drake took a deep breath, inhaling the fresh air. The view was good—no covered bridge or wide open meadows, but lovely nonetheless. A grove of mature trees served as a backdrop to a sizeable garden spot where Bea had planted parsley, thyme and rosemary—an herb garden. Patricia had already decided that next year she would plant tomatoes, lettuce, green beans and peas. She had never lived on a farm, but how difficult could gardening be?

The lake was only a short walk away—a pleasant walk at that. Drake had already checked out the possibility of clearing a section of the trees to allow at least a limited view of the water from the house. Aesthetic values—the beautiful and the sublime—were important to Drake as an artist and nature lover.

Patricia remembered the casserole in the oven, necessitating postponement of any further discussion of flora and fauna. *The way to a man's heart is through his stomach?* She begged to differ—the way to Drake's heart had been love, loyalty, and the courage to forgive.

Her dinner was a great success, served in the dining room with white placemats and candles. Drake's appetite proved she was more than just adequate in the kitchen. What he didn't know was her earlier near panic that her first meal would not go well. Bea's well-used cookbooks had come to her rescue. Afterwards, Drake helped her with the clean-up which took a long time—the chore frequently interrupted by impromptu gestures of affection and playfulness. Neither wanted the evening to end. They finally moved to the porch where night creatures—cicadas and a distant whippoorwill—serenaded them with a nocturnal lullaby

Fifty-one

"I have found the paradox, that if you love until it hurts, there can be no more hurt, only more love." Mother Teresa

The night before the wedding, Drake had a vivid dream. Thank goodness, unhappy dreams of his earlier years no longer haunted him. In the dream he saw an old man step onto a long Victorian porch. He had a full head of pepper-sprinkled silver hair. His body was slightly stooped and he walked with an awkward limp of one who had traveled far and accomplished much.

He settled into a rocker and his eyes sparkled when he turned to see a woman, with raven hair frosted by silver, puttering in a vegetable garden—a garden mostly taken over by hybrid roses. Her hair was partially hidden beneath a large yellow sun hat. She smiled and waved to him. A few feet away an easel held an unfinished painting of a woman, this time in a soft lavender hat, carrying a basket overflowing with rose blossoms. A mourning dove fluttered in to perch on the porch railing. It flew off again as two very young boys, still in pajamas, climbed onto the old man's lap, one on each knee. He hugged them to him while the lady in the hat hurried across the lawn to join them.

The dream then seemed to speed up, with fleeting images of the gallery, a red covered bridge with a bubbling stream beneath it,

DECENT DECEIT

a very old country church at the top of a hill, a soldier throwing a hand grenade, graveyard headstones carved with names he couldn't make out, a hillside meadow where sheep grazed while spring lambs frolicked nearby.

Drake awakened slowly, holding on tightly to remnants of the dream. His room was dark and he didn't want to move—still remembering and wondering what it all meant. It was his wedding day. Did the dream promise him a long life with Patricia—and children—even grandchildren? He smiled, remembering the two happy little boys in his dream. Would he and Patricia live to be old on that hallowed ground? As the dream indicated, would their love remain strong as the years passed?

Sunlight finally crept in around the vertical blinds at his window, snapping him back from his state of euphoria and a realization that his dreams were all coming true. Most of his belongings, except the bare necessities, had already been moved to the B&B. He opened the blinds to the awakening of a beautiful new day that promised he would no longer be alone. His perfectly pressed tuxedo hung from the door, causing no panic or ambiguity—only a heart filled to the brim with love. This ending of his bachelorhood and the beginning of a new phase of his life caused him no fear—only anticipation.

He went to the tiny kitchen and filled a mug with coffee, stepped out onto the deck the same as he had done throughout all the seasons. The day he had moved into the apartment he was a disillusioned, deceived and lonely young man searching for a new way of life. He had certainly found that, but it had taken three men—a father and son, the latter a Veteran with PTSD—and an unlikely local sheriff. All three had befriended him and became his family. The influence of Tanner and Oscar, Charlie, and most of all, Patricia, had helped clear the way for him to become a better man—a person with a purpose. He was now a man without deceit, a man who had forgiven the deceit of others—a man finally comfortable in his own skin. He was tremendously grateful. Less than a year before he had ridden into Porterville on a Harley-Davidson, having no idea what to expect, never dreaming his life was about to change in unimaginable ways. He hadn't expected much. What he got was a new beginning, a new profession, and a young lady he had never expected to see again.

He paused and looked out over the valley and saw a mirage—or was it another dream—Patricia waving to him from the covered bridge, her lithesome gait gaining speed as she hurried toward him. He shook his head. Yes, he had a lot of making up to do and couldn't wait to get started. The mulberry tree, the birdsong, and the low-lying fog on cool mornings would become a memory. So would the mournful sounds of Oscar's saxophone or violin flowing from the upstairs window of the main house to the open window of his humble apartment. They had met—Drake and Oscar—soldier and civilian, in a small rural community of a terror torn world, and found a common cause.

Drake looked at his watch. No time left for reminiscing. Soon he would be locking the door of the apartment for the last time. A very special lady would be waiting for him at the altar of a small church in Porterville—a small town with a big heart. Also waiting would be any number of people to help them celebrate their marriage. Charlie would be there in a tux instead of a sheriff uniform to stand as his best man—a man who might have been his father if the stars had written their story differently. Alice would be lovely as Patricia's maid of honor. Tanner and Roy would escort the guests to their seats. Also attending would be art students and their families, exhibiting artists and staff from Kaiser College, Tom Henson who was rescued by Drake and Oscar the night of his accident, and his wife Eloise. It was a small town but a large turnout was expected. With his Second Chance Art Center, Drake had started a renewal in the town. Patricia was warmly embraced as the new proprietor of Bea's B&B—a lovely Victorian landmark that was to become their home.

He would join Patricia at the altar as a changed man—not the old Drake, but a sober and much wiser man—a man with no lingering animosity toward those who had deceived him. Through sheer determination and the help of friends he had become the man he felt destined to be. He had learned to trust and believe again, and now his future—a future including his beautiful Patricia— awaited him just a few miles away. He couldn't wait to get started—he couldn't wait to say "I do." Friends had become his new family and the town of Porterville had become his permanent home.

THE END